A Quiet Belief in Angels

R. J. Ellory

W F HOWES LTD

This large print edition published in 2007 by
W F Howes Ltd
Unit 4, Rearsby Business Park, Gaddesby Lane,
Rearsby, Leicester LE7 4YH

1 3 5 7 9 10 8 6 4 2

First published in the United Kingdom in 2007
by Orion

ISBN 978 1 40741 009 8

Typeset by Palimpsest Book Production Limited,
Grangemouth, Stirlingshire
Printed and bound in Great Britain
by Antony Rowe Ltd, Chippenham, Wilts.

Dedicated to Truman Capote
(1924–1984)

ACKNOWLEDGEMENTS

Perhaps, somewhere, there are creative
endeavours accomplished alone.
This was not one of them.
As always, my endless thanks to Jon, to
Genevieve, Juliet, Euan and Robyn.
To Paul Blezard, Ali Karim and Steve Warne
for their constant support
To Guy.
To Victoria and Ryan.

What we remember from childhood we remember forever – permanent ghosts, stamped, inked, imprinted, eternally seen.

Cynthia Ozick

PROLOGUE

S ound of gunshots, like bones snapping.

New York: its endless clamor, harsh metallic rhythms and hammering footsteps, staccato and relentless; its subways and shoeshines, gridlocked junctions and yellow cabs; its lovers' quarrels; its history and passion and promise and prayers.

New York swallowed the sound of gunshots effortlessly, as if it were no more significant than the single beat of a lonely heart.

No-one heard it amidst such a quantity of life.

Perhaps because of all these other sounds.

Perhaps because of no-one was listening.

Even the dust, caught in a shaft of moonlight through the third-floor hotel window, moved suddenly by the retort of the shots, resumed its errant but progressive path.

Nothing happened, for this was New York, and such lonely and undiscovered fatalities were legion, almost indigenous, briefly remembered, effortlessly forgotten.

The city went on about its business. A new day

1

would soon begin, and nothing so inconsequential as a death possessed the power to delay it.

It was just a life, after all; no more, nor less than that.

I am an exile.

I take a moment to look back across the span of my life, and I try to see it for what it was. Amidst the madness that I encountered, amidst the rush and smash and brutality of the collisions of humanity I have witnessed, there have been moments. Love. Passion. Promise. The hope of something better. All these things. But I am faced with a vision, and wherever I turn now I see this vision. I was Salinger's 'Catcher', standing there on the edge of a shoulder-high field of rye, aware of the sound of unseen children playing among the waves and sways of color, hearing their catch-as-catch-can laughter, their games – their childhood if you will – and watching intently for when they might come too close to the edge of the field. For the field floated free and untethered, as if in space, and were they to reach the edge there would never be time to stop them before they fell. Hence I watched and waited and listened and tried so hard to be there before they went tumbling away into the precipice beyond. For once they fell there would be no recovering them. They were gone. Gone, but not forgotten.

This has been my life.

A life spooled out like thread, strength uncertain, length unknown; whether it will cease abruptly or run out endlessly, binding more lives together as it goes; in one instance no more than cotton, barely sufficient to gather a shirt together at its seams, in another a rope – triple-woven, turk's-head closures, each strand and fiber tarred and twisted to repel water, blood, sweat, tears; a rope to raise a barn, to fashion Portuguese bowlines and bring a near-drowned child from a flooded run-off, to hold a roan mare and break her will, to bind a man to a tree and beat him for his crimes, to hoist a sail, to hang a sinner.

A life to hold, or to see slip through uncaring and inattentive hands, but always a life.

And given one, we wish for two, or three, or more, so easily forgetting the one we had was spent unwisely.

Time travels straight as a hopeful fishing line, weeks gathering to months gathering to years; yet, with all this time, a heartbeat of doubt and the prize is gone.

Special moments – sporadic, like knots tied, irregularly spaced as if crows on a telegraph wire – these we remember, and dare not forget, for often they are all that is left to show.

I remember all of them, and more besides, and sometimes wonder if imagination hasn't played a part in designing my life.

For that's what it was, and always will be: a life.

4

Now it has reached its closing chapter I feel it is time to tell of all that has happened. For that's who I was, who I will always be . . . nothing more than the storyteller, the teller of tales, and if judgement is to be made on who I am or what I have done, then so be it.

At least this will stand as truth – a testament if you will, even a confession.

I sit quietly. I feel the warmth of my own blood on my hands, and I wonder how long I will continue to breathe. I look at the body of a dead man before me, and I know that in some small way justice has been seen to be done.

We go back now, all the way back to the beginning. Walk with me, if you will, for this is all I can ask, and though I have committed so many wrongs I believe that I have done enough right to warrant this much time.

Take a breath. Hold it. Release it. Everything must be silent, for when they come, when they finally come for me, we must be quiet enough to hear them.

CHAPTER 1

Rumor, hearsay, folklore. Whichever way it laid down to rest or came up for air, rumor had it that a white feather indicated the visitation of an angel.

Morning of Wednesday, July Twelfth, 1939, I saw one; long and slender it was, unlike any kind of feather I'd seen before. It skirted the edge of the door as I opened it, almost as if it had waited patiently to enter, and the draft from the hallway carried it into my room. I picked it up, held it carefully, and then showed it to my mother. She said it was from a pillow. I thought about that for quite some time. Made sense that pillows were stuffed with angels' feathers. That's where dreams came from – the memories of angels seeping into your head while you slept. Got me to thinking about such things. Things like God. Things like Jesus dying on the cross for our sins that she told me about so often. Never took to the idea, never was a religious-minded boy. Later, years behind me, I would understand hypocrisy. Seemed that my childhood was littered with folks that said one thing and did another. Even our minister, the circuit rider, Reverend Benedict Rousseau, was a hypocrite, a charlatan, a fraud: one hand indicating the Way of the Scripture, the other lost amidst the boundless pleats of his sister's skirt. Way back then, my time as a child, I never really saw such things. Children, perceptive as they may be, are nevertheless selectively blind. They see everything, no question about it, but they choose to interpret what they see in a manner that suits their sensibilities. And so it was with the feather, nothing much of anything at all, but in some small way an omen, a portent. My angel had come to visit. I believed it, believed it with all my heart, and so the events of that day seemed all the more disparate and incongruous. For this was a day when everything changed.

Death came that day. Workmanlike, methodical, indifferent to fashion and favor; disrespectful of Passover, Christmas, all observance or any tradition. Death came – cold and unfeeling, the collector of life's taxation, the due paid for breathing. And when Death came I was standing in the yard amidst the scrubbed earth and dry topsoil, surrounded by carpetweed and chickweed phlox and wintergreen. He came along the High Road I think, came all the way along the border between my father's land and that of the Krugers'. I believe He walked, because later, when I looked, there were no horse tracks, nor those of a bicycle, and unless Death could move without touching the ground I assumed He came on foot.

Death came to take my father.

My father's name was Earl Theodore Vaughan. Born September twenty-seventh, 1901, in Augusta Falls, Georgia, when Roosevelt was President, hence his middle name. He did the same to me, gave me Coolidge's name in 1927, and there I was – Joseph Calvin Vaughan, son of my father – standing amidst the carpetweed when Death came to visit in the summer of '39. Later, after the tears, after the funeral and the Southern wake, we tied his cotton shirt to a branch of sassafras and set it afire. We watched it burn down to nothing, the smoke representing his soul passing from this mortal earth to a higher, fairer, more equitable plain. Then my mother took me aside, and through her shadowed and swollen eyes she told me that my father had died of a rheumatic heart.

'The fever took him,' she said, her voice cracking with emotion. 'Fever came down here, winter of '29. You were caught but a babe Joseph, and your father was racked with phlegm and spittle sufficient to irrigate an acre of good soil. Once the fever grips your heart, it weakens, it never can recover, and there was a time, maybe a month or more, when we were just biding the hours until he died. But he didn't go then, Joseph. Lord saw fit to leave him be for a handful of years more; maybe the Lord was figuring he should wait until you began your adult years.' She reached into the pocket of her apron and took out a gray rag. She wiped her eyes, the kohl smearing further across her upper cheeks; she possessed the hangdog demeanor of a ruined bareknuckle fighter, spirit-broken and defeated on a Saturday night. 'The fever was in his heart, you see,' she whispered, 'and we were lucky to keep him for the years we did.'

But I knew that the rheurm hadn't taken him. Death took him, coming down from the High Road, heading back the same way, leaving nothing but His footprints in the dirt by the fence.

Later my thoughts of my father would be fractured and distended with grief; later, thinking of him as Juan Gallardo perhaps, as brave as that character in *Blood and Sand*, though never inconstant, and never as handsome as Valentino.

He was buried in a broad coffin, plain deal and warped, and the farmers from adjoining tracts, Kruger the German amongst them, drove his body along the country blacktop on a flatbed truck. Later they congregated, dour and suited, in our kitchen, amid the smell of onions fried in chicken fat, the aroma of bundt cake, the scent of lavender water in a pottery jug by the sink. And they spoke of my father, airing their reminiscences, their anecdotes, telling tall tales within wider narratives, each of them embellished and embroidered with facts that were fiction.

My mother sat wordless and watchful, her expression one of artless simplicity, her kohl-limned eyes deeper than wells, dilated pupils as black as antimony.

'One time I watched him all night with the mare,' Kruger said. 'Lay there 'til sunrise feeding the old girl handfuls of crow corn to stop the colic.'

'Tell you a story about Earl Vaughan and Kempner Tzanck,' Reilly Hawkins said. He leaned forward, his red and callused hands like bunches of some dried foreign fruit, eyes going this way and that as if forever searching out something that held a purpose to evade him. Reilly Hawkins farmed a tract south of ours, had been there long before we arrived. He welcomed us like long-lost even on our first day, raised a barn with my father, and took nothing more than a jug of cold milk for his trouble. Life had sculpted him a patina, features crazed with fine wrinkles, eye-whites close to mother-of-pearl, kind of eyes washed clear and clean by tears for fallen friends. Family too, all of them long gone and near forgotten; some from war, or fire or flood, others from accident and foolish misadventure. Ironic now, how impulsive moments – in and of themselves nothing more than efforts to affirm and grace existence with a rush of vibrant life – resulted in a death. Like Reilly's younger brother, Levin, all of nineteen years old at the Georgia State Fair. There was a half-drunk and garrulous stunt pilot, owned a Stearman or a Curtiss Jenny, crop-dusted in season; out to scare the tops of trees and graze the roofs of barns with his senseless and arrogant tricks, and Reilly had goaded and cajoled Levin into taking a flight with the man. Words went back

10

and forth between the brothers like some *pas-de-deux*, a precision two-step, a tango of dares and provocations, each phrase a step, an arched foot, a bowed back, an aggressive shoulder. Levin didn't want to go, said his head and heart were built for ground-level observation, but Reilly kept at it, worked his fraternal angle despite knowing better, despite the haunt of sourmash around the pilot, despite the closing evening light. Levin conceded, went up on a wing and a prayer for a quarter dollar, and the pilot, a good deal braver than he was adroit, attempted a bunt followed by a hammerhead stall. Engine died its death at the apex. Long breathless silence, a rush of wind, and then a sound like a tractor hitting a wall. Killed the pair of them. The pilot and Levin Hawkins like two helpings of scorched roadkill. Plume of smoke three hundred feet high and still a ghost of it come morning. Pilot's rungofetch assistant, kid no more than sixteen or seventeen, walked around for some hours with no expression on his face, and then he too disappeared.

Reilly Hawkins' folks died soon after. He tried to keep the small farm together after they passed on, both of them broken-hearted after Levin's death, but even the hogs seemed to look sideways at him like they understood his guilt. Never a word of blame in Reilly's direction, but old man Hawkins, chewing ceaselessly on his Heidsieck champagne tobacco, would watch the older brother, watch him like there was a debt to be repaid and he was waiting for Reilly to offer up. His eyes would twitch back and forth like a quit smoker in a cigar store. Never a word spoken, but the word always present.

Reilly Hawkins had never married, some said because he couldn't give children and had no shame to admit it. I believed that Reilly never married because his heart was broken once, and thought to have it broken a second time would kill him. Rumor said it was a girl from Berrien County, pretty as a Chinese baby. Figured not to risk such a venture as he had other reasons to live. Choice between some wide-mouthed girl from an over-stretched family, girl who wore cotton print dresses, rolled her own cigarettes and drank straight from the bottle – that, or loneliness. Seemed to have chosen the latter, but of this he never spoke directly, and I never directly asked. That was Reilly Hawkins, the little I knew of him at the time, and there was no guessing his purpose or direction, for more often than not he seemed a man of will over sense.

'Earl was a fighter,' Reilly said that day in our kitchen, the day of the funeral. He glanced at my mother. She didn't move much, but her eyes and the way she glanced back was permission for him to continue.

'Earl and Kempner went up beyond Race Pond, over to Hickox in Brantley County. Went up there to see a man called Einhorn if I remember right, a man called Einhorn who had a roan for sale.

12

Stopped in a place on the way just to take a drink, and while they were resting a brute of a character came in and started up hollering like a banshee in a warbonnet. Upsetting folk he was, upsetting them and getting people riled and omery, and Earl suggested the man take his business outside and into the trees where no-one could hear him.'

Reilly looked once more at my mother, and then at me. I didn't move, wanted to hear what my father had done to calm this brute of a character near Hickox in Brantley County. My mother didn't raise her hand, nor her voice, and Reilly smiled.

'Cut a long story down to size, this brute tried to level Earl with a roundhouse. Earl sidestepped and sent the man flying out through the doorway into the dirt. Went after him, tried to talk some sense into the devil, but the man had a fighting heart and a fighting head and there was no reasoning with him. Kempner went out there just as the man came up again and went for Earl with a plank of wood. Earl was like one of these Barnum & Bailey Chinese acrobats, dancing back and around, fists like pistons, and one of those pistons just connected with the big man's nose, and you could hear the bone break in a dozen places. Blood was like a waterfall, man's shirt was soaked, kneeling there in the dirt and howling like a stuck pig.'

Reilly Hawkins leaned back and smiled. 'Heard that the old boy's nose never did stop bleeding . . . just kept on running 'til he was all emptied out—'

'Reilly Hawkins,' my mother said. 'That was never a true story and you know it.'

Hawkins looked sheepish. 'No disrespect, ma'am,' he said, and bowed his head deferentially. 'I wouldn't want to be upsetting you on such a day.'

'Only thing that ever upsets me is untruths and half-truths and outright lies, Reilly Hawkins. You're here to see my husband away to the Lord, and I'd be obliged if you'd mind your language, your manners, and keep a truthful tongue in your head, especially in front of the boy.' She looked over at me. I sat there wide-eyed and wondering, wanting to know all the 'more gory details regarding my father: a man who could right-hook a brute's nose and deliver death by exsanguination.

Later I would remember my father's burial. Remember that day in Augusta Falls, Charlton County – some antebellum outgrowth bordering the Okefenokee River – remember an acreage that was more swamp than earth; the way the land just sucked everything into itself, ever-hungry, never satiated. That swollen land inhaled my father, and I watched him go; I all of eleven years old, he no more than thirty-seven, and me and my mother standing with a group of uneducated and sympathetic farmers from the four corners of the world, jacket sleeves to their knuckles, rough flannel trousers that evidenced inches of worn-out sock. Rubes perhaps, more often uncouth than mannered, but robust of heart, hale and generous. My mother held my hand tighter than was comfortable, but I said nothing and I did not withdraw. I was her first and only child, because – if stories were true, and I had no reason to doubt them – I had been a difficult child, resistant to ejection, and the strain of my birth had ruined the internal contraptions that would have enabled a larger family.

'Just you and me, Joseph,' she later whispered. The people had gone – Kruger and Reilly Hawkins, others with familiar faces and uncertain names – and we stood side by side looking out from the front door of our house, a house raised by hand from sweat and good timber. 'Just you and me from now on,' she said once more, and then we turned inside and closed the door for the night.

Later, lying in my bed, sleep evading me, I thought of the feather. Perhaps, I thought, there were angels who delivered and angels who took away.

Gunther Kruger, a man who would become more evident in my life as the days went on – he told me that Man came from the earth, that if he didn't return there would be some universal imbalance. Reilly Hawkins said that Gunther was a German, and Germans were incapable of seeing the bigger picture. He said that people were spirits.

'Spirits?' I asked him. 'You mean like ghosts?'

Reilly smiled, shook his head. 'No, Joseph,' he whispered. 'Not like ghosts . . . more like angels.'

'So my father has become an angel?'

For a moment he said nothing, leaning his head to one side with a strange squint in his eye. 'Your father, an angel?' he said, and he smiled awkwardly, like a muscle had tensed in the side of his face and would not so easily release. 'Maybe one day . . . figure he has some work to do, but yes, maybe one day he'll be an angel.'

CHAPTER 2

Along the coast of Georgia – Crooked River, Jekyll Island, Gray's Reef and Dover Bluff – roads that were more half-bridges and causeways wishing they were roads, every now and then skipping stretches of water like flat stones spinning from the hands of children; a flooded swell of islands, creeks, sounds, salt marshes and river inlets, trees shrouded in Spanish moss, split-logs bound together to navigate a corduroy track across the deeper swamps, while the flatlands in the southeast rose gradually across the state to the Appalachians. The Georgians grew rice, and then Eli Whitney came with the cotton gin, and field-hands harvested peanuts, and settlers tapped the pines for curing rope, calking the seams of sails with pitch and turpentine for paint. Sixty thousand square miles of history, a history I learned, a history I believed in.

A tablet-arm chair; a one-room schoolhouse; a teacher called Miss Alexandra Webber. A wide-jowled open prairie of a face, eyes cornflower blue, simple and uncomplicated. Her hair was flax and linen, and forever she smelled of licorice and peppermint, and something beneath that like ginger root or sarsaparilla. She gave no quarter, expected none in return, and her depth of patience was matched solely by the spirit of her anger if she felt you had willfully disobeyed her.

I sat beside Alice Ruth Von Horne, a strange, sweet girl I found myself caring for in some inexplicable way. There was something simple and affecting in the way she twirled her bangs as she concentrated, every once in a while glancing back at me like I had the answer she couldn't find. Perhaps I gave her the impression I understood this thing she sought, perhaps for no other reason than appreciating her attention, but when she was absent I was aware of that absence in some manner other than physical presence. I was eleven, soon to be twelve, and sometimes I considered things that would not have been appropriate to share with others. Alice represented something that I did not fully understand, something that I knew would be altogether too difficult to explain. For the four years I had attended the school Alice had been there, ahead of me, beside me, for one term seated at the desk behind. When I looked at her she smiled, sometimes blushed, and then she would look away, only to wait a moment and look at me again. I believed her sentiment was uncomplicated and flawless, and I believed that one day, perhaps, both of us might recall it as a perfect memory of who we had been as children.

Miss Webber, however, represented something

else entirely. I loved Miss Alexandra Webber. My love was as clear and simply defined as her features. Miss Webber conducted her classes along Robert's Rules of Order, and her voice, her silence, everything that she was and everything I imagined she would ever be, was an anodyne and a panacea following the death of my father.

'Gentleman Johnny Burgoyne . . . who has heard of Gentleman Johnny Burgoyne?'

Silence. Nothing but the sound of my heart as I watched her.

Seventeen of us were crowded in that narrow plankboard room, and not one raised their hand.

'I *am* disappointed,' Miss Webber said, and smiled understandingly. Apparently Miss Webber had come all the way from Syracuse to teach us. People from Syracuse breathed different air, air that made their heads clear, their minds sharp; people from Syracuse were a different race.

'Gentleman Johnny Burgoyne, born in 1722, died in 1792. He was a British General during the Revolution. He found himself surrounded by our troops at Saratoga on the seventeenth of October, 1777. It was the first great American victory and a truly decisive battle of the war.'

She paused. My heart missed a beat.

'Joseph Vaughan?'

I damn near swallowed my tongue.

'Where have you gone to, Joseph Vaughan . . . surely you're not on this earth?'

'I am, miss, y-yes . . . yes, of course I am.'

19

The sound of cupped laughter, like the ghosts of trick-or-treat children. Children I knew from Liberty County and McIntosh, others from Silco and Meridan. Alice was amongst them. Alice Ruth Van Horne. Laverna Stowell. Sheralyn Williams. They came from all around to learn of life with Miss Alexander Webber.

'Well, I am very pleased to hear that, Joseph Calvin Vaughan. Now, in order to demonstrate how much attention you have been paying this afternoon, you can stand beside your desk and explain to us exactly what happened at Brandywine, South East Pennsylvania in the same year.'

My précis was stale and insubstantial. I was instructed to stay late and wash the blackboard rags.

She stood over me, at first I believed to ascertain whether I would shirk my duty, perhaps to reprimand me further for my lack of concentration.

'Joseph Vaughan,' she started.

The schoolroom was empty. It was mid-afternoon. My father had been dead the better part of three months. I would be twelve in five days.

'Our lesson today . . . I have the definite impression that you were bored.'

I shook my head.

'But you were not paying attention, Joseph.'

'I'm sorry, Miss Webber . . . I was thinking about something else.'

'And what would that have been?'

20

'I was thinking about the war, Miss Webber.'

'You have heard about the war in Europe?' she asked. She seemed surprised, though I would not have known why.

I nodded.

'Who told you?'

'My mother, Miss Webber . . . my mother told me.'

'She is a cultured and intelligent woman, isn't she?'

'I don't know, Miss Webber.'

'Believe me, Joseph Vaughan, any American woman living in Georgia who knows about Adolf Hitler and the war in Europe, I'll tell you now that that woman is a cultured and intelligent person.'

'Yes, Miss Webber.'

'Come sit down, Joseph,' Miss Webber said. I looked up at her. I was a handful of years younger and perhaps half a foot shorter.

She indicated her desk at the front of the classroom. 'Come,' she said. 'Come sit here and talk with me for a moment or two before you leave.'

I did as I was told. My skin felt too big for my frame. I could feel my skeleton struggling as it dealt with such flexibility and inexactitude.

'Tell me another word for a color,' she said.

I looked at her, my puzzlement evident.

She smiled. 'It's not an exam, Joseph, just a question. Do you know another word for a color?'

I nodded.

'Tell me.'

'A hue, Miss.'

'Good,' she said, and smiled wide. Her corn-flower eyes blossomed beneath a Syracuse sun.

'And another word?'

'Another?'

'Yes, Joseph, another word for a color.'

'A shade perhaps, a tint . . . something like that?'

She nodded. 'And can you think of another word meaning many?'

'Many? Like a host, a multitude?'

Miss Webber tilted her head to one side. 'A multitude?'

I nodded.

'Where d'you find a word like that, Joseph Vaughan?'

'In the Bible, Miss Webber.'

'Your mother has you read the Bible?'

I shook my head.

'You read it yourself?'

'A little.'

'Why?' she asked.

'I wanted—' I could feel the color flushing my cheeks. *How many words for such a feeling?* I thought.

'You wanted what, Joseph?'

'I wanted to learn about angels.'

'Angels?'

I nodded. 'The seraphim and the cherubim, the celestial hierarchy.'

Miss Webber laughed, and then she caught herself. 'I'm sorry, Joseph. I didn't mean to laugh. You merely surprised me.'

I said nothing. My cheeks were hot; like the summer of '33 when the river dried up.

'Tell me about the celestial hierarchy.'

I shifted awkwardly in the chair. I felt something like embarrassment. I didn't want Miss Webber to ask about my father.

'There are nine orders of angels,' I said, my voice catching at the back of my throat like it had encountered a crab-net. 'The seraphim . . . fiery six-winged creatures who guard God's throne. They're known as the Sacred Ardor. Then there are the cherubim, who have large wings and human heads. They are God's servants and the Guardians of Sacred Places. Then there are Thrones, Dominations, Virtues, Powers, Principalities, and then come the Archangels, like Gabriel and Michael. Finally there are angels themselves, the divine intermediaries who protect people and nations.'

I paused. My mouth and throat were dry. 'Michael fought Lucifer and cast him down to Gehenna.'

'Gehenna?' Miss Webber asked.

'Yes,' I said. 'Gehenna.'

'And why did Michael fight Lucifer?'

'He was the lightbringer,' I said. 'That's what his name means . . . lux means light and ferre means to carry. Some people call him the morning star, other people call him the lightbringer. He used to be an angel. He was supposed to bring his light forward and show God where Man had sinned.'

I glanced toward the door. I felt stupid, like perhaps I was being tricked into talking about things. I looked back at Miss Webber and she was just smiling, her expression one of interest and curiosity.

'He brought his light and showed God where Man had sinned, and he collected evidence, sort of like a policeman would. He then told God, and God would punish people for what they'd done.'

'So what was wrong with that?' Miss Webber asked. 'Seemed like he was just doing his job.'

I shook my head. 'He did at first, and then he became more interested in pleasing God than he did in the truth. He started tricking people into doing bad things so he could tell God all about it. He brought temptation to Man, and was tempted himself. He started to tell lies, and God got real mad at him. Then Lucifer tried to start a mutiny amongst the angels, and Michael fought with him and he was cast down to Gehenna.'

I stopped talking. My mouth had run away with itself. By the time I realized where it was going it had crossed the horizon. The dust left in its wake parched my throat and made me cough.

'You want a drink of water, Joseph?' Miss Webber asked.

I shook my head.

She smiled again. 'I am impressed, Joseph. Impressed that you know so much of your Bible.'

'I don't know much about the Bible,' I said. 'Just a little bit about angels.'

'You believe in angels?' she asked.

I nodded. 'Of course I do.' It seemed strange to me that she would ask such a question.

'And why did you want to learn about angels, Joseph?'

I swallowed my fear loudly. It made a lump like a walnut in the front of my throat. 'Because of my father.'

'He wanted you to learn about angels?'

'No, miss . . . because Reilly Hawkins told me that if my father worked real hard he might become one.'

She paused for a moment. She looked at me, perhaps more closely than before, but she did not smile, nor did she laugh. 'He died, didn't he?'

'Yes, miss.'

'When did he die, Joseph?'

'July the twelfth.'

'Just a few weeks ago?'

'Yes, Miss Webber, about three months ago.'

'And how old are you now, Joseph?'

I smiled. 'I'll be twelve in five days.'

'Five days, eh? And you have brothers and sisters?'

I shook my head.

'Just you and your mother?'

'Yes, Miss Webber.'

'And who taught you to read?'

25

'My mother and my father . . . my father used to tell me it was one of the most important things you could ever do. He said you could stay in a one-room shack in a two-horse town for the whole of your life, but you could see everywhere in the world right there in your mind's eye so long as you could read.'

'He was a wise man.'

'With a bad heart,' I said.

She looked momentarily taken aback, as if I'd said something out of turn.

'I'm sorry—' I started.

She raised her hand. 'It's okay.'

'Maybe I should go now, Miss Webber.'

She nodded. 'Yes, perhaps you should. I've kept you too long.'

I edged along the chair and stood at the side of the table. I took my small heart in my hands, fragile like a bird in a straw-built cage. 'It was nice to talk to you, Miss Webber,' I said, 'and I'm sorry for not paying attention about Brandywine.'

She smiled. She reached out her hand and touched the side of my face. Just for a heartbeat, a fraction of a second. I felt energy surging through me, energy that filled my chest, swelled my stomach, gave me a feeling like I needed to pee.

'Never mind, Joseph . . . I can imagine you were some place a whole lot more important.' She winked. 'Go,' she said, 'away with you now, and keep your mind's eye open.'

★   ★   ★

My birthday was a Saturday. I rose to the sound of Negroes singing in Gunther Kruger's field. On the stoop was a brown paper-wrapped parcel, my name printed in clear and unmistakable letters – JOSEPH CALVIN VAUGHAN. I carried it inside and showed my mother.

'So open it, boy,' she insisted. 'It'll be a gift, perhaps from the Krugers.'

The Long Valley by John Steinbeck.

Inside it bore the inscription: *Live life with a bold heart, Joseph Vaughan, as if life is too small to contain you. Best wishes on this, your twelfth birthday, your teacher, Miss Alexandra Webber.*

'It's from my teacher,' I said. 'It's a book.'

'I can see that it's a book, child,' my mother said, and, drying her hands on her apron front, she took it from me. The cover was stiff board, the pages smelled like fresh ink, and when she handed it back to me it came with the entreaty to care for it well.

I held the book in my hands and pressed it close against my chest, almost afraid to drop it, and then I paused before I opened it. I closed my eyes and thanked whatever had inspired Miss Webber to demonstrate such an act of generosity.

THE CHRYSANTHEMUMS

The high gray-flannel fog of winter closed off the Salinas Valley from the sky and from all the rest of the world. On every side it sat like a lid on the mountains and made of the great valley a closed pot.

27

I carried the book outside, sat there on the porch steps, the sound of the black people in the fields, the smell of pancakes and a new morning all around me, and I read – page after page, flying by words I neither understood nor cared to understand, because there I found something that challenged and frightened me, excited me with a rush of fever and passion that I could not describe.

Later I told my mother that I wanted to write.

'Write to whom?' she asked.

'No,' I said. 'I want to write . . . write a book, write several books. I want to be a writer.'

She leaned over me, pulled the covers up around my throat and kissed my forehead.

'A writer, is it?' she said, and smiled. 'Then it seems to me you better start carrying a pencil.'

On Friday, November third, 1939, Alice Ruth Van Home's body was found. I knew her better than anyone in my class. She had green eyes, and hair that was neither gold nor red nor brown but the myriad colors of a thousand fallen leaves. When she laughed it sounded like some exotic bird had mistakenly flown in through our window. In her lunch pail she brought sandwiches which I knew she'd made herself. The crusts were cut off and wrapped separately.

'Why d'you do that?' I asked her one time.

'You want one?' She held out a thin brown twig.

I shook my head.

'Try it,' she said.

I took the thing gingerly, smelled it.

She laughed. 'Try it,' she repeated.

Tasted like something warm, like cinnamon, like nothing similar to anything. Tasted quite wonderful.

She tilted her head to one side. 'Good, huh?'

I nodded. 'Real good.'

'That's why they're separate. Don't taste them so much if you leave them on the sandwich.'

She was found naked in a field at the far end of the High Road, where Death must have begun his journey when He came to collect my father. Seemed that Death had not come to take Alice; she had saved Him such trouble by walking out there to meet Him. Her lunch pail was found beside her. It was late in the day, long after school, and there was nothing inside the pail but empty wrappers and the smell of crusts.

She was eleven years old. Seemed someone had stripped her and beaten her, done things to her 'that no normal human being would do to a dog, let alone a little girl'. Reilly Hawkins said that; said it in our kitchen, seated there beside Gunther Kruger who'd brought a clay pitcher of lemonade from Mrs Kruger, and my mother told him 'Hush, Reilly, I don't want to be talking about such things while the boy is here.'

Later the boy they spoke of went to bed. I waited until the house had ceased its creaking and stretching, and then crept away from my room and hung like a ghost amidst the shadows and memories at the top of the stairs.

'Raped her they did,' I heard Reilly say. 'Little girl, nothing to her . . . and some animal raped her and beat her and choked her to death, and then left her in the field at the top of the High Road.'

'Seems to me it's gonna be one of them nigras,' Gunther Kruger said.

My mother turned on him, her words firm and unrelenting. 'Enough of such talk, Gunther Kruger. Even as we speak your countrymen are allowing a tyrant to push them into a war that we have all prayed would never happen. The Polish government is exiled in Paris; I even heard a rumor that Roosevelt will have to help the British to buy guns and bombs from America. Thousands, hundreds of thousands, maybe millions of people are going to die . . . all because of the German people.'

'Such a viewpoint is unjust, Mrs Vaughan . . . not all Germans—'

'And not *all* Negroes, Mr Kruger.'

Kruger fell silent. The wind had turned and collapsed his sails. He drifted aimlessly toward the shoal of embarrassment and did not look back toward the opposing vessel.

'And such talk I will not permit in my house,' my mother said. 'We're not in the Dark Ages. We're not ignorant people. Adolf Hitler is a white man, just as Genghis Khan was a Mongol and Caligula was a Roman. It is not the nationality, nor the color, nor the religion . . . it is always just the man.'

'She's right,' Reilly Hawkins said. 'She's right, Gunther Kruger.'

Kruger asked if Reilly or my mother wanted more lemonade.

I crept away to my bed and thought of Alice Ruth Van Horne. I remembered the sound of her voice, the way she smiled at the most darned fool things. I remembered a game we had once played in the field with the broken fence, a game where she had fallen and scuffed her elbow and I had walked her home to her mother.

She was a sweet-tempered girl, always cheerful it seemed.

I remembered the way she looked at me, the way she smiled, turned away, looked at me once more . . . always waiting for an answer that I never gave.

I cried for her.

I realized that my memory of Alice, a memory I believed would always be flawless, would now be nothing more than a shadow on my heart.

I tried to imagine the kind of human being who would do such a thing to Alice Ruth. Whether such a person was a kind of *human* being at all.

When I woke my pillow was still damp, I believed I must have cried in my sleep.

I figured that God made Alice an angel immediately.

The following morning I cut an article from the newspaper, and hid it in a box beneath my bed.

CHARLTON COUNTY JOURNAL
Saturday November 4th, 1939

Local Girl Found Murdered

On the morning of Friday November 3rd, the body of a local girl, Alice Ruth Van Horne (11), was discovered in Augusta Falls. Alice, a student of the Augusta Falls Junior School, was discovered by a local resident. Sheriff Haynes Dearing was quoted as saying, 'We are at once alert for the presence of any vagrant or unknown person in the area. With immediate effect we are implementing a countywide state of emergency for any suspicious person or persons. The murder of a young girl, a member of our own community, in such a brutal fashion, has given us all a reason to be aware of any uncommon or noticeable occurrence in our midst. I would ask all citizens to refrain from panic, but to be alert to the whereabouts of their children at all times.' When asked for more details of the investigation into this horrific murder, Sheriff Dearing refrained from making further comment. Arthur and Madeline Van Home, the murdered girl's parents, have lived in Augusta Falls for eighteen years. They attend the Charlton County Methodist Church. Mr Van Home farms his own property within the Augusta Falls town limits.

I tried not to think about how it would feel to be beaten and choked to death, but the more I tried not to think the more it filled my mind. After a few days I let it go, which seemed to be what everyone else in Augusta Falls wanted to do.

And there are times I remember – summer days mostly; hazy, fat with air and sunshine, and Mr Tomczak dragging his Victrola gramophone out into the yard, and bakelite records as heavy as plates; and the adults kind of unbuttoned themselves, and despite the fact that no-one had any money, and more than likely never would, it didn't matter because there was a richness in friendship and community.

And the kids out in the fields playing catch-and-kiss, and someone had a crate of beer for the dads, and someone else made watermelon juleps for the ladies.

My mom would put on a summer frock, and one time she waltzed with my dad, and he wore a smile like a medal: for valor, for fidelity, for love.

And the days I remember were days that had gone. Slipped away silently into an indistinct past. Not only gone, but forgotten. They were days that I believe we will never see again. Not here, not in Augusta Falls. Not anywhere. Everything awash with the heady delirium of spontaneous celebration, a celebration for no other reason than being alive. And the sound of something familiar but distant – a baseball game on the radio, the clunk-snap-hiss of emerald Coca-Cola caps – and all of a sudden the past is there. Technicolor and Sensurround: Cecil B. DeMille, King Vidor. And then a welcome silence after an endless noise.

And spiked through these memories, like rusty jags of metal, were other memories . . .

The girls.

Always the girls.

Girls like Alice Ruth Van Home, whom I had loved as only a child could love someone – simply, quietly, perfectly.

Their lives like twists of damp paper, screwed tight and tossed away.

And then something would happen – something quiet and beautiful – and I'd start to believe there was hope that the world might set itself to rights.

I did not. Not then.

Perhaps I some small way what I have now done will redress the balance.

Perhaps now the ghosts that have haunted me all these years will slip away.

Their voices will fall silent – finally, peacefully, irrevocably.

In my hand I hold a shred of newspaper. I hold it up, and through the thin paper, now smeared with my own blood, I see the light from the window, the silhouette of the dead man before me.

'See?' I say. 'You see what you did?'

And then I smile. I am growing weaker. I perceive some sense of closure.

'Never again,' I whisper. 'Never again.'

CHAPTER 3

'Y ou pick a word,' Miss Webber said. 'You pick a word and then you think of as many words that mean the same or similar thing. They are called synonyms, words that mean the same or similar thing. You write them in your notebook, Joseph, and when you wish to make a sentence you look in your notebook and use the most interesting or suitable words you can find.'

I nodded.

She stepped around the desk and eased into the tablet-arm chair beside mine. The classroom was empty. I had waited behind on her instruction. It was two weeks before Christmas and the final days of school.

'You have heard of the Monkey Trials?' she asked.

I shook my head.

'Some years ago, 1925 I think, there was a biology teacher called John T. Scopes. He came from a town called Dayton in Tennessee, and he taught his pupils about something called evolution. You know what evolution is, Joseph?'

'Yes, Miss Webber . . . like the idea that we were

all monkeys in the trees a long time ago, and before that we were fish or something.'

She smiled. 'Mr Scopes taught his pupils about the theory of evolution instead of the theory of Creation as it is taught in the Bible. He was taken to court by the state of Tennessee, and the prosecuting lawyer was a man called William Jennings Bryan, a very widely known orator and three-time presidential candidate. The man who defended Mr John Scopes was Clarence Darrow, a very famous American criminal lawyer. Mr Scopes lost his battle and he was fined one hundred dollars, but at no time did he relinquish his position.' Miss Webber leaned a little closer to me. 'At no time, Joseph Vaughan, did he say what he believed people wanted to hear. He said what he thought was right.'

She leaned back. 'You're wondering why I'm telling you this?'

I said nothing, merely looked back at her and waited for her to speak further.

'I'm telling you this because we have a Constitution and the Constitution says we should say what we feel, and maintain our right to speak the truth as we see it. That, Joseph Vaughan, is what you should do with your writing. If you want to write, then you should write, but always remember to write the truth as you see it, not as other people wish it to be seen. You understand?'

'Yes,' I said, believing I did.

'Then, during your Christmas vacation, I want you to write me a story.'

'About what?'

She smiled. 'That is something you have to decide. Choose something that has some meaning for you, something that you feel provokes an emotion, a feeling . . . something that makes you angry or hateful, or something that makes you feel excited perhaps. Write a real story, Joseph. It doesn't have to be long, but it has to be about something you believe in.'

Miss Webber rose and stood over me. Once again she touched my cheek with the flat of her hand. 'Have a good Christmas, Joseph, and I will see you at the start of 1940.'

Gunther Kruger was the richest man in Charlton County. The Kruger house was twice the size of ours. In the parlor they had an Atwater Kent crystal radio, and the Kruger family – Gunther, his wife, their two sons and one daughter – would sit before it with headphones and listen to music and talking that travelled from Savannah, all the way through Hinesville and Townsend, Hortense and Nahunta. Those sounds somehow crossed the Okefenokee Swamp and did not sink. It was magical and strange, an aperture into a world I could not fathom. In the kitchen they had a Maytag washing machine and a Sunbeam Mixmaster, and Mrs Kruger, who wore coarse woolen skirts, would make wienerwurst and potato salad and talk to me in her pigeon-English accent.

'You are a sceercraw,' she would say, and I would frown and tilt my head and say, 'Sceercraw?'

'For sceering buds,' she said. 'Like he is med of stigs and olt clodes, yes?'

'Sticks and old clothes,' I repeated, and then smiled widely. 'A scarecrow!'

'Yes,' Mrs Kruger chimed. 'Like I have set, a sceercraw! Now eat before the buds come or you weel sceer them. Ha ha!'

I started visiting with the Krugers a week or so before Christmas. Oftentimes Mr Kruger would not be there, and my mother would tell me to stay only until Mr Kruger returned from whatever business he was engaged in. 'Man has enough children around his feet,' she said. 'He returns home you say your thank-yous and come home, understand?'

I understood; I did not wish to outstay my welcome. Besides, Elena Kruger, all of nine years old, too many teeth for her mouth, ears like spinnakers awaiting a gulf stream, seemed to have her heart set on goading me into violence each time I was there.

It took the patience of Job to restrain myself from horsewhipping Elena Kruger for her catcalls and slanderous indignities. Her brothers, Hans and Walter, both somewhat older than me, seemed oblivious to her invasive behavior, but she was there – needling and hankering, baiting and

39

badgering – from the moment I arrived until I heard Mr Kruger's rich tones of welcome when he came in back through the kitchen.

She was a sweet enough child I'm sure, but to a twelve-year-old boy a nine-year-old girl seems the worst kind of harpy. Her voice was shrill, like a rusted spike jabbing my ears, and though later she would mellow and soften, and in her own way become really quite sensitive and beautiful, at the time she was like bitter-tasting medicine for an illness long gone. Elena Kruger was as welcome as a pitcher of fizzy milk, repeating endlessly, each belch that little bit more sour.

Only once did I see her bruises. It was late after-noon, days before Christmas, and Mr Kruger was not yet back from the fields with Walter. Mrs Kruger called for her daughter to help her in the kitchen, and Elena went. I stood in the hallway that separated the parlor from the back half of the house, and from there I could see through the doorway.

Elena was told to turn up the sleeves of her blouse, and turn them up she did, all the way to her shoulders, and there, in numerous colors – purple, sienna, yellow and carmine – bruises were punched and painted along the upper halves of her arms. The impression given was of some forceful and terrible grip placed on her, large hands holding her upper arms, perhaps shaking her, perhaps doing nothing more than holding her still.

40

'Epilepsy,' my mother said when I had told her what I'd seen.

'You mustn't say a word, not a word, mind,' she stressed. 'Elena Kruger has epileptic fits, grand mal seizures they are called, and both her mother and father have sometimes to hold her tight to the mattress or the floor to stop her injuring herself.'

I asked why did she have fits, and my mother smiled and shrugged her shoulders. 'Why does one man have a crooked leg, or an eye that doesn't work? Who knows, Joseph . . . it is the nature of things.'

I imagined strong hands holding Elena down, hands that would prevent her shuddering and trembling across the floor, how her skirt would soil, how she would perhaps bite down on six inches of roughhewn leather belt to prevent her severing her own tongue.

After that Elena's needling and name-calling never bothered me as much. I just had to picture the terrifying violence of such a physical affliction and my heart, small and insubstantial though it was, went out to her. She already hurt more than she could ever hurt me, and I believed if I took some of that hurt she might get better. I was naïve, foolish perhaps, but it seemed to make sense at the time. I believe that was the point at which I began to see her in a different light, and though she had two elder brothers – Hans was twelve, and Walter all of sixteen and the better

41

part of a man – I felt some fraternal pull toward her. She seemed fragile and disconsolate, adrift in a world where the words of her father, her brothers, seemed to hold sway. I imagined her as some gentle, lonely soul, a soul without tether or anchor, and I determined that I – in some small way – would attempt to make her life somehow happier.

Christmas came and went. I wrote my story. It was called The Broken-Field Run', and it was about Red Grange, how he used to catch the ball and take off down the field like a long dog after a short rabbit. I had seen him at the movies one time, a Saturday afternoon matinee with my father: an RKO Radio Pictures newsreel, a half-hour Pete Smith Specialty, and then a short before the main feature. Red Grange, perhaps the greatest runner in football history, legs like steam pistons going one after the other. I used words like *fleet* and *mercurial, athletic* and *Herculean*. Miss Webber changed them to words she thought everyone would understand, and then she stood ahead of the class and told everyone to close their eyes.

'That's right,' she said quietly. 'Close your eyes . . . and don't open them until I'm done.'

She read my story to the class. I wish she hadn't. My heart, thundering like a traction engine, could have powered a steamboat all the way from Minnesota to the Gulf of Mexico. It was a feeling

I would never forget, and it almost served to dissuade me from pursuing my dream to write.

When she was done there seemed to be a small chasm of silence into which I fell. No-one said a word. Miss Webber reached out her figurative hand and rescued me from that chasm.

She did not compliment the story, nor negate it. She did not hold it up as some sort of example to the other children in the class. She merely asked who had been able to see Red Grange as he struck out on his broken-field run.

Ronnie Duggan raised his hand.

So did Laverna Stowell. Virginia Grace Perlman. Catherine McRae, her brother Daniel.

I kept my head going forward and my eyes inside it. The color swelled in my cheeks.

Soon there were more children with their hands up than those without.

And then Miss Webber said, 'Good . . . good indeed. That is called *imagining*, and imagining is a vital and necessary ability in this world. Every great invention came about because folks were able to *imagine* things. You should nurture and cultivate your ability to imagine. You should let your head fill up with pictures of the things you think about and describe them to yourself. You should *make believe* . . .'

I listened to her. I loved her. Years later, a very different time, I would think of stopping my work, and then I would remember Alexandra Webber and let my head fill with pictures.

I would make believe, that's all, and somehow things would seem less dark.

February came. The weather turned. Gunther Kruger visited with my mother, told her that they were driving the length of St Mary's River to spend a day at Fernandina Beach.

'We would very much like it if you would both accompany us,' he said, and my mother – barely glancing at me – explained to Mr Kruger that she was most grateful, but unfortunately would not be able to come.

'Joseph, however, would be thrilled,' she said. 'I have promised Mrs Amundsen that I would do the butter-churning with her, and if we miss it today the milk will turn—'

Mr Kruger, ever the gentleman, raised his hand and smiled widely. He saved my mother the embarrassment of explaining her refusal. 'Perhaps next time,' he said, and then told me that they would be leaving from the Kruger house at six in the morning.

'Do not send any food,' Mr Kruger told my mother. 'Mrs Kruger will make enough to feed the five thousand and many of their relatives.'

The following morning it was raining, lightly at first, and then heavier. Nevertheless, we drove along the edge of St Mary's River all the way to Femandina Beach, and by the time we arrived the sun had broken forth and the sky was clear.

It was a rare day. I watched the Kruger family – Mrs Kruger, Walter, the two younger children – and they seemed to represent some idyll, some standard against which all families should have been judged. They did not fight, or argue; they laughed frequently, and with no clear reason to laugh; they appeared to me as some symbol of perfection in an indiscriminately imperfect world.

By the time we left the sun had softened its temper and was considering retirement. The haze of late afternoon hung like a ghost of warmth around us, its arms wide and embracing, and when we carried the baskets and blankets to the car Mr Kruger walked beside me and asked if I had enjoyed the day.

'Yes, sir, very much,' I said.

'Good,' he said quietly. 'Even you, Joseph Vaughan . . . even you must have some memories to cherish for when you grow older.'

I did not understand what he meant, and I did not ask.

'And Elena,' he said.

I turned and looked up at him.

He smiled. 'I want to thank you for your patience with her. She is a delicate child, and I know you spend time with her when perhaps you would rather be rough housing with Hans and Walter.'

I felt awkward and embarrassed. 'I – it's okay, Mr Kruger, no trouble at all.'

'You mean a great deal to her,' he went on. 'She speaks of you often, Joseph. She has found it difficult to make friends, and I thank you for being there for her.'

'Yes, sir,' I replied, and set my eyes straight to the road ahead.

For more than nine months I had watched the wound heal. I believed there would always be a scar, right there beneath my skin, invisible to anyone but myself, and the scar would remind me of what had happened to Alice, that winter of 1939 – the things I'd overheard from the landing as Reilly and my mother spoke in the kitchen . . .

For more than nine months Augusta Falls had made believe that what had happened was a dark and awkward dream. Something had happened somewhere else, not here in their own town, and they had heard rumor of this terrible thing and thanked God that it had not happened to them. They had dealt with this thing in such a way, and they had survived. They had made it through the shadows and come out the other side.

For nine months they told themselves everything was going to be okay.

But it was not.

Laverna Stowell was found murdered in the late summer of 1940. She was nine years old, would have been ten on August twelfth, three days after the discovery of her body in a field near the outskirts of Silco, Camden County. She was found on a Friday, just like Alice Ruth Van Horne. She was naked, nothing but her socks and a single shoe on her right foot. I knew this because I read

46

a newspaper report the following Wednesday. I cut out her picture and the article beneath.

CHARLTON COUNTY JOURNAL
Friday August 9th, 1940

Second Girl Found Murdered

On the morning of Friday August 9th, the citizens of Augusta Falls were once again witness to a terrifying discovery. The naked body of Laverna Stowell, daughter of Silco couple Leonard and Martha Stowell, was found naked but for her socks and a single shoe on her right foot. The second murder follows the November death of Alice Ruth Van Horne. Camden County Sheriff Ford Ruby refused to comment, but did allow that a dual-county operation would be established by himself and Charlton County Sheriff, Haynes Dearing. Miss Alexandra Webber, teacher at the Augusta Falls School where Laverna Stowell was a student, said that Laverna was a bright and outgoing child who had no difficulty making friends. She said that the children had been informed of this situation, and prayers would be said at each morning roll-call for the forthcoming week. Already citizens of Augusta Falls and Silco have met, and a town meeting to discuss the possibility of united action will be arranged. Sheriff Haynes Dearing once again stressed the importance of citizens in both towns and surrounding areas to remain calm. 'There is nothing worse than panic in such situations. I am here to reassure everyone that there is a police procedure employed in any murder investigation, and it is the duty of the police to establish and carry out this procedure. If people wish to assist they can be alert to any strange or unfamiliar individuals, and also take care to ensure the safety and welfare of their own children at all times.' When asked if any progress had been made in the investigation of the killing of Alice Ruth Van Horne, Sheriff Dearing refused to comment, saying that 'all details of an ongoing investigation need to remain confidential until the perpetrator has been arrested and charged.'

I held the cutting in my hands and felt my eyes fill with tears. I imagined how I would feel if it had been Elena. I cried again, but this time there was something else beneath the sense of loss: fear. A bone-deep jag of fear that pierced right through me, and around it was a sense of anger, of near hatred for whoever had done this thing. Laverna had come each day from Silco in Camden County, and though I'd shared no more than half a dozen words with her outside of Miss Webber's class, I still believed that somehow I had failed her. Why, I did not know, but I believed that both of them – Alice Ruth and Laverna – had been my responsibility.

'You can't blame yourself,' my mother told me when I explained my feelings. 'There are people out there, Joseph, people who do not see life the way that we see it. They grant it no importance, no value, and they are almost incapable of stopping themselves when it comes to such terrible things.'

'There must be something we can do—'

'We can be watchful,' she said. She leaned closer to me as if imparting a secret not to be shared with the world. 'We must take to watching for ourselves, and watching for everyone else. I know you feel responsible, Joseph, that is your nature, but responsibility and blame are not the same thing. You should be responsible if you feel it is your duty, but you must never blame yourself. You cannot punish yourself for the crimes of another.'

I listened. I understood. I wanted to do something, but I did not know what.

Two men came. They wore dark suits and hats. My mother told me they were from the Georgia Bureau of Investigation, that they had been assigned to assist Sheriff Dearing. They criss-crossed the state asking forthright, indelicate questions, and from what I overheard from the kitchen it seemed that people quickly began to resent their presence. Dearing had apparently requested that he accompany them, but agents

Leon Carver and Henry Oates declined his request, said it was Federal business, that objectivity was the key. I saw Carver once, a tall and imposing man, whose nose looked like a clenched fist scattered with purple veins. With eyes set back far into his head beneath heavy brows, he appeared to be squinting out of a permanent shadow. I did not speak to him, nor he to me. He watched me like I could not be trusted, and then turned his back. They stayed in Augusta Falls for three days, then they headed south, made a wide clockwise circuit through the surrounding towns, and then disappeared. We heard no more, and they were never mentioned.

Later I spoke to Hans Kruger.

'Boogeyman,' he said. 'There's a boogeyman out there and he comes to eat children.'

I snorted in contempt. 'Who told you that?'

'Walter,' he said defensively. 'Walter told me it was a boogeyman, someone who's come back from the dead and needs to feed off living people to stay alive.'

'And you believe that horseshit?'

Hans hesitated for a moment.

'And he says these things to Elena?' I asked.

Hans shook his head. 'No, he doesn't say these things to Elena. I have to tell Elena so she knows—'

I grabbed him suddenly by the collar of his shirt. He tried to step back but I held on tight. 'You don't say anything to Elena!' I snapped. 'You leave

50

Elena alone. She's frightened enough as it is without you telling her horseshit stories about things that don't even exist!'

Walter appeared around the corner of the house. 'Hey! What is this here? You boys should not be fighting!'

Hans ducked away, wrenched himself free of my grip and ran back to the front of the house.

I stood there feeling ashamed, a little frightened by Walter.

'What's happening here?' he asked.

'I told him not to tell boogeyman stories to Elena,' I said. 'I don't want her to be frightened. Hans said he was going to tell Elena about the boogeyman.'

Walter laughed suddenly. 'He did, did he? Let me sort that out, okay?'

'Don't hurt him, Walter.'

Walter placed his hand on my shoulder. 'I won't hurt him, Joseph. I'll just teach him a lesson.'

'It's not a boogeyman . . . it's a person who's doing these things, a terrible person.'

Walter smiled understandingly. 'I know, Joseph, I know. Let the police take care of it, okay? The police will find out who is doing these things and stop them. You let me take care of Hans and Elena.'

I said nothing.

'Okay?' he prompted.

I nodded. 'Okay,' I said, but I did not mean it. Walter was out with his father, working the farm, earning keep for the family. I had decided to look after Elena, and nothing would change my mind.

'Now go,' he said. 'Home with you. I will speak to Hans and make sure he doesn't frighten his sister.'

I turned and ran back to my house. I said nothing to my mother. I stood at the window of my bedroom and looked across at the Krugers house. I believed that if anything happened to Elena I would never be able to forgive myself.

After the Federal people left, sheriffs from each county – Haynes Dearing, a man in his mid-thirties, already looking older than his years, and Ford Ruby – had a sit-down meeting at the Quinn Cumberland Diner, a respectable and clean establishment on the north side of Augusta Falls owned and run by two widows.

Haynes Dearing was a Methodist, attended Charlton County Methodist Church. Sheriff Ford Ruby was Protestant Episcopal and frequented the Communion Church of God in Woodbine, but despite their differences regarding John Wesley and scripture interpretation they considered that the death of a little girl was more important than religious distinctions.

The death of a second little girl brought them together, and they pooled their resources. There was even talk of a man coming from Valdosta, a government man with a lie machine and a female assistant, but no-one ever showed. Sheriffs Dearing and Ruby, deputizing pretty much every man that could walk a straight line unaided, searched the woods and banks around Silco, even went back and searched the far end of the High Road once more, just to see, just to be sure. Of what, I did not know, and I did not ask, for once again there were hushed conversations in the kitchen of my house.

Nothing ever came of the searches, and finally, inevitably, Haynes Dearing and Ford Ruby went back to arguing about John Wesley and the scriptures, kept on arguing until they concluded it had been a mistake to work together, to even think they could work together, and they vowed such a thing would never happen again. By the end of August I no longer heard mention of Laverna Stowell. Perhaps she was an angel too, she and Alice Ruth Van Horne, and maybe my father, if he'd managed to keep his hands clean and worked hard enough to make the grade, was sitting right alongside them. Perhaps I convinced myself that the nightmare had now really ended. Perhaps I believed that some itinerant vagabond, crazy and brutal and vicious, had passed through our lives and now had disappeared. For some unknown reason he had visited twice, but this I did not consider. The truth and what I imagined might be the truth were not the same thing. I wondered if some other county, some other state, was now losing its children to this bogeyman. I kept my eyes wide and my ears alert, even at night; the sound of animals moving between our house and that of the Krugers sometimes woke me, and I would lie there chilled and afraid. After some time, steeling myself for what I might see, I would slip from beneath the covers and make my way tentatively to the window. I saw nothing. The night unfolded before me in a cool static monochrome, and I would wonder if my imagination wasn't feeding my mind with small and fragile lies. I hoped with all I possessed that the nightmare had passed, but deep down, right there inside my heart, I knew it had not.

CHAPTER 4

'A competition,' Miss Alexandra Webber said. Five months had passed since the death of the Stowell girl, five months and another Christmas.

Christmas had been hard on my mother. She and Mrs Kruger, whose name I now understood to be Mathilde, had volunteered their services to assist in an influenza epidemic that had broken out amongst the Negro families. For many days she came home late and left early, and I spent much of my time at the Krugers' house. I was thirteen years old, a few months older than Hans Kruger, a few years younger than Walter. Nevertheless, despite our similarity in ages, there was little we held in common. There were as many opinions as there were words about the war; there were rumors that Adolf Hitler was a madman, that America would be drawn into the fighting. Roosevelt was inaugurated for the third time, and already there was talk of the British using American arms and equipment, the cost of which would not be requested until after the conflict was over. Some – Reilly Hawkins in particular – said

55

that it was the first step on a short road to collab-
oration.

'They'll call for us,' he said. 'They'll call for us
to go and fight in Europe.'

'And would you go?' my mother asked him.

'No question about it,' Reilly said. 'You gotta
die for something, right? Seems to me it'd be better
to die in a field in Europe fighting for something
you believe in than die out here in the swamps
from nigra influenza.'

'Reilly,' my mother admonished.

'Yes, ma'am,' he said sheepishly. 'Beg your pardon,
ma'am.'

'What is it you believe in?' I asked Reilly. 'You
believe in war?'

Reilly smiled and shook his head. 'No, Joseph,
I don't believe in war. I'll tell you what I believe
in—' He stopped suddenly and looked at my
mother as if for permission to speak.

'Go ahead, Reilly Hawkins, but remember I'm
listening, and I'll let you know if you've gone too
far.'

'What I believe in,' Reilly said, 'is the freedom
to think and believe and say what you feel is right.
This man, this Ay-dolf Hitler, well he's nothing
but a fascist and a dictator. He's getting those
German people all fired up and hateful about the
Jews, about travelling people, about people who
don't look the same or talk the same or go to the
same churches. He's forcing his own views on a
country, and that country is going mad. That's the

56

kind of thing that travels like an airborne virus, and if good people, honest people – people like us – if we don't do what we can to stop it then we'll find it everywhere. That's why I'll go if they ask me.'

The following day I asked Miss Webber about the war, about what Reilly Hawkins had said about the Jews and the travelling people.

For a moment she looked surprised, and then there was something in her face that spoke of grief, of suppressed tears perhaps.

That's when she spoke of the competition. She changed the subject – suddenly, unexpectedly – and I forgot all about Adolf Hitler and how he was getting folks all fired up and hateful.

'What competition?'

'A story competition; a competition for people to write and submit stories.'

I leaned my head to one side.

'Don't do that, Joseph Vaughan,' she said. 'Makes you look like you have only half a brain and your head's lopsided.'

I set my head straight.

'So write a story,' she said. 'It can be about anything at all, but like we discussed before it is always better to write about something you're personally interested in, or something you have experienced. It should be no longer than two thousand words, and if you write it neatly enough I will set it correctly on my Underwood typewriter and we will send it all the way to Atlanta.'

I didn't say a great deal. I didn't remember the moment too well. I think I had my eyes wide and my mouth slightly open.

'What?' Miss Webber asked. 'Why are you standing there like that?'

After a moment I shook my head. 'No particular reason,' I replied.

'Now you look like the sort of boy who needs his mouth wiped every fifteen minutes . . . go sit down at your desk, Joseph.'

'Yes, Miss Webber.'

'And start working on some ideas. Deadline for your story is a month from today.'

Three days later I came across a word: 'monkeyshines'. I don't remember now how I came across it, but I did. It was from the late 1800s, and it meant tricks and japes, the kind of things kids do when they're in a mischief and mayhem mood. The word pleased me, made me smile, and so I used it as the title for my story.

I wrote about being a kid, 'cause that's what I was. I wrote about being thirteen and having no father, about the war in Europe and some of the things that Reilly Hawkins told me. Alongside that, I wrote about the things I did to keep my mind occupied, to make me forget that my mother was tired, that Hitler was a madman, and somewhere some thousands of miles away people were being killed because they thought different or spoke different. I wrote about practical jokes me and the Kruger boys had done. About the time we found a dead raccoon and buried it. We dug up some mountain fly honeysuckle and planted it on the little grave, and we said some words and wished the raccoon would find Alice Ruth and Laverna and keep them company in Heaven. I wrote about these things and signed it neatly at the bottom – Joseph Calvin Vaughan – and I put my age and my date of birth because I figured the story people in Atlanta might want to know such details.

I gave my story to Miss Webber on Friday the eleventh of February. On Monday she told me she'd typed it up and mailed it to Atlanta, and she showed me Atlanta on the map. It seemed an awful long way away. I wondered if my story would have changed at all by the time it got there.

I thought about it a lot for some time, and then I forgot about it. Seemed to me that writing things down was a way of making them go away.

'You could look at it that way,' Miss Webber told me. 'Or you could look at it from the viewpoint that writing things down makes them last forever. Like that book I gave you last Christmas . . . that was written and it's still here. There's thousands of copies of that book all over the country, all over the world. Right now there might be someone in England, someone in Paris, France, someone else again in Chicago, reading that very same book, and what they read and what they think is going to be very different from what you felt you were reading. A story is like a message that means something different to everyone who receives it.'

I listened to what Miss Webber said because everything she said made sense.

When spring came my mother got sick. She grew pale and anemic. Dr Thomas Piper visited several times, and each time he looked concerned and important. Dr Piper wore a dark suit with a vest and a pocket watch with a golden chain, and he carried a leather bag from which he produced tongue depressors and bottles of iodine.

'You are how old?' he asked me.

'Thirteen, sir,' I told him. 'Fourteen in October.'

'Well, good enough. You are a man as far as I'm concerned. Your mother has weak blood. Weak in nutrients, weak in iron, weak in most everything that should be strong. She must have bed rest and quiet, perhaps for as much as a month, and she must have a diet rich in green vegetables and good meat. If she does not do this you will not have a mother for very much longer.'

I walked across to the Krugers' house after Dr Thomas Piper had left.

'We will take care of her,' Mathilde Kruger said. 'I will send Gunther every day with soup and cabbage, and when she is stronger we will feed her sausages and potatoes. Don't worry, Joseph, you may have lost your father but you will not lose your mother. God is not that cruel.'

Three weeks later, the day that Reilly Hawkins told me President Roosevelt was sending American

60

soldiers to Greenland, Miss Webber had me stay after class.

'I have a letter,' she said, and she reached into her desk and produced an envelope. 'It is a letter from Atlanta, Georgia. Come sit here and I will read it to you.'

I walked to the front of the classroom and sat down.

'Dear Miss Webber,' she started. 'It is with great pleasure that we write to inform you of our competition results. We were greatly impressed with the standard of material submitted this year, and though the adjudication of such a vast array of different styles and subject matter is never easy we believe that this year it has been harder than ever.'

Miss Webber paused and glanced at me.

'It is with a degree of commiseration that we must tell you that 'Monkeyshines' by Joseph Vaughan did not reach the final stage of judging, but nevertheless we wished to communicate to you our collective enjoyment regarding this most excellent piece. 'Monkeyshines' raised more than a few tears and a good degree of laughter amongst our readers, and when it was made clear that the piece had been penned by a boy of thirteen there were serious questions regarding the validity of authorial identity. Such a question was immediately refuted as we are, of course, more than aware of your own reputation and credibility as a teacher. Nevertheless, it still came as a surprise

61

that a composition demonstrating such a natural narrative style and so astutely perceptive was the work of someone so young.'

Again Miss Webber paused. All I understood was that I had won nothing. I felt little if any emotion regarding the matter.

'And so, in closing, I would like to heartily commend Mr Joseph Vaughan for his story, 'Monkeyshines': a thoroughly enjoyable reading experience, and evidence that we have in our midst, right here in Georgia, a bright and immensely talented young author who, we trust, will continue to go from strength to strength in his literary ventures. With our best wishes. The Atlanta Young Story Writers Adjudication Board.'

Miss Webber turned to me and smiled. She frowned, then tilted her head to one side. I wanted to tell her she looked like half her brain was missing.

'You are not pleased, Joseph?' she asked.

I said nothing. I wondered what she thought I might be pleased about.

'The Adjudication Board wrote to you, all the way from Atlanta, to tell you that your story had received a special commendation. They say that you are bright and immensely talented. Do you understand that?'

'I understand that we didn't win, Miss Webber,' I said.

She laughed suddenly, and it was like a wealth of sunshine breaking forth. 'Didn't win? Winning is not the *only* reason to do something. Sometimes you do something for experience, or simply for pleasure; other times you do something to prove to yourself that you *can* do it, irrespective of anyone else's viewpoint or belief. You wrote a story, only the second complete story you've ever written, and the Atlanta adjudication board sent you a special commendation and expressed their wish that you go from literary strength to strength. That, my dear Joseph Calvin Vaughan, is something of which to be very proud.'

I nodded and smiled. It was fifteen minutes past the end of lessons and I wanted to get home. When I'd left that morning my mother had seemed particularly frail.

Miss Webber folded the letter carefully and returned it to the envelope. 'This is for you,' she said, and handed it to me. 'You should keep this letter, and whenever you feel that your ability is in question, whenever you feel that you should do something other than write, you should read it once more and feel your purpose resolve. Writing is something that is a gift, Mr Vaughan, and to deny its importance, or to do something other than use your ability, would be a grave and significant mistake.' She smiled once more. 'Now go . . . home with you!'

I thanked Miss Webber and left the room. I walked quickly, taking the High Road and staying close to the fence. Mr Kruger had told me that after the rain the ground was too soft to bear the weight of a child, let alone a young man such as myself, and that if I walked along that way I was to stay close to the fence and away from the trees.

When I arrived home I stood in the kitchen for several minutes. In hindsight, always our most astute adviser, I realized I had granted no importance to the letter from Atlanta. It was my first real acknowledgement, and yet it seemed to mean nothing. I took the letter from my pocket and read through it once more. The words were received but they were not absorbed. Later, the letter would mean a great deal, and in some small way it would act as an anchor amidst the storm of critical and trenchant self-doubt that would come, but then – standing in the kitchen – it was merely a message of failure. Miss Webber was not to blame. The letter told me I could do better, and perhaps, in some small way, I had already determined the standard to which I would aspire.

It was then that I heard voices, above me I believed, and I was puzzled. My mother was alone and unwell in the house, and yet the voices sounded like a conversation. Had the disease she suffered driven her to madness?

I tucked the letter into my pocket and backed up to the bottom of the stairwell. I heard nothing. Was I imagining things?

I took the risers one at a time, my ears sharpened and alert. When I reached the upper landing I heard the voices again – my mother, her clear and distinct lilt, even a hint of laughter, and another voice – deeper, perhaps accented?

I walked down the hallway to her door. It was firmly closed, but it was undoubtedly from behind that door that the voices came.

I knocked once.

'Mother?' I asked.

There seemed to be a moment of confusion, the sound of rustling, something else, and even as I reached out to turn the door handle she called out, 'One moment, Joseph, one moment, please.'

I waited, perplexed and confused.

Thirty seconds, perhaps more, and then the door was opened from within and Gunther Kruger stood there looking at me, smiling widely, his cheeks reddened.

'Joseph!' he exclaimed, pronouncing it 'Yosef' the way all the Krugers did. He seemed more surprised than pleased. 'Hullo there. What a surprise!'

I shook my head. Why would it be a surprise? I always came home from school.

I looked around him to see my mother laid up in the bed, the covers pulled tight to her throat. She withdrew one arm and extended her hand toward me.

'Come in, Joseph,' she said. 'You are home early.'

'I'm not,' I said. 'I always come home at this time.'

She frowned. 'But your extra tutorial with Miss Webber—'

'Is on a Monday,' I interjected. 'Today is Friday.'

She smiled. 'Of course it is. How silly of me.

Mr Kruger here was just bringing me some soup.' She glanced toward the dresser, and there – in the clay pot that Mrs Kruger sent over almost daily – was the soup. It looked untouched, the lid still firmly set.

'Oh,' I said.

'Well,' Mr Kruger said, 'I think it's time I should be going. It was nice to see you, Joseph, as always. You should come over later and see Hans and Walter, yes?'

'Yes,' I said, still a little mystified.

Mr Kruger snatched his jacket from the chair behind the door, and without putting it on he hurried past me and went down the stairs. I heard his footsteps as he crossed the tiled kitchen floor, and then the back door slammed abruptly. He had forgotten to say goodbye to my mother.

'Come to me,' she said. 'Come and sit by me on the bed.'

I crossed the room. Everything smelled of lavender and boiled chicken.

'Sit here,' she said, and patted the mattress with her hand. 'How was your day, Joseph?'

'I got a letter.'

'A letter?'

I nodded.

'A letter from whom?'

'From the people that judge the story competition in Atlanta.'

She sat up, her eyes wide, her expression one of intense interest. 'And?'

I withdrew the letter from my pocket and showed her.

She read it without speaking, and then she looked at me with tears in her eyes and reached out her hand. She laid her palm flat against the side of my face.

'My son,' she said, her voice a broken whisper. 'You have found your vocation it seems.'

I shrugged.

'Don't stop,' she said. 'Don't ever stop writing. This is the way the world will find out who you are.'

For some reason I felt like crying, but I did not.

I was thirteen, almost a man, and though both Miss Webber and my mother thought the letter a great deal more important than I did, it was nevertheless no reason to be sad.

I gritted my teeth. I lay down beside my mother, right there on the patchwork quilt, and closed my eyes.

She stroked the hair from my forehead, and then leaned down and kissed me.

'Your father would have been so proud,' she said. 'His son, the writer.'

CHAPTER 5

The third girl was all of seven years old. She was found on Saturday, June seventh, 1941. Just as with Alice Ruth Van Horne and Laverna Stowell she was left naked and beaten. Her name was Ellen May Levine. A wide and deep incision centered her body, as if someone had attempted to cut her in two. Perhaps they had started such a thing and could not bear to finish it.

I had known her less than three months. She had come all the way from Fargo, near the Suwannee River in Clinch County, to attend Miss Webber's classes in March that year. She was found in a shallow grave no more than half a mile from our house, there in the trees at the edge of Gunther Kruger's boundary.

Sheriff Haynes Dearing met with Sheriff Ford Ruby, and they drove over to meet with Clinch County Sheriff Burnett Fermor. Rumor had it that the three of them spent more than two hours together; they called for detailed maps of the three counties and at least two orders of sandwiches and coffee. When the meeting was done it seemed

68

they were none the wiser than when they'd started, but at least they hadn't argued about John Wesley and the scriptures.

At least a dozen men were deputized. They came with pickup trucks and dogs and scoured the countryside from one horizon to the other. There were huddles of people talking in the street. Seemed that every day the newspaper had something else to say without saying very much of anything at all. Folks even mentioned the names of Georgia Bureau of Investigation agents Carver and Oates, as if in bringing them back something would be different from their previous investigation. Carver and Oates never came, nor the man from Valdosta with a lie machine and a female assistant. Sheriff Dearing looked perpetually exhausted, as if sleep was a cohort of the killer and was evading him with great skill. There was talk of murder weapons, of knives, meat cleavers, other such suppositions. I watched it all, every single thing, and I wondered how someone would be found who had made it their business to remain undiscovered. Everyone knew they were innocent, and yet everyone knew they were a suspect, and would remain so until the guilty one was identified.

He was not, and for some reason I believed it would stay that way.

'This is a bad, bad thing,' Reilly Hawkins said. Once again he was seated in our kitchen. My mother had recovered from her illness, though Mr Kruger still brought soup and sausages two or three times a week from his wife's kitchen. I knew this was the case, because often, after school, my mother would send me over to the Krugers' with washed pots and plates and her thanks.

'This thing with these children—'

My mother shook her head. 'It's not something I want to discuss, Reilly,' she said.

'I want to talk about it,' I told her. 'I'm old enough to know what murder is, and I'm old enough to know that there are crazy people. Miss Webber told us that the Germans are putting Jewish people in prison camps and that many, many thousands have died—'

'Is she now?' my mother interjected. 'I don't know that that's suitable material to be teaching young children.'

'Not so young,' I said. 'I know that the French police are arresting Jews in Paris and handing them over to the Germans, a thousand at a time. I also know that James Joyce died in Switzerland, and that Virginia Woolf drowned herself in a river—'

'Enough,' my mother said. 'So you know a lot of things, Joseph Vaughan, but that does not necessarily mean that we will discuss the murdering of young girls in our kitchen.'

I looked at Reilly Hawkins. He looked away.

'I knew all three of them,' I said. My voice broke with emotion. I felt tears coming. 'I knew all three of them. I knew their names, what they looked like. I sat in Miss Webber's class with them, and

70

sometimes Miss Webber would have me read a story to everyone, and Ellen May would sit right up close like she wanted to hear every single word I said.' I could not hold myself. I stood up. 'I want to talk about it! I want to know what's happening and why we can't do anything about these terrible things!'

'Enough already!' she snapped. 'You have chores to do. Go and clean the window in your bedroom, and then you can go over to the Krugers if you wish.'

Anger rose inside me. I glared at my mother, and for a moment I saw right through her determined expression. She was afraid, as afraid as I; she did not know what to say to make this thing any better.

I felt I should reach out to her. I believed it would have been right to apologize, to tell her I was confused and afraid and I needed to tell someone how I felt. But that, in my small and narrow view, would have been tantamount to admitting defeat in the face of authority. I made a performance of stamping my way upstairs and along the corridor. When I reached my door I opened it and slammed it shut as if I had gone inside, then I turned back the way I'd come and crept along the hallway to the top of the stairs.

'—willful yes, but rarely disobedient,' my mother was saying. 'He has a bright and inquisitive mind like his father, and once he has hold of something he will not let it go.'

'I'm not one to judge,' Reilly said. 'He's the only boy I've ever been close to and I care for him a great deal. These recent things . . . these killings . . . are terrible things. Something like this happens, well, you cannot even begin to imagine how the parents must feel.'

'I know the second girl's parents, just as acquaintances mind,' my mother said. 'Leonard and Martha Stowell. Sweet people. Never met their daughter. She was the youngest, I think. Seem to remember there were three others, two boys and a girl.'

'A tragedy, a terrible tragedy. And to think, such a thing is the work of a human being.'

'In the very loosest sense of the term. Barely a human being I think.'

Reilly cleared his throat. 'I don't know, Mary, it seems a terrible place the world is becoming, what with this war in Europe, the awful things we're hearing about the Polish people and the Jews. I have heard rumor that the Germans are searching out and killing all the intellectuals – musicians and artists and writers and poets, even professors and teachers – anyone who in any way opposes their views. They are searching them out and sometimes just executing them right there in the street.'

'It is not the world, Reilly. It is simply a few insane men using their power over ignorant people. This propaganda against the Jews has been going on for twenty years or more. Adolf Hitler has been slowly poisoning the minds and hearts of the German people, and he was doing this long before he went to war. I only hope that this war is over before we are drawn further into it.'

'I don't know that such a thing can be avoided,' Reilly said. 'As a free and democratic people it's our responsibility to stand up against this kind of persecution.'

'So it is,' she said, 'but first it is our duty to protect the children of our neighbors and friends against the monster in our midst.'

Later I crept back along the hallway and went into my room. From my window I watched as Elena Kruger helped her mother hang washing in the back yard.

Three days later Elena Kruger began attendance in Miss Webber's class. She sat one row to my left, one desk down.

She sat where Ellen May Levine had sat before someone cut her in half.

It seemed an injustice to me, the affliction Elena Kruger suffered. I was never witness to her grand mal episodes, but the bruises on her arms and shoulders were clearly visible when we went swimming in one of the small tributaries that escaped from the Okefenokee. June was hot, but July it went off the barometer sufficient to split stones, and when school finally broke for the vacation in the first week of August it was all we could do to stand straight in the brutal temperature. The sun broke high and bright, hard like a fist, stayed resolute until nightfall and then rested to gather strength for tomorrow. Reilly said it was the hottest summer on record; Gunther Kruger said Reilly had access to no such records, and how would he know such a thing anyway. Seemed to me it didn't matter what any other summer might have been like, the one we had was enough to go around, and more besides. Walter Kruger worked much of the day with his father, and so the three of us – myself, Hans and Elena, we took to crawling beneath the Kruger house and hiding from the heat. Beneath the house it was cool and damp, almost another world, and despite the scritching of bugs and the sensation of moist crawling that was always on our skin, the shade it afforded was far more tolerable than the harsh and un-relenting sun.

'I think . . . I think if this goes on for another three weeks the swamps will be hard enough to walk on,' Hans said. I considered Hans a little slow – well meaning, yes, but somehow a little dense, as if all his thoughts had a prearranged time for arrival and yet managed to be overdue. He worshiped Walter, however; looked upon him as the fountainhead of all wisdom and truth. If Walter uttered it, well then it was gospel. A little of that carried through Hans to Elena, and I later felt it my duty to defend her against their pranks and pratfalls. One time, years before, Hans had told

Elena she was to eat a worm. He said that Walter had given him the message, that it was a definite instruction from Walter that she eat a worm. A whole one. She didn't ask questions; she spent a good four or five minutes looking for one until Walter himself appeared and happened to ask her what she was doing. Perhaps it was a Germanic thing, the view that one should always obey one's elders. If anyone had told me that Walter instructed I eat a worm, well, I would've told them to go stick that worm where the sun didn't shine, and I wouldn't have meant beneath the Kruger house.

The heat didn't continue for another three weeks, it continued until the latter part of September, and by then the Okefenokee was struggling to make it as far as the county line. We never did discover if the swamps dried out sufficiently to walk on. The colic came like Death Watch Mary and infected horses as far north as Winokur, as far south as St George. Lines were drawn on maps, and those maps were handed out at town meetings right across the state. The lines were territorial divides, and people were forbidden from crossing those lines in case they carried the infection into new areas. Oddly enough, though we were neighbors, one line ran right between us and the Krugers. I could not visit with them until Christmas was on the horizon, but each week my mother would sent me to the end of the High Road, and there – wrapped in a cloth and tucked beneath the same rock – was a package left by Mr Kruger. Countless times I went for that package, nothing more than a piece of leather rolled up and tied with a string, and each time I ferried it back to my mother without a question. Finally my curiosity took a hold and wouldn't let go. I fetched the leather from beneath the stone, and knelt there in the dirt for a moment. I thought of what my father would think; whether he had worked hard enough to become an angel, and even then could see right down into my thoughts. The question in my mind was greater than the threat of censure, and I untied that string, remembering each turn so I could tie it once more when I'd looked inside.

Seven dollars.

A five and two one-dollar bills.

It seemed strange to me that Gunther Kruger would send seven dollars to my mother each week.

I tucked the bills back; I rolled the leather around them; I tied it in such a way as only I would ever know, and then I ran home.

I gave her the money and never said a word.

For some reason I felt like Judas.

December of 1941.

In October we had heard that Adolf Hitler was near the gates of Moscow; that an American battle-ship – the USS *Reuben James* – had been attacked while on convoy duty west of Iceland. Seventy sailors died, forty-four were rescued. We held our breath, afraid to move perhaps. Reilly Hawkins said something bad would happen, that he'd been seized by a premonition while on an errand to White Oak.

Reilly Hawkins' premonition came true.

On December seven the Japanese bombed Pearl Harbor. Three hundred and sixty Japanese warplanes attacked the US Pacific Fleet in Hawaii. They also attacked US bases in the Philippines, on Guam and Wake. Twenty-four hundred people were killed.

Four days later Hitler and Mussolini, the fascist dictator of Italy, declared war on America.

Within six weeks American troops would land in Northern Ireland. They were the first to set foot in Europe since the Expeditionary Forces landed in France during the Great War of 1914–18.

Reilly Hawkins drove all the way to Fort Stewart, itself no more than a stone's throw west of Savannah, but the Army told him his feet were flat and his arches were fallen and he couldn't carry a gun for Roosevelt. I'd never seen a man so dejected and broken; he stayed in his house for three days straight, and when he appeared he'd neither shaved nor changed his shirt. My mother said that nothing could crush a man's spirit so much as telling him he could not help.

Four days before Christmas Gunther Kruger came to see my mother. Hans was ill – sharp elevations of temperature, relapsing fever, muscular pains, delirium. My mother called Dr Piper and he examined the boy.

'Streptobacillus moniliformus,' he pronounced sonorously.

'In English,' my mother said.

'Rat-bite fever,' Dr Piper told her. 'The boy's been bitten by a rat. See here,' he said, and indicated a suppurating weal at the back of Hans's ankle. 'Rat bite.'

'You can treat it?' she asked.

'Sure I can treat it,' Dr Piper said, 'but there needs to be a program to rout out and destroy the rats.'

My mother smiled and nodded. She turned to me. 'Go,' she said. 'Run to Reilly's house and tell him that Dr Piper needs him at the Krugers'.'

Reilly started work on his own, but by the end of the following week there were seven men in all. The Augusta Falls Vermin Unit. That was the name my mother gave them, and Dr Piper told them that if the infected rats were not found then every child in Augusta Falls was at risk. It was necessary for morale, for the well-being of the families, that this task be undertaken with efficiency, with military discipline, with speed. Reilly was the chief. He was to be addressed as such. There were to be .25 caliber rifles, all ammunition paid for from the town purse; there were traps, nets, heavy boots, other incidentals and requirements, all of it official, all of it – in its own way – vital to the war effort.

Vermin Unit Chief Hawkins shaved every day, wore a clean shirt, patrolled routes that the children took to school. He carried a rifle on his shoulder, his pockets full of bullets, and he worked conscientiously to rid Augusta Falls of the rats.

'There will always be rats,' Dr Piper told my mother. 'You can't possibly believe that Reilly Hawkins is going to somehow clear the entire county of rats . . . and even if he does, I've heard rumor that the rats in Clinch and Brantley are far bigger and far uglier than any we might have in Charlton.'

My mother smiled at him. 'I never said such a thing was possible, Thomas, but go and see Reilly Hawkins when you have a moment, and then tell me he doesn't possess a greater sense of self-worth and respect than he ever has.'

Dr Piper smiled. 'Would that all the women of Augusta Falls were as sagacious as yourself, Mrs Vaughan.'

My mother bowed her head slightly. 'Would that all the men were as easily directed to constructive action, eh, Dr Piper?'

Nothing further was said. Reilly Hawkins and his Vermin Unit went on finding and destroying rats. The kept a logbook, detailed and precise. By February of 1942, as the Japanese invaded somewhere called Sumatra, the Vermin Unit claimed responsibility for the deaths of more than four hundred and thirty rats. No quarter was given. No prisoners of war. An eight-foot-deep hole had been dug in the middle of a cottonwood and tupelo grove at the very edge of Gunther Kruger's southernmost field, and dead rats were not only tipped down there by the bucketload, they were burned as well.

That was the last time Gunther Kruger and Reilly Hawkins saw eye to eye on very much of anything, because once Christmas was done and we turned the corner into '42 the color and pitch of everything in Augusta Falls seemed to change.

It was the war that did it; perhaps not so much the war, but what the war began to represent. It told us that there was a difference between people; that someplace thousands of miles away our own people were dying for something that we didn't even start. It told us that the German people couldn't be trusted, that somehow America had been maneuvered into a conflict that was not of its own making.

'Religious intolerance,' Miss Alexandra Webber told us. 'Prejudice, religious intolerance, a veritable witch hunt if you like . . . that's what is being perpetrated against the Jewish peoples. It is a challenge to everything that the United States of America believes in, a challenge to the Constitution. There is no way we can honestly continue to disavow involvement. This isn't a war between England and Germany, nor America and Japan. This is a war between the Allies and the Axis Powers, and the Axis represents everything that we abhor and condemn. This is a war for freedom, for power of choice, for religious forbearance.

80

Believe me, if I were a man I would be down there at the recruiting office myself.'

Outspoken she might have been, but Alexandra Webber was honest. The consensus of opinion turned against non-nationals – against the Italians, the Germans, even some Eastern European immigrants that had settled farms near Race Pond. There was a tension present at town meetings, something intangible yet unmistakable. The non-Americans started to withdraw from visible life. Even Gunther Kruger kept his children home. It was that obvious.

The tension broke on Wednesday, March eleventh, 1942, with the discovery of a fourth murdered girl.

Her name was Catherine Wilhelmina McRae. She was eight years old. Her decapitated head was discovered by children playing near the same grove of cottonwoods and tupelos where the rat-pit had been sited. Her body was found thirty-five yards away in a stream gully. There was no reason to assume that Catherine McRae's killer was not the same person who had killed Alice Ruth Van Home, Laverna Stowell and Ellen May Levine, and so the assumption was made.

I knew Catherine's brother, Daniel, better than I knew her. Daniel was a month younger than me. I was there when his father came to collect him from Miss Webber's class. We watched him go in silence. His father's face was red-raw from crying. Daniel was chalk-white and stunned.

81

The three sheriffs – Dearing from Charlton, Ruby from Camden and Fermor from Clinch – met once more. This time there were no maps, no sandwiches and coffee; this time there was a tri-County task force mobilized to scour the fields and surrounding countryside for anything that might relate to the murder of the McRae girl.

Reilly Hawkins' Vermin Unit was established under a different name. Men came from Folkston, Silco, Hickox, Winokur. Twin brothers came from Statenville in Echols County, related by blood to Sheriff Fermor on his mother's side; they drove more than a hundred miles in a beat-to-hell flatbed to join the line. That line was more than seventy men by the morning of Thursday the twelfth, and without a word, with no direct statement or edict, the foreigners were evident in their absence. There was not one German, not one Italian; even the Poles and the French stayed home. It was just Americans, Irish-Americans, a couple of Scots, and a Canadian with one eye called Lowell Shaner. Perhaps that was when the trouble really started. Perhaps that was the moment that ill-will and hearsay became the fuel for some violent fire of accusation, at first nothing more than a spark, an ember, but after two days of searching fields and gullies for any small indication of the McRae girl's killer, the talk that was spreading became incendiary.

'An American wouldn't do something such as this.'

'Who could have killed four girls? Surely it would have to be someone who didn't respect life the way we do.'

'Man who could do this wouldn't be a church-going man, believe me.'

And so, in its own small and narrow-minded way, the people of Augusta Falls began their own line of inquiry. There was talk – hearsay, rumor, scuttlebutt – some of it slanderous, some of it fiction, some of it generated by the type of people that liked nothing more than to incite ill will and bad feelings between people who previously were neutral toward one another.

There was so much talk of the killings I found it a difficult subject to avoid. Perhaps it was the first time I was scared of the world. The war frightened me – if only from the perspective Miss Webber forwarded.

'We know, as a race of peoples, that we are in trouble when war simply becomes a matter of dropping bombs from planes and killing hundreds, if not thousands of people. History has shown us one thing: that as we become more technologically advanced, we also become more able to kill more people without ever seeing their faces. One day, I am sure, someone will invent a bomb that is capable of destroying a whole town, if not a county. And that, sure as anything, will mark the point at which this civilization begins it slow and inevitable decay.'

So said Miss Webber, but despite her disturbing

prediction the war was still something that wasn't even being fought in my own country, something that existed many thousands of miles away. Even the attack on Pearl Harbor had resulted in American soldiers leaving the United States. The war was not being fought on American soil, and so – in a way – we managed to convince ourselves that it was something that did not involve us.

The killings were different. The killing of the four girls was right there amongst us. They were children I had known, and that – despite the smallness of its reality compared to the European front – was all the more terrifying.

One day, another day I stayed behind to wash the blackboard rags, I told Miss Webber of my fears.

She smiled and shook her head. 'So write your heart out,' she said. 'Writing can be an exorcism of fear and of hatred; it can be a way to overcome prejudice and pain. At least if you can write you have a chance to express yourself . . . you can put your thoughts out into the world, and regardless of whether anyone actually reads them or understands them they are no longer trapped inside of you. Bottle them . . . bottle them up, Joseph Vaughan, and one day you're likely to just explode.'

Later, many years later, how accurate her words would prove. But then, all of fourteen years old, I just wanted to understand why these things frightened me so much. I believed if I could understand the man then I would no longer fear him. The man who had done these terrible things to these little girls. I tried to imagine what life he might have led, how he would see the world, ostensibly the same world I saw, but somehow different. When I saw sunlight, did he merely see shadows? When I woke from a nightmare, relief washing through me like sea-foam, did he attempt to claw his way back into the nightmare to experience even more of it?

I gritted my teeth. I clenched my fists. I closed my eyes and tried to imagine how crazy you'd have to be to kill someone. To kill a child. And I wrote:

His eyes were swollen from crying, or maybe from looking for something. Or maybe his eyes were swollen because he was a crazy man, kind of man you'd keep a picture of to scare children when they were bad.

Smacking hard against the bad edge of life. Smacking hard against the corners, against the rougher angles, the angles that should have been smoothed down by such things as love and tolerance and patience.

And people would watch him from the corners of their eyes, and they would ask themselves what it would take to make a man so dark and crazy. Scattered hair, pinpoint eyes, brooding lips, a strong jawline – but strong with anger and passion,

85

not the strength that comes from character and determination. Man like that would know darkness, they'd think. Man like that would know shadows and hidey-holes, cellars and dungeons and catacombs, and he'd know all too well the chingle-changle chains dragged by headless horsemen as they galloped into dreams.

Man like that you didn't talk to, didn't make eye contact, didn't even think that he was there when he walked right by you. Give him thoughts and he'd see them, know you were thinking about him, and it would be like an energy magnet that pulled him in. And once he'd got you, well, he'd got you. There'd be no getting away, you see.

But no-one really knew what he was thinking, because no-one had ever asked him. He was just there, had always been there; he was the strangest familiarity along the footpaths and down the byways, hanging back beneath the trees when the rain came down, maybe smoking a cigarette and speaking in tongues to the ghosts that walked with him, beside him, inside of him even.

He's part of our town, a part of our home, and perhaps everyone believes that if they ignore it, if they don't think about it, then he will go away. Disappear into the shadows between the broken down shacks on Cooper's

Row. Vanish. Dissolve into nothing and be forgotten forever.

No such luck, friends and neighbors.

His name was unknown, his face as well. Come springtime, when folks believed in the basic goodness of all things on God's green earth, he came home to the people of Augusta Falls, Georgia, in many more ways than one.

Things don't disappear if you ignore them; a lesson learned.

Maybe lessons have to hurt sometimes so they come on home for keeps.

I showed what I had written to Miss Webber. She read it silently, her face expressionless, and then she closed my notebook and slid it across the desk toward me.

'Not one for the Atlanta Young Story Writers' Adjudication Board,' she said quietly, and then she smiled, but she smiled with her mouth and not her eyes, and I knew somehow – perhaps through nothing more than intuition – that I had upset her. I did not possess the nerve to ask her outright, and therefore I stayed silent.

'I know it's Monday, Joseph,' she said, 'but I have such a headache, and I was wondering if you wouldn't mind staying over for your extra tutorial tomorrow perhaps.'

'No problem,' I said. I gathered up my things. 'I think—'

I looked up at her.

She smiled. 'It's nothing,' she said. 'Go. Go on home. Tomorrow we will talk about James Fenimore Cooper and the Mohicans.'

At the end of the school road I looked back. Miss Webber had walked out beside me and paused there on the veranda at the front of the building. She was looking out at the horizon, her eyes fixed on some distant and indistinct point. She seemed pensive, lost almost. I wanted to walk back and ask her what was wrong. I did not. I turned and hurried home.

Now I see and understand that this is the only way it could have ended.

Perhaps so.

What did the Bible say?

'Who so sheddeth man's blood, by man shall his blood be shed.'

An eye for any eye.

One life in exchange for thirty.

I try to remember when I realized the truth, when I understood that the man before me could be the only one to have done these things.

But memories slide across one another and slip out of sequence.

They are like reflections on mercury, forever seeking the path of least resistance. They gravitate like magnets. They merge and become one.

All that remains is a reflection of myself. I see the distant image of the child I once was, the reality of the man I have become.

I close my eyes.

I try to breathe deeply, but it hurts.

I know that I am dying.

CHAPTER 6

It was that Monday – Monday, March twenty-third 1942, twelve days after the discovery of Catherine McRae's decapitated head; twelve days during which the men of Augusta Falls and Folkston, Silco and Winokur had found nothing that told them the identity of the child-killer in their midst . . . it was that day that everything changed.

And it started in my house, the house where I lived, where I had been born and had grown up, where I had lost my father when Death came walking down the High Road and left nothing but footprints and irreparable loss; it started when I returned from the schoolhouse, leaving Miss Webber with her headache and her faraway gaze . . .

It started with the sound of laughter from the upper floor of the house, the same voices I'd heard before, and me creeping along the landing, my heart in my mouth, pulse racing, forehead varnished with sweat – the tension of some indescribable fear pushing me forward.

My hand on the handle of my mother's bedroom door.

The sounds from within.

An intuitive sense of *knowing*, an understanding perhaps of why the money came every week, the money wrapped in a piece of leather and tucked beneath a heavy stone. It had been up there, alongside the fence that ran adjacent to the High Road. The road along which Death had walked.

Even now, all these years later, I can see her face.

I opened the door and saw them there – she on the bed on her hands and knees, as naked as the day God made her, and he – Gunther Kruger – right there behind her, naked also, his hands on her shoulders, his face flushed and sweating, their clothes scattered across the floor as if they possessed no value whatsoever.

No-one spoke.

Three people and no-one spoke.

I pulled the door to. I slammed it, I think. I turned and started running – down the stairs, across the lower hallway, through the kitchen and out the back door into the yard. I kept on running.

Heard a story one time. Was a story about a boy whose father was forever threatening to beat him. Boy was no bigger than a fence post, and he was scared of getting beaten. Didn't see himself standing up to such a generous thrashing, for his father was like a tree, kind of tree still standing after a hurricane. So the boy started running. Every day. Running to school, running home afterward, running around the field near his house

91

three or four times before dinner. Mother thought he'd lost his mind, brothers and sisters teased him. But the boy kept on running, running just like Red Grange on the broken-field. Later the doctor said he had an 'athlete's heart', enlarged from continual exertion. Later, they said a lot of things. Boy's heart gave out it seemed. Just damn near exploded. Running away from the thing that scared him most finally killed him. Ironic, but true.

Ran like that away from my house. Ran along the fence bordering the High Road, cut through the tupelo grove and across the corner of the Kruger fallow until I reached Reilly Hawkins' place.

Reilly was away, maybe after rats, maybe after a child-killer, and I waited in the cool silence of his house for more than two hours.

'Jesus Mary Mother of God!' he hollered when I appeared from the darkened corner of his kitchen. And then, 'What the hell . . . ? Christ, Joseph, what happened? You look like someone damned near walked over your grave.'

I told him what I saw.

He was silent for a good while. He shook his head and sighed. He seemed to be thinking, not about what to say, but how to say it in such a manner as I would understand.

'Folks is complicated,' he started. 'Folks get lonely, they get afraid, and sometimes the only way they can make themselves feel better is by being close with another person, close like it says in the Bible.'

'They were having sex, weren't they?' I asked.

'Yes, from what you tell me it certainly seems as though they were.'

'And that's not in the Bible.'

Reilly smiled. 'Sure it is—'

'I know,' I interjected. 'I know that sex is in the Bible, but not that kind of sex . . . not the kind of sex that a man has with another woman than his own wife.'

Reilly nodded. 'Got me dead square on that one, Joseph. Bible says that *that* kind of sex is the sort of thing you get in trouble for.'

Neither of us spoke for a while.

'She'll be worried sick, you know?' Reilly eventually said. 'She'll be out in the fields looking for you.'

I shrugged.

'You gotta stay here, Joseph,' he said. 'I'm gonna go over there and tell her where you are. I'll tell her you're staying with me tonight.'

I shrugged again.

'There's some fresh milk and pieces of fried chicken in the cold box,' Reilly said. 'Times like this it's good to eat. You eat, I'll go and find your mother, and then I'll come back and show you where you can sleep.'

'I don't want you to go, Reilly,' I said.

Reilly walked across the kitchen and sat down beside me. 'I gotta go tell her, Joseph . . . she'll be worried half outta her mind, you know?'

'I don't care.'

He smiled understandingly. 'Now you say that, but in the morning you'll be sorry for thinking such a thing.'

'Thinking and doing ain't the same thing.'

'No, they're not, but nevertheless it isn't good to think or do something you're gonna be sorry for later.'

I let Reilly go. He was away a good half an hour, and when he returned my mother was with him. She looked like she'd been crying, and when she stepped into the room I steeled myself not to look at her. Not directly. I wanted to cry too, but I didn't dare. I knew if I cried I'd be sorry in the morning.

'Joseph,' she said, her voice soft like a breeze, like the feeling of a clean cotton sheet billowing over you as you lay down to sleep. 'My God, Joseph, I don't know what you're thinking now, but I'm sure it can't be good.'

I turned my head even further away from her. I felt the muscles stretching in my neck. I wanted to cover my head with something. I was mad at Reilly for bringing her to his house. I felt like he'd betrayed me.

My mother sat facing me, right there at the kitchen table. She reached out her hand toward me and I tried to withdraw further even though there was no place for me to go.

'You want to tell me what you're thinking?'

I shook my head. I closed my eyes and wished she would disappear.

'Joseph . . . I'm speaking to you. It's disrespectful to ignore people when they're speaking to you.'

I turned suddenly, my eyes wide. 'Disrespectful to take your clothes off and do those things with someone else's husband!'

She looked shocked, stunned. She blinked several times. After a moment she rose from the chair and stood there looking down at me.

Reilly was there too – I could sense him just outside the kitchen door.

'Is that what the money was for?' I asked. 'Is that what the seven dollars was for every week? So he could come and do those things?'

My mother lowered her head, not in shame; she was too proud to be ashamed. She lowered her head as if acknowledging a small defeat, the beginning of a war she knew she could not win at such a time.

'When you are ready to speak to me . . . speak to me like a grown-up, like a young man, then I will listen,' she said. 'You can stay here as long as Reilly Hawkins is willing to have you, and when you are ready to come home the door will be open. I am not going to apologize to you, Joseph Calvin Vaughan, because you do not have the right to judge me. I am sorry that I have upset you, but that is *all* I am sorry for.'

She nodded once and left the kitchen. I heard her share a few words with Reilly Hawkins, and then the back door closed and I knew she was gone.

Reilly appeared in the kitchen doorway. 'I have a spare room upstairs,' he said, his tone compassionate, infinitely understanding. 'You can sleep here tonight, and then we'll figure out what we're gonna do tomorrow.' He paused for a little while and shook his head. 'Or maybe the day after.'

Three days later – Thursday, twenty-sixth March the same day that the Nazis started deporting huge numbers of Jews to a place called Auschwitz in Poland – I spoke with Miss Webber.

'How heavy is it?' she asked.

I looked at her askance.

'The weight you've been carrying,' she said. 'How heavy is it?'

I smiled and shook my head. 'As much as a house,' I said.

She looked at me in a manner I would see in years to come, a way that only girls looked at you: her eyes, her entire expression carrying more complex messages than words could ever convey.

'It's good to talk at times like this.'

'Reilly Hawkins said it was good to eat.'

'I imagine Reilly Hawkins is right enough, but right now he knows an awful lot more than I do.' She lifted her satchel and started to fill it with our notebooks, the meager offerings of literary vagueness we had submitted for her consideration. She said nothing more, but I could hear the machinery of her mind turning over.

'It's personal,' I said.

She nodded. 'Seems to me that anything to do with one's life is personal, Joseph.'

'I mean . . . I mean this is *really* personal.'

'I am not trying to intrude, Joseph, I am merely expressing my concern as your teacher and your friend for your well-being.'

She closed her satchel and snapped the buckle closed. She hefted it off the desk and set it on the floor. She stood motionless, motionless but for the circuitous convolutions of her mind.

I could feel her drawing me in. I knew what she was doing. She was perhaps better than anyone I had known, anyone I would ever know, at gently, cautiously, soliciting communication. There was something in her voice, something earthy and seductive. Even amidst a group, Miss Webber leading the recitation of times tables, the conjugation of perfect verbs, you could hear the singular pitch of her voice, both above and beneath the sound of the class. When she read stories you could hear the sounds she described, smell the woodsmoke of ranchers' fires beneath the Red Top Mountain or the Amicalola Falls, see the endless waves of brushstroke maize, feel the raw and unrelenting sun cursing the back of your neck . . . all these things were present. It made you want to listen, and when she asked, it made you want to speak.

'My mother—' I started. I looked at her, my eyes wide as tears crept up behind them, threatening to break the surface and make a run for my cheeks. 'My mother was unfaithful, Miss Webber.'

I looked down at the floor.

Miss Webber stepped forward. I felt the warm certainty of her hand on my shoulder.

My mind felt like a drought-field, arid and cracked, and my conscience like an aged tree, its roots clawing desperately at parched dust, hoping against all hope to remain. Conscience was slipping, losing its hold, and soon it would tumble. Within the branches of that tree had once flowered loyalty, faith, trust and duty, everything that had once represented family. In speaking I had broken some bond of silence, some unspoken consent that defied any word be spoken beyond the walls of our house.

'I don't understand,' Miss Webber said. 'Your mother is a widow—'

'With another woman's husband,' I interjected, and after the words left my lips there was a stony silence.

Miss Webber exhaled slowly and sat down.

I looked at her; she was misty and insubstantial through my tears.

'Not everyone is perfect,' she said quietly. 'Not everyone can live up to your expectations, Joseph. Human beings are *human*. We all fall from grace at some time.'

I nodded slowly. My breath came short and fast. 'I know,' I whispered. 'I know, Miss Webber . . . but something like that would never be forgiven, and that means she will never be an angel . . . and that means she won't ever see my father again . . . and . . . and you have no idea how much that will hurt him.'

I stayed with Reilly Hawkins for another day. He spoke with me about inconsequential things. He gave me a book called *The Life and Times of archy and mehitabel*. Archy was a poet reincarnated as a cockroach who typed letters to the author of the book. Being a cockroach he could not reach the shift key, and thus everything he wrote was typed in lower case. Mehitabel was an alleycat, worldly-wise and cynical. Archy was philosophical, more tolerant and forgiving, and together they set the world to rights in their own inimitable way. I read the book and it made me smile, and for minutes at a time I would forget about my mother.

In the evening Reilly told me stories of his family, first and foremost of his brother, Lucius.

'I thought you only had one brother,' I said.

'Levin? Yes, there was Levin. But Lucius was older than both of us.'

'What happened to him?'

'Lucius was a man with a fire in his belly. He used to work for Daly & Hearst's firm, the Anaconda Copper Mining Company, and then he heard of the war in Spain. He left America in '36 to fight with the loyalists against Franco. He was killed by one of his own people, trampled to death by a horse and rider as they tried to escape from a burning barn. Lucius was crazy and beautiful, dark-haired with eyes like back-lit sapphires. My father used to say that he would either be a genius or a fool and he could never tell which. But then my father was crazy too.' Reilly laughed; sounded like a frog in a bucket on its way down a well. 'You know what a laxative is?'

I nodded.

'There was this laxative preparation called Serutan. Had a catchphrase . . . used to say 'Serutan is natures spelled backwards.' Get it? Well my pa used to drink that stuff 'cause he liked the taste, and then he used to break wind until the house smelled like an egg fried in sulphur. Me and Lucius and Levin, my ma as well . . . we used to leave the house and stand in the yard and wait until the air cleared before we could go back inside.' Reilly shook his head. 'He looked the better part of normal, sounded the same way until you started to hear the words, and then you realized John Hawkins was as crazy as a March hare in November. He had his eyes hung low, his lip curled up one side of his face like some crazed cartoon of a crazier man, and when he got mad and shouted at us kids, thin strings of spittle would weave back and forth over his teeth like a water spider was in there building defences for the winter.' Reilly shook his head. 'Crazy he was – him, and probably every single one of his ancestors. Crazy like bugs on a griddle.'

'What happened to him?' I asked.

'He got the cancer, you know? Ate him up from inside. He was always smoking these filthy black cigarettes that came from God only knows where. Anyways, the cancer got him in the lungs and the throat. He shoulda died quick, but he sure as hell took his time about it. He figured to see some scenery on the way out maybe, and he took the long way round to the boneyard. Used to sit on the veranda, sit there in his rocker, smoking his filthy black cigarettes and wheezing up a hurricane of spit, and he'd just look toward the horizon. There was nothing out there, nothing much of anything but weather and distance – and more than likely some extra weather beyond – but still he would sit there as if he was waiting for something.'

'He was waiting for Death to come get him,' I said. 'Same way Death came along the High Road to fetch my pa.'

Reilly nodded wisely and cocked an eye at me. 'Figure you'd be right there, Mister Joseph Vaughan . . . figure you'd be right.'

Saturday morning Reilly made chicken-fried steak, told me that it would be my last meal in his house this time around, that I should chew it well, good nutrients in steak you see, and then I should make my way out to the yard where I was cutting timber the day before. Should finish and bind the stack, and when all was swept and washed I'd be making my way home. Not back to Reilly's house, but the house I was born in.

101

'You ever see flowers at the side of the road?' he asked.

I nodded.

'You know what they're there for?'

'Some damn fool got drunk and ran his car into a tree and died I reckon.'

Reilly nodded. 'Mourning should last as long as the flowers, and then it's done. Life goes on. Truth? I'll tell you some truth. More talk of the war these days. Used to be talk of the Depression. Whichever way it goes there's people dying every minute of every day. Don't matter if it's hunger or cold or sickness, or Ay-dolf Hitler's bullets. Dead is dead whichever way it lays down to rest or comes up for air. Times like these is when people get busy in their beds. New people is made almost as fast as the old ones can die. New people are made with greater ease and less fuss than making chokecherry pancakes. Seems nature's way of cleansing the past and arranging the future. You understand me, Joseph Vaughan?'

I nodded.

'So let the past be what it was, the present what it is, the future the best it can be. There's the Devil in angel's clothing if ever you wanted to see him.'

I smiled. I didn't really understand what he meant, but by then it didn't matter. I'd already decided I would go home that day.

My bitterness, my sense of betrayal, was as transient as the narrow twists of dry flowers at the side of the highway, flowers for someone drunk, or someone hurrying, or someone merely absent-minded; someone who lost their life and all that went with it in a heartbeat. Nature's way of pruning back the weak, the sickly, the fragile. Maybe not. Maybe just the Devil in angel's vestments: white on the outside, black within.

My mother and I never spoke of the episode with Gunther Kruger. What could I have said? What could she have said in return?

Things naturally gravitated towards routine and normalcy. I did not resist the gravitation. Only once did my mother say anything which seemed relevant. That Sunday night, leaning over me, kissing my forehead as I turned my face into the pillow, she whispered, 'Pray for me too, eh, Joseph . . . pray for me too.'

I smiled, I said I would, I held her hand for a moment and also her gaze.

I felt her relax within, as if by acknowledging her request I had granted her absolution and forgiveness. I possessed no such authority, but then recognized that the authority considered by self was nothing compared to the authority bestowed by others. My mother gave me as much as she needed me to have, and then accepted my unspoken blessing.

I had decided never to see Gunther Kruger again, nor his deceived wife, but I felt for Elena. I could not let her go. I would watch her in class, and I would think of the girls that had died, and then I would think of her father and my mother and how I had found them. Perhaps I decided to believe something else, that I had been mistaken, that I had not witnessed any such incident. I pushed the shadow to the back of my mind, and there it stayed, growing ever more weak and feeble, craving sunlight, craving attention, receiving nothing.

Some days after I returned home I walked with Elena to the end of the road. Here she turned and started toward her house, but I reached out and touched her arm. She hesitated, uncertain of why I stopped her, and even though I smiled as sincerely as I could she seemed nervous.

'Slow up a minute,' I said.

She frowned.

'You in some kinda hurry?'

She shook her head. 'No. Why d'you ask?'

I looked down at my shoes. I felt awkward for a moment. 'I just wanted to—' I looked at her. She seemed so fragile.

'What, Joseph? Wanted to what?'

I shook my head. 'I just wanted . . . wanted you to know that I will always be here if you need anything.'

Elena didn't say a word in response. Her expression barely changed. She turned and looked away towards her house. She seemed distant for quite some time, and then she looked back at me and smiled. 'I know,' she said, her voice so quiet I barely heard her. 'I know, Joseph.' She reached out and touched my arm. 'Thank you,' she whispered, and before the words had left her lips she was walking away, running almost. I watched her go. I had said what I wanted to say. I hoped it would be enough.

Years later, after all the terrible things seemed to have ended, I believed that that was the point at which the darkness began. A shroud, a weight, a veil, the shadow in the back of my mind having found nourishment sufficient to grow.

I did not know, and perhaps never would.

I went on writing: wrote my hand sore and my heart out. But writing did not exorcise my fear, my anger, my sense of responsibility for what had happened. It was then that I decided to do something. It was then that I resolved to do all I could to ensure that no other little girls would die.

I spoke to Daniel McRae, to Hans Kruger; I spoke in hushed tones with other boys from the class – Ronald Duggan, Michael Wiltsey, Maurice Fricker. Six of us in all. I was seven months shy of fifteen years old, and there was less than a year between us. We agreed to meet after class, down amongst the trees at the end of the broken-fence field, and for an hour before school ended my palms sweated.

I ran home and collected the newspaper clippings from the box beneath my bed. Alice, Laverna, Ellen May and Catherine. We gathered down there, the six of us huddled together, and I held out the shreds of paper, turned at the corners like yellowed fall leaves.

Watched Daniel as he saw his sister's name there in newsprint before him. Felt him flinch, like his soul had touched an electric fence. Glanced down at his shoes for some reason; small hole in the toe, skin so dirty beneath you'd never have noticed until you looked hard and long. Maybe his folks – too submerged in grief – hadn't seen that hole either. Said everything that needed saying. Looked like he was set to cry, but the muscles twitched along his jawline, and I could feel him holding himself together.

No-one said a word. Tension like a held breath.

'So . . . so what're we gonna do?' Ronald Duggan said eventually. Stood there, bangs in his eyes, a head shorter than me, the pallor of his skin like someone raised on leftovers, thin varnish of sweat shining up his forehead. He looked nervous. Hell, they all looked nervous, but I sensed the spirit, the fellow feeling that came when I stood alongside one, two, three of them and knew that they wanted to do something to help.

'Something,' Hans Kruger said. 'We gotta do something.'

'Seems to me we should let Sheriff Dearing do what he's paid to do,' Maurice Fricker said.

'But he's not doing nothing,' Hans said.

'Anything,' Daniel said. 'He's not doing *anything*.'

'It's that cuckoo clan,' Michael Wiltsey said. 'It's them that's doing these things. Can't think of anyone else wrong enough to do such things to little girls.'

'Ku Klux Klan,' I said. 'They're called the Ku Klux Klan, and they're not interested in white girls, Michael. All they're interested in is black folks . . . they just hate black folks for no simple reason. It's nothing to do with them.'

'So who is it?' Daniel asked. 'If you're so dam smart then you tell us who's doing these things.'

I shook my head. I wondered if it was a mistake to be discussing this, as if by talking about it we were bringing the nightmare ever closer. 'I don't know who's doing it, Daniel, and neither does Sheriff Dearing, nor Ford Ruby. That's the problem here. Something's happening and no-one knows why, and no-one knows what to do about it.'

'And you figure we can do something about it?' Michael asked.

'Hell, Michael, I think we should at least try.' I held out the newspaper clippings again, in such a way as they could all clearly see. 'I don't want to read these things about people we know. Look at Daniel—'

They all looked up one by one, slowly, tentatively – almost as if they were afraid to see.

Daniel McRae stood motionless. He looked like he'd backed up out of his head and left his body standing right where it was.

'Daniel's lost his sister. You have any idea what that must be like?'

Daniel looked like he was ready to break up. Tears filled his eyes. 'Don't . . . don't want to—' he started, but I reached out and put my hand on his shoulder. He bowed his head, and from the depths of his chest I could hear the small hitches as he suppressed his sobbing.

'We have to do something,' I said. 'Something is always a dam deal more than nothing. We're old enough to keep an eye out for these children, aren't we?'

'So that's what we're going to do,' Hans asked. 'We're going to . . . we're going to watch out for the girls?'

'We're going to be guardians,' I said.

'Like a secret club,' Ronald Duggan piped up. 'We can call ourselves that. We can call ourselves the Guardians.'

'Name don't mean a thing,' Daniel said. His voice cracked mid-sentence. 'Don't matter what you're called. Matters what you do . . . that's all.'

'The Guardians,' Michael said. 'That's what we are . . . and we should take an oath. We should do that thing where you . . . where you . . . you know that thing?'

'What the hell are you talking about?' Maurice asked. He frowned and scowled simultaneously; looked like someone had sewn his eyebrows together across the bridge of his nose.

'The blood brother thing,' Michael replied. 'Where you cut your hand and press your palms together, and then you make an oath about what you're going to do.'

'Nobody's going to be cutting anybody's hands,' I said.

'We should,' Daniel said. He spoke quietly, his voice almost lost in the back of his throat. 'We should do it because it means something, and because this is important, Joseph. My sister was killed by this . . . this bogeyman.'

'Lord God almighty, you've been talking to Hans Kruger,' I said. 'It ain't no bogeyman. There's no such thing as a darn bogeyman.'

'Just a name,' Daniel replied. 'Name don't mean anything. We call ourselves the Guardians, we call him the boogeyman. Just names, that's all. Means we know what we're talking about, nothing more. And we should do something to show we're all in this together. I think we should do this, and we should make an oath, and then we should work out what we're going to do so this doesn't happen again.'

Hans Kruger had a penknife. Blade no more than two inches long, but it was sharp. 'Have a stone, and I work it on the stone until it can cut paper longways,' he said. He held out his hand, and when he drew the edge of the blade across the soft pad beneath his thumb he squealed. Blood followed the line of the knife, and within a few seconds it had crept along the creases of his palm.

I took the knife. I held it for a second. I pressed the blade against my palm, closed my eyes, gritted my teeth. It felt like nothing at first, and then a sharp needle of pain lanced through me. I saw blood, and for a moment felt faint.

Each in turn, one after the other, and then we pressed our palms together.

'Gonna die of blood poisoning,' Maurice Fricker said. 'Darn crazy fool kids the lot of you.' But when we held our hands out ahead of us, each of us bleeding, there was a grim determination in his expression that told me he believed in what we were doing.

'We make an oath,' I said 'We make an oath to protect the little girls—'

'Elena,' Hans Kruger said.

Michael Duggan looked up. 'And Sheralyn Williams . . . and Mary.'

'And my sister,' Ronald Duggan added.

'Your sister?' Daniel said. 'Your sister's nineteen. She rooms in a three-decker and works in the post office in Race Pond.'

'We watch over all of them,' I said. 'We the Guardians hereby promise to watch over all of them, and we promise to keep our eyes and ears open at all times, and we promise to stay up late and watch the roads and fields and—'

'And meet every night right here,' Hans said. 'And then we go out and patrol the town and make sure that nothing happens—'

'What are you talking about?' I said. 'What the hell's gotten into you? These girls weren't taken from their beds. They were taken in broad daylight, taken from right under our noses and killed where anybody could have seen them.'

'Which means that it must have been someone

110

they knew, right?' Ronald said. 'Otherwise they would have run away. They all know well enough to stay away from strangers.'

There was a cool silence. Everyone looked at everyone else in turn. I felt like a ghost had walked right through me.

'No-one's going anywhere alone,' I said. 'And we're making a promise to keep our eyes and ears open, and if we see anything suspicious we tell Sheriff Dearing, okay?'

'That's what we're going to do,' Maurice said.

'I agree,' Daniel said.

'We're done then. The Guardians have been founded. No-one speaks of this,' I said. 'If this is someone we know then we don't want everyone blabbing about it. We don't want to give this . . . this boogeyman any chance to find out we're watching for him.'

Minutes later I walked away, the newspaper clippings folded and stuffed into my pants pocket. My hand was sore, and before I went into the house I washed it in the rain barrel at the end of the yard.

I felt like a child. Perhaps for the first time I really felt like we were up against something that we could never hope to understand. I was frightened. We all were. Whatever was out there was an awful lot more terrifying than some war in a different country. But there was something else, something small but nevertheless significant. Took a while to get my finger on it, but when I did I looked underneath and found it.

111

It was the first time I'd ever felt part of something. That was all it was, but it seemed important
and special. The first time I'd ever really belonged.

Three days later we met after school and agreed
the location of our first meeting.

'End of Gunther Kruger's field,' I said. 'The
furthest one from the road toward the bend in the
river.'

'I don't know where that is,' Daniel McRae said,
and for a moment I wondered whether it was
simply fear that prompted such a thing. I got the
impression he didn't want to come, that he'd made
an oath to do everything he could and now felt
afraid.

'You know where the road from your house
meets the road to school?' Hans Kruger said.

Daniel nodded; there was no way he could deny
where that was.

'I'll meet you there,' Hans said. 'Meet you there
and I'll show you the way.'

Daniel's eyes flashed nervously. He glanced at
me. I smiled reassuringly. He did not smile back.

After school we went our separate ways, each of
us to our own homes for dinner. My mother had
plans to be away most of the evening. She asked
what I would be doing.

'Reading some,' I said. 'I have some work to do
as well.'

'You get hungry there's milk and corned beef in
the cold box.'

She left a little after seven. I waited until eight, nervous things in the base of my gut, and then I put on a dark jacket, took a box of matches from the stove, and from beneath my bed I retrieved a four-inch knife with a leather sheath that my father had given to me a year or so before he died.

'You can't be giving him that,' my mother had said.

'Lord's sake, Mary, he's a grown boy. Anyway, the thing's as sharp as a lettuce leaf. Maybe if he's lucky he could crease someone to death with it.'

They shared words for a minute more. I had to give the knife back. Later my father took me aside, said he'd hidden it beneath my bed, that I shouldn't say a word. Our secret.

I tucked the sheath into the waistband of my pants, tugged my shirt down over it. I looked once more at the kitchen, and then I left by the back door and crossed the yard toward the fields.

By the time I reached the end of the road I was joined by Hans and Daniel. They had walked the long way round. We said nothing, took forthright and confident steps as if we were trying to convince ourselves that we knew what we were doing.

By the time we reached the end of the Krugers' field everyone was there save Michael Wiltsey. No-one said a word. We merely nodded at one another, tried to smile, each of us waiting for someone else to say something of meaning. Ten minutes went by. Maurice Fricker suggested we go look for Michael, but I told them to stay put, that he'd be along soon enough.

By the time he arrived it was gone nine. Ronnie Duggan had brought his father's pocket watch and a lantern. He suggested we light it. I said that lighting a lantern would be nothing better than an advertisement of who we were and what we were doing. Regardless, he insisted on carrying it with him.

'So where are we going then?' he asked.

'We walk around the edge of this field and start down toward the church,' I said. 'Back of the church we turn toward the school, but before we reach the road we cut across behind my house and head toward the Sheriff's Office—'

'The Sheriff's Office?' Michael Wiltsey asked.

'We're not going *to* the Sheriff's Office,' I said, 'just toward it, just as far as the bend in the road, and then we're heading back this way.'

'Hell, Joseph, that's gotta be the better part of two or three miles,' Daniel protested. 'That's most of the way round Augusta Falls . . .'

'Isn't that the point?' Hans asked. 'Isn't that the point . . . to try and search as much of the town as we can?'

No-one said a word, not until Maurice Fricker stepped forward, eyes wide, skin dead-white, and said, 'We made an oath. We made a promise we were gonna do this. So let's do it, huh? Or is any of you chickenin' out?'

No-one chickened out. I started walking. Hans right beside me and the others following in silence.

Less than an hour. The air was chill, the sky a deep midnight blue that made our faces and hands glow almost white. I could see how frightened Daniel McRae was, starting at every sound – the slightest rustle from the hedgerow at the side of the road, the wings of some bird launching itself from a tree. At one point I sensed his fear, and I wondered whether he believed that the killer would find him by his smell, would recognize him as a McRae. Would come to finish the work he'd started with his sister. Wanted to tell him not to worry, that the killer was only after little girls, but I was insufficiently convinced of this to make it sound genuine. I practised the words in my head but they did not work. I said nothing. I watched Daniel, and when we reached the turn in the road and started back the way we'd come I held his gaze for a moment. I knew he wanted to leave. I knew he wanted to run like the Devil all the way home, to bolt the door, to hide in his room, to bury himself beneath the bedcovers and make believe that none of this had ever happened. But he could not ask. He could not break his oath, so I made it easy for him.

'Daniel,' I said.

Daniel seemed to jump inside his skin.

'I need you to go back to your house.'

His eyes widened.

'What's going on?' Hans Kruger asked.

The others gathered around us. We'd been stumbling about in the dark for more than an hour. We had seen nothing, believed now that there was nothing to see, and perhaps all of them were hoping that some sort of reprieve had been granted, that they were going to be sent home.

'I need Daniel to go back to his house,' I said.

'Why?' Maurice Fricker asked. 'Why should he be allowed to go home?'

I looked at Maurice, each of them in turn. 'Daniel's the only one who's lost a member of his family,' I said. 'I'm concerned that the man who murdered his sister might be watching the rest of the family. I need Daniel to go and make sure they're okay.'

It was a foolish and shallow reason. All of them knew that, but no-one dared challenge Daniel McRae, because he *had* lost his sister, he had been the only one to lose a family member, and I knew they would give him some sort of leeway because of that.

Daniel's eyes were wider than ever. He looked as if he was holding his breath.

'Yes,' Hans Kruger said. 'He should go.'

I looked at Hans. I could tell from the way he returned my gaze that he understood what I was doing.

'Go,' Hans said. 'Run quickly, and on the way you can look around my house and make sure there is no-one after my sister.'

116

Daniel moved – suddenly, unexpectedly. He tried to smile at me, tried to say something, but it seemed that every muscle in his body was geared for running and nothing besides. He took off – Red Grange on a broken-field – and we stood there watching as he vanished toward the end of the road and finally disappeared.

A handful of minutes later we heard it.

The sound came from out amongst the trees to my right. Hans heard it too, Maurice Fricker, Michael Wiltsey also. We stood breathless and silent, and then – almost like an afterthought – I caught a flicker of something within the trees.

My heart stopped dead. My whole body stopped a second later.

I wondered if I'd imagined something, if the strength of my fear had projected something into the darkness, something that existed solely in my imagination.

'You see that?' someone hissed, their voice a rush of desperate sound.

I wondered how many frightened children it took to create a ghost.

The light again, this time for sure. I took a deep breath. I felt my eyes widen. A feeling of abject terror worked its way out from the base of my gut and trembled through my entire body.

I heard Ronnie Duggan's voice then, nothing more than a petrified whisper.

'Jesus Christ almighty . . . it's him . . .'

I backed up. Hans was beside me. I turned and

started toward the low wall that bordered the edge of the field. I felt for the handle of the knife in my waistband, gripped it firmly, wondered whether I would have any chance at all to inflict damage on this thing if it came for us.

Ronnie dropped the lantern. I heard the glass break. It sounded extraordinarily loud. 'Oh shit,' I heard him say, and I knew it was not because he'd broken his father's lamp, but because now we had made it undeniably obvious where we were.

'Behind the wall,' Hans whispered, his voice like a hiss of steam escaping from a tightly lidded pan.

Five of us, falling over our own feet, each of us trying desperately to reach the wall.

I looked back, and where we had heard something – out amongst the trees – I saw a sudden flicker of light. My heart thumped violently in my chest, and even as we reached the rough stone wall I had wrenched the blunt knife from its sheath. I crouched there with my thudding heart, a film of sweat varnishing my entire body. All I could hear was the sound of five children trying their damnedest not to breathe.

I tried to pretend the killer had not seen us, that he would pause for a moment, glance along the road, see nothing, turn and walk back the way he'd come.

In less than a minute I knew this was not the case. I saw the beam of light bounce along the trees and come to rest on the road no more than fifty feet from where we hunkered down against the wall.

I began to pray, and then I knew there was no point. All of them had prayed. Every single one of them had prayed, if not for themselves then for one another. Miss Webber had had us pray for Alice Ruth Van Horne, for Laverna Stowell. She had us pray to God that He would see fit to prevent this killer from taking any more children. And what good had it done? It had accomplished nothing. Instead I gripped the knife. I turned and looked at Hans, and I could see in his wide, white-staring eyes, that he was as scared as me.

Heard the sound of footfalls. The glow of the torch illuminated the road no more than thirty feet from where we hid. Down behind the wall, five kids, frightened as hell, and a killer on the road, torch in hand and eyes waiting to catch sight of any one of us . . . perhaps could smell us, perhaps was fast enough to outrun us, strong enough to hold all of us, both arms stretched wide, and crush us wholesale.

Ronnie Duggan let out a cry. A tiny, whimpering, terrified cry, but it was enough.

The torchlight was still. The footfalls stopped.

Could hear his breathing, more like rasping, like something huge with blood bubbling in his chest . . .

Could smell the rank and poisoned haunt of his breath, the smell of leather, of a rusted metal cleaver . . . could hear his thoughts, sense what he wanted, see myself strung upside down from a tree and flayed alive, stripped of every inch of my skin . . . I would take hours to die, and every second would be a living Hell . . .

When he spoke . . . when those first words were uttered by the killer on the road, Michael Wiltsey screamed loud enough to be heard in Camden County.

Remember the Guardians.

A welcome memory, like a cool silence after endless noise.

Remember their faces. Ronnie Duggan with bangs that his ma never saw fit to trim. Michael Wiltsey, the King of Fidget. Maurice Fricker, spit of his dad, and how he could cross his eyes and then send them sideways like he was looking left and right both at the same time. Scared kids we were, each and every one of us. And then there was Hans. Remember Hans for the first time in as long as remembering can get. Seems like I pushed him out of my mind, because thinking of the Krugers was altogether too painful. Too painful by half. The night we were caught by Sheriff Dearing, the way we believed we'd been cornered by the killer. The trace of his torch as it bounced along the edge of the wall where we'd crouched, each of us white with terror, dry-sweating, teeth chattering. Skin raised like chicken-flesh, and nerves tighter than tourniquets for bleeding wounds. Me holding onto my blunt knife as if it would have served some purpose.

'Who's there?' he shouted.

Michael had screamed, loud enough to be heard in another county.

No-one dared move, not a twitch.

And Sheriff Dearing's voice hadn't sounded like anyone I knew. But we knew one thing . . . one thing for sure. Knew we were all done for. Done and dead twice over and then some.

Caught us hiding down there behind the wall, his torch illuminating our stricken faces, the momentary sense of relief that seemed to wash right through his features like water through paint, as if he'd been scared too, real scared, as scared as us, and then he was mad, mad as hell, shouting at the top of his voice in the darkness, hollering about how we were all going to be grounded, that out mas and pas would be waiting for us with a darn good thrashing . . . kind of thrashing we'd never forget.

Bundled us wholesale into the back of his car, drove half an hour to ferry us all back home, and when my mom saw me climbing from the back of that police car she started crying. Crying like she did when my dad was buried, but somehow different.

Madder than anything she was, as mad as I'd ever seen her, but wouldn't let me go, holding me tight until I couldn't breathe, telling me I was the worst kind of child a mother could ever have – willful, disobedient, ornery, cruel even. But still hugging me, hugging me and crying, saying my name over and over and over.

'Oh Joseph . . . Joseph . . . Joseph . . .'

Sheriff Dearing came to the schoolhouse the

following day. He didn't identify us by name, but as he spoke he looked at each of us in turn, pinned us with a steely eye right where we sat and said as how there'd been some trouble, that things were getting out of hand, and how he'd imposed a curfew on us kids.

Home by six, no later. Home, and locked up tight where we couldn't be causing any trouble. For our own good, he said, and then he stood there silently while Miss Webber nodded in agreement.

We met after school, the Guardians. Stood in a huddle and tried to pretend to one another how we hadn't been that scared, that if it had been the killer we'd have overpowered him, brought him to the ground, kicked him left, right, up, down, north, south and sideways. Kicked him so far down to Hell he'd never come back.

We knew we were kidding ourselves. We knew just exactly how frightened we'd been that night.

Frightened like little girls.

CHAPTER 7

We fought the Japanese at the Battle of Coral Sea, and then at Midway. A man called Churchill came from England and talked to Roosevelt. Eisenhower went to London as commander-in-chief of all American forces in Europe. More and more often there were reports on the radio about the war. Each week Miss Webber would tell the class of another child's father, another mother's son having gone to fight. Some of them would come back broken, defeated-looking. Some of them didn't come back at all.

Time, in some small and narrow way, seemed to heal the rift that had existed between myself and my mother. I went back to visiting with the Krugers. I even learned how to look Mrs Kruger in the eye without thinking of her husband and my mother in the biblical way. Routine and predictability brought not only acceptance, but also forgetting. Some of the things I wrote then, things I would later look back on, even suggested there was a sense of happiness within me. I was approaching fifteen years of age. I looked at girls in a different way. I thought of Miss Webber, and some of the thoughts embarrassed even myself. But it seemed not to matter. Nothing seemed to matter. We heard enough of the war to realize that any hardship or awkwardness we might suffer was inconsequential and irrelevant in the face of the real suffering that was taking place. Miss Webber told us that we were old enough to understand the truth of what was happening. She said that there were more than half a million Jews in the Warsaw ghettos, that medical supplies were denied to anyone under five or over fifty; that all Jewish children were made to wear the Star of David on their coats; that the Nazis had murdered seven hundred thousand Poles, a hundred and twenty-five thousand in Rumania, and more than a quarter of a million in Holland, Belgium and France. She showed us where such places were on the globe. We looked in silence. Some of the girls cried, Elena Kruger amongst them. I reached out to hold Elena's hand, but she smiled awkwardly and wiped her eyes with the sleeve of her dress. She said she was fine. Miss Webber said that often the men of the village were forced to dig many graves, and then those same men, their wives and children too, were executed by squads of German soldiers. I thought of the girls that had been murdered right here in Augusta Falls. I thought of how evil men could be. I sometimes took out the newspaper clippings and pored over them, trying hard to make the monochrome faces come to life in my mind. But I never could. I felt

125

like those girls had passed away into some vague and indefinable netherworld. Perhaps they waited for redemption, for salvation from their pain. In truth, I hoped they were angels, but it seemed my faith was as insubstantial as their memory.

Late that month I went home and started to write a story. It had no title – seemed to me it didn't need a title until it was done. Made me feel awkward, for I put myself in the mind of a Jewish child in Paris wearing a Star of David and a mournful, broken look. Sat at my window, chin almost touching the sill, and looked out into the night sky. Sky as hard as flint, the scudding clouds thin and fragile, like they'd disperse with nothing more than a fingersnap, but all of it beautiful in a broken-up, haphazard kind of way; the ghosts of day-clouds, backlit afterthoughts to remind you of morning. The morning gone, the morning on its way . . . which one it didn't seem to matter. In the air the crisp snap of lodgepole pine and bitter juniper made the taste of breathing sour and electric. Stars looked down at me, maybe angels too – Alice Ruth Van Horne, Laverna Stowell, Ellen May Levine. Remembered the McRae girl, how they'd found her head lying in the cottonwoods and tupelos, her body in the stream gully. Men from four counties had looked hard and long for any sign of the killer, through daylight and then after dusk with torches. People came with dogs – dogs no more scent-quickened than a cat – and yet they brought them, and there was noise enough to raise the dead, but they found nothing. Those people had homes and jobs, they had children, all manner of livelihoods, but they dropped their livelihoods like fire-bottom potatoes and came running. Did they come out of fear? Fear that it could be their own children next? No, I didn't believe so, because many of them left their children unminded in their houses, unminded even after nightfall so they could walk out and help. No, it wasn't so much fear that drove them, it was something altogether more generous and compassionate.

We had felt fear then. All of us. Believed at least that that was what we were feeling. In truth, we had seen nothing as yet. In truth, we had no idea how bad it was to become. The real fear came with the fifth girl. That's when it came. Came just like Death along the High Road. Like the mailman, like the windmill-pump salesman, like anyone else walking into Augusta Falls with wares to sell, snake-root oil or self-lubricating tractor gears, ready to catch people who should've known better on a bad day with a short fuse. And just to get him away from the door they would take whatever was offered and only slow up and make time to curse themselves later. But by then the man would be gone. Gone like the narrow whirlies that sprang up along the horizon, force enough to disappear a cow – not some sick thing or some rubber-legged calf, but a full steer, all horns and slobber and bad manners. Tornadoes, whirlwinds, whatever they were – you saw them, and then they were gone.

But the real fear was different. Came as fast, but moved right in like there'd been an invitation to visit family. Times were it seemed that Death had come to collect all of us, every single sorry one, and had merely started with the children because the children didn't have the mind to fight back.

Fifth girl was the one who sat beside me in Miss Alexandra Webber's class. Sat so close I knew her name, how she drew the number five backwards. Hell, she sat so close I knew how she smelled.

Found her Monday, August third, 1942.

Found most of her, to be precise.

The bad dreams came. For a while it was every night. Always the same, perhaps small variations in time and place, but always the same.

Started with a sound.

Bang!

Bang!

Bang!

Like the sound of a heavy pole dragged along a picket fence, or down the stairs, but heavier than that, like somebody whacking something, giving it a goddamned good whack for all it's worth. And a sound back of it, coming up close but definitely back of it, almost like an echo, but not an echo 'cause it wasn't the same sound, 'cause the sound that followed the *BANG!* was a wet sound, like something bursting, like a watermelon maybe, but a sour watermelon, sour and soft, and gone too yellow, sort of watermelon you hurl off the veranda just for laughs, just for kicks, just for . . . *monkeyshines!*

And then I would see her.

Lying down she was.

Lying down like she was taking a rest.

A long rest. Long rest of her life kind of rest.

Could see the soles of her shoes.

Coming up toward the brow of the hill, just a little hill, couldn't have been more than fifteen or twenty feet of hill, and just over the brow of the hill I saw the soles of her shoes. New. White soles of new shoes. Soles of shoes facing me, and for a moment there was a ghost of embarrassment haunting my cheeks because I figured that if I could see the soles of her shoes, then I could've seen right up her dress to her little white—

Tried not to think of anything, except: *Why was she lying down?*

Why would someone . . . someone like a girl, a little girl . . . why would a little girl come up here and lie down on the hill, lie right there so's anyone coulda come walking on up and see the white soles of her new shoes?

Didn't seem to be any kind of answer to a question like that.

And then I heard Miss Webber's voice, and she

was saying, 'The sour contradiction of doing every-thing you can to succeed, and then apologizing for it when you did . . . what kind of life is that?'

Over my head there were fall leaves curling up on their branches like children's hands, infants' hands: some final, plaintive effort to capture the remnants of summer from the atmosphere itself, and hold it, hold it close as skin, for soon it would be hard to recall anything but the brooding, swollen humidity that seemed to forever surround us. Winter in Georgia was a thing all its own; a bold and arrogant enormity of a thing, like some bilious and uncouth relative, come to stay and charging into private moments and conversations with clenched fists and sounnash-breath, all the etiquette of a Unionist firing squad.

Miss Webber again: 'This is not Aristotle, Joseph Calvin Vaughan. This is not black and white with no single shade of gray in between . . . this is life, and life happens, and life will keep on happening whatever you might do to stop it—'

And then, *Stop it!* the little girl screams, but it's dark, Georgia dark, and there isn't a light on earth but for some farmer's truck a thousand miles away; or perhaps a fire somewhere out in a clearing where ranchers sit and eat something rank-smelling, their boots off and upended so bugs and spiders and creeping things don't climb inside and bite their toes come sunrise.

Stop it! Help me . . . oh Jesus, help me!

Girl like that, arms like twigs, legs like sapling

branches, hair like flax, smell like peaches, eyes like washed-out sapphire stones, quartz perhaps, something that runs in a seam beneath the ground for a million years until it shows its face . . .

And she, the little girl, she digs and scrabbles, her hands like tight little bunches of knives as she scratches at the ground, as if by scratching at the ground some deep, almost subliminal message will be transmuted by osmosis, absorption, something, anything . . . as if the earth will be able to see what is happening to her and relay the message through soil and roots and stems, through the eyes and ears of worms and bugs and things that go scritch-scritch-scritch in the night when no-one can see them, sort of things that cannot be seen with the human eye, things that bug-scientists catch and peer at through microscopes; and when you see them looking up at you through the polished black tube of an eyepiece you gasp, because they have night eyes, wise eyes, eyes that see everything, and their face has a knowing smile, like they know they're dead and squashed between glass slides, but somehow it doesn't matter, because all the wisdom that seeped through the ground still resides within them. All that wisdom is something that you could never take away – even by killing something with a face like that you could never take it away.

Maybe something like that would carry a message?

So maybe . . . maybe . . . maybe that's what the

little girl hoped – that by scratching, clawing, fighting, kicking, punching the ground . . . that by doing those things someone might hear her . . . someone might hear and come running and see the man hunched over here, the man with bowed shoulder and sweated brow, the man with rusty blade and skin that stank of hole and outhouse and fetid swamp, of swollen river dirt, of raw fish, and raw chicken – so raw and aged it's blue and withered and punky to the nostrils . . . sort of chicken you'd feed a dog and know the veterinarian will need to visit . . .

Someone would come and see that man, hunched and working, working hard like it's his *job*, and a *real* job, not like these pale, anemic desk-jockeys in their pressed pants, busy filing things, like filing things mattered a damn in Hell . . .

But no-one came.

No-one . . .

But I came. I came the next morning, and by that time she'd been out all night, lying there in the grove of trees at the edge of Gunther Kruger's land, and when I stumbled upon her she was all of four – no, five – pieces, and each piece cast asunder, but the biggest and the best was her head, because *the man with the job* had kind of sawn down through the side of her neck and then cut a diagonal line, and the line had ended beneath her right arm, and there it was – her head, her right shoulder, her right arm, her right hand all by itself. One of the hands that had clawed and scratched and dug at the ground—

And in the air was the memory of her screaming: *Help me help me oh God Jesus Jesus Mary Mother of God Our Father who art in Heaven hallowed be thy name thy kingdom come, thy will—*

But that noise only went on for a handful of heartbeats because the man with the job leaned up and then leaned down, and with the point of his rusty blade he found a spot between her ribs and then he pushed slowly down on the handle and felt the rusty blade resisted by nothing much of anything at all.

Her eyes widened, and for a second it looked like everything was gonna be okay, 'cause there seemed to be a light, a real light like a star coming down, and she smiled, a rare and pretty smile, and wondered whether she was going to be an angel right away, or if thinking some of those bad thoughts about her gramma last Christmas meant she had some work to do . . .

By the time he started *doing things* to her she was dead, which was probably a good thing.

Name was Virginia Grace Perlman, and her father was a short man who worked in the bank in town, nothing much of a bank, kind of bank a bank robber would turn down if it was offered, but a bank all the same. And he was a Jewish man, and she was his Jewish daughter, all of eight and a half years old, and someone pushed a rusty blade through her heart, and then did things, biblical things, things that would cause a man to break a sweat. And he did those things to her in the trees by the stream – same stream that had a gully where most of Catherine McRae had been found five months before – and when he'd finished doing those things he cut her into five pieces, and one of those pieces was her head and neck with her right arm and shoulder attached, and another was the rest of her torso – her left arm and shoulder, most of her side, but without her left hand . . . and they looked for some long, long time and never found that left hand, and yet another of those pieces was most of her lower half, and that was positioned in such a way as you'd see nothing but the white soles of her new shoes as you walked towards the brow of the hill . . .

And that's what I found.

I was gonna be fifteen in two months' time, and on the morning of August third I found a dead girl in five pieces without her left hand less than a mile from where I lived.

The next day I cut out the newspaper column and put it in a box with the others. I broke a sweat while I did it, and I couldn't cut with a straight line.

For a week I could write nothing, and then I wrote about something else.

Maybe it would have been different had she not been Jewish. But she was. I remembered her from class. I liked her. She didn't say much, never had, and now never would.

Maybe it would have been different if there hadn't been a war going on in Europe. Or maybe there could have been a war, but with no Americans involved.

The war was the fault of the Germans.

The Germans, evidently, conclusively, were bad people.

The Germans didn't like the Jews, disliked them enough to kill more of them than you could ever picture in your mind's eye.

Maybe that was how it all started – the word that travelled, a word that possessed no substance or evidence or backbone.

A nothing word.

Maybe it was something to do with *who* she was.

Maybe because she was Jewish.

A Raggedy Ann little Jewish doll, broken up and left for dead.

The nightmares came, and that's how they were.

I saw all of it, at least what I imagined. How she had fought and struggled, how she'd clawed the ground with her fingers, how he'd stopped her screaming by pushing the rusty blade right into her heart.

Closed my eyes and saw it.

My mother would come through when I woke, come right on into my room and sit with me, cradling my head against her breast, and I felt like a handful

135

of nothing that would disperse with less than a breath. That's how I felt. Like there was nothing left. Felt like a ghost.

Tried to read no importance into why it was me who'd found Virginia Grace Perlman. Tried not to make that the focus of my attention, but it was hard, damned hard, to let go.

And so many times – lying there, shivering – I imagined how different it could have been.

I made believe I'd come upon them when it was happening. Early evening he'd taken her, at least that's what Sheriff Dearing surmised. Taken her at dusk, taken her right from the road as she'd walked home alone. We – the Guardians – had had our eyes and ears closed that evening. Could not remember what I'd been doing at the time. So important I couldn't even remember. Made believe I'd been there. Made believe that I'd seen that man leaning over Virginia Grace, seen her fighting, seen her struggling to hold onto her life, and I'd gone roaring and charging at them, and suddenly the Guardians were right there back of me, all of them shouting and hollering like banshees, and the man had known it was all undone, and he'd gone haring away like the mad thing that he was, and we'd carried her down the hill to my kitchen, and my ma and Reilly Hawkins had been there, and Mrs Kruger had been sent for, and someone had gone running for Sheriff Haynes Dearing . . .

And Laverna Stowell's father had come with two

dogs – ugly bastards, but scent-quickened – and they'd taken a haunt of the girl's clothing, and they had him, got a hold of *his* smell, and they were away, and Laverna Stowell's father had to hold the dogs until someone brought a truck round, and there were men in the back, men like William Van Horne and Henry Levine and Garrick McRae, and each of them had axes and rough shillelaghs cut from shagbark or black walnut, and the truck would fly after the dogs, and they'd follow the stream gully, and all the way down the hill until they cut across the edge of Lucas Landry's pasture, and then they'd see the man, running like something crazed and feral, like an animal hunted . . .

Caught him near Dr Piper's picket fence, and Sheriff Haynes Dearing was there, and later he swore that there was nothing anyone could've done because the madman, the one who'd killed the girls, was running so hard and so fast, and his legs were going faster than his body, and even as they'd seen him running right into the fence there was nothing they could've done to slow him down . . . 'cause he was running like a hurricane, you see, and when he hit that fence he went over it like a felled tree, and the fence broke, and one o' them picket poles just came rushing up to meet him like a long-lost, and it went right through his middle.

And they hadn't wanted to move him, despite the fact that he was screaming blue mercy something-or-other to God and the Devil simultaneous, laying there with a picket pole right through his guts, and Dr Piper had come out and seen what was happening, and he hadn't been able to do nothing 'cause he was just a drugstore doctor, he wasn't no surgeon, and someone thought to call the veterinarian from Race Pond, but they all figured that the way the killer was spiked, the way the blood was swelling up around the pocket pole and rushing to the ground, there wasn't a great deal of point in calling anyone . . . so help me God that's the Lord-livin' truth right where I stand, so strike me down with a bolt of Holy lightning if I've told a word of a lie.

Had to be true, because there was a doctor and a sheriff and three eyewitnesses, one of whom – William Van Horne – used to be an usher for the Clinch County Courthouse 'til he heard the water ran better near Augusta Falls and decided to move himself and his wife, his children and his stock over here.

But it didn't happen like that.

I came alone, and I came late. Many hours late. Virginia Grace was dead already.

Hell, it was not my fault, but because I found her I couldn't get away from the idea that it all had something to do with me.

Like guilt when there'd been no crime.

'Want to help you, Joseph,' my mother said. Tears in her eyes. 'Blame is a bitter and indigestible thing, even when the blame is a coat you cut for yourself, even when you stood right there and got

138

yourself measured so you could wear it right.' Her eyes were wide and wet and somehow lost. 'I've done some things—'

'Mom—'

'Hear me out, Joseph. You're old enough to know the difference between right and wrong. Time you looked something square in the face and seen it for what it was. This thing that happened between me and—'

'Mom, please,' I said. 'It's gone, all been and gone and past. This isn't something I need to know anything about.'

'Your father used to say there was nothing, just nothing in the world you shouldn't know something about. Used to say that ignorance was a stupid man's defense.'

She'd mentioned my father; there was nothing I could say in response.

'This thing that happened . . . happened between me and Mr Kruger, and the money that you'd go up and get.' She turned away toward the window. 'Truth, Joseph? Truth is that sometimes we do whatever we have to do to keep our lives working in the right direction. Some of those things were done for company, because even at my age you can get awful lonely when there's nothing to see but distance and weather. Missed your father bad, so terribly bad you wouldn't believe—'

'Miss him too, Ma . . . I know what you mean.'

She turned, reached out her hand to touch the

side of my face. 'I know you do, Joseph, but missing your father is a different kind of thing from missing your husband . . . thirteen, fourteen years we spent minding each other's business and finishing each other's sentences.' She smiled. 'Anyways, he was one in a million, and it was a long time before my mind even considered the fact that the heartbreak I felt at losing him had become the ache of loneliness. Out here,' she whispered, 'out here in the middle of no real place at all, it's hard to be a woman and a mother. It's hard being on your own with no man beside you. Money is hard. You don't find work, and Mr Gunther is a dear friend of ours, he and his wife, and sometimes grown-ups have a different way of expressing their gratitude for the kindness of others than young folks do.'

I shook my head. 'You don't need to tell me, Mom . . . and you don't need to feel sad or like I blame you for something. I never asked you to talk about this, and I didn't ask 'cause it wasn't my business. What's been and gone is what's been and gone. Dad is dead. I found a little girl on the hill. Someone did terrible things to her. Sometimes I don't sleep so good and I don't know how long it will be before I do. I'm nearly fifteen. I think about Miss Webber in a biblical way—'

My mother laughed suddenly. 'A what?'

'A biblical way. You *know*.'

She nodded, smiling to herself. 'Right,' she said. 'A biblical way.'

'So that's where things are, and that's how I feel, and you're my mom and I love you whatever's happened. Hell, Mom, it don't matter if you went and got comfortable with Mr Kruger every other Sunday from here to Thanksgiving. I don't know what to say. Things is all upside down and back to front anyways. I have nightmares and I wish I could have done something to save that little girl. When the little ones would come in to Miss Webber's class, like Wednesday and Friday afternoons to get a story . . . well, that little one, that Virginia Grace, she used to sit right by me. I can remember how her laughter sounded. Hell, Mom, I can remember what she smelled like . . . like strawberry, like bitter strawberries, something like that. That's what I thought of when I saw her up there . . . saw her up there all cut into pieces and thrown about like something that wasn't worth nothing at all. That's what I saw, and I figure that when you see something like that there isn't anything you can do to wipe out the pictures in your head, and they'll stay right there in my mind until I'm worm food. Makes me think differently about things. Makes me think that there's nothing you can do with your life except live it the best way you can, and if you make some mistakes then at least you made them trying to do something good, or trying to do something better, or at least taking a degree of comfort and love where you could get it even though a minister would have called it sin.' I laughed, a dry and bitter sound.

141

'Hell, seems to me from what I've heard from ministers that anything with a good taste or a nice feeling is gonna buy you a one-way ticket to Gehenna.'

My mother shook her head. 'You sound more like your father than your father did.'

I held her hand. I raised it and kissed her palm. 'What's gone is gone,' I said. 'Seems to me that nothing since Dad died is as important as what's happened to these little girls. Everything in between seems . . . Jesus, Mom, it all just seems pointless in the face of something like this. And I'm sure Mr Kruger would agree.'

'I'm sure he would,' she said quietly, and then we didn't speak anymore, and later it would seem so ironic that in light of all we'd said, things about guilt and blame, things about my father and the recent murders, in light of all of it the final word went to Mr Kruger. Gunther Kruger the German, richest man in Augusta Falls, man with an Atwater Kent crystal radio and a Sunbeam Mixmaster in his kitchen.

Gunther Kruger, who'd gotten biblical with my mother, who'd helped her through the rough times by leaving seven dollars wrapped in leather beneath a stone by the fence.

Gunther Kruger, whose kids were like the Katzenjammers, whose wife was a handful of warm sourdough rolled into a shape of a woman and made to fit a kitchen like a hand fits a glove, and the way nothing was ever too much trouble for her, because her life was her children, anybody's children, and that's why her door was always open for me . . .

Gunther Kruger, father of Elena.

The body grows cool. The front of his shirt is black with drying blood. For some reason I am hungry, and I glance at my watch. Two hours I've been sitting here. Two hours all told. I am so tired, so utterly devoid of strength. Tired with thinking, with remembering, tired of talking to someone who never replies. Never will reply. Inwardly I am quiet, and the rush of sounds that has filled my mind for so many years appears to have grown still.

Perhaps I can will myself to die: just sit here and slow my own heart, slow it right down to nothing, like them Buddhist fellows can, and then finally, irreversibly, it will stop.

Perhaps I could do that, and they would find us both dead together, and they would wonder what had happened here, right here in this third-floor hotel room.

Because no-one heard the sound of shots. No-one screamed. No sound of running feet from the hallway. No pounding on the door, no hollering of 'What's happening in there? Hey! Open the door! Open the door or we'll call the police!'

Nothing but silence – inside and out.

I shift slightly. My legs are numb. I put the gun on the floor before me and take a moment to massage my right thigh. I feel the ache of blood creeping along my veins, along my arteries, and as I move I can hear the rustle and crumple of the newspaper clippings that fill my pockets.

I pause. I hold my breath for just a second. I lean closer to the dead man. I can see my reflection in his eyes.

'One thing I know for sure,' I whisper. 'I know that you're never gonna be an angel.'

CHAPTER 8

S ummer was bunched up against us, tight-fisted and tense; heat like a smack in the face when you stepped outside the porch; appetites were narrow, thirst was relentless, and people got weak and willful despite knowing that dehydrating and absence of nourishment were a quick way down a short road into frayed tempers and spite.

The sun, high and bold, no stranger to the Georgian landscape, blanched the sky like water through albumin tempera, itself the whole and unblemished yolk, the air white and sparse and rarified. The ground that underscored the horizon was a shadow of ochre, a rust-stain barely washed from cotton; ghosts of colors, imprecise and lacking certainty, and everywhere dust motes and citrus blackflies and greenhouse thripes, the atmosphere seemingly possessed of insufficient substance to carry anything of weight. Finally you grew unaware of the heat or – more accurately – you were aware of it as you'd be aware of breathing or daylight: conscious only of its absence.

I used to sit in the shade beneath the porch steps

and watch a family of Old World tussock moths who'd gotten the same idea. Used to hear the sound of voices in the fields and imagine they were the little girls, still playing catch-as-catch-can games, their squeals of laughter rolled up with relief as someone played a hose out across them in the mid-afternoon heat.

I could hear the sounds of their lives, their voices as they skipped together.

'Two-six-nine . . . the goose drank wine . . . the monkey chewed tobacco on the streetcar line . . . the line got broke . . . the mon-key choked . . . they all went to Heaven in a little rowboat . . .'

'Clap hands . . . clap hands . . . clap hands . . .'

Fear sat inside me like a ball of muscle, like I had an extra heart – a heart that knew fear and hopelessness and the feeling that life could throw something right at you, right out of left field with a curve like a billowed sail, and there was nothing, just nothing in the whole goddamned world you could do about it. Bit my nails and thought about Virginia Grace Perlman. Closed my eyes and could see the white soles of her new shoes over the sharp brow of a small hill. Smell of pine in the air, pine and something earthy, something that hung beneath everything like a shadow.

Took me a while to figure out what it was. Blood, that was all. It was the coppery smell of spilled blood that had seeped into the earth.

Took a walk up there a while later. Stood amidst the trees and looked down toward my own house, the Krugers' too. Saw Elena out on the back steps rubbing something on her bruised shoulders to keep the sun's cruelty at arm's length. Wanted to wave to her. Wanted her to see me. Would've called out her name had there been a chance she'd have heard.

Wanted to let her know I was there; that I could see her, and as long as I could see her she was safe.

No-one's gonna come get you, not while I'm here, not while I'm watching. Was too late last time, but this time . . . if there's another time, the Guardians are gonna be ready . . .

Wanted to let her know that everything was going to be fine.

It wasn't, and I kind of knew I was kidding myself. I heard the words, and the words were bitter and dark, and it seemed the heat of high summer did nothing but encourage the growth of such words. It was the war; it was the Germans and what they were doing to the Jews; it was the fact that five girls had died within the space of less than three years, and the sheriffs of three counties still no wiser than they were when Alice Ruth Van Horne was found naked in a field at the end of the High Road.

That was the truth, and the truth was sour like a bad lemon.

Late that same night. Couldn't sleep. Afraid perhaps. Twisting and turning in the sheets and pillows like a boy dreaming of drowning. Rose in the cool half-light of nascent dawn and stood at the window, looking out across the fields.

I watched and waited, every once in a while holding my breath for as long as I could. Squinted out through half-closed eyes, made colors flat, perspective disappear. *A one-eyed man sees everything flat*, my dad had once told me. *Can't judge distance. Misestimates proximity of one thing to another.* Tried not to think of my father, the sound of his voice, the smell of him – bitter apples, coal tar, sometimes cigars. I closed my mind down to nothing. Waited and watched, and then waited some more. Tried to breathe deep and even and slow. Tried to close out the sound of bugs and trees, of the wind and the stream. Tried to hear other things. Things that came from darkness.

Tried to be brave. Tried to be a Guardian.

Everything was still. Still like cemeteries, like empty shacks, like stagnant ponds that looked as if they'd support your weight if you dared to walk across them.

A creaking sound.

Felt the jolt, the sudden rush of needles across my lower back, the way those needles danced up my spine and raised the hairs on the nape of my neck. Turned toward my bedroom door, and for a moment, just a brief moment, I imagined I saw the handle begin to turn. A narrow and frightened sound escaped my lips – an involuntary sound, the sound of my body reacting to something my mind didn't want to understand.

I watched. I waited for the door to swing slowly open, but nothing happened. I closed my eyes, realized I had clenched my fists so hard I was digging small crescents in my palms with my fingernails.

Opened my hand. Saw the thin line of healed skin where we'd cut ourselves and made an oath. An oath to protect. An oath to keep our eyes and ears open.

Whoever was out there had perhaps heard us, had read our minds, had perceived what we were doing, and in seeing me there, standing there amidst the others, had singled me out as the ringleader, the troublemaker.

I'll show him, he'd thought. I'll show him how it feels to be afraid.

And he'd taken Virginia Perlman and killed her just for me.

I opened my eyes, turned back toward the window.

And I saw him.

My breath stopped cold and hard, tight like a knot inside. I scrunched my eyes tight, willed myself to think clearly, to close down my imagination and see nothing but what was right there in front of me.

I opened them again.

Still there. A dark figure standing motionless at the end of the road that led away from our front yard.

Just standing there. Doing nothing. Listening perhaps, watching the fields and paths for the sign of someone alone, another girl, someone he could steal away into darkness and . . .

I felt tears coming, felt the sheer paralysis of being able to do nothing, not even to cry out, my hands clenched and ready to beat against the glass of the window, and yet redundant, terrified, stricken dumb and without the ability to move . . .

And then he turned.

Turned as if to face me.

Gunther Kruger paused for a moment, and then he started to walk away, back toward his own house, his long coat swaying around his legs like a cloak.

The sense of relief was overwhelming.

I started to cry, not in fear or terror, but out of deliverance.

I watched him disappear between the houses, and then I heard the sound of a door opening and closing.

A Guardian, I thought, and for a moment imagined him as one of us, standing out there in the darkness to ensure that no-one came along the High Road to steal his daughter into the night.

It was a long while before I slept, but when I did I slept without dreams.

The following day the Guardians met in the trees near the broken-fence field.

'We have a problem,' Hans Kruger told me. He stood close, a little distance between us and the others. 'My sister,' he said. 'She thinks we're up to something. She thinks we're involved in something, and unless I say she can come she's going to speak to my father.'

'So tell her you're not doing anything—'

Hans laughed abruptly, suddenly, and I wondered for a moment if he hadn't already told her about the Guardians. Perhaps he sought some sense of approval from her; perhaps he believed he could shine like his elder brother in her eyes. 'You know Elena as well as anyone,' he said. 'She's crazy for things like this. She gets the idea there's something going on she won't let it go until she knows all about it. You remember that time with the raccoon . . . the one we buried?'

I remembered it all too well, how she'd whined and cajoled and needled until we told her what we were going to do, and then she insisted she come with us even though she screamed when she saw it, screamed and cried because the raccoon had been hit by a truck or somesuch and had lost much of its hind.

I nodded. 'I remember,' I said.

'So what am I going to do?' Hans asked, and then he turned as someone came through the trees and appeared at the edge of the path.

Elena Kruger, all of eleven years old, her hair tied in symmetrical pigtails that jutted from the side of her head like flower stems, a bright bow tied at each end like a bunch of irregular petals, and smiling like she knew everything there was to know in the world.

'Elena!' Hans snapped.

'I saw you come down here,' she said. 'I saw you all coming down here and I want to know what's going on . . . you have to tell me what you're doing or I'll tell.'

I stepped ahead of Hans. 'Let me handle this,' I said emphatically.

I walked toward her, my expression stern, an expression of authority, and I stood before her, a good head and a half taller, and I looked down at her the way Miss Webber sometimes looked down at me.

'You have to go home,' I said.

'Don't have to do anything you say,' she sniped.

'Elena . . . I'm serious. This is not something you can be involved in. You have to go home now and say nothing to anyone.'

She tilted her head to one side. She batted her eyelids and looked at me with an expression that made me blush inside.

'Elena, I mean it. This is serious business.'

By this time the others had started toward us. I could feel their eyes on my back, and then Maurice Fricker stood beside me and looked down at Elena Kruger. 'What the hell's she doing here?'

'Could ask you the same thing, Maurice Fricker,' Elena said. 'I know your brother, know your mom

153

and dad too, and if you don't tell me what's going on I'm going to run all the way to your house and tell them I saw you smoking cigarettes.'

Maurice raised his hand. 'Why, you little—'

I stepped between them, right up close to Elena; I took her arm and swiftly guided her away from the gathered crowd.

We walked a little way toward the trees, and then I slowed and stopped. 'Sit down,' I said. 'Sit down here and listen to me.'

I told her who we were. I told her about the Guardians. I told her about the promise we'd made to keep our eyes and ears open for anything that happened. I told her why, and then I explained how she could never be part of such a thing. She was there to *be* protected, not to protect.

'But I've got ears and eyes like anyone else,' she said, and for a moment she looked like she was going to cry.

I glanced back toward the five boys. Ronald Duggan was standing with his hands on his hips, his face like someone had slapped him. Hans just looked awkward, like the appearance of his sister was somehow his fault and responsibility alone.

I turned back to her. 'Elena, I mean it. You can't get involved in this. This is dangerous for you.'

She shook her head. 'Because I'm a girl, isn't it?'

I laughed. 'No, for Christ's sake, Elena, it's not because you're a girl.'

'Then why? Why can't I be part of this?'

I looked back at the gathered crowd. They were waiting for me to get mad at Elena and send her home. They were waiting for me to say something harsh and direct and meaningful. I could do no such thing; not to Elena Kruger.

'Elena . . . the thing is this . . . the thing is that you're too important to me.' I turned and looked at her. There was something in her eyes I had never seen before. I was trying to plan what I was saying, but there was no control; words kind of fell out despite myself. 'I care for you too much, Elena . . . I really do. I can't bear the thought of something happening to you, I really can't. You have to trust me on this. You have to understand that making sure nothing happens to you is the most important part of my job. I watch the road toward our houses. I stay up late and watch the road. I make sure nothing happens . . . I *will* make sure that nothing happens to you, and the idea of you out in the darkness somewhere, doesn't matter who might be with you . . . the idea of you out there in the darkness where something could happen to you is just too much for me to stand.'

I stopped talking. I was looking down at my fingers, twisted them together, feeling butterflies in the base of my gut.

I turned slowly as I felt her hand on my arm.

Elena Kruger, eyes wide and tearful, hair tied in pigtails, some long distant memory of a skinny little girl with bruises on her arms, leaned up and kissed me on the cheek.

I looked at her. Saw innocence, naivete, the sense of blind trust in her eyes.

'Okay,' she whispered, and then she slowly rose to her feet, brushed the dust from her skirt and smiled.

'My Guardian, right?' she said, and in her voice was a tone of triumph. 'My Guardian, Joseph Vaughan.' A look in her eyes as if she now trusted me with her life.

I felt my cheeks color up and I had to look away.

'I won't say a thing,' she said, and then she turned – suddenly, unexpectedly – and ran away.

I stood up and watched her disappear down between the trees.

Yes, I thought. *I'll be your Guardian. Whatever happens, I'll be there.*

Late August. The Germans arrested a further five thousand Jews in France; Marines landed on Guadalcanal and the Gilbert Islands; someone threw a stone through Gunther Kruger's car windshield. Sheriff Haynes Dearing organized the posting of notices on trees and gates around Augusta Falls. The notices showed the silhouette of a man – just a shape, like an upright shadow – and beneath the shadow were the words: DON'T TALK TO STRANGERS. DON'T GO WITH STRANGERS. STAY ALERT. STAY SAFE.

Seemed to make things worse, not better. Reminded everyone that something was in our midst, and if you happened to forget about it the notices were right there to remind you. Whether he was a boogeyman or not, he now seemed more real than ever.

Then on August twenty-seventh, a Thursday, a single gun shot punched a hole through the window of Gunther's bedroom.

Gunther Kruger called out Sheriff Haynes Dearing; Sheriff Dearing was sorely concerned, had never heard of anything like it, at least not directed toward white folks, but he never questioned whether the shot had been an accident.

Friday night there was a ruckus out near the cottonwood grove, and when Gunther Kruger walked up there come morning he found someone had killed his dog, cut it open from throat to tail and left it to bake in the sun.

He called Sheriff Dearing out a second time; Sheriff Dealing asked questions about folks Kruger might have upset, about whether someone had a mind to seek vengeance for something. Had he cut into someone's land, edged a fence ten yards closer than he should have, let his dog kill some chickens on someone else's patch?

'Isn't about chickens or fences or anything else, and you know it!'

Sheriff Dearing said how Gunther Kruger should mind his manners when speaking to an officer of the law.

'So do something,' Kruger insisted. 'My wife and children are in danger from these maniacs . . . America is the land of justice and freedom—'

Sheriff Dearing told Mr Kruger that he better have a mind to say nothing negative about America or the American people.

'But American people . . . American people have put a stone through my automobile window. A shot was fired through my upstairs window, could have hit me or my wife or any of my children, and now an American has killed my dog, cut him right down the middle and left him out for everyone to see. You know how much my daughter loved that dog?'

Sheriff Dearing raised both his hands, looked like he was surrendering up on something, and he backed away a step and started shaking his head. Told Kruger that there was nothing to be gained from such inflammatory accusations, and that if Kruger was of a mind to be so slanted, well, there wasn't a great deal of anything gonna be accomplished by Sheriff Dearing standing there talking. Could talk 'til the sun went down and neither of them would be any further forward.

'But at least if you stayed until dark we might see another American violate my home and my family,' Kruger said, stuttering his words out rapid-fire, dimes from a slot-machine jackpot, and that was pretty much all that was needed to see Sheriff Dearing in his car and off down the dirt road to the highway without even so much as glancing back.

I wondered if someone had seen Gunther Kruger out that night, the night I saw him from my window. Seen him out there and made five out of two plus four.

Sheriff Dearing should've said nothing, but it was Saturday night, and Clement Yates, who'd once been temporarily deputized and helped Dearing catch a runaway from the juvenile home in Folkston, was having a birthday. Clement Yates possessed a flat and unremarkable face, aside from his right eye which was slanted up at the corner with a neat scar, like someone had caught his brow with a fish hook and finally tugged it free. More than that, he was a little slow, and the slope of his mouth, the slackness of his jawline, gave the impression that he had in fact swallowed that hook, the line and sinker too, and was even now waiting patiently to consume the rod. When Clement had an idea there was a dawning light in those dull eyes, a light like St Elmo's fire, and more than likely there would be an announcement on the wireless.

There were a good few men down at the Falls Inn, which was nothing more than two beer tables, one pump, a corner booth for couples, a plankboard table for sitting and eating, a sawdust and spit floor and a moose head on the wall with its right eye missing. The name of the place was a pun. Owner was called Frank Turow, and first

159

day he opened the place he slipped and fell down the cellar steps and near busted his back. Frank carried a strange face, as though his skull had never hardened; a sharp push, a backyard tussle, something such as this had brought undue pressure to bear against his face. Features yielded, stayed such a way thereafter. Neither handsome nor ugly, but the indecisive middle-ground inhabited by all those enduring double-takes and puzzled glances.

Attending Yates's birthday, aside from Sheriff Dearing and Yates himself, were Leonard Stowell and Garrick McRae, Lowell Shaner – the one-eyed Canadian who'd walked with the seventy-man line in March after the murder of Garrick McRae's daughter, Frank Turow, who was all of sixty-eight years old and tough as a floorboard, six foot of stringy muscle and agile enough to bury any of them who had a mind to dare him, and finally Gene Fricker, father of Maurice, fellow Guardian. Gene Fricker worked at the grain store, smelled like a canvas sack of damp seed; he was heavy-set, slow like Yates, but slow in a methodical and diligent kind of way, never stupid, but selectively ignorant of those things that didn't interest him. Seven men, two kegs of rough beer that tasted like yeast dissolved in raccoon piss, and tongues loosened by camaraderie, one-upmanship and, most of all, unhinged by a bottle of Calvert that Turow had preserved for the occasion.

'It's not an American,' Yates said.

'What's not?' Leonard Stowell asked.

'This one here who's doin' these things to these kids.'

Haynes Dearing raised his hand. 'Enough already. I'm still the law, and I'm layin' it down. This here's a birthday party for Clement Yates, and that's all it's gonna be. We ain't rattlin' our cans about nothin' like that this evenin'. We got Leonard Stowell and Garrick McRae here, both of them lost little 'uns.' Dearing raised his eyes and then nodded at each man in turn. 'Different news for a different day, agreed?'

'Didn't come here to say nothin' 'about nothin',' McRae said, 'but while that pie is on the table I'll cut a slice . . . I agree with Clement, birthday or no birthday, it ain't no American.'

'Last one was a Jewish girl,' Frank Turow remarked.

'Ain't important what kind of girl she was,' Lowell Shaner said. 'Fact of the matter was that she was someone's daughter, and I was out there on the line after Garrick's daughter was murdered . . . I was out there watching grown men who'd never even seen her before, and I saw those men darn near break down in tears. They went out there 'cause they wanted to help . . . and I'll tell you something right here and now Sheriff—'

Dearing leaned forward, his head set between his hunched shoulders like some kind of fighting dog. 'And what're you gonna tell me, Lowell Shaner?'

For a heartbeat Shaner looked doubtful, but he glanced at Garrick McRae, could see the grim line of the man's tense jaw, the flinty hardness of his eyes, and the dense substance of that expression seemed to give him the resolve he needed.

'That if something ain't done sharpish—'

'Then you good ol' boys are gonna get yourselves a lynching party all soaked up with spirits, pour yourselves into the back of a flatbed, and go haring off down to St George or Moniac and hang yo'selves some poor dumb defenceless nigra. Tell me I'm wrong and I'll give ya each a dollar.'

An awkward silence joined the party.

'Nigras is Americans,' Clement Yates said quietly.

'Well, right enough,' Dearing said. 'I'm sorry, I missed the drift of this thing. What you're talking about is finding some *foreign* child-killer . . . like an Irisher perhaps, or maybe one of them Swedes that came through here on the way to the logging camps . . . or hell, what about a German? We got plenty of Germans here. Germans are causing all this war trouble, killing our boys in Italy and God only knows where, and they're killing Jews over there too, and the last little girl that got killed was a Jewish girl. Hell, how could we have forgotten that? That means it has to be a German. It *must* be a German.'

'Haynes,' Gene Fricker spoke up. 'You're getting'

all riled and wound for no reason. No-one's sayin'—'

'A deal of anything that makes any sense at all, Gene,' Dearing stated matter-of-factly. 'That, my friend, is what no-one is saying.' He sort of leaned back in his chair and straightened the hitch on his gun-belt. It was an insignificant action, would've gone unnoticed at any other time, but at that point it seemed to serve a purpose; reminded everyone present that Dearing was the law, that he was the only one carrying a gun, and he carried it because the law said he could.

'We're not gonna have any trouble here in Augusta Falls,' he said quietly. He leaned forward once more and laid his hands flat on the table, palm down. 'We're not gonna have any trouble here, and it ain't gonna be because I said so, it's gonna be because what we got here is some straight-thinking, sensible citizens, all of you more than capable of stringing some words together into a short sentence, all of you wise in the ways of the world, all of you suffering a little with the heat, the bad crops, perhaps . . . but none of you suffering from the hot-headed and foolish malady called witch-hunting. We agreed on this point?'

There was a moment's hesitation as each man scanned the faces of the collective remainder.

'Are we agreed on this point?' Dearing asked a second time.

A murmur of consent traversed from left to right.

'I heard word there was trouble made for Gunther Kruger,' Dearing said. 'I'm trusting to a man that none of you had anything to do with it, and I ain't askin' for confessions nor denials. I'm telling you that whatever trouble might be made for Gunther Kruger is all spent and over, and it'd be an ill-advised and foolish man who didn't take that message to whatever neighbors he might find around him. Hidebound I might be, a little too conventional and rooted, but I'll not be happy cutting folks down from trees this summer.'

'We got it all,' Gene Fricker said. 'You've built the wall, Haynes, no need to go shoring it with two-bys. The thing will stand by itself.'

'Just so's we have an understanding boys . . . just so we do in fact have an understanding. People are frightened, and when people are frightened they don't think straight. This thing has changed how everyone sees everyone else. You may have your complaints about how we're handling this, and I can't say I blame you, but the fact of the matter is that we are all good citizens here and none of us want to see this thing happen again. You keep your eyes open. You look for anything out of the ordinary, and if you see something you come tell me and I will investigate it forthwith and without delay. You get me?'

And that seemed to be all that was said, or so it went from mouth to ear to mouth again, because that meeting was talked over and over, even by Reilly Hawkins some days later. Perhaps none of those present had a mind to cause further trouble, but trouble came, and it came fast and furious. The following night, Sunday, August thirtieth, was a night that would mark a watershed in my life, and the lives of many people in Augusta Falls.

Perhaps I should have seen it coming, for there was tension about, an electricity that was tangible. Maybe I convinced myself that there was in fact nothing. I even recall the Saturday night, lying there in bed while Sheriff Dearing, Leonard Stowell, the others at the Falls Inn, celebrated the birthday of Clement Yates. The world revolved, people went quietly about their business; I read Steinbeck until my eyes closed with no assistance from me, and it seemed that the next day would be the same as any other Sunday that had been or was yet to come.

Had I known then what I knew later – hindsight ever the most astute and cruellest adviser – I would have fetched the Guardians from their beds, and together we would have stolen the girl from the house ourselves and hidden her somewhere until it was all over.

But I did not know, and neither did she, and my mother for all her wisdom was ignorant too.

Death came back to Augusta Falls, walked all the way along the High Road; workmanlike, methodical, indifferent to fashion and favor; disrespectful of Passover, Christmas, observance or tradition; Death came cold and unfeeling, the collector of life's taxation, the due paid for breathing, a debt forever in arrears.

I saw Him take her, saw Him up close, and when I looked in His eyes I saw nothing but a reflection of myself.

CHAPTER 9

The sound like a fist through glass, a fist wrapped in a towel, a towel snatched from the line that ran from back door to gate post, wrapped around a fist and punched through the glass, like a dull *crump* of sound, a *hot* sound somehow, hot and tight, a hot tight sound that pushed its way into my mind even though I was sleeping.

The heat close, too close, the skin a snake aches to shed; the heat of Georgia in late August, a gorgeous heat that challenges you to sleep despite it, and once sleep is gained you don't want to let it go, don't want to surface out of it, like surfacing from safe darkness into painfully bright light, and sucking yourself back into unconsciousness as the hot crump sound from outside becomes something like knives and glasses, glasses and knives, all bunched together in a leather bag and shaken, shaken, shaken . . .

Someone is shaking me.

Slurring muscles, unlocking themselves as if from premature rigor, each nudging the next, alerting it, the domino effect from neurone to

167

synapse to nerve to resistance as sleep threatens to burst open like a water-filled balloon. Give itself up, surrender, but all unwilling, for once lost it will not be recovered. Like Johnny Burgoyne at Saratoga: gentlemen or not he still surrendered.

'Joseph!'

An urgent hiss.

'Joseph! Wake up!'

Dreams perhaps, dreams of Miss Webber, her wide-jowled open prairie of a face, eyes cornflower blue, simple and uncomplicated; how those cornflower eyes blossomed beneath a Syracuse sun.

Joseph!

Sounded like my father – sudden and urgent, not mad, not angry, just insistent. I was fighting something, something heavy, something pressured, like drowning perhaps.

The sensation of movement, hands beneath me, and then I was opening my eyes and Reilly Hawkins' face looked down at me, my mother right beside him.

'Hurry, Joseph!' she urged.

'Come, Joseph . . . get dressed quickly, we need to be out of the house!'

It was then that I could smell the smoke – acrid and bitter. I believed I could feel the heat through the walls, but perhaps that was imagination embellishing memory.

I hurried on my clothes, uncertain, agitated, but understanding that speed was of the essence.

Something had happened; something bad I believed. My mother and Reilly Hawkins went on ahead of me. I heard their footsteps clattering down the wooden stairs, like a stick dragged across a picket.

Once downstairs I found the kitchen floor flooded with water. There were buckets and saucepans scattered across the tiles and out of the door into the yard . . . a rushing disarray of voices from outside, and suddenly Clement Yates appeared, his face reddened, his shirt soaked with sweat and water, his eyes wide, his skin grayed and streaked with black.

'A bucket!' he yelled at me. 'Get a bucket, boy . . . get a bucket of water and hurry! Hurry, for God's sake!'

The bucket was heavy. I almost skidded and lost it as I left the door and headed into the yard.

It was then that I saw the flames, bright fists of orange clenched on the roof of the Kruger house, and then lunging out toward the sky as if in anger. The smell was thick and claustrophobic, a smell of burning wood and cotton, of wool and scorched stone, of earth baked in the intense heat; it was like nothing I had smelled before, because beneath it – caught like a deceptive undercurrent below the surface – was the smell of Death.

How many people were out there I did not know. Gunther Kruger's house was on fire, and it seemed all of Augusta Falls had rushed to help him extinguish the flames. The roar and spit was brutal, the dull *crump* as windows gave against the heat, the creaking yaw of stretched beams finally yielding to the furnace, the hot *snap!* of clay tiles, like gunshots, like whipcracks, the smell of juniper and yaupon bursting into orange life behind the house, the screams, the fear, the pounding feet, the two lines of men – one from our kitchen to the back of Kruger's house, the other from the gully; two lines of men passing buckets hand to hand, and in amongst those men were Gunther Kruger, Hans and Walter, Clement Yates, Leonard Stowell, Garrick McRae and Gene Fricker. Sheriff Dearing, he was there too, could hear his voice but didn't see his face. Later, I heard he was the one in the raw red guts of the building, the one breaking doors and fighting back the smoke. Eyes too blind to see a thing, could hear voices, and stumbling through gray and darker gray, through black and acrid filth, all to no avail.

They got them out – Gunther and Mathilde, Walter and Hans.

She didn't make it: Elena Kruger, with her bruised arms and her grand mal seizures. All of eleven days from her twelfth birthday, and she died somewhere on the basement stairs, heading down into darkness to escape the heat.

Remembered the promise I'd made, standing on the hill where I'd found Virginia Perlman, the promise to watch over Elena and ensure no harm came to her. Broke that promise like it had never meant a thing. Knew . . . knew deep inside, that somehow I had made this happen.

170

My mother was there, her voice cracked from shouting, her clothes filthy, her hands and knees caked in wet charcoal and mud. Reilly Hawkins had to drag her back when the roof finally gave, for they all knew that the girl was lost. Before that moment there had been hope – misguided, optimistic, but hope nevertheless. When the upper timbers shuddered down one after the other, when those huge roiling arcs of flame billowed out through each door and window aperture, they all knew there was nothing they could do. Elena Kruger was still inside, and then the walls hitched sideways and leaned inward drunkenly, and anyone venturing beyond the limits of the plot would have burned from inside out before they'd even reached the blackened brickwork.

I stood and watched, my heart red and hot, a bloody stampede of rhythm, my fists clenched tight, my teeth gritted so hard it hurt, and tears running down my face, tears from smoke and painful breaths – and devastation, as I realized what had happened.

Someone had fired the Kruger house.

It was later that I saw Death. Nothing more than a shadow, a specter, but He was there. Same one that took my father.

Early hours of Monday morning, maybe two o'clock, or three. Still awake, all of us still awake, but delirious from the heat, the smoke, the fatigue, the grief. Flames were dead, the Kruger house nothing more than a black shadow across the plot, here and there studded with the memories of walls like broken teeth jutting from the gums of the earth. Could see where the kitchen once stood, could smell the wiernerwurst and potato salad Mrs Kruger had made to feed the sceercraw.

They brought Elena up then. Gunther Kruger, Sheriff Dearing, one-eyed Lowell Shaner and Frank Turow. They found her lying on the steps of the basement, her body burned beyond recognition. They wrapped a blanket around her, carried her up into the thin shadows of impending dawn. Mrs Kruger stood back and watched, beyond all hope, beyond emotion, incapable of crying anymore. At some point she seemed to fold effortlessly into the ground, and my mother was there, my mother and Reilly Hawkins, and they held her up, guided her away to the back of our house and into the kitchen.

I watched from the window of my room, the window that overlooked the Krugers' yard. I saw Him then, alongside the crude funereal procession that ghosted its way between the trees and down toward the River Road. Frank Turow had a flatbed truck, and there they would lay the body of Elena Kruger for the drive to Dr Piper's house. Death was there, neither walking nor floating, for He was in the shadows between the trees, the shadows of the men that walked with Elena, in the sound of heavy boots crushing wet leaves and broken sticks, in the sound of gravel on the hot top, in the mist that issued from their mouths as they cleared throats and whispered words, as they hoisted the body upwards and laid it on the truck. He was there. I knew He could see me, that I was watching Him. For some strange reason I felt He was as afraid as I.

It was then, the moment before they carried her away, that I felt the tension and disturbance of my own worst fears.

Just as had occurred with Virginia Grace, the thought came.

The thought that *he* knew what we were thinking, that *he* knew what had passed through our minds, and in allowing Elena to know of us, in promising I would protect her, I had consigned her to this terrible, terrible fate.

He was taunting me.

He was as good as inside me, and I shivered uncontrollably and could not still myself.

The engine started. The truck pulled away with Frank Turow and Sheriff Dearing up front. Gunther Kruger knelt in back beside the dead body of his only daughter, his head bowed, his spirit broken. Lowell Shaner stood at the side of the road. He didn't move until the truck had vanished from sight, and then he sat down in the dirt, right there at the side of the road, his forehead on his knees, and he didn't move for a long, long while.

Had I known I would have called out Mr Kruger's name, even though he would not have heard me. Had I known that Gunther Kruger would be gone for so long I would have shouted something, some word of comfort, of hope, something that might make him feel that the world and all it owned was not against him. But I did not know, and was therefore silent.

Mrs Kruger and her two sons stayed with Reilly Hawkins that night. The following day Mr Kruger came to collect them, took them and the clothes they had slept in, for that was all they possessed, and Frank Turow drove them north to Uvalda in Toombs County. There was a farm up there, a farm owned by Mathilde Kruger's cousin's wife, a widow now, but still maintaining some land, some pigs, a modest livelihood.

I did not ask after the Krugers. Perhaps they had been cursed, and I was afraid it was contagious. Their land, the footprint of their house, was washed clean by rain and the shift of seasons. The basement was filled in and covered over with deep sod and the tramp of feet. Someone planted a tree, a small thing no more than three or four feet high, but it shifted in the breeze and made me think of Elena and the terrible sufferance of her brief extinguished life.

The Krugers were there, as much a part of our lives as anyone we knew, and then they were gone.

Sheriff Haynes Dearing did not ask questions about the fire. He did not want to know; I felt he too was afraid of what he might discover. There was talk, as there would be, and people's minds turned to explanations and justifications, reasons why such a thing might have happened.

The rumor began, the words about Elena's bruises, that her father might have inflicted them on her, that she'd been abused and mistreated, violated even; that such things had taken place over many years, and finally her father had to do something to stop her speaking. I remember Sheriff Dearing visiting my mother. I did not hear the words they spoke, but I sensed the atmosphere. He was warning her, telling her that he had suspicions, that Gunther Kruger was gone and that she should refrain from making any contact with him.

Why had all the Krugers survived, all of them but Elena? he asked.

Why had she been found in the basement when all the others had been upstairs?

Was Gunther Kruger guilty of the things that had been suggested? Were Elena's bruises caused by his hand after all?

Was there any possibility that Gunther might have killed his own daughter to stop her talking?

I remembered the night I had seen Gunther Kruger standing on the road, standing silent and unmoving, his long coat like a shroud, the fear I had felt when I'd imagined who he might have been.

How I'd seen him as nothing more than a shadow.

I heard the things that people said, tried my best to believe none of them; felt that dark minds generated darker thoughts. Always there would be reason enough for people to accept such things. Possibly because they could not bear to think of someone, some unknown person, having set the Kruger fire for motives of prejudice and discrimination. Maybe because the human mind sets things to rights any which way it can, and if Kruger himself was guilty, that would make it all the easier to categorize and resolve. Besides, he was a foreigner, a *German*, and if word from Europe was true, if the Germans were in fact responsible for the atrocities over there, then surely it was in their blood, some hereditary affliction that prompted acts of violence and abuse. Augusta Falls was a small town. The Krugers left it behind, and there was nothing but the memory of their daughter.

The Guardians, once six, were now five. Hans Kruger was gone, and in some way I was relieved. I did not believe I could have faced him each and every day.

The rest of us didn't meet for a month, and when we did the mood was somber and reserved.

'You think the killer set the Kruger fire?' Michael Wiltsey asked.

We were sat in a line, backs to the old stone wall at the edge of Lowell Shaner's field. It was the last day of September 1942, a Wednesday, and while the rest of the world would remember that month for the killing of fifty thousand Jews and Hitler's offensive against Stalingrad, the five of us would remember that day for another reason entirely.

I shook my head. 'No.'

'Makes you so sure?' Ronnie Duggan said. He wiped his bangs out of his eyes and squinted at me.

'Maybe it was someone who thought Gunther Kruger was the child-killer.'

'You think?' Daniel asked. His sister had been dead a little more than six months, but he carried her shadow wherever he went. See him from a distance and he looked like he was being followed. Sometimes I caught Miss Webber watching him when he wasn't looking.

It had been eighteen months since the Guardians had first met, and I recalled that day as if it had been no more than a week before. Eighteen months that had seen the deaths of Ellen May Levine, Catherine McRae and Virginia Perlman. Elena had gone too, and despite being the one to find Virginia, it was the death of Elena that had hurt me the most. Perhaps she followed me. Perhaps I too looked like I was carrying a ghost. Perhaps such things were visible only to others.

'I think,' I said. 'I think that's what happened.'

'My dad has a gun, you know,' Maurice Fricker said.

'Everyone's dad has a gun, Maurice,' Ronnie Duggan said. 'My dad stands out back in the yard and shoots stupid kids. Figure you better walk home a different way.'

'I'm serious,' Maurice said.

'I . . . I could get one too,' Michael said.

'Christ, no,' Daniel said. 'Give you a gun, hell, the way you fidget you'd kill everyone standing.'

'Enough already,' I said. I stood up, buried my hands in my pockets. 'This is just crazy talk. No-one's getting hold of any guns, all right?'

'So what're we going to do?' Daniel asked.

'We've got to arrange some kind of system,' I said.

'System?' Maurice said. 'A system for what?'

'To patrol the town . . . to patrol the town and make sure that we see everything that's going on.'

'Remember what happened last time?' Ronnie Duggan interjected. 'Dearing came to the school. My dad was so pissed he could barely breathe. I sure as hell ain't doing that again.'

'I don't mean like that,' I said. 'I'm not talking about sneaking out in the dark. I'm talking about arranging some way to keep track of people's movements.'

'Five of us?' Michael asked. I could see he was nervous. His fidgeting was even more pronounced at such times. 'How the hell are five of us going to watch a whole town?'

I stepped forward, turned and looked at the four of them sitting there against the wall.

'Who's got paper?' I asked. I took a pencil from my pocket.

'I have,' Ronnie Duggan said. He stood up, pulled a wad of small pages from his back pocket.

'What the hell is that for?' Daniel asked.

Ronnie looked awkward, glanced at me as if I might have some answer for him. I shrugged.

'You know,' Ronnie said. He wiped his bangs out of his eyes. 'If I'm out . . . you know?'

'Out?' Daniel asked. 'Out where? What are you talking about?'

'Goddammit,' Maurice Fricker said, and started to laugh. 'It's if he needs to take a shit when he's out.'

Daniel looked shocked. He seemed to be holding himself together, but suddenly he erupted into sputtering hysterics.

Ronnie Duggan threw the bundle of paper at me and I caught it. I held it for a moment and then dropped it, almost involuntarily.

'Christ, it's only paper,' Ronnie said.

'But it's shit-paper!' Daniel shouted, and I stood and watched the three of them – Maurice, Michael and Daniel – as they fell sideways in fits of laughter.

Ronnie Duggan just stared at me through the curtain of bangs. 'Darn it, Joseph . . . will you tell them to stop, please?'

I leaned down to retrieve the paper.

'Don't touch it!' Maurice howled. 'Don't touch the shit-paper!'

I stood looking at them. I wanted to laugh but I couldn't. For Ronnie's sake, for the sake of why

179

we were there. I sat cross-legged on the ground, held the paper and my pencil ready, and waited for them to settle.

'Like darn children,' Ronnie said, and he sat down as well.

Not so far from children, I thought. I was a month from fifteen. The Guardians were all I had. It seemed that Augusta Falls was not the town where I had grown up. This town was a shadow of itself, its own darker half, and I sat in that field with a wad of paper on my knee and I looked at the only real friends I had that were still alive. Ronnie, Michael, Maurice and Daniel. I had somehow wound up their unelected leader, their spokesman, their captain. I was perhaps more afraid than any of them, and as I watched them laugh I knew their laughter was an escape, a release, a brief respite from the onerous burden that was burying us all.

'So who do we know for sure?' I said. 'Who do we know that couldn't possibly be the killer?'

My words stilled them. They settled down.

'My dad,' Daniel McRae said.

'And mine,' Maurice echoed.

'And mine,' Michael and Ronnie added.

I wrote down the names. If my father had been alive his name would have gone down on the list as well. If my father had been alive there would never have been a second girl. I wanted to believe such a thing, and so I did.

'Sheriff Dearing, Lowell Shaner, Reilly Hawkins,' I went on. 'And Dr Piper.'

'Dr Piper is weird,' Daniel said. 'He gave me a medical check one time. Made me drop my pants and he held my balls and told me to cough.'

I smiled at him. 'That,' I said, 'is one of the very unfortunate duties of a doctor.'

'Seriously,' Michael said. 'Who else do we know that couldn't be doing this?'

'All the family members of the murdered girls,' Maurice replied. 'Their fathers, brothers, any of those people. I mean, for Christ's sake, you just don't go murdering your own kin, do you?'

I wrote down the surnames of the ones, besides Catherine McRae, that we'd lost – Van Horne, Stowell, Levine and Perlman.

'Frank Turow,' Ronnie said. 'Clement Yates, Gene Fricker.'

Their names went on the list. They were all people I knew, had known all my life. They were amongst those who'd walked the seventy-man line after the death of Daniel's sister.

'This is just people from Augusta Falls,' Maurice Fricker said. 'I don't believe it's someone from here.'

'That's not the point,' I said. 'We're eliminating people. We're taking out of the equation anyone we know it *couldn't* be. Then we know who we're not looking for, right?'

'And we pay attention to everyone else,' Ronnie said. 'We can't watch a whole town, but we don't have to, right, Joseph?'

I nodded. 'That's right. We just look out for everyone who isn't on the list.'

'But it could be anyone at all,' Michael said. 'It could be someone from Camden or Liberty or Appling. Anyone could come from anywhere around here, and we wouldn't know.'

'We have to,' I said. 'That's why we're doing this. We keep diaries. We meet once a week, right here, and we go over anything that seems odd, anything that's out of place. We do what we always said we were gonna do . . . we keep our eyes open, we look out for one another, and most of all we look out for the little ones.'

'It's not going to happen again,' Daniel McRae said.

I turned to look at him and there were tears in his eyes. The memory of laughing at Ronnie Duggan belonged to some other life altogether.

'It *can't* happen again,' I said, and I prayed – prayed with everything I possessed – that I was right.

October became November became December; we met each week as we'd planned. We spoke of who we'd seen, where and when. We tried to find anomalies and oddities in schedules and routines. We went down to the edge of the disused railroad track one afternoon and found a man sleeping in a ditch near the edge. He smelled like a dead raccoon, and when he woke and saw us standing there he hollered like a stuck pig and went haring into the trees and across Lowell Shaner's fallow field. Our collective spirit was dulled and blunted with each new meeting. We knew we were accomplishing nothing. We made believe that the killer had long since left Charlton County, perhaps been killed himself, maybe fallen down a ravine, drowned in a swamp, even committed suicide from shame and guilt and the horror of what he'd done.

Even the silhouette on the posters started to look like something from the imagination of frightened children. Sometimes we would have nothing to report, and we'd look at each other a little lost, a little desperate. Times like that I felt at sea, without anchor, that the focus I willed to give them was just not there anymore. I wanted to be their leader, their fearless and forthright captain; I wanted to give them guidance and positive direction. Once I canceled a meeting because I couldn't face them again.

I believed that we all understood our failure. Elena Kruger had died, and though we knew that she had not been taken by the killer directly, she had still been taken. We had elected ourselves responsible for the children of Augusta Falls, and I myself had promised to keep her from harm, whatever the cost. As individuals we had failed, as a group we had failed, and after a while our meetings became nothing more than a constant and painful reminder of that failure.

Nothing was said directly, it was more a tacit agreement. We drifted apart. The Guardians ceased to exist. Perhaps we believed that we had in some way contributed to Elena's death. I did not know then, and I imagined that in looking back I would be none the wiser. I thought of Michael Wiltsey, of Maurice Fricker, of Ronnie Duggan and Daniel McRae. I thought of Hans Kruger who must have felt worse than all of us combined, for he had been there inside the house when the fire started. He could have done something. I imagined he believed he *should* have done something. Perhaps he tried, and in trying he failed. We all felt that way. We had done our best, but our best didn't even come close to the mark. The Guardians were finished.

With Christmas on its way, we just seemed to be watching and waiting for Death to take another.

CHAPTER 10

President Roosevelt ordered a freeze on rent, wages and farm prices; the Allies routed Rommel at El Alamein; one hundred and forty thousand American troops landed in North Africa to fight something called the Vichy French; we could no longer buy coffee or gasoline; the Germans surrounded in the devastated city of Stalingrad finally surrendered to the Russians. They had survived for three weeks by eating the Rumanian Cavalry Division's horses.

My mother gave me a fountain pen for Christmas, Reilly Hawkins gave me a book in which to write, its pages of thick, watermarked paper, the cover embossed leather. I wrote my name inside, the date, my age, and then closed it.

A new year was on its way. The war had not ended. Many things had changed since the death of Elena Kruger and the departure of her family. I did not see Reilly so often, and one time I overheard someone saying that I was *her child*. Later I would learn that the rumor about Gunther Kruger had continued, though now it had grown to include my mother, that my

185

mother had not only consorted with Gunther Kruger, but had been aware of the terrible violations he had inflicted on his daughter, and had done nothing. Sheriff Dearing came to visit her, and they talked in hushed tones in the kitchen. Seemed to me she was no less worried when he left than when he'd arrived.

'Words are merely words,' Miss Webber told me. I voiced my thoughts frequently. Often I would stay late to have her read something I had written, and if I seemed distracted, perhaps disturbed, or if I had failed to show her something new for several days, she would take me aside and ask me what was happening.

'Words are not actions. Words spoken are forgotten just as quickly as they're uttered.' She told me this in all sincerity, but what she told me wasn't true. Words were not forgotten. Words were remembered, and time seemed to give them nothing but strength. Dark thoughts seemed to mature and grow with age, and the more people with whom they were shared the more influence and validity they possessed.

My mother heard them. She saw the way people shunned and excluded her. She was not oblivious to the whispering that she encountered, how some women would turn and leave a store when she entered. She was told that a running credit facility was no longer available at the town mercantile. Reilly Hawkins did his best to help us, but there was no denying the fact that money came slow

186

and short. My mother would not have taken charity, let alone asked for it. She made it known that she would take in washing, mending, other such chores, but with ever-increasing rarity people came to see us.

After a while, Christmas having gone, it seemed that the Vaughan lot was a small and distinct ghetto surrounded by a picket fence in dire need of paint. Augusta Falls had isolated us. They had isolated my mother. She had lost her husband, her livelihood, her sense of community, her friends. Whatever small measure of companionship she may have shared with Gunther Kruger had been taken from her also. Seemed all that was left was me; she could not lose me because I did not plan to do anything but stay. So she lost her mind. Little by little, inch by inch, the slow deterioration of sense, of judgement, gave way to outright dementia.

'I am not an alienist,' Dr Piper told me.

It was the third time I had spoken to him, the second time he had visited my mother. The first time I had called him out she would not leave her room. I could hear her in there, sometimes crying gently, sometimes silent, and nothing I said or did resulted in her unlocking the door from within. I hurried across to the grain store and asked if Gene Fricker could reach Dr Piper on the telephone. By the time Dr Piper came she had come out of the room and was standing in the back lot looking at the memory of the Kruger house. Dr Piper appeared and she was as clear-minded and rational as she'd ever been.

The second time I spoke to Dr Piper on the telephone directly. He said he couldn't come out. He was on his way to deliver a baby.

The third time I got Gene Fricker to call him because my mother hadn't eaten for the better part of a week. I knew this because there was little enough food in the house. When I returned from school each day none of it had gone. I knew she hadn't left to eat elsewhere because I wedged a small piece of paper in the door lock, back and front. Those papers were still there when I returned. When she spoke to me she spoke of things that had happened many years before, gave them far greater consequence than they deserved, acted as though they'd occurred most recently. She asked if I'd been across to the Krugers; she asked after Walter, Hans and Elena.

'When you see Miss Webber next you must tell her to pass on my regards to Mr Leander . . . you know, the old man who lives next door to her?'

I nodded. 'Yes, ma'am, I will.'

She knew all too well, as did I, that Mr Leander died in the winter of '38, found him on his knees stiff and frozen in his back yard, his eyes wide open, his mouth too, his hands adhered to the back door handle.

I told Dr Piper everything I could remember of the things she'd said.

'She is suffering some sort of mental stress,'

Piper told me, 'but like I said, boy, I'm no alienist. Colds and coughs, delivering babies, high temperatures, pronouncements of death. That's what I do. I don't look no further than what I can see, and whatever your mother's got I can't see it. Best I can do is make arrangements for her to see one of the head doctors at the nervous hospital in Waycross, up there in Ware County. They got people up there who've got more letters after their names than letters in 'em. Them's the folks you'll need to be speaking to.'

I talked to Reilly Hawkins. I spoke with Alexandra Webber. They were good people, kind people, but they knew nothing of mental illness.

Dr Piper made arrangements. Reilly Hawkins drove us. My mother sat silently beside me, a feeling of tension present that I'd never experienced before. I missed my father. I missed the warmth of Mrs Kruger's kitchen. She would have seen to my mother. She would have made broth and sauerkraut; gotten her talking about children and making clothes, about useless husbands and defiant sons. Mrs Kruger would have been there for my mother, regardless of what she might have suspected about Gunther and his infidelities.

Tuesday, February tenth, 1943. Waycross Community Hospital, Ware County, state of Georgia. I was fifteen years old, perhaps older in my head and heart. I stood beside my mother at a large desk in the hospital's entrance foyer. I could

189

smell medications, that bitter-sweet alcohol-infused combination of astringents and anodynes. I was scared, overawed by the size and presence of the place. The people were white-coated, white-faced, stern, seemingly indifferent and dispassionate. Had I not possessed a voice, had Dr Piper not arranged an appointment for us to see a Doctor Gabillard, I believe we would have stood right where we were for the remainder of the day.

My mother said nothing of consequence. She asked if I'd left the sandwiches she'd made in Reilly Hawkins' truck. She asked if the doctor was going to make her headaches disappear. She reminded me to tell my father that we promised Haynes Dearing a lunch on Saturday, that a chicken would be good.

I waited patiently, all of two hours alone. Sat on a plain deal chair in a corridor on the third floor while my mother spoke with Dr Gabillard. Gabillard was younger than I'd imagined, perhaps thirty-five or forty. Figured anyone who understood the human mind would need to be at least a hundred. But the doctor's hair was gray already, thin on top, and through the windswept mess of recession I could see how shiny his scalp was. Could've seen my own face reflected had he leaned over. Figured perhaps he buffed it with a French polish, made it shine like a Sunday shoe. He smiled too much, like he was trying to reassure everyone present that everything, just everything, was gonna be just fine. Fine an' dandy.

It wasn't.

I knew it wouldn't be even before she went in there. I wanted to go out and wait with Reilly Hawkins, or have him come in and wait with me. Rock and a hard place. Didn't want to leave in case she came out. Reilly wouldn't come in, said that if a head doctor took one look at him he'd be consigned to the institution in Brunswick.

'That's where they send crazy people,' he said. 'I mean, *real* crazy people, kind of folks who put things on their heads and bark at folks. That kind of crazy.'

I asked him and he laughed. 'No,' he assured me in his most certain and assured tone. 'Your mother will not be going to Brunswick.'

I waited in the corridor. I figured by five p.m. I would pee myself.

'She's sedated,' Dr Gabillard said. 'We're going to keep her here for a little while and let her take some rest.'

He asked me about my father, about living relatives, about friends of the family I could stay with while she was being treated.

'You're a bright boy,' he told me, 'and so I'll tell you a few things about what we're going to do and why. Is that okay?'

'You're gonna make her better, right?'

Gabillard smiled. Smiled with his mouth and not his eyes. 'Not necessarily that simple,' he said. 'The brain is a complex piece of machinery,

191

and there isn't a great deal we know about it. Fixing someone's brain isn't like fixing a broken arm, Joseph.'

'I don't think there's anything wrong with her brain,' I said. 'I think it's her mind that's been overwhelmed by all the losing she's suffered.'

Again Gabillard smiled, and laughed, and reached out and touched my shoulder like he was being patient and understanding with someone who couldn't possibly have the faintest idea what was going on.

I figured not to say anything else, got the idea if I disagreed then I might find myself on the way to Brunswick.

'Chloral hydrate-induced sedation,' Gabillard said at one point. At other points he mentioned carbon dioxide treatment to limit the supply of oxygen to the brain and thus diminish the life of the mental viruses that afflicted her; he spoke of Librium to help her sleep, Scopolamine to elicit underlying thoughts and feelings that even my mother didn't know, Veronal to sedate, and to encourage susceptibility to hypnotism; and later he talked about a Hungarian called von Meduna who'd invented Matrazol shock therapy.

'You see,' he concluded, 'there are many things we can try, and all of them, I *assure* you, are going to contribute to your mother feeling an awful lot better. Now, Joseph . . . I understand there was an insurance policy your father signed for medical purposes?'

I saw her once before I left. She was lying on a bed in a white room. Through the glass porthole in the locked door all I could see were the soles of her shoes.

Like Virginia Grace Perlman over the brow of a hill.

I saw my mother once a week for eleven months. For a while I would drive up there with Reilly Hawkins, but in April of '43 he said he didn't want to go anymore.

'I can't be doing this every week, Joseph . . . for sure and for certain I can't be doing this anymore. It's not that I don't care a great deal for both you and your mother, but hell, Joseph, I can't bear to see that place another time. I can't bear to think what they might be doing to her inside those walls, and I sure as damn don't wanna go in and see for myself.'

I understood. I made it easy for Reilly. I couldn't bear it myself, but I went anyway. Took a bus most of the way and walked the rest.

My mother, Mary Elizabeth Vaughan, née Wheland; born December nineteenth, 1904, in Surrency, Appling County, not far from the banks of the Little Satilla River; married Earl Theodore Vaughan after a thirteen-month courtship, married him on her twentieth birthday; bore his only son October eleventh, 1927, buried her husband in July of '39 after just fourteen years of marriage; a widow at thirty-four, a widow who

193

would never marry again because she started to lose her mind. Seemed to me the hospital at Waycross finished the job for her.

She moved out of this world into a world of her own. The move was incremental. By the summer of '43 she no longer recognized me. I was a little older, but my looks hadn't changed so much. Gabillard told me that Haynes Dearing had visited twice, perhaps three times, but Dearing never mentioned it to me. I believed he would have found it too hard to speak of what she'd become.

The alienists and doctors at Waycross kept telling me there were signs of her recovery.

'Recovery from what?' I asked, and they would smile and shake their heads, and say, 'It's not quite as simple as that, Joseph.' After a while I stopped asking and they stopped talking. I would go up to the third floor and sit by her bed, hold her hand, wipe her brow, and she would look at me and tell me things that I knew were just imagined.

I never saw Death. He never sat beside me. He never haunted the room in which she slept waiting for His moment to take her. There were times, nothing more than seconds, when I wished He would come. Not for me, but for her. I believed I had lost the better part of my mother on the night of Sunday, August thirtieth the year before. The night Elena Kruger died. The night my mother recognized that the life she'd wished for and the life she possessed would never be the same. I believe she saw the world for what it was, and the thought of making it alone was too over-whelming. I knew nothing of people. I knew nothing of their complexities and anomalies. But I did know my mother. She found a way to escape, and it was all I could do to go on seeing her for the years before she died.

Later, hindsight and maturity as company, I recog-nized my own quiet and gradual retreat.

I stayed in the house, the home where I'd been born and raised. I worked after school, any jobs I could find, and it seemed – through sympathy and compassion – people were willing to let me undertake things they could have done themselves. In the summer months I would work until it was too dark to see. Simple jobs. Fencing, clearing ground for plowing, cutting down trees, such things as this. And then I would go home and write. I wrote down my thoughts, my feelings; I filled the leather-bound book that Reilly Hawkins had given me, and I asked Miss Webber to get me a dozen exercise books. When I'd filled those I asked for more. She wanted to know what I was writing.

'What I think . . . sometimes what I feel,' I said, but I never brought them for her to read. Perhaps I believed that if I wrote enough of reality then I would finally empty out, and into the vacuum would appear the fruits of imagination and inspir-ation. I would then write something like Steinbeck or Fenimore Cooper, a work of fiction as opposed to a work of incident. It was only later that I understood how the two were related: that experience, fashioned by imagination, became fiction, and life, viewed through the tint and hue of imagination, became something one could better tolerate and understand. I colored my memories with sounds and pictures that I knew had not occurred, at least not the way I wrote them. I thought for a moment that perhaps I was losing my anchors to reason and rationale, but I appreciated the fact that there was conscious choice on my part. Regardless of what I wrote, regardless of now I portrayed something, I knew with certainty what was fact and what was fiction. I read voraciously, borrowing books from Miss Webber, from Reilly Hawkins, from the Augusta Falls Town Library. Regardless of author, location, time, regardless of likes or dislikes, styles of subject matter, I read them all. Reading became a *raison d'être*.

Sometimes I thought of the Guardians, but I tried not to think. We had been children, nothing more than that, and the world that we faced had always been vast enough to swallow us. I did not see Maurice or Michael, or Ronnie Duggan with his bangs in his eyes; perhaps I did not wish to see them, for they would simply remind me once again of how we had failed to protect the children. To see their faces would have been to see Elena, the way her body was carried to the flatbed the night of the fire. Such things would feed the ghosts, and I wanted to leave those ghosts behind.

By the time I turned sixteen in October of '43 I believed that the war in Europe couldn't continue much longer. Perhaps I also believed that the terrible things that had happened in Augusta Falls were part of some best-forgotten past. The flyers that Sheriff Dearing had pinned to trees and fences had long since dissolved beneath rain and weather. Lives went on regardless, and those that had lost their children had somehow absorbed the loss and survived. People had stopped asking after my mother, and the trips I made to Waycross, trips that took the better part of three hours each way, now occurred no more than once a month, sometimes less. In the coming December she would be thirty-nine years old. To see her at Waycross, laid up in bed, sometimes seated in a wicker chair by the inched-open window, her hair greying, her face drawn and anemic, you'd believe she was fifty. Whatever spirit she might have possessed had been stolen or broken, I couldn't tell which, but the woman I visited was not my mother. She was a shell, twisted up inside with fear and desperation, perpetually elsewhere, her eyes seeing me but translating something else. In her own mind her words sequitur and rational, to me nothing more than murmurs and ramblings and disconcerting noise. I knew that Haynes Dearing visited with her. I spoke with Gabillard once, another time with a nurse, and they told me that the sheriff had been. I thanked him silently for that. I sent out a wish that he would continue to visit, that it was not just me and my mother against the world. I never spoke to him of his visits, and he never mentioned them to me. I think we would both have been too awkward and embarrassed to know quite what to say.

After my birthday I started to think of leaving, and though my departure would not ultimately come for another few years, the seed was nevertheless planted. Perhaps the things I read, perhaps the realization that there was in fact a world beyond Augusta Falls, a world where small-minded bitterness and recriminations of the past would not matter, precipitated such a thought. Anonymity appealed to me, the anonymity one would experience in a city suffused with life and people, so rich with noise that a single face, a single voice, would barely be noticed. Perhaps this thought was my own means of escape from all that had happened, but for the years that my mother continued to live at Waycross I could not leave her behind.

So I stayed. I held my tongue and my temper. I lived alone. I earned sufficient money to hold mind and body together, to buy pencils and exercise books, to take the bus out to Ware County once a month and see the woman who was once my mother.

Perhaps, had it not been for Miss Alexandra Webber, I would have slipped into obscurity, but in the summer of '45, as the world exhaled the tension of a spent war, she came to visit me.

'To see what you've been writing all these years,' she said, and she smiled with such warmth, her Syracuse eyes cornflower blue, her features clear and certain and beautiful.

'I came to hear you read, Joseph Calvin Vaughan,' and she sat across from me at the kitchen table, she all of twenty-six, me all of seventeen, and I remembered the cool rush of longing that would fill me as a child.

I had thought of Alexandra Webber, and the thoughts were as defined as shapes cut through paper. My head, my hands, my heart, my hopes; prayers like wishes, made and then forgotten.

Loneliness is a drug, a narcotic; it grows through veins, through nerves and muscles; it assumes some right of possession over your body and mind; it feeds itself, and creates its own requirement. Loneliness and solitude are walls.

Alexandra Webber came to see what I had written on those walls, and though I believed there was no doorway she somehow found one.

I chose to step back quietly and let her through.

I shift again as numbness turns my legs to stone. I look over the man's shoulder, out through the window toward the lights of New York. I see cars passing in the streets below, and out beyond them the myriad lights of a million windows, and behind each one the life that is played out, each oblivious to the next, each bound up tightly in its own importances and singular moments.

My voice sounds like someone else, as if my body stands before the window but I am somewhere removed.

'I never asked you why,' I say. 'I never asked you how these things happened, did I?' I look at the body seated in the chair in front of me, the head lolled back, the color of hair, the width of shoulders. I know there will be no answer, but for some reason the silence unsettles me.

'Did you even understand what you were doing? Did you ever think about what you'd done? Did you never feel guilty? Suffer remorse?' I clench my fists. 'How could you do such things? How could any human being do such things to a child? A child, for God's sake.'

I close my eyes. I try to remember faces. Any of them. Alice Ruth Van Home. Virginia Grace Perlman. I try to remember Alexandra, how she looked when she arrived that day, the day she invaded my solitude and made me believe that I could live again.

I try to picture my mother, how she looked when I visited her at Waycross.

But there is almost nothing. The shapes and features are vague and indistinct.

'Did you ever think about what happened to their parents, their brothers and sisters? Did you?'

I shake my head. Look down at the floor. I feel as if I am floating near the ceiling and there beneath me is my body, small and inconsequential. My voice is like a whisper in a storm. Nothing. Less than nothing.

I consider what I have done.

I wonder – just for a heartbeat – if I am little more than the worst type of hypocrite.

An eye for an eye?

Could such a thing ever be right?

But now it's too late. This thing is done.

I sit quietly.

I wonder how long it will be before they come.

In these final hours all I can do is try to remember all that happened, and even as I do I believe I can feel the past coming up to meet me, can feel—

CHAPTER 11

Clean air, a breeze from the coast; carried with it the smell of sour gum, juniper, sassafras perhaps. Stood at the window of the house, looked right through and over the Kruger lot, empty now, and but for reminiscence and memory would never have known it was there. Shadows cast behind trees were indigo, gray, darker gray, running to midnight blue. Smell of fresh-cut wood stacked back of the shed, the pine sap leaking into the earth, catching thripes and blackflies, preserving them in grain and grit until their time to burn.

It was from the same window that I saw her coming.

Heart like a clenched fist.

Can hear her downstairs. Can hear her making food, said she could make the best eggs this side of the Altamaha River.

In my dreams she was younger, hair down one side of her face, a cascade across her shoulder: raw, dark silk in ochre, sienna and umber. Her scent was fresh, like citrus, punky and seductive. Her skin unblemished, innocent, as clean and clear as her eyes, and smelling of soap, of the thin film of sweat that would break across her forehead when she leaned over me in a one-room summer schoolhouse and made me recite something significant. Or insignificant. It didn't matter to remember.

Footsteps across the ceramic tiles below. Flat Syracuse soles, schoolteacher shoes – predictable, pragmatic, functional. Fingers lifting eggs from her cool-box sockets, holding them, breaking them, the white and yolk running out like the guts of something into a bowl. The sound of the fork as she whipped them into a frenzy.

Sound of my heart, my pulse; sound of blood rushing through me; sound of sweat escaping the pores of my skin; sound of hair and nails growing; sound of waiting.

She came early, the fractured, awkward light of dawn still filling the gap between night and day.

I watched her as she approached the house, was there to open the door when she arrived.

'Joseph Calvin Vaughan,' she said, as if my name was something I didn't know.

'Miss Webber,' I replied.

'You're a young man now, Joseph, no longer a child. I haven't taught you for the better part of two years. You can call me Alexandra.'

'Alexandra,' I said.

'That's my name,' she said, and she smiled with her eyes as well as her mouth.

There was silence between us for a dozen or more heartbeats.

'You're going to invite me in,' she said, more a statement than a question.

I tilted my head to one side. 'I am?'

She nodded. 'You are,' she whispered, and she stepped beside me and squeezed past into the narrow hallway.

I had on jeans, a shirt buttoned no more than once or twice. My feet were bare. I had washed but was not yet fully dressed for the day. There was a quarter-mile of fencing to raise along the narrow side of the clearcuts. Frank Turow was paying half, Leonard Stowell's brother-in-law the other. It was good money, and I didn't want it gone to some other itinerant journeyman with a hammer and a bag of nails.

But then Alexandra Webber came to my house to make eggs, to make small talk, to make-believe.

Later, when she called from the bottom of the stairwell, I almost slipped from my skin. I had put on my shoes but they seemed to gain no purchase on the floor beneath me; I went carefully, tentatively, like a new foal, my knees too flexible to easily bear my weight.

'You have taken care of the house,' she said. She stepped into the kitchen, looked around, nodded at the table. 'May I sit down?' she asked.

'Sure,' I said. I remembered that this was *my* house, if not mine then my mother's, and I did not need to feel like an uninvited guest.

'How are you, Joseph?'

I stepped away from the door and to the right. I kept my eyes on Alexandra Webber. I moved sideways until I felt the edge of the rough wooden counter against the small of my back. I put my hands behind me and gripped the edge with my fingers. Felt like I needed to hold onto something. Something I knew, something familiar.

'As good as,' I said. 'You know how it is, right?'

She shook her head slowly. She reached up and fingertipped a stray lock of hair away from her cheek and over her ear.

Things happened in parts of my body that I had not experienced before. There was an ache in the base of my groin, a sensation like something pulling from within. My mouth was dry, a taste like copper and dirt.

'How is it?' she asked. 'No, I'm not sure that I do know how it is, Joseph . . . tell me.'

I smiled, shrugged shoulders. 'It's been tough . . . the last couple of years have been tough, Miss Webber—'

'Alexan—'

'Alexandra,' I interjected. 'I'm sorry . . . can't help but think of you as my schoolma'am.'

Alexandra laughed. 'I *was* your schoolma'am,' she said. 'But I was your friend as well, wasn't I?' She hesitated for a moment, her eyes questioning.

205

'You were,' I said.

'You used to come and speak to me about all manner of trials and tribulations, and then, when this thing happened with your mother . . .' She looked away toward the window. 'When this thing happened with your mother, I imagined you might come and speak to me again, come and ask for my help with her . . . but you didn't. I wondered whether I'd done something to upset you.'

I laughed, suddenly, abruptly, more nerves than humor. It was a reaction, nothing more than that. 'Upset me?' I shook my head. 'Even if you tried . . . even if you tried you couldn't upset me.'

She'd brought a *Writer's Digest*. There were details of a short-story competition inside. I laughed. I remembered 'Monkeyshines' and the letter from Atlanta.

'You still have it?'

I nodded. 'Upstairs.'

'You wanna go fetch it?'

'You want me to?'

'Sure, go get the letter . . . I can't remember what it said. I'll make us something to eat.' She tilted her head to one side. 'You okay with eggs . . . I make the best eggs this side of the Altamaha River.'

I rose from my chair. I took a step toward the doorway. 'Yes,' I said, almost as an afterthought. 'Eggs are fine.'

I went upstairs. I could hear her in the kitchen

beneath me, breaking eggs into a bowl, whipping them.

Closed my eyes and imagined everything I had ever wanted to imagine about Alexandra Webber.

Believed I loved her. Every which way. Biblical included.

She read the letter. She smiled, she laughed, she asked me questions I later forgot. Was too interested in watching her.

We ate the eggs. Uneeda crackers and watermelon pickle too. It was good. Didn't know if it was better than anything else this side of the Altamaha, but it was good enough for me.

Thought about the fencing, about the clearcuts, about Frank Turow and Leonard Stowell's brother-in-law.

To hell with them, I thought. They were grown men. They'd have understood my situation.

'So how *have* you been?'

I pushed my plate aside. 'I've been okay.'

'And your ma?'

I shook my head. 'She's gone, Miss Webber, she's gone south for the winter and ain't comin' home.'

'It's a tragedy . . . everything seems to have been a tragedy for you. Your father, the thing that happened with the Krugers, and now your ma.'

'It's life . . . figure that life gives as good as it gets, right?'

She reached out and touched my hand. There it was; the snap and hum of electricity; felt the hairs stand to attention at the nape of my neck. Felt a cool rush of hope fill my chest.

'Missed having you to teach,' she whispered.

'Missed being taught.'

'Always my favorite pupil.'

'Always my favorite teacher.'

She laughed. 'That's not fair . . . I was your only teacher.'

I smiled. 'Blow, blow, thou winter wind . . . Thou art not so unkind as man's ingratitude.'

She frowned, her brow creased in the center like a seam. 'Shakespeare?'

I nodded. '*As You Like It*.'

'You're saying I'm ungrateful, Joseph Vaughan?'

'Saying you didn't see a compliment when it came.'

'I saw it well enough.'

'So I'll say it again . . . always my *favorite* teacher.'

'And you're reading Shakespeare?'

I shrugged. 'Sometimes . . . more often than not I read *Red Ryder* and *Little Beaver* comics.'

'You do not.'

'Do too.'

'You're teasing me, Joseph Vaughan.'

I looked down at my hands. They were folded neatly together on the table like they belonged to someone else, as if someone had left their gloves behind and I had arranged them ready for collection. 'Wouldn't know what you were talking about, Miss Webber.'

'You don't have to call me that . . . there really aren't that many years between us.'

'Same number of years there's always been.'

Silence for a moment. Heart beating, right there in my mouth. Mouth so full of heart I wondered how I'd managed to say so much. My thoughts were broken up small like shards of ceramic. Could see every one of those thoughts, and they all were of Miss Alexandra Webber, and for the most part they were biblical.

'You have to go to work today?'

I shook my head. 'Don't *have* to do anything.'

'You want to spend the day with me?'

I looked right at her, direct and unflinching, and then I smiled. 'Maybe,' I said.

She blushed visibly. 'Only a maybe?'

'Maybe is good, Alexandra Webber. Maybe isn't no.'

'What are you saying, Joseph Calvin Vaughan?'

Smiled. Took the heart from my mouth and held it in my hands. 'Saying nothing, Miss Webber. Nothing and everything. Think I've felt a good number of things that I don't know that I understand. Always thought of you as beautiful, and always figured you were smart, and how you always had just enough time for everything I wanted to say . . . and I s'pose I kind of looked up to you like a kid should look up to a teacher, I guess. Then I grew up, started to think a different way, kind of way people think about each other when they want to get close

209

and comfortable, and whichever way I looked at it, whenever I had such a thought, you were right there in the middle of it like you belonged—'

She gripped my hand. 'Stop,' she said, in her voice a sense of urgency.

'Why? Who's gonna hear me? Who's listening aside from you?'

'You don't know what you're saying!'

'Don't I?' I'd walked half way to the end of the road, figured it was just as far back as to journey to the end. 'So tell me why you came here?'

Miss Alexandra Webber looked away.

'Miss Webber?'

She raised her hand, her voice also. 'Okay, that's it, Joseph! If this is going where I think it might be going then the first thing you can do is call me by my first name.'

I nodded. 'So tell me why you came here, Alexandra?'

'Alex,' she said matter-of-factly.

I held my tongue and my gaze.

The awkward recognition of unfamiliar breathing; the realization that scent, skin, the touch of hair between my fingers was not my own.

'It's okay,' she whispered, and her voice came like the sound of the sea from within a shell. 'You'll know what to do.'

I looked at her, close enough to feel the flicker of her lash against my cheek. 'And if I don't?'

'Then,' she said, her voice almost lost within the sound of her heart. 'Then I will show you.'

'Why did I come here?' She shook her head and turned away. 'I don't know, Joseph . . . perhaps because I believed you were lonely.'

'Lonely?'

She smiled. 'Sure. Lonely. You know what lonely means.'

'I do,' I said. 'I know all about lonely.'

'Like it was your job, eh?'

'My job?' I smiled, started to laugh. The feeling inside was one of emotional release, like a belt too tight now unbuckled. 'Yes, you could say that . . . loneliness was my job . . . And you?'

She leaned to one side, the flat of her hand against her cheek, her elbow on the table to support her chin. 'Me?'

I nodded. 'Yes, you. You were lonely too, right?'

Alex kissed my eyes, each in turn; the dampness of her lips, the ghost of her fingertips, the pressure of her breast against my arm, the heat of her body . . .

The way her waist vanished to her thigh, and then up and back across her stomach. There were buttons back of her dress, and she turned slowly, took my hand, showed me where they were. She stepped out of the fabric as if from a second skin. The rush of cotton as it kept its promise with gravity.

She stepped back.

My breath caught in my throat, a trapped bird, frightened.

She laughed.

She shrugged. A lock of her hair fell from behind her ear and caressed her cheek. She raised her hand and tucked it back where it had come from. 'Everyone gets lonely, Joseph.'

'And that's why you're here . . . 'cause you figured we were both lonely and you wanted to do something about it?'

She nodded, half smiled. 'Maybe,' she said.

'Maybe?' I asked. 'I get to say maybe. You? You were never a maybe person, Alex . . . always simple, straightforward, black and white.'

'Does it matter why I came?'

I shook my head. 'No, Alex, it doesn't matter why you came.'

She got up from the chair. She stepped backwards, and then stepped forward, just a single step, but it felt like she'd closed the gap between imagination and reality. 'You want me to go?'

'No, Alex . . . I never want you to go.'

Later, I could not remember how we'd found our way upstairs. Later, trying to remember, I believed it did not matter.

I raised my hand and touched her arm, her shoulder, the nape of her neck.

Her hands found my waist, the buttons of my pants. 'Off,' she exhaled.

I fought with my clothing.

The breeze lifted the curtains at the window behind me, raised the hairs on my skin, made me shudder for a moment.

She stepped back, back again, and sat on the edge of the bed.

I stood in front of her, my right hand against the side of her face, her cheek, her hair between my fingers.

She kissed my stomach, encircled my navel with the tip of her tongue, and then she dipped her head and opened her mouth. A small fire lit up inside me.

No more than seconds and she looked up at me. 'You know how this goes, right?'

I nodded.

She edged forward, slipped off her underskirt. She laid down on the mattress and reached out her hand.

'Come on, then,' she said, 'before I die of antici-pation.'

Somehow we found a rhythm, awkward at first, but we found it. We followed it: took us some place we hadn't planned to go. Kind of place you didn't want to come home from.

There were moments I remembered laughing, though later I could not recall why.

Alex lay beside me, her body pressed against mine, her arm angled to support her head, and every once in a while I would turn my face to look at her as she spoke, to interrupt her words by kissing her, and after another while I said, 'Again', and she closed her eyes and laid down and I folded up against her.

We did not leave my room until it was close to evening.

Weeks went by.

The dreams came back. Dreams that were haunted by the left hand.

The hand of Virginia Grace Perlmari. The hand they never found.

Augusta Falls had convinced itself to forget the killings. Three years behind them, the collective mind of a town had managed to close itself on the past. I had not.

Alex visited with ever-increasing frequency, and I spoke with her about the girls, the murders, about who might have done such things; we talked of the Krugers, the death of Elena, all that had transpired.

'Whatever happened,' she said, 'it's over . . . it was so long ago.'

'It wasn't anything to do with the Krugers,' I said. 'I knew Gunther Kruger . . . I knew his wife and children.' I paused and looked away toward the kitchen window. It was approaching the end of November. For the better part of three months Alex had been visiting two, three, sometimes four times each week. We made love – sometimes furiously, like there was something inside each of us that had to be discovered, and only with force and

214

passion was there a chance to break it free, to discover it; other times slowly, as if under water, every word, every breath, every single second of physical contact drawn as far as possible. I had turned eighteen a month before. Alex Webber would be twenty-seven in February of '46. The better part of nine years didn't seem a great deal of time. It was close to four years since Reilly Hawkins had driven me and my mother to Waycross Community Hospital, since I'd spoken with the head doctor about carbon dioxide to starve the brain, Librium to aid sleep, Scopolamine to find her true, unspoken feelings, Veronal to sedate. Seemed to me my mother had slipped into some dark and silent place, and no matter the drugs they gave her, no matter the things they did, they seemed to serve no purpose. The darkness and the silence remained. The treatment merely prevented her from crying out for help.

Alex had filled a void, a vacuum. Whatever she brought I consumed, and still remained hungry. We read books together, sometimes all night. Steinbeck, Hemingway, William Faulkner, Walt Whitman, Flaubert, Balzac, Dumas' *Chicot the Jester*, Hawthorne's *The Scarlet Letter*, Stendhal's *Scarlet and Black*. Those things I did not understand she explained. Those things she could not explain she showed me. My work fell slack. There were people who would no longer hire me. I started shaving, and then decided to grow a beard. My hair went past my shoulders.

'Bohemian,' Alex said, and laughed, and kissed my forehead, and gripped my beard with her fingers and led me to the mattress.

Later I spoke with Alex about New York, my vision, my ideal.

'Superb-faced Manhattan! Comrade Americanos! To us, then at last the Orient comes. To us, my city. Where our tall-topt marble and iron beauties range on opposite sides, to walk in the space between.'

'You what?'

'Walt Whitman,' she said, and laughed at me. 'You ignorant Bohemian scribbler!'

'Ignorant? I'll have you know I started a book.'

'You what?'

'A book. A novel,' I said. 'I started writing a novel.'

She sat up straight. The sheet fell from her throat and ruched at her waist. Her perfect breasts, the arc of her shoulder, her throat, the line of her jaw. I reached out my hand. She slapped my wrist, grabbed it, held it down.

'Tell me!' she snapped. 'Tell me what this is, Joseph.'

'It's nothing . . . hell, Alex, it's just an idea I had. I started it last night—' I paused, frowned. 'No, two nights ago . . . the night you said you were gonna come and then didn't.'

'So tell me,' she urged. 'Tell me what it's about.'

I tugged a pillow from beneath me and positioned it behind my head. Alex's expression was animated, enthused; she seemed genuinely excited.

'It's just a rough thing,' I said.

'Like you,' she joked.

'I'll give you rough,' I said, and playfully grabbed a handful of her hair.

'No,' she said. 'Seriously . . . tell me what you're writing.'

'It's about a man,' I said.

She smiled, tilted her head to one side. 'Good start . . . like "Once upon a time there was a man" kind of thing, yes?'

'Too smart, Alex Webber, too smart by half.'

'So tell me,' she said. 'Tell me what it's about.'

'About a man called Conrad Moody . . . and he does something terrible. He kills a child. An accident, but he's a fatalist, he believes in Providence and the Three Sisters . . . he knows that somewhere he must have committed a crime and escaped his punishment, and now his punishment has been brought to him. He spends the rest of his life in atonement for killing the child, a child he promised to protect.'

Alex was quiet for a moment.

'What?' I asked.

She shook her head. 'You have some you could read me?'

'Now?'

She nodded. 'Yes,' she said.

I leaned across the bed and put my hand beneath. I felt along the floor until I touched my notebook. I retrieved it and sat up, Alex beside me, watching me, something cool and distant in her expression.

'You want me to read this now?'

'Yes,' she whispered. 'Just a little.'

I opened the book, found a page. I cleared my throat and started.

'He thought of something like a white-knuckled solar plexus fist, but that was no real way of describing the tension within. He thought of a dam, like seven hundred thousand pounds per square inch pressure, breaking point, something more than that, but he felt that this did not define it. An understatement; a definite understatement of fact. Tension like whipcord strung taut, a piano wire, a wire that creaked and strained and could not have twisted a fraction more without snapping, lashing back, slicing through something perhaps. Ironbound, he was. Imperfect, yes, but ironbound. And believing those imperfections made him human. This is what he had been told, and he never cared to disbelieve, for belief had always been his firm foundation, and without that the walls within would have fallen. Conrad Moody wrote upon those walls, and they listened. They heard everything he wished to say. Simple enough. Strong enough also. Strong enough to bear it all alone—'

'Stop,' she said.

I looked up at her. A single tear had edged its way from her eye and started down her cheek.

I frowned, tried to smile. 'What?' I said. 'What is it? Hell, Alex—'

'It's about you, isn't it?'

'Eh?'

'You . . . it's about you and the Kruger girl, isn't it? You promised to look after her, didn't you, Joseph? That day you told me about, looking down from the hill and seeing her in the yard. You promised to yourself that you'd make sure nothing bad happened to her.'

I didn't reply; there were no words in my mind.

'But it didn't work, did it?' Alex said. 'You couldn't keep your promise and she died.'

I was silent.

'How long will you torture yourself over that?' she asked.

'I don't think—'

She raised her hand, pressed her finger to my lips. She shook her head, closed her eyes for a second, and then pulled me close toward her. 'Ssshhh,' she sighed. 'Don't say anything. It's okay . . . gonna be okay, Joseph. We're going to make a baby. It's that simple. We're going to make everything okay. We're going to bring a child into the world and redress the balance . . . we're going to break the spell.'

'Alex—'

'Ssshhh, Joseph . . . enough. We're going to make everything all right again . . .'

My heart thundered in my chest, a trapped fist. I was sweating, my skin varnished, but I was cold, shivering almost. Alex pulled up the sheet and encircled us with it. She lay down, and I went with her, down onto the mattress, my notebook tumbling to the floor.

'Now,' she whispered.

CHAPTER 12

There days before Christmas we visited my mother in Waycross Community Hospital. I borrowed Reilly's pickup and we drove there. Saturday, December twenty-second, 1945, an overcast and oppressive sky, the trees along the highway like hands grasping for something.

I did not want Alex to see her, not how she was, but Alex insisted.

'It's Christmas. She's your mother. This isn't the sort of thing you negotiate or postpone.'

Fifty-some miles, give or take, but that was with the crow. We took the circuitous route, watched the sky open up for morning, chase shadows as the sun lifted, houses appearing as if from nowhere. Thunderheads jostled for space along the horizon to the west like an impending threat, the promise of revenge for something unspoken, but every once in a while a spike of brilliance sliced through, like a whittler's knife cutting back the deadwood to find the true grain within.

We spoke little, Alex Webber and I, but every once in a while I glanced at her profile, and she seemed content. Optimism ran in her veins.

We saw shapes picking cotton in the field; men stacking logs for the corduroy road, others splitting those same logs for railroad sleepers. We drove for more than an hour and were no more than halfway to Waycross. There was no hurry. Road unravelled behind us, ran out ahead of us like a black ribbon, and we followed it simply because a decision had been made. We were going up to see Mary Elizabeth Vaughan, the woman who bore me, going there because Alex believed she was family, now as much her own as mine. She said she loved me. I'd reciprocated, to which she'd replied: 'So when you love someone you take all of them, every attachment, every obligation. You take the history, the past and the present. You take all of it, or none at all. That's the way it goes, Joseph, that's just the way it goes.'

Alex did not argue, she did not contest; she stated viewpoints matter-of-factly. I would set my mind to a challenge and she'd take the wind from my sails before I'd weighed anchor. I consigned myself to let such things go. She was from Syracuse, and such people thought differently.

Mid-morning broke sultry and humid, breeze up close and personal with too much moisture. I pulled Reilly Hawkins' pickup to the side of the road, a wheel-beaten mud and ditches affair that ran the tires left and right simultaneous and made driving a chore rather than a pleasure. Alex said she was thirsty, wanted to open a flask of coffee she'd brought, and for a while we sat up front, sipping from the same cup one after the other, and talking little of nothing to pass the time.

'We've got a blanket,' she said after a while.

'Sure,' I said.

'I wasn't asking, Joseph, I was saying.'

I shrugged. 'So we got a blanket.'

'We've got a pickup with a flatbed in back. We've got a blanket. We've got an open road with no-one in sight.'

'What're you saying, Alex?'

'Whatever you think I'm saying, Joseph.'

I turned and looked at her, mischievous smile an' all. 'You're saying you want to get in back of the pickup and break a sweat—'

'So romantic! God, let's just call it the way it is.'

'Well, hell, Alex, you were the one who thought it.'

She shrugged. 'So it ain't complicated . . . put the blanket in back of the pickup and come fuck me, okay?'

'Christ, Alex, you just can't get in back of a pickup truck right in the middle of the road and fuck someone.'

'Why the hell not? Where the hell does it say that you can't do that?'

I was amazed. 'Alex, this is not the way you're gonna get pregnant.'

'Hell, Joseph, this isn't about getting pregnant, this is about wanting to have sex in the back of a pickup.'

'You really want to do this? You really want me to put a blanket back there—'

'And fuck me. Yes, that's what I want. I want you to do that right now, before I change my mind, before you manage to kill every ounce of spontaneous romance that might have occurred, okay?'

I put the blanket in back of the truck.

Alex came around and tugged her underwear down from beneath her skirt and threw it at me. She clambered up onto the flatbed and lay down. I was laughing by then, laughing so hard it took a while for me to get arranged sufficiently to undertake the task at hand.

I was conscious of the open air, the sound of birds in the trees, conscious of the way Alex sort of wrestled me onto my back and then straddled me. I was laughing too much to take her seriously, and then in a moment of wonder it seemed remarkable to me that I was there at all, that Alex Webber – schoolteacher – was with me.

'What?' she asked.

I frowned, shook my head. It was difficult to breathe with her entire weight pressing down on me.

'Tell me?' she said. 'Tell me what you're laughing about?'

'I'm not laughing,' I breathlessly replied. 'Jesus, Alex, you gotta get off me before I suffocate.'

'Suffocate? I'm not suffocating you. I don't weigh anything at all.'

'Nothing at all? Okay—'

'You're saying I'm heavy? You're saying I'm too heavy. Is that what you're saying, Joseph Vaughan?'

'Don't call me that!'

'Why the Sam Hill not? 'S your name, isn't it?'

'It's my name, yes. Hell, Alex, you say it like I'm in school.'

She laughed raucously. 'Joseph Vaughan! You better turn your homework in on time else you're gonna be washing blackboard rags.'

'Alex!' I said. 'Seriously . . . you gotta get off me before I die.'

She shifted sideways, took the weight off my chest, and then she eased backwards, her hand beneath her, finding me, guiding me, laughing even as she lowered herself down.

I reached out and held onto her waist, looked up at the tent of blanket draped over her head.

She looked down at me, held her hands out sideways. I took them, our fingers woven together, and she started rocking back and forth.

It seemed so right, too right perhaps. It seemed to be an encapsulation of everything I had ever wanted in someone. Was the first one you ever loved always this way?

I was conscious of her scent, her smile, the pressure of her over me, the feeling of almost being consumed by something extraordinary.

Conscious finally of the sound of an approaching car, of lying flat on my back, Alex on top of me, pressed close, the pair of us damned near buck-naked, covered with nothing but a blanket, trying not to laugh, to make no sound at all, conscious of my hand on her ass, her skirt up around her waist, my pants around my ankles, and the way the car drew to a halt alongside us.

'Oh Jesus,' I whispered.

'Ssshhh,' she whispered back.

My eyes were bug-wide. The car drew to a halt. I had never felt so vulnerable. The sounds of the car door opening, slamming shut, the sound of boots on the road, the kick and skid of loose gravel scattering beneath the chassis.

'Cab's empty,' a voice said. 'Cab's empty, and sure as hell don't see no-one in the road or amongst the trees. Better come on out from beneath that horse blanket and show your faces.'

Alex shifted sideways, just a fraction, but I felt myself draw out of her. The spontaneous romance of the moment died an abrupt death. Like Cupid got a bullet.

'This here is the Sheriff talking, Sheriff of Clinch County, name's Burnett Fermor, and whatever you're doing in the back of your pickup . . . well you're doing it right here on one of my roads. Gonna ask you to come out from under there, whoever the hell you are, and show your faces, or things ain't gonna stay friendly.'

My eyes wider, Alex's expression something close to sheer terror, my heart making a break for the trees.

'I'm counting to three now, people. Three's all I got. Got no more than that. So here we go . . . one . . . two . . .'

'Okay!' I shouted. I reached up and pulled back

the blanket, peered over the edge and looked down the length of the flatbed, looked down the length of Alex's shrouded body, aware of my pants around my ankles, her skirt around her waist, that if I pulled the blanket back any further her ass would be right there for the world to see.

Sheriff Burnett Fermor, tough-looking, face like a sack of awkward angles, thumb of his left hand tucked neat in his belt, heel of his right hand resting on the handle of his revolver.

'Well, howdy there, boy,' he drawled. Muscles along his jawline twitched when he spoke. Eyes squinted against the sun, gave him the appearance of someone coming out of the cellar into daylight, someone who'd been locked under the house for his own and others' safety. 'You under that blanket alone, or we got company this morning?'

Alex shifted. Her fingers appeared along the edge of the blanket and she drew it back a fraction. She smiled uneasily.

'Well, hello there, miss,' Fermor said. He took a step closer to the back of the pickup.

Alex leaned up slightly. She smiled weakly. 'Hello, Sheriff,' she said.

'Well, we ain't kids here, are we?' he said. 'Think there's very little being left to the imagination this morning. I'm gonna have to ask you fine people to come out of there and stand by the side of the road.'

'Could you give us just a moment?' I asked.

'A moment, son? What would you be requiring a moment for?'

I felt the tension of nerves in my stomach. 'To get ourselves smartened up a little before we come out of here.'

Sheriff Burnett Fermor squinted at me. 'Seems to me we have us a difficult situation. I wouldn't want to be embarrassing you folks, but at the same time I wouldn't want to be looking the other way while you come out of there. I don't have any idea who you people might be, and I'm sure not likely to turn my back on you until we have a chance to get acquainted.'

'I can assure you, Sheriff—'

Burnett Fermor raised his hand and smiled. 'Excuse me interrupting you there, son, but I don't see how you're in any kind of a situation to be assuring me of anything. I'm gonna avert my eyes a little, just to save you as much embarrassment as I can, but the truth of the matter is that I'm gonna be needin' you to come right on out of there and stand by the side of the road.'

'But the lady—'

Fermor shook his head. 'Son,' he said, in his voice a tone of resignation, a little exasperated. 'Once again, I'm not gonna be playin' word games with you. Let's not talk about the lady, huh? Seems to me that any young woman who finds herself in the back of a pickup truck in broad daylight involved in some kind of bedroom activity . . . well, I don't think we're gonna be discussing the finer points of decorum and etiquette, right? Gonna ask you just this one time now, and then

I'm gonna be making a call to my office for a deputy to come out here—'

'We're coming out,' I said. I looked down at Alex. She closed her eyes, shook her head from side to side.

I moved awkwardly from beneath her, turned the blanket aside and scooted down to the end of the pickup on my ass. I dropped over the end to the ground and pulled up my pants. Fermor just watched me coolly. Alex did the best she could to conceal herself behind the blanket, tugging her skirt down and making her way to the back of the truck on her knees. She looked harassed and humiliated, her hair tousled up on one side, her feet bare, her shame evident to the world.

Fermor glanced at his watch. 'Ain't even eleven o'clock, and you pair are out here cavorting and fooling around in the back of this here vehicle. What the hell kind of way is that to behave?'

I opened my mouth to speak.

Fermor shook his head. 'Tell you the truth, I don't wanna hear nothin' but your name, son.' He took a notebook and a pen from his shirt pocket. He looked up at me, nudged the peak of his hat back from his brow.

I said nothing, glanced left at Alex.

'Your name?' Fermor repeated.

'Vaughan,' I said. 'Joseph Calvin Vaughan.'

Fermor printed my name laboriously in his book. 'And where are you from this morning, Mr Joseph Calvin Vaughan?'

229

'Augusta Falls,' I said.

'Augusta Falls? That's in Charlton County, right?'

'Yes, sir.'

'Augusta Falls, Charlton County . . . seems you would know my contemporary down there, Sheriff Haynes Dearing.'

'Yes sir, I know Sheriff Dearing.'

Fermor looked up, squinted beneath the brim of his hat. 'You had words with Sheriff Dearing in Augusta Falls, Mr Vaughan?'

I shook my head. 'No sir, I haven't.'

Fermor raised his eyebrows. 'So how would you be acquainted with him?'

'It's not a big place, Sheriff. Pretty much know everyone around there.'

'You do, do you?'

'Yes, sir.'

'And what do you do down there in Augusta Falls, son?'

'I work on fences, felling trees, any kind of thing like that . . . some farm work when it's harvest, whatever's going.'

'You gotta house down there, somewhere you live?'

'Yes, sir.'

'And how old are you, Mr Vaughan?'

'I'm eighteen years old.'

'Is that so? All of eighteen years old.'

Fermor wrote something else in his book, and then he turned his attention to Alex. 'And now you, miss . . . your name?'

230

'Alexandra Madigan Webber.'

'Alexandra Madigan Webber . . . and you're from Augusta Falls too, right?'

'Yes, Sheriff, from Augusta Falls.'

'And what would you be doing travelling out here this time of day?'

'We were on our way to the Community Hospital in Waycross.'

'Right, right,' Fermor drawled. 'And why would you be going to the Community Hospital, Miss Webber?'

'We're going to see—' She glanced sideways at me. She looked strained and anxious.

'To see?' Fermor prompted.

'We were on our way to see Joseph's mother.'

Fermor nodded slowly, his eyes never leaving Alex. 'And was there any particular reason you felt it necessary to stop over here, Miss Webber . . . instead of just driving right on through to Ware County?'

Alex looked at me, then back at Fermor. He'd asked the question just to embarrass her further and she knew it. She shook her head slowly. 'No, sir,' she said, and her voice cracked with emotion.

I felt the lift of anger as it rose from my stomach to my chest.

'Well, all right,' Fermor said, and wrote something else in his book.

'We're real sorry,' I said. 'We were driving along, and we decided to stop for a little while—'

231

Fermor raised his hand. 'I don't know that it's real necessary for me to know all the awkward details of this tryst of yours, Mr Vaughan, 'cept to know that this here is a public highway. Kind of highway where people come walking or riding horses, even folks in cars, and the last thing in the world they want to be witness to is two folks engaging in the kind of behavior that we've seen this morning. Fact of the matter is that it's gonna be the violation of some law somewhere—'

Alex opened her mouth to speak. She took a step forward. 'Sheriff—'

Fermor took a step forward himself. There was something menacing in the way he did it, a counterpoint to Alex, a challenge. 'Let me ask you something, Miss Webber,' he said. 'How old are you?'

She frowned. 'What does it matter how old I am?'

'I asked a polite question, Miss Webber, expect a polite answer.'

She shook her head. 'I'm twenty-six, Sheriff.'

'And what would you be doing down there in Augusta Falls?'

Alex cleared her throat. 'Schoolteacher,' she mumbled.

'You say schoolteacher, Miss Webber?'

She nodded.

'You're the schoolteacher in Augusta Falls?' Fermor asked, something of surprise in his voice.

'I am, yes. I am the schoolteacher in Augusta Falls.'

Fermor nodded at me. 'And this young man here . . . this young man is one of your students, Miss Webber?'

She laughed nervously. 'No, sir, he's not one of my students.'

Fermor adjusted his hat on his head. 'Well, thank the Lord for small mercies, Miss Webber, because that would be just about as interesting an abuse of one's position and respectability as I could imagine.'

'There is nothing in the law that says an eighteen-year-old—'

Fermor smiled, took another step forward. '*I* am the law here, Miss Webber, and if anyone's gonna be quoting chapter and verse on the law then it's gonna be me. Truth of the matter is that you pair of troublemakers have upset me greatly with your pickup truck shenanigans, and I'm gonna take you in and book you for something or other, and maybe you'll learn a lesson, eh? Maybe next time you drive into Clinch County on the ways to some-place else you'll just keep on going 'til you get to that place . . . as opposed to pulling over on the side of *my* highway and doin' stuff that should only happen behind closed doors when the sun's gone down.'

'Oh for Christ's sake—' Alex said.

'For *Christ's* sake, Miss Webber? You a church-goer down there in Augusta Falls? You responsible for the moral and religious education of your charges in that schoolhouse of yours? I would say

233

you were, if that schoolhouse is anything like ours, right?' Fermor shook his head. 'So I wouldn't be taking anyone's name in vain right now, least of all the Lord's, considerin' the position you people have found yourselves in this fine morning. I'm gonna ask you to get your shoes and clothes arranged properly, one at a time, and then step right over here to the side of my car and wait for me to handcuff you.'

'Handcuff us?' I asked, now disbelieving, now beginning to worry that something vindictive and unjust was taking place.

'Why yes, Mr Vaughan, handcuff you. That's what I'm gonna do, and you people are gonna co-operate, or like I said before I'm gonna make a call to my office and a couple of deputies are gonna come down here and we're gonna make a party of it.'

The heel that was rested on the gun shifted back an inch. I looked at Alex. Her eyes were wide, tear-rimmed. She looked like a frightened child.

We co-operated. We put our shoes on and straightened ourselves up. We walked one after the other to Fermor's car and he handcuffed my left hand to Alex's right, and then cuffed my right to a bar that ran above the upper edge of the window.

Neither Alex nor I spoke a word as we drove. As we neared a dip in the highway I glanced back at Reilly Hawkins' pickup at the side of the road. I wondered if it would still be there when we returned.

★   ★   ★

Clinch County Sheriff's Office was a featureless block at the side of the road on the outskirts of Homerville. It looked like something someone had dropped on the way into town, and then considered it of insufficient worth to return and collect. So there it had stayed, and once inside, each of us sequestered in a separate cell but facing one another across a narrow corridor, I began to think that perhaps this event was the high point of Sheriff Fermor's week. Stationed at the end of the corridor was a deputy, no older than me, tight-lipped and serious-looking, overcome with the grandeur and sobriety of his task. He informed us that there was to be no talking. I looked through the bars at Alex. She sat on the bunk with her back against the wall, her knees drawn up, her chin resting atop them, and every once in a while she looked back at me, wide-eyed and confused. I shook my head and smiled. It's gonna be okay, I tried to communicate. It's not a big deal, nothing's gonna come of this . . . and no, I don't blame you.

She smiled back weakly, and then she closed her eyes and lowered her head. I think perhaps she fell asleep.

The commotion started after an hour or so. The door at the end of the corridor was flung open and Fermor stood there.

'Let these deviants out of here,' he said matter-of-factly. 'We got one helluva lot more important thing to be attending to.'

The deputy looked nervous, seemed uncertain.

'Go!' Fermor barked.

The kid came haring down toward us, keys on his belt jangling, and he fumbled and struggled to get the cage door open.

Alex sat bolt upright. 'Wha—'

'We're outta here,' I said, and stepped up to the cell door. My hands instinctively gripped the bars.

Fermor walked down and stood beside the deputy.

'You're Joseph Vaughan from Augusta Falls,' he stated sonorously.

I nodded. I felt the tension in my hands, felt my knuckles whiten.

'You were the one that found the Perlman girl back in August of '42.'

I nodded again. 'Yes sir, I was.'

'Well, son, we got another one – out in Fleming, Liberty County. I'm going up there, taking Deputy Edgewood here with me, so I ain't got time to process any paperwork on you people.'

I sensed my eyes widen. The blood retreated from my face. My heart missed several consecutive beats; my legs felt like they were filled with nothing but liquid. For a moment I couldn't register what he was saying.

Another girl. Three years after Virginia Grace Perlman, another girl had been killed.

'You're sure . . . sure it's—' I stammered.

'Not sure of anything yet,' Fermor said. He cleared his throat, tucked his thumbs in his belt.

'Just gonna say this one thing before I throw you people out of here. Don't much appreciate that you came into my county to commit this misdemeanor. I looked it up. What you were doin' was a misdemeanor, plain and simple. Exposin' yourselves in a public place, and engaging in lewd and lascivious conduct. And the fact that you're a schoolteacher, Miss Webber—' He paused for effect, and then nailed Alex with a steely and disapproving glare. 'Fact that you're responsible for the edification of Augusta Falls' young 'uns, well, I don't wanna use the language I'd like to use 'cause I been better raised than that . . .'

Fermor's voice was a blur of meaningless sound in my ears. I watched his mouth move, the way his expression changed as he spoke, and it meant nothing to me. All I could see was the white soles of Virginia's shoes over the brow of the hill.

'I'd see to it that you take stock of what's happened here today, take it as a fortunate lesson – fortunate that I was the one who came across you and not someone else with a harsher view. Only reason I ain't gonna book you is 'cause of this terrible thing up in Liberty County, and I gotta go up there and assist my contemporary, Sheriff Landis.' Fermor nodded, and then turned to his deputy. 'Deputy Edgewood is gonna drive you back to your vehicle, and then I would ask you to be on your way, go on up to Waycross to the Community Hospital and attend to your affairs. That is all I gotta say, but I will pray for you come Sunday as is my predilection in such matters. I wish you well, but I'll not be sorry to see you out of my county.'

Fermor nodded one more time, and then turned to Edgewood. 'Take the second car, drive these people back to their pickup, and then you come on out to Fleming.'

'Yes, Sheriff,' Edgewood said, and watched as Fermor strode out toward the front of the building. Moments later we heard the engine of his car gun into life.

Deputy Edgewood stood there for a moment, nervous, perhaps uncertain of what lay ahead, and then he stepped forward and raised the key that would unlock my cell door.

'Let the lady out first,' I said.

He paused, looked at me, glanced back over his shoulder at Alex, and then said, 'Yes, of course. The lady. Yes . . . er, sorry.'

Alex came out, waited patiently while Edgewood fumbled and dropped the keys, found the right one, unlocked my door and stepped back so I could gain the corridor between.

Edgewood told us to walk out to the front of the building and wait for him. I took Alex by the hand, and once we exited the narrow corridor I put my arm around her shoulder and pulled her tight.

'A lucky break,' I whispered, but what I really wanted to say was *Another girl . . . they found another girl.*

She turned and looked up at me, her upper and lower lids smeared gray with kohl, her skin pale. She merely nodded, didn't say anything, and while we waited for Edgewood I just held onto her as tight as I could.

The drive was without conversation. I don't think Edgewood would have known what to do had I started speaking to him, but I was incapable of speech. I felt the past three years close up against me like a shadow, felt my heart thundering in my chest, felt the presence of something I had tried so hard to forget overwhelm me.

Edgewood dropped us off at the pickup, turned around and headed back toward the junction where he could turn toward Liberty County.

'I want to go up there,' I told Alex.

'Where?'

'Fleming.'

She frowned. 'Why, Joseph, why d'you wanna go up there?'

I shook my head. 'I don't know, Alex . . . hell, I don't know, I just feel like I need to go up there.'

'And see what? Some other little girl who got herself murdered?'

We stood each side of the pickup, looking at one another over the hood. I glanced down at the ground, at my shoes, and when I looked up I realized that there was no way for me to explain what I felt.

I'd found Virginia Perlman. I'd made a promise to Elena Kruger, a promise to ensure no harm came her way, and I had failed. I'd been the one to stand and watch as unjustified bitterness and anger was directed toward Gunther Kruger and his family, and how that had indirectly resulted in not only the death of his daughter, but also the loss of my mother as I knew her. I was drawn to this thing, that's all I could feel, but I knew there was no way I would make Alex understand that. I thought of the Guardians, where they were now, what they were doing . . . and I knew again that everything we had tried to accomplish had been nothing but the fool-ishness of children.

'You really wanna go?' she asked.

I nodded. There was no hesitancy or uncertainty in my mind.

'And your mother? When do you figure on seeing her?'

I shrugged. 'I don't know, Alex, maybe on the way back . . . but if you don't want to come with me I could take you home.'

She shook her head. 'I wanted to go see your mother,' she said quietly. 'I sure as hell don't want to go to Fleming.'

'I want . . . I *need* to go, Alex . . . don't ask me why, for Christ's sake, I don't know why myself, but there's something about this that just . . . it just . . .'

'If you're going, well then you're going alone,' she said. 'If you really have to do this then that's the way it's gonna be . . . I don't want to be involved. I don't want any part of this godawful thing.'

'I understand,' I said. 'I'll take you home.'

It took me two hours to get to Fleming. I drove northeast, took a route through Hickox, Nahunta, followed the Glynn-Brantley county line to Everett, and then headed north through Long County into Liberty. By the time I arrived it was late afternoon, overcast and oppressive. The outskirts of Fleming showed no indication of police presence, but three hundred yards in I saw a gathering of black and whites, representatives from Charlton, Clinch, Camden, Liberty itself; another car with the Tattnall County shield on the door. I pulled the pickup over to the left and waited there for some minutes. The feeling I had was compelling, a feeling of having to know what had happened, having to know who it was, what had been done, if it was attributable to the same person responsible for the earlier deaths. Over to the right of the highway was an embankment, behind it a higher ridge which ran upward to an outcrop of shrubs and low trees. A wooden sawhorse had been placed at each end of a thirty-foot expanse, a rope strung between them; on the other side indications of movement and activity amongst the woods. I got out of the pickup and came around the right-hand side, circumvented the rope and crossed the line of trees about fifty yards further down. I wished they'd been with me – Maurice, Michael, Ronnie, even Hans.

From twenty yards away I could see Sheriffs Burnett Fermor and Haynes Dearing, and a third man I presumed was the Liberty County Sheriff. Edgewood was there, standing back and to the left. He was standing rigid, looked like he was having difficulty dealing with whatever was there. I kept on walking, slowed down somewhat, and even though I knew there would be trouble, even though I knew Fermor and Dearing would have words to say, I couldn't help myself.

First appearances were of a confusion on the ground. From where I stood, the handful of seconds it took for Fermor and Dearing to see me, to place who I was, to ask me what in Sam Hill's name I was doing there, whether I'd followed Edgewood, had Edgewood brought me, and the girl . . . where was the girl, and what the hell did I think I was doing coming out into the middle of a murder scene . . . Jesus Christ goddammit, what the hell was this? In those few seconds I struggled to make sense of what was in front of me. I don't know that I even managed to correlate the evidence of my eyes with the procession of thoughts and questions that followed until Edgewood and Dearing were standing over me at the edge of the highway.

The girl had been cut in two. Body had been cut in two right across the middle, each part buried in a different shallow grave, but each grave no more than a couple of yards from the other, and in unearthing the two separate parts of her the apparency was of a eight- or nine-foot body, the upper half protruding from the ground, the middle submerged, the lower half appearing some distance away. It was not an image that found any point of reference to anything. It was an illusion, a deception, a chimera.

Once again I felt the blood draw from my face, my hands, my legs. I felt everything inside me draw back, as if it was attempting to retreat from the horror I was witnessing. I felt weak at the knees, and for a moment I heard nothing, even though Sheriff Dearing was barking questions at me one after the other.

'—doing, and now you're here—'

'—exactly is going on, and I better get some straight answers—'

'—some kind of—'

I put my hands over my ears and dropped to my knees. It was then that I felt the handcuffs snap onto my wrists for the second time in the same day. A shadow closed around my heart. I looked up at them, all of them – Edgewood, Dearing, Fermor, Landis of Liberty County – and I opened my mouth to speak.

'Don't say a goddamned thing!' Fermor barked at me. 'I don't know what the hell is going on here, boy! Where's the girl? Where's the girl that was with you? What have you done with her?'

I couldn't speak.

Dearing grabbed the chain between the cuffs and dragged me to my feet. The pain in my wrists and forearms was excruciating. I had difficulty breathing, and when he turned and started shoving me toward the road I felt my legs give beneath me once again.

They bundled me into the back of Sheriff Landis's car. Landis and Fermor stayed behind, Edgewood was told to drive, and Sheriff Haynes Dearing of Charlton County, a man I had known for as many years as I'd been alive, climbed into the back of the car alongside me and told Edgewood to drive to the Liberty County Sheriff's Office.

'Don't know what the hell is going on here, boy,' he said, his voice sharp, accusative, 'but before this afternoon's out there's gonna be some goddamned straight answers.'

I started to say something.

'Not a word,' he hissed. 'Not a goddamned word there, boy. You're in enough trouble as it is. You ain't gonna do nothing but make it worse by telling me anything right now.'

I felt my mind shut down. I thought of Alex, of my mother. I turned and looked out of the window. Thunderheads had gathered along the horizon. It had started to rain.

Elena.

You sweet, silent, lost little girl.

I think of the woman you would have become. I wonder if somewhere there is a place that holds all these unfinished lives. Another plane, another world running parallel to our own, and there we will find the dead, picking up their incomplete lives and living them out.

And I recall times when I tried so hard to understand the kind of person who could have killed so many children.

There were my mother's imagined sins – terrible, even murderous, and there were my own sins – sins born out of fear, a fear so great it made me believe that what I was doing was somehow justified. But this sin was different. So, so different. The sins we committed were driven by a sense of rightness, of justice, of the necessity to see this thing ended.

But yours . . .

Even now I cannot bear to think of the mind that must have prompted such actions.

I recall Sheriff Dearing's face as we walked away from what we had done. The way he looked at me, the way he turned back and glanced over his shoulder.

Perhaps he knew even then.

Perhaps we both knew.

And earlier, before everything changed, there was that day in Liberty, Fleming County, a day they believed that perhaps I was the guilty one . . . I remember it so vividly. I believed that Virginia Grace had been the last one, back in August of '42. But no, there were more, and not just the one that was found there.

How I sat across from Dearing, a man who had walked through my childhood with me, and the way his face sort of folded around the eyes, a sense of defeat, a ghost upon his shoulders, and the tone of his voice as he said . . .

CHAPTER 13

'Esther Keppler.'

'Who?'

'Esther Keppler,' Sheriff Haynes Dearing repeated.

I sat facing him. It was late. I had no idea how late but I could tell from the way the cold had drawn in that the sun had already gone down. Couldn't see any windows from where I sat in the small back office of the Liberty County Sheriff's Department. I'd been there two, perhaps three hours. Much of the time I'd been alone, wondering what the hell I was doing there. I'd asked at one point, to which Dearing had replied, 'We have exactly the same question for you, Joseph, exactly the same question for you.'

He then shook his head and left the room without requiring an answer from me. I was relieved because I did not have one.

I asked how long I was going to be there; said I was hungry.

'Don't know how long,' he'd said, 'could be a while yet . . . I'll have someone bring some food for you.'

An hour later Deputy Edgewood came into the

room with a plate of sandwiches and a bottle of Coke.

'Can you tell me what the hell is going on here?' I asked him. He couldn't have been much older than me; figured there might be some slight hope he'd help me out.

Edgewood shook his head. 'No,' he said flatly. 'I can't tell you anything.'

He backed up to the door, stepped out and closed it behind him. Locked it, as had been done every time before.

I ate the sandwiches. I drank the Coke. After a while I needed to use the restroom. I approached the door, banged on it with the heel of my fist.

'Hey!' I shouted. 'Anybody out there?'

There was nothing – no response, no sound. I banged again, louder, and was startled when someone banged the door on the other side.

'Shut the hell up in there!' a voice came through, clear as daylight.

'I need the bathroom!'

'Well, you can goddamned wait!'

'You can't do this to me! I haven't done anything! I have rights—'

'Rights? What the hell are they then?' the voice came back, and then there was silence.

I banged on the door again. Nothing.

I returned to the plain deal chair and sat down.

Waited another half an hour, perhaps more, and it was then that Dearing appeared, told me the name of the girl they'd found.

'Don't know anyone of that name,' I said. 'She's from here?'

Haynes Dearing drew the chair out from beneath the table and sat down. 'Yes, she's from Fleming. Nine years old.'

'She was murdered like . . . like the others?'

Dearing nodded. 'Seems that way . . . and there have been two others since the one you found in Augusta.'

'Two others?'

'Yeah, two others . . . making it a total of eight.'

My mind stopped working. I felt my skin crawl. The hairs rose on the nape of my neck. My mouth was dry, bitter-tasting. Eventually I found my voice, and I said: 'Nine, Sheriff Dearing . . . there have been nine.'

Dearing frowned. 'Nine?'

'Elena Kruger . . . remember?'

'Sure I remember, but she wasn't killed by the same person. She was killed in the fire.'

'Not by the same person,' I said, 'but you can count her death amongst these, because it was directly caused by what happened.'

'Be that as it may,' Dearing said. 'I have eight killings, all of them young girls, this last one killed yesterday, cut in half for God's sake, and each separate part buried.' He paused and looked at me. 'True about this morning . . . that Burnett Fermor came across you and Alexandra Webber doing whatever the hell you were doing in the back of a pickup truck?'

249

I nodded.

'Jeez, what the hell is that all about? Whose truck is that anyway . . . sure as hell ain't yours.'

'Reilly's.'

'Reilly Hawkins?'

'Yes, Reilly Hawkins.'

'And what were you doing, Joseph? Where were you headed?'

'See my mom at Waycross Community.'

'And what did you stop for, eh? That's not the sort of thing I'd expect of you, and certainly not of Miss Webber. She's the schoolteacher, you know?'

I smiled. 'I know, Sheriff, I know she's the schoolteacher.'

'And how long has this thing . . . this relationship been going on between you and Miss Webber?'

I shrugged. 'I don't know, better part of six months maybe.'

'Six months?'

'Yes, about six months.'

'And you are how old?'

'Eighteen.'

'And Miss Webber?'

'She's twenty-six, twenty-seven come February.'

Dearing nodded slowly. 'Twenty-seven come February . . . okay, okay.'

There was silence between us for a little while. I was aware of the pressure in the middle of my body. I still hadn't used the bathroom. I believed

I was concentrating on it in order to think as little as possible about what Dearing had told me. Two more girls. Eight in all. I wanted to ask him who they were, what had happened to them, why such information had not been communicated to us. I wanted to know why he had accomplished nothing, not only him but the combined sheriffs' departments of several counties.

'Can't believe you got yourself arrested,' Dearing said. 'But the fact that you were arrested gives you a very substantial alibi, doesn't it?'

I frowned, shook my head. 'What d'you mean, alibi?'

'That you were locked in a police cell when she got herself killed tells me that you couldn't have done this thing—'

'I couldn't have done this thing? What in Christ's name is that supposed to mean?'

Dearing raised his hand and silenced me. 'You have any kind of an idea how this would look to someone who didn't know you? I mean, for God's sake, Joseph . . .' His voice trailed away. He shook his head slowly, sat in silence for a little while, and then he said, 'And how did this thing come about, this *relationship*? This is something that started six months ago . . . it didn't start any earlier?'

'Earlier, Sheriff? Like did she seduce me when I was under the legal age for consensual sex?'

Dearing looked a little surprised.

'Is that what you're asking, Sheriff? If you're

251

asking that, then hell, go on and ask. It's not complicated. What you see is what you get as far as I'm concerned.'

Dearing cleared his throat. 'Well, okay then . . . is that the case? Did she seduce you into some sort of sexual relationship before you were legally responsible for such decisions?'

'No.'

'No?'

'That's right,' I said. 'No, she did not seduce me into anything. Miss Webber and I have known each other for many years—'

'You were one of her pupils, right?'

'*Was* one of her pupils, Sheriff. She and I were friends after I left school. We remained friends. Now we have a relationship, and we were on our way to see my mother in Waycross this morning when we—'

Dearing raised his hand. 'I know enough about what happened. I don't need any further details.'

'Okay . . . can I use the bathroom now, Sheriff Dearing?'

'In a minute, son, in a minute. First I gotta ask you what the hell you're doing out here in Fleming when there's been another little girl murdered.'

I looked at Dearing. His question brought me suddenly down to earth. I had been speaking of Alex, defending my situation. I had almost forgotten where I was, and then there it was – the reason for my presence in Fleming. Another girl had been murdered. Before her, another two.

'You said that two others had been murdered?'

Dearing nodded. 'Seems that way. One down in Meridan back in September of '43, another in Offerman, Pierce County last February . . . and those are the ones we know about.'

'So whoever killed the girls in Charlton and Camden left after the Kruger fire . . .'

'We're not jumping to any conclusions, Joseph. We don't know for sure that all these killings were carried out by the same man.'

'But the way in which these girls went missing, the way they were found . . . there's enough similarities to connect them?'

Dearing shook his head. 'I'm not saying anything . . . I *can't* say anything, and I wouldn't even if I could. Fact of the matter is that another girl has been killed, and we want to know what you're doing here, Joseph. You live in Augusta Falls, your ma's in the Community Hospital in Waycross, and yet you're all the way north in Fleming because you heard a girl had been murdered. Tell me something that makes sense, will you? You're from my jurisdiction. You're one of my people. I know you, I've known your ma for I don't know how many years . . . tell me something I can make sense of, huh?'

I sat silent for some moments.

'Joseph?'

I looked up at Haynes Dearing. I shook my head. 'I don't have an answer for you, Sheriff.'

Dearing nodded. 'How did you know about this?'

253

'About the girl?'

'Yes, about the girl . . . about what happened here in Fleming.'

'Sheriff Fermor told us . . . well, he came and got Deputy Edgewood to let me and Alex out because he had to come to Fleming.'

'So you overheard him telling his deputy?'

I smiled, shrugged my shoulders. 'I wouldn't say I overheard him, Sheriff. He didn't exactly make it a secret.'

'Okay,' Dearing said thoughtfully. He glanced towards the door, more an involuntary reaction to something, as if a thought had occurred which made it difficult for him to face me.

'What?'

Dearing shook his head.

'No, what?' I asked again. 'What are you thinking?'

'I'm thinking coincidences, Joseph . . . that four of these girls have been from Augusta Falls—'

'Three,' I said. 'Three from Augusta Falls. Alice Ruth Van Home, Catherine McRae and Virginia Perlman.'

'Ellen May Levine as well.'

I shook my head. 'Ellen May was from Fargo in Clinch County. She was found in Augusta Falls, but she wasn't from there.'

'You seem to know more about this than me, Joseph.'

I laughed, and realized the sound I made must have come across as a nervous response. It had not been intended that way. 'It's my home town,' I said. 'These things upset me, Sheriff, especially after I was the one who discovered Virginia's body.'

'Right, of course you were,' Dearing interjected. 'I'd forgotten that you were the one to find her.'

'No you hadn't,' I stated matter-of-factly. 'What the hell is this? What's happening here, Sheriff? You got some kind of idea that I had something to do with these killings?'

Dearing smiled. It was a genuine smile. He seemed the model of avuncular authority he'd always appeared to be from my distant and awkward childhood. 'I have no such idea, Joseph. If anything, you've created this situation for yourself.'

'What situation? What are you talking about?'

Dearing leaned back and folded his arms across his ample stomach. 'You have hair grown almost to your shoulders. You have a beard, Joseph, a damned beard of all things. You got yourself arrested for cavorting with a twenty-six-year-old schoolteacher in the back of a pickup truck belonging to Reilly Hawkins. You live in the same town as three of the murder victims, and the fourth was found there as well. You lived next door to the Krugers, and if the fire at the Krugers did anything it gave everyone some kind of idea that maybe Gunther Kruger had something to do with what had happened. And then . . . damn it, Joseph, then there was this thing with your mother and Gunther Kruger, something it was very hard for a lot of folks to ignore, and as soon as he left Augusta your mother wound up at Waycross Community, and everyone's thinking that maybe she knew something, something big enough to feel real bad about, and it turned her mind, and now she's in the care of these special doctors up there—'

'Everyone?' I asked, interrupting Sheriff Dearing as he disgorged his awkward monologue. 'This is what *everyone* thinks?' I thought of him visiting her, that he'd never told me, didn't seem set to tell me now.

Dearing laughed. 'It's an expression, Joseph, a turn of phrase. You know what I mean.'

'I do? You're sure that I do, Sheriff?'

'Okay, okay, enough already . . . this isn't meant to be a confrontational thing, Joseph. This is one concerned member of the county police department following a line of enquiry.'

'A line of enquiry about who? Me? Whether I was involved in any of these killings? Or maybe about my mother and why she went crazy . . . hell, Sheriff, maybe she killed all these girls. What d'you think about that? How about following that as your line of enquiry?'

Sheriff Dearing smiled understandingly. 'You're tired, Joseph. You've had a long day. I'm gonna have someone take you back to your pickup. Figure you should make your way back home tonight. But this I need you to understand.' Dearing leaned forward. 'I might trust you. I've known you long enough to consider it unlikely that you're involved in these things, but Burnett Fermor, the others here . . . hell, they don't know you from Adam. They want to keep you here. Despite the fact that this little girl died while you were in Burnett Fermor's lock-up, he still doesn't have to let you go. Your alibi is circumstantial, that's what he said. He said that the medical examiner could be wrong, that the estimated time of death is *estimated*. He wants to ask you some questions, to start looking at whether or not you have an alibi for the others.'

I was horrified, stunned that anyone could even consider such a thing. I opened my mouth to speak but Dearing raised his hand. 'You take Reilly Hawkins' pickup and drive it straight back to Augusta Falls. Don't go anyplace but home. Be there when I come to see you in the next day or so.'

'And where the hell would I go, Sheriff . . . oh yes, of course, some other town where there's little girls being murdered, right?'

Dearing nodded patiently. 'I'm gonna grant that comment the importance it deserves, Joseph.' He eased back his chair and rose to his feet. 'I'll have Deputy Edgewood take you back to your vehicle. I *will* be speaking to you in the next couple of days, and you *will* be answering my questions truthfully, you understand?'

Dearing rose from his chair.

'Sheriff?'

He paused and turned; looked down at me. For

a brief moment I felt like the child I'd once been. He knew what I was going to ask him; I could read it in his eyes.

'Why is it still happening? How can this still be going on after all these years?'

Dearing stepped back and sat down once again. 'You can't ask me that,' he said quietly. 'That is a question we've been asking ourselves for a little more than six years.'

'And you have nothing?'

He made a sound like he was going to laugh, and I recognized the utter desperation in his eyes. 'Nothing? We have eight dead girls, Joseph . . . I wouldn't call that nothing.'

'You know what I mean, Sheriff.'

Dearing bowed his head. He placed his hands together, palm to palm. A man praying. 'We have had our suspicions,' he said. 'We have gone house to house through numerous different counties. We have requested assistance, but there's been a war going on in case you hadn't noticed. The people we need are needed elsewhere, you understand? These things have crossed town limits, county limits.' He stopped suddenly. 'I don't even know why I'm telling you this.' He smiled weakly, shook his head. 'Let's just say that I make believe I'm going to step out one day and see him, and even though I have no idea what he looks like I'm just going to *know* it's him, and—' He paused for a moment, looked away thoughtfully. 'I'm not going to ask questions, Joseph . . . I'm not going to put handcuffs on him and drive him to the Sheriff's Office. I'm just going to shoot him right where he stands, and then it will all be over.'

'Six years,' I said. 'Eight girls, if we don't include Elena Kruger. And these last two, the ones in Meridan and Offerman?'

'What about them?'

'The same thing . . . the same manner of death?'

'Yes, exactly the same . . . like he's trying to bury what he's done. Like he's trying to break everything up and cast it to the four corners of the earth, but he can never bring himself to do it. He just leaves them lying there where they can be found . . .' Dearing stopped talking. 'Enough,' he said. He rose from his chair once more, and for a moment he looked awkward, as if he realized he'd been speaking out of turn. If ever I'd seen someone who needed to talk, needed to talk their heart out, it was Haynes Dearing.

'The first ones were all connected to Augusta Falls, weren't they?' I asked. 'But now they're spread out, right?'

Dearing shook his head. 'Time for you to go home, Joseph, time for you to go home.'

'Don't talk to strangers,' I said. 'Don't go with strangers. Stay alert. Stay safe.'

Dearing looked at me closely. 'You remember that?'

'You remember the Guardians?'

He frowned.

'Me and Hans Kruger and the others. Daniel

McRae, Ronnie Duggan, Michael and Maurice. That's what we called ourselves. The Guardians. And the flyers you posted all over the place. You remember those, right?'

'I remember catching a crowd of you out one night,' Dearing said. 'Often wondered what the hell you thought you were doing.'

I smiled. 'We were doing something, Sheriff, that's all. We were just trying to do something to help catch him.'

'Jesus, you kids could have gotten yourselves into a whole heap of trouble.'

'We were already in trouble, Sheriff. Someone was out there murdering children. Seems to me that that would classify as trouble enough, don't you think?'

Dearing nodded, and then he turned toward the door. 'I have to go,' he said. 'I have this thing to handle. Someone has to go and tell her parents.'

'This is Fleming County. Shouldn't Sheriff Landis be doing that?'

Dearing looked down at me, and once again I felt like a child. 'These days,' he said quietly. 'These days we go in twos.'

Fifteen minutes after Sheriff Dearing left the room, Deputy Edgewood came to drive me to Reilly's pickup. I said nothing for the entire journey.

CHAPTER 14

'Fried catfish,' my mother said. 'We could have Oysters Rockefeller to start, and then Country Captain with hush puppies, sweet potato pie and some fried catfish.' She laughed, flicked her hair back from her brow. 'I do so *love* fried catfish, don't you, my de-ah?'

Alex glanced at me. I nodded. Alex turned back and smiled at my mother.

'And then I could make pies. I make a mighty fine pie. Black bottom perhaps, even honey walnut or blueberry slump. We could make hand-crank ice cream too, you know. My nurse could come. She loves a good pie. Her name's Sister Margaret. She used to be a nun. The Holy Order of the Immaculate Heart of Mary. Mary, see? Like my name. I do hear a lot of nuns like pie . . . you've heard that, Joooph?'

'Yes, Mom, I've heard it,' I replied, consigned to the fact that my mother was of the belief that she would be entertaining Alex, her family, perhaps the better minority of Georgia at some sumptuous Southern banquet.

'A brain fever,' she whispered to Alex. 'I was

261

taken with a brain fever last summer. Such an affliction, and I was overcome with such malaise and enervation. You've never seen the like of it. Anyway, I do hope everything works out fine with you and Joseph. Lord, I am so proud, just *so* proud of you both. You're going to be married, of course?'

I looked at my mother. Her hair was white and fine, flyaway grandmother hair. She was forty-one years old. She looked the better part of sixty. The skin on her face and hands was swollen, that was the only way I could describe it. Apparently the medication she took caused such a side-effect. I couldn't bear to think what they were giving her, and so I did not ask.

It was Sunday. The previous night I had returned from Fleming. I'd stopped at Alex's house and explained what had happened, that Sheriff Dearing had been there, that I'd spent some time with him.

'Why?' she'd asked.

'He had some questions, Alex, nothing important.'

'Questions? Questions about what, Joseph?'

'About the Krugers, that was all. They lived next door to us, we knew them well, perhaps better than anyone, and he wanted to know if there was anything that happened back then that might help him.'

'And?'

'Nothing,' I'd replied. 'I couldn't tell him anything.'

I did not tell her about the other two girls, the ones from Meridan and Offerman.

I'd stayed the night, slept beside her, aware that she'd lain awake for some considerable time, but I'd said nothing.

Eventually she drifted away. I waited until the sound of her breathing was deep and even, and then I crept from the room, padded barefoot along the upper landing, and stood looking through the narrow window at the end. The fields were flat and blue, the mist crawled in from the Okefenokee and made ghosts that hovered above ground. Somewhere amongst those ghosts were the children, each and every one of them, and I'd closed my eyes and made-believe. Made believe if I concentrated hard enough I could hear them, their catcalls and laughter, their sudden interrupted rush of life now bursting forth in some other way, some other ethereal reality. They were all there. Ghost children. Children of the dead. Walking now, their breath visible in the mist, hand in hand, each step leaving footprints in the moist earth – and back of them, bringing up the rear, watching them and making sure no harm came their way, was my father. My father, the angel.

For a time I'd held my breath, thought about Alex. Thought about my mother. Thought about the life that had come running at me and caught me off guard. There were times I felt I'd had no time at all. Eighteen years – the blink of an eye, the beat of a heart. Other times it seemed that every emotion I could experience had been crammed into those years, handfuls jammed in one after the other until the very seams of my being were stretched and distended. What did I have? My parents were gone – my father physically, my mother in spirit and mind. I had Alex, that's what I had, and even as I considered this I knew that the time would come when it could no longer exist. It was not so much the years between us, certainly not my viewpoint about such a difference, but the viewpoint of the world.

A relationship was a trade-off: companionship against control of one's life. There was no doubt in my mind that I loved Alexandra Webber, and even as I considered the events that had brought us together it still seemed unreal to me. I did not think of her as a schoolteacher, and perhaps never had. She had been a friend, that first and foremost, and I seemed to have lived my life with few friends. Reilly Hawkins, the Kruger children, Mathilde and Gunther themselves, for a time and in some particular way, the Guardians. Aside from such people there seemed to have been no-one but Alex Webber, the woman who forced my hand and made me write.

I'd walked back after a while, stood at the side of the bed and watched her as she slept. I'd listened to the sound of her breathing, even reached out and placed my hand above her breast so I could feel her heart. She was all I had. She meant so much to me, and yet I knew that whatever I might gain I would somehow lose, and thus I struggled internally.

Later, I slept – restlessly, fitfully – and I dreamed of dead children walking through the fields of Georgia.

The following morning, rising before Alex, I went out and bought a newspaper. I cut the clipping from it, a small two-inch column about a dead girl in Fleming. I placed it with the others – six in all – and thought of the two that were missing.

'We should go and see my mother,' I said. 'Her birthday was the nineteenth. Christmas is the day after tomorrow. I should go, Alex, I really should, and I want you to come with me.'

'So we go.' Like that, so matter-of-fact. 'Reilly will let us use the pickup?'

'Sure he will . . . but this time we don't stop on the way.'

She smiled, reached out toward me. I stepped toward her, taken her hand, drew her close and held her. 'Think we should cut your hair and shave your beard,' she said. 'Make you look less like the crazy mountain man come down to scare up the villagers.'

'Not now. Now we go see my mother.'

Which is what we'd done, and we arrived without incident, and once we found my mother – in the sun-lounge at the back of the building – I told her that Alex was my girlfriend.

'Such a modern word,' she said. 'Girlfriend.' She laughed. The sound was of someone else, not the woman who'd raised me. 'You can stand in the sunlight,' she went on, raising her hand and indicating the lawns behind the building through the high windows of the sun-lounge. 'You can stand in the sunlight . . . feel the warmth of the sun. Feels like the fingerprints of God on your soul.' She turned and smiled at Alex, seemed to look right through her, like there was no recognition. I wondered if my mother even remembered her name. 'And you can hear the voices of angels.' She looked at me directly. The sensation of something moving across the back of my neck made me shudder. Fleeting, like the shadow of a cloud on a field.

'Angels?' I asked.

My mother nodded, smiled again, but this time there was a heartbeat of connection, like she was looking at me and she saw her son. For real, she saw her son.

'Angels,' she whispered. 'Voices of angels . . . like those little girls, Joseph, the ones that went with the Devil, remember?'

I nodded. I felt uncomfortable.

She leaned closer to me. 'Come,' she whispered, her tone conspiratorial, perhaps paranoid.

I leaned closer.

'I know who took them,' she said.

I frowned.

'The little girls, Joseph . . . I *know* who took them.'

'Took them?' I asked. I wondered what had really happened to my mother. I wondered about the mind, the way it worked, the manner in which it could malfunction and close down with such finality.

'Took them all to Hell,' she hissed.

I felt suddenly and intensely overwhelmed. I glanced sideways at Alex. She looked as nervous as I felt.

I reached out and took my mother's hand.

Her eyes were clear blue and fixed, like a light shone back of them. 'They're all out there,' she said. 'Alice and Laverna, Ellen May, Catherine . . . the one you found, Joseph . . . what was her name?'

I shook my head. 'You know her name, Mom.'

'Virginia, right?'

'Right, Mom, Virginia Perlman.'

'I hear them all . . . hear them, hear your father too, and sometimes I can hear Elena, and she's lost, Joseph, she doesn't know where she came from and she sure as dammit doesn't know where she's supposed to be going. Says she's waiting for me, and she'll wait as long as it takes, and when I get there I can hold her hand and show her the way . . .'

'Mom . . . please . . .'

She paused for a moment, perhaps offended by my interruption, and then she nodded, winked as if we were engaged in some unspoken collusion. 'It's okay, Joseph, not another word. But you must promise me something, Joseph . . .'

'What, Mom, what do you want me to promise?'

'That you'll speak with Sheriff Dearing, tell him what I've said . . . in fact, tell him to come and see me. Tell him that I know the truth. Tell him that *I* know who this child-killer is.'

My heart was closed like a fist. 'Yes,' I said, and even as the word left my lips I wondered if I would ever really speak with my mother again. Ever speak with the woman who had raised me, the woman who'd loved my father, the woman who'd buried him and somehow carried on living for no other reason than her son. 'I'll tell him,' I whispered, my voice cracking with emotion, my fists clenched, every ounce of will I owned required to hold back my tears. 'Soon as I get back I'll tell him.' I smiled as best I could. I hoped beyond hope that she wouldn't say such things to the doctors, to the other patients. God knows what they would have done to her had she told them she was talking with dead husbands and murdered little girls, that she knew the identity of a child-killer who'd evaded the police of several counties for so many years.

And it was then that she spoke about Oysters Rockefeller and blueberry slump, about the banquet she would prepare for us, for her nurse, for the elite of Georgia. She became the vague and distant woman I had come to expect, and there was no light behind her eyes, and there were no words about the dead.

We stayed a while longer, as long as I could bear

to sit with the woman who'd once been my mother, and then we wished our goodbyes.

'So sad,' Alex whispered. She took my arm and sort of pulled me close as we walked away. 'Such a cultured and intelligent woman . . . and now . . .' Her voice trailed away into a fragile, emotional silence.

We found Nurse Margaret, my mother's nurse. She was painfully thin; her features seemed almost vague, like a watercolor painting. Her eyes were pale gray and washed-out, as if she'd spent the vast majority of her life in tears. A Southern spinster I guessed, her lips thin and pursed, her manner tied up tight like a corset, the kind of woman that longed for love but would never find it.

'She told you that . . . that I was a nun?' she said. 'Lord almighty . . . I can imagine I'd be the last person in the world to be considered for such a thing.' She shook her head. 'No, I'm just Margaret, straight and simple, nothing more complicated than that.' She smiled warmly, and then steered Alex and me away from the people who sat waiting in the room beyond the sun-lounge.

'She manages somehow,' Margaret said. 'Every once in a while you can see something, like there's a light behind her eyes, and that's the real Mary Vaughan, the one that existed before the illness.'

'What *is* wrong with her?' Alex asked. She

glanced at me, almost as if she was afraid I'd be offended by her asking.

Margaret smiled sympathetically. 'I'm no psychiatrist, dear,' she said. 'I'm here merely for my medical skills, nothing else. You want an opinion then you should speak with her doctor. All I know is what I hear, and what I hear doesn't make a great deal of sense. I don't know that anyone really understands what happens when people . . .' Margaret looked at me, then at Alex. 'You know what I mean . . . no-one really knows what happens when people *turn*.' She sighed and shook her head. 'I wish I did know, then at least I'd feel like I could do something to help.'

Alex turned to me. 'We should see her doctor.'

I shook my head. 'Seen him. Seen him numerous times. They don't know what's wrong with her, never have, probably never will. All they're trying to do is keep her quiet.'

'It's the voices she hears,' Margaret said, and she glanced at both of us in turn, something fearful in her gray, washed-out eyes. 'The little girls?' she added, and then looked directly at me as if I would elucidate for her.

I said nothing.

'She can speak about the weather, about flowers in the gardens, about other patients.' Margaret was fussing with the edge of her dress pocket. 'Seems she's all there, you know? Can sit and talk for an hour, sometimes more, and you think she's

270

mending fine, making sense . . . and then suddenly, out of nowhere she's talking to someone else, someone you can't see. So I say to her, I say "Mary? Who are you talking to dear?" and she turns and looks at me like I'm the crazy one, and she says, "Why, Margaret, I'm talking to—" and then she says some name, some little girl's as far as I can gather, and off she goes, telling whoever she sees something about her day, talking to someone called Earl.'

I nodded. 'Earl was her husband . . . died back in '39.'

Margaret smiled, like she'd been asked a question and got it right. 'Yes, Earl,' she repeated. 'Talking about something she did with Earl, and even when you walk away she's still there talking away, talking like there'll not be any time to talk tomorrow.' Margaret stopped suddenly. She looked awkward, looked like she'd said too much. 'I'm sorry,' she blurted. 'It's not my place to be speaking about such things. I do apologize. It's just that you're the only ones who've visited with her in such a long time. There's the other gentleman. He's been a few times, but he never stays long . . .'

'Haynes Dearing,' I said.

Margaret shook her head. 'I don't know his name. He never told me and I've never asked.'

I reached out my hand and touched her arm. 'It's okay,' I said. 'You've been real helpful, Margaret. It's been very good speaking with you.

Please don't feel as though you've said anything out of turn.'

Margaret smiled. With her washed-out eyes she glanced back and forth as if expecting someone to appear. I wondered how long it would be before Margaret was having conversations with people who weren't there.

We left without seeing Doctor Gabillard. I didn't even ask if Gabillard was still attending to my mother. There was no purpose in speaking further.

'You really think there's nothing else that can be done?' Alex asked me as we drove away from Waycross Community Hospital.

'She's been there nearly four years, Alex.'

Alex opened her mouth to say something, perhaps to ask another question, but nothing came forth. She looked at me, seated there in the passenger seat as we drove in Reilly Hawkins' pickup toward the highway. I glanced back at her and there was nothing in her expression, a simple statement of nothing. Her eyes were empty, as if she'd seen all there was to see and little else remained.

I reached out and gripped her hand for a moment. 'I've been coming out here for an awful long time. After a year, eighteen months, it stopped feeling like I was visiting my mother. Now I just come out of duty . . . perhaps more for the memory of my father than anything else.'

'You remember telling me about the angels?' Alex asked.

I smiled. 'Don't remind me of that.'

'Why not?'

'Because I was very young at the time, and you were most definitely my schoolteacher, and that makes what we're doing now awful strange.'

'You feel that way?'

I shook my head. 'Not until you start talking about angels and the Atlanta Short Story Competition, and giving me a book by Steinbeck for my birthday.'

'You should write a book about all of his,' she said.

I frowned. 'All of what?'

'Your life. Your father, the little girls that were killed, what happened to the Krugers, what happened to your mother, us . . . all these things. You should write your autobiography.'

I started laughing. 'I'm eighteen, Alex, eighteen years old. You make it sound like I haven't got a great deal more life to live.'

'Do you think she knows?'

'Eh?'

'Your mother? Do you think she knows who did it?'

'Did what? What are we talking about now?'

'The little girls that were killed, Joseph. You heard what she said.'

I shook my head. 'Alex, my mother is crazy.

273

She's in the psychiatric wing of the Waycross Community Hospital. She has conversations with my father, and he's been dead since July of 1939. I am sure she has absolutely no idea who was responsible—'

'*Is* responsible, Joseph . . . the killings are still going on.'

'Okay, okay . . . I am quite certain that she has absolutely no idea who *is* responsible for these things.'

'But what if she does know? What if knowing this and not being able to do anything about it is what has made her this way—'

'Made her crazy, Alex. What if knowing this thing has made her *crazy*. Let's say it how it is. We know each other well enough not to walk in circles around this thing. She's crazy. She's bughouse, nuts—'

'Stop it!' Alex snapped. 'Enough!'

'And enough from you, Alex. Jesus, I don't wanna hear anymore about this thing, okay? She does not know who killed these girls . . . sorry, who is *killing* these girls. She does not know. She has never known and I am sure she never will. She will go on living at Waycross. She will probably be there for the rest of her life, and I will keep on visiting her until I can't take it anymore, or until she doesn't even recognize who I am. Then I will be sorry, but at the same time I will feel a tremendous burden lift from my shoulders, because you have no idea, no idea at all, how it

274

is to go out there and listen to your own mother holding rapt conversations with dead people, especially when one of them happens to be your own father.'

'I'm sorry—' she started.

I looked at her. I reached out my hand and touched the side of her face. 'Alex, I love you. I love you more than anything or anyone in the world. I'm not mad at you. I'm not even slightly angry at you. I'm upset about the situation. There's nothing I can do about it except get upset every once in a while, but it's not about you. If anything, it's directed at the people at Waycross, the ones who said they would do something to help her and seem to have made her worse. That's all there is to it. What happens to my mother, who she is, how she behaves . . . these are not things that you should concern yourself with. They're certainly not things that I want to have come between us.' I paused to catch my breath. 'That's all there is to it, nothing more, nothing less, and really, *really*, I don't want to talk about it anymore, okay?'

'Okay,' she said quietly. She reached up and held my hand, kissed my palm. She smiled, and in the vague light of a Georgia evening, with the warm breeze coming through the open window of the pickup, she looked like more than I could ever have wished for.

She closed her eyes, squeezed my hand once more, and then let it go.

I looked back toward the empty road ahead of us.

We did not speak for a long time, and when we did the words we shared were of no particular consequence.

After the killing in Fleming of the Keppler girl, after visiting my mother and listening to her talk her own special kind of crazy, I wondered if I was destined to carry the weight of these ghosts for all time. If I, somehow, could have done something to stop these killings, and in doing nothing I had consigned myself to carrying a burden of guilt for the rest of my life.

After the Keppler girl the dreams came more frequently.

I dreamed I was murdered. Dreamed I had run like the wind through trees and fields, the awareness of something behind me, something I could not see but could perceive with as strong a sense of certainty as my own name.

I dreamed I was being hunted. Tracked down. Chased. Dreamed I was growing ever more tired with each step, a bone-deep exhaustion, a fatigue of the mind, the heart, the soul. Dreamed that each step I took was always the last, and yet somehow I took another, another, another. Slowing down though, slowing and stumbling, until the thing behind was upon me, and I looked up into deadlight eyes, and screamed a scream of silence, and when the silence ended there was a deeper, greater silence, a silence that swallowed me whole and would never release me.

And then I was lifted to the back of a flatbed truck, and Kruger was there, and he wept over me, and his tears fell down and touched my skin. Lowell Shaner, Frank Turow, Reilly Hawkins . . . they were all there, and looking from the back of the truck as we dipped below the rise I could see my mother, behind her the ghosts of dead children. And they wept silently, and there was a sense of everything coming to an end . . . and a sense of knowing something, knowing who had been there, who was inside my invisible certainty as I ran across fields and through under-growth, as my feet staggered heavy and slow through the edges of the Okefenokee Swamp . . . and there was music, music like they played in church . . .

And then I was buried, my expression frozen in terror for all time. I was lowered into the ground in my Sunday bows and brights, my shined shoes, my combed hair, and people stood around the hole as it grew deeper and deeper, and there was the sound of earth falling onto me, and I knew I would lie right there for eternity, and the grass would grow, and the seasons would change, and people I had loved would age and die, and there would be silence in my mind instead of voices . . .

I would be there, my thoughts forever touching the edge of certainty . . . that I'd known who it was . . . that I'd known who it was . . . that I'd known who it was . . .

And he wasn't a silhouette on a flyer pinned to a fence post. He wasn't any kind of silhouette at all. He was a human being – a real flesh and blood, eating, breathing, talking human being.

And he was out there.

Somewhere.

CHAPTER 15

Christmas 1945. 'Old Blood and Guts' Patton died from injuries he sustained in a car crash in Germany. The man who'd conquered Sicily in thirty-eight days, who had suffered two demotions as a result of his cantankerous and difficult attitude, was fatally wounded on a lonely stretch of road. It seemed the darkest irony, and in some way a perfect reflection of how the world deemed it necessary to treat us human beings. Alex went to see her folks in Syracuse two days after Christmas. She planned to be gone for a week or so. I drove her to the bus station in Augusta Falls, and I waited with her. When the bus pulled away I realized that I had no reason to go home. I stayed in town for a while. I sat in a diner on Manassas Street and watched people walk from one place to another. Despite the season they all seemed eager to leave and unwilling to arrive, faces slow and expectant, their lives stretched out between ungrateful kids and senile parents. Little enough for themselves in the middle. Perhaps, I figured . . . perhaps that's just how it was. When I left I saw Sheriff Haynes

Dearing across the street. He raised his hand and waved me over.

'Out and about?' he asked.

'I drove Alex up here to take the bus to Syracuse.'

'Seeing her folks?'

'Yes, she's gone to see them for the New Year.'

'You didn't want to go with her?'

I shrugged. 'I don't much care for the airs and graces necessary when you're someone's guest.'

'I'm the same,' Dearing said. 'Wife has her sister and husband over, and though it's our house she's always fussing and minding things in such an irritating manner. I can't be doin' with such business myself.'

I nodded. I wanted to head home.

'You on the way back?' Dearing asked.

'I am, yes.'

'You're in a hurry, right?' he asked, but the way he asked it wasn't so much a question as a challenge to refuse his company.

'A hurry? Hell, no more than any other time, Sheriff. There's things to be done, always things to be done, as you well know.'

'But you have a little time for me, time to share a cigarette and talk about some things?' Once again the question he asked was more a statement or an invitation to counter him.

'Never did get the hang of smoking cigarettes,' I said. 'Tried a few times, made me feel rough and awkward. Talking I can do . . . never had much of a problem with that.'

281

'So walk with me down to my office, just social, nothing official, and see if you can't clarify some things for me, why don'tcha?'

'That really a question, Sheriff?'

Dearing smiled and shook his head. 'Hell no, I don't s'pose it is, Joseph.'

'I'll come, and of my own volition. Wouldn't want you thinking I had anything to hide.'

'Good enough, Joseph, good enough,' Dearing said, and he turned and led the way.

Sheriff Haynes Dearing's office was like an outhouse for pieces of his personality he didn't want to carry. Up on the wall he'd hammered some boards, nothing more than plain deal sheets, upon which he'd stabbed thumbtacks through photos, tickets, certificates of this and that, coupons, vouchers from Hot Shoppes and Howard Johnson's, the side of a Cream of Wheat cereal box, a Betty Crocker recipe for apple pandowdy that looked like it'd been cut from a newspaper, a kid's wax crayon drawing of 'Sheref Derin', a chart detailing the phonetic alphabet, a scale telling all kinds of weights and measures and distances; other such things. Far right-hand corner was a printed legend headed U.S. Postal Service, beneath it their motto: 'Neither snow nor rain nor heat nor gloom of night stays these couriers from the swift completion of their appointed rounds'. Dearing noticed how it caught my attention.

'My father,' he said. 'Delivered the mail. Helluva

thing. Forty-some years. Hang that up there to remind me of his persistence and resilience, and because it kinda fits with what I do.'

I frowned.

'Not delivering mail. More like delivering the facts, you know?' He smiled, sort of shrugged his shoulders, and sat heavily in his chair. The chair – wooden-slatted, wheels on its base – creaked uncomfortably beneath his weight. 'Hell, I don't know, Joseph, maybe there's no similarity at all . . . maybe "To Protect and Serve" didn't seem important-sounding enough.' He laughed to himself. 'Sit down,' he said. 'You want some coffee or something?'

I shook my head.

'So, you finally get out to Waycross to see your mother?'

'Yes, we saw her last Sunday, two days before Christmas.'

'And?'

'I don't know what to say, Sheriff . . . she isn't my mother anymore. I have conversations with her . . . hell, they aren't really conversations.' I shook my head. 'Last visit, she told me she knew the identity of the child-killer.'

Dearing raised his eyebrows, and then he looked concerned, sympathetic. He shifted in his chair and then leaned forward to look at me closely. 'I'm sorry to hear that, Joseph, I really am. I don't know what to say. What happens here . . .' He raised his hand and tapped his brow with his forefinger. 'Damned if I know what makes people tick, you know?' He exhaled slowly and leaned back. 'I've been out there to see her a few times,' he said.

'I know, Sheriff . . . I know you've been to see her and I really appreciate it.'

'Seemed the right thing to do. I've sat and talked to her and I don't know that she even remembers who I am.'

'I don't . . .' I looked down at the floor, shook my head resignedly. 'Whatever they're doing to her isn't fixing anything. They've given her drugs and all manner of special treatments. Every time I go they got something else cooked up that's the magic-bullet wonder cure. Seems all kinds of snake oil and jimson weed to me. Doctor comes down, seventy-five-dollar suit, all sniptious and superior, and what he tells me has about as much use to anyone as so many parcels of chickenshit.'

'I'm sorry to hear it, Joseph. Though it don't necessarily surprise me when it comes to medics an' the like. Seems such people spend all their time lookin' where folks has been instead of lookin' where they're going.'

I raised my hands and shrugged resignedly. 'It is what it is, Sheriff.'

'What does Miss Webber think?'

I looked up, puzzled. 'Alex?'

'Sure, she's a schoolteacher, ain't she? Smarter than three or four ordinary folks rolled together. She ain't your regular punchboard, right?'

I laughed. Dearing's words came out straight and blunt, a prizefighter jabbing holes in the space between us. Words like that seemed made of something more physical than sound; bareknuckle words, kind of bloody-nosed and ugly. That was a quality I could appreciate. 'What does she think?' I replied. 'I don't know . . . I haven't really asked her. This is the first time I've taken her out there. She spoke a little on the way, nothing much of anything really, but I'm not in the most talkative frame of mind when I've been out to Waycross.'

'What was the deal with Gunther Kruger?'

The question came out of left-field with a curve ball. I ducked but it caught me sideways and hurt some. Tomorrow I would still feel it, maybe a bruise. 'Gunther Kruger?' I parried.

'We see what we see, Joseph.' Dearing said. Seemed a simple enough statement, but the way he said it made it sound like something else. 'You're a writer ain'tcha?'

'Some.'

'Wanna know what I think about writers?'

'Fascinated.'

'You don't think I read some? Read that Rider Haggard feller, Hemingway, people like that. Read *The Informer* by the Irisher, what was his name?'

'O'Flaherty,' I said. 'Liam O'Flaherty.'

'That's the man.'

'I'm surprised.'

'That I can read?'

'No, Sheriff, that you read things like that.'

'Have a cousin who works in the Georgia State Library in Savannah. Every year they clear out God knows how many books . . . she selects a couple dozen for me and sends them down.'

'You were gonna tell me what you thought about writers.'

'I was on my way,' he said. 'Sometimes like to make a journey of what I'm saying so it feels more like a destination when I get there.'

I sat silent and waited.

'Writers see things other folks don't see.'

I raised my eyebrows.

'I'm right,' Dearing said. 'Maybe more accurate to say they see things in a way that others don't. You agree?'

I shrugged. 'Figure that everyone sees what they see, and they all see it a different way.'

'Maybe so,' Dearing replied. 'But a writer notices details and such that others don't, and he sees those details because he's looking with different kinds of eyes.'

'Perhaps,' I said. 'And you're telling me this because?'

'Because of what happened with your mother and Gunther Kruger.'

I didn't reply.

Dearing smiled, something understanding in his expression. 'We ain't at school anymore, Joseph.' He leaned forward and rested the palms of his hands on the table. I figured he was gonna use the support to stand up but he just kind of leaned forward and looked at me. 'I'm not of a mind to dredge through people's personal lives. Don't consider it's any of my business, and don't think I'd want it if it was offered. Your mother and Gunther Kruger made a habit of sharing one another's company, that's a fact. I know it. You know it. Sure as hell Mrs Gunther Kruger knew it. Don't know about the kids. Kids can be deceptive. Wide-eyed and innocent, but they hear every word.' Dearing paused, pushed himself back into his chair. The chair, perhaps reconciled to such punishment, merely groaned a little. 'Remember a time, three, four years ago. Man said his wife was poisoned—' Dearing stopped mid-flight. 'Hell, you don't wanna be hearing second-hand stories about such things. Another time we'll do that. Anyways, where the hell was I?'

'My mother and Gunther Kruger.'

'Right, right. So, like I said, I got an idea that maybe there were things that went on back then that you didn't think to speak about at the time. Maybe they didn't seem important. Maybe they weren't, you know? Hindsight gives us a different slant and situation. I wondered if there was anything that you can remember that might give us something.'

'About the girls that were killed?'

'Sure, about the girls that were killed.'

'And you think I might know something about this because I lived next door to the Krugers.'

'No, not because you lived next door to the

Krugers . . . because three of the girls were from here, another one from Fargo, but she was found on Kruger's land—'

'Hold up,' I said. 'I feel like I'm being given a ride somewhere, Sheriff.'

Dearing smiled and shook his head. 'No-one's giving anyone a ride, Joseph.'

'So ask me what you wanna ask me and I'll tell you the answer.'

Dearing cleared his throat. 'I know I came and spoke to you afterwards, but I don't know that I ever really understood about what happened with the Keppler girl.'

I frowned.

'Tell me the truth, Joseph . . . why did you go to Fleming that day?'

I smiled and shook my head. 'This is a railroad train, right? You should've told me I'd won a ticket, I would've packed some things for the trip.'

'Ain't no railroad ticket, Joseph. Tell ya something. Curiosity I have is about yay big.' Dearing held his hands wide as a measure. 'I find it strange that you would hear about the death of a little girl, little girl you never heard of before, and drive all the way out to Liberty County. Got me thinking.'

'Thinking what, Sheriff . . . something about how a murderer might return to the scene of a crime?'

'Not only the murderer, Joseph, maybe someone who knows something about the murder.'

I didn't reply.

'You've heard of such things before?'

I shook my head. 'You think it was Gunther Kruger, don't you? You think Gunther Kruger killed those girls back then, and he's back to killing again, right?'

'What d'you think?'

'I don't think anything, Sheriff Dearing.'

'He seem like the sort of man capable of murdering someone?'

'Capable of murdering someone? I think everyone is capable of murdering someone. You give them the right motive and opportunity, well, who the hell knows, eh? Maybe even you, Sheriff.'

'This isn't a discussion about me, Joseph. This is about whether or not there was anything that happened back then that made you feel Gunther Kruger might have had something to do with these killings. There was a certain viewpoint at the time—'

'The viewpoint that set fire to his house and killed his daughter?' I asked. I was starting to get angry.

'A terrible thing,' Dearing said. 'What happened back then, no question about it. It was a terrible, terrible thing, and I, for one, feel a tremendous sense of responsibility—'

'Why would you feel responsible? You didn't light the fire, did you? Or *did* you, Sheriff? Was that a situation where there was sufficient motive and opportunity—'

Dearing raised his hand. 'There are lessons to be learned in life, Joseph. You can try something once and learn a lesson from it. Kind of lesson you need to be taught twice says you're nothing but plain dumb.'

I frowned.

'You upset me once, heading on out there to Fleming. Hell, last person in the world I expected to see out there was you. I don't want you to be upsetting me another time, Joseph.'

I raised a conciliatory hand.

'Gunther Kruger was a suspect back then. I don't mind telling you that. You know something? I'll tell you this for a nickel and dime and you don't gotta pay me straight away. There was nothing, *not one thing* anywhere that said his little girl had the spasms—'

'She was an epileptic, Sheriff—'

'Was she now?' Dearing leaned back in his chair. He tucked his right thumb in his belt and looked pleased for himself.

'You're saying she wasn't?'

Dearing shook his head. 'I'm saying there was no record anywhere that that little girl had the grand mal or anything like it.'

'So the bruises I saw . . .'

'Were simply the bruises you saw, nothing more or less than that. Hell, Joseph, whichever way you dress it up and take it out there was something awry with that family. Me, I'm a Republican, as much as Bob Taft ever was, and I don't know that

I'm in favor of selling up Georgia land to foreigners and the like, but I got a basic respect for my fellow man and no ill will toward him. However—' Dearing paused melodramatically. He leaned forward to emphasize his position and the importance of his viewpoint. 'When it comes to killing little girls I have no opinion about anyone, 'cept that they might or might not be involved. I ain't one of these ignorants that hates folks just 'cause they're from someplace else. Don't matter who they are, what color, what language they speak, they all get the same degree of interest when it comes to the law. Fact that your ma, God bless her, makes like Lana Turner in that *Postman* picture with Mr Gunther Kruger . . . fact that she was a decent and God-fearing woman . . . well, hell, Joseph, I can't take the fact that your ma got personal with Gunther Kruger as any kind of reference for his character. I . . . we . . . figured him for beating the little girl, me and Ford Ruby, and Sheriff Fermor . . . he's the one you had the pleasure of meeting that afternoon with Miss Webber, right?'

I nodded. 'I remember him, yes.'

'So the three of us had a couple of meetings, and we did what we did, we asked our questions and followed our clues, and we didn't come back with anything for the Show 'n' Tell. Nothing 'cept the coincidence of where the little girls were found. That and the fact that we took Gunther Kruger for a child-beater.'

'Which ain't one helluva lot to hang a murder rap on someone.'

'True, true, but bright you may be, all full of ten- and twenty-dollar words, and I might be slow and methodical, and have no more sparks in my head than a damp firecracker, but I'll tell you something I have got, Joseph Vaughan . . . I've got persistence, you see? Persistence. I'm the sort of man who gets ahold of an idea, and I ain't gonna let go of it 'til it's been wrestled off of me, and even then whoever's doin' the wrestling knows they've been through a fight.'

'So what're you saying?' I asked.

Dearing leaned back. He took on the resigned, philosophical aspect of someone attempting to solicit information by nonchalance, almost as if whatever I might say really didn't matter a great deal. 'What I'm saying is that I got Alice Ruth Van Horne, Laverna Stowell, Ellen May Levine, Catherine McRae and Virginia Perlman all dead between November of '39 and August of '42. Then this thing happens with the Krugers. The fire. The little girl dies in the fire, right? The Krugers are gone out to wherever—'

'Uvalda, Toombs County,' I interjected. 'Apparently one of her cousins had a farm up there.'

Dearing nodded. 'That's where they went,' he said, 'but that's not where they stayed.'

I frowned. I had lost track of the Krugers, had never asked of their fortune. Perhaps, in some way, it had been a relief to see them go. Their continued presence would have reminded me of Mr Kruger's infidelity and the death of Elena.

'They wound up in Jesup.'

'Where?'

'Jesup,' Dearing said. 'Right in Wayne County.' He opened one of his desk drawers and pulled out a map. He unfolded it across his desk, stood up, and motioned for me to come look. He stabbed his finger on a spot and I peered down at it. 'The sixth girl, Rebecca Leonard, found September tenth, 1943, right here in Meridan, McIntosh County. Put your finger there.'

I complied.

'Seventh girl, Sheralyn Williams, found February tenth, 1945, right there in Offerman, Pierce County.' Dearing took a nickel from his pocket and put it on the spot. 'And then the eighth girl, as you know, found right here in Liberty, Fleming County. Esther Keppler. That was just days ago, December twenty-first.' Dearing looked up at me, the two of us on opposite sides of the table, leaning over this map with our fingers on it like we were Blücher and Wellington at Waterloo. 'So whaddya see?'

'I see three locations, with Jesup right in the middle.'

'I see the same thing. From Jesup all of them are no more than thirty miles by crow.'

'Which doesn't mean a great deal.'

'But at the same time doesn't mean nothing.'

'And just because those three locations make a triangle with Jesup right in the middle tells you that Gunther Kruger did these killings.'

Dearing snorted contemptuously and folded up the map. 'No, shee-it, it don't tell me nothing of the sort.'

I was puzzled. I didn't know where Dearing was going with his implications and innuendoes.

'I got eight dead girls, Joseph, nine if you count the Kruger girl. She doesn't figure in this thing in my mind. Kruger wouldn't have set fire to his own house. That fire was set by someone who figured Kruger had it coming. Either that, or an accident. So, like I said, I got eight dead girls, youngest seven, oldest eleven, and four sheriffs from four different counties unable to answer any questions from the victims' respective parents about what might have happened and who might have done this. I got one suspect, maybe two, and nothing on either of them. That's where I am, and this thing started all of six years ago—'

'We think,' I interjected.

'You what?'

'Six years ago, we *think*,' I repeated. 'This could have been going on an awful lot longer, we could have just been unaware of it.'

Dearing shook his head. Up close I realized how much he had aged. His face was striated with fine creases, not so much wrinkles as points of collapse, where the invading force of time had usurped the territory of youth. He looked like a crumpled picture, unfolded, that would never lie straight again. 'I don't know that I wanna hear such a thing,' Dearing said quietly. He sounded tired, a little overwhelmed.

'I'm sorry, Sheriff, I didn't mean to—'

Dearing raised his hand and shook his head. 'Forget about it. I'm just of a mind to talk, and I've known you since you were yay high, and this thing with Miss Webber . . .' Dearing paused and looked at me. 'How old is she, Joseph?'

I sat down and looked up at him. 'She's twenty-six, Sheriff, I told you that before.'

Dearing sat down also, pushed the map to the edge of the desk. 'Sure you did, sure you did. It's just that—'

I smiled at Dearing. 'You know something? I don't think in anything but straight lines and right-angles, Sheriff. You got an opinion, I'm gonna hear it. Ain't any real issue of whether we agree or not. People think what people think, always have done, always will. I'm sure there are people that find some solace in leveling a criticism here or there. Such people, as far as I'm concerned, are full of bitterness and *schadenfreude*.'

'Sharda what?'

'*Schadenfreude* . . . it's a word that describes the sort of person who gets a kick out of other people's miseries. You know what I mean, right?'

'Hell, do I know what you mean,' Dearing said. 'That about sums up my wife's sister, twisted old bitch that she is.'

I laughed at Dearing's facial expression, like he'd taken a mouthful of copper filings.

'Anyway, you got something to say then you can say it. I'm not the easily offended type.'

Dearing shrugged. 'Dammit, Joseph, you look like . . . Christ, I don't know what the hell you look like. Rasputin or something, right? Your hair's too damned long, and this beard you seem so intent on wearing makes you look like a crazy person. And now this thing with the schoolteacher. You were damned near up ahead of the circuit court for exposing yourself in a public place, for lewd and lascivious conduct . . . you were lucky that was all, lucky that Burnett Fermor didn't strip your hide raw out there. That kinda thing, along with the way you look . . . well, hell, Joseph. Burnett Fermor wasn't the first one to look in your direction for these killings.'

My heart stopped. For a while I couldn't breathe. I tried to say something but nothing came out.

'You found the Perlman girl,' Dearing went on. 'Several of the victims were found very close to your house. Even the possibility that the fire was set by you to direct the focus of attention elsewhere.'

'You what?'

'It's just nothing, Joseph . . . it's just scared folks with more fear than common sense. That's how any kinda prejudice is gonna start. People get afraid, ignorant people mainly, and they have nothing to do with their time, and then the time fills up with anxieties. It's an easy thing . . . look at the way it goes with Negroes. Anything goes missing, well it's gotta be a Negro. Someone hears that someone's house got broken into, well it's gotta be a Negro. You sure ain't doin' yourself any favors in Augusta Falls, and I gotta be the one to tell you because sure as hell no-one else is going to.'

'I don't believe this!'

'You gotta understand what's happening here, Joseph. This has been going on for years. People have gotten real scared. They want to know what's happening. They don't want to hear about the number of leads we've followed, the rumors we've heard. They don't want to hear about the vagrants we've dragged out of boxcars and held for two days and nights before they were sober enough to answer questions. They want us to bring them a child-killer's head, that's all they want.' Dearing sighed exasperatedly. 'Anonymous phone calls. Jesus, you want to hear about anonymous phone calls, and every one of them, every *single* one of them, has to be followed up . . .' He closed his eyes. 'The thing that you have to appreciate Joseph, perhaps more than anything else, is that you have to abide by other folks' expectations or there's going to be a prejudice.'

'This is insane, Sheriff,' I interjected. 'This is just so beyond—'

'Just calm yourself there,' Dearing said.

I was gripping the arms of the chair so hard my hands were hurting.

'This isn't an accusation, Joseph. This isn't anything but hearsay and rumor and tittle-tattle out of the mouths of people who should know better. This is people who are scared, people who have lost daughters, and they want answers, they want to know who's responsible, and when you have scared people talking together their natural instinct is to look toward anyone who's a little different, a little out of the ordinary.'

'But you can't be serious . . . you can't tell me that people honestly think that I might have had something to do with murdering little girls?'

'What people think and what's the truth ain't the same thing, believe me. All I'm saying is that when Gunther Kruger was here they saw a foreigner, a German, and a little girl with bruises on her arms. There was a war going on. There was already sourness in the atmosphere, and someone managed to convince themselves that Kruger was their man. I know it wasn't you that fired the house. I don't think you got a murderous thought in your head. But now Kruger's gone, might as well have disappeared from the face of the earth, and people have got nothing. So what they gonna do, eh? What the hell they gonna do 'cept look for the next one who stands out, the one who looks a little different.'

Dearing paused to gather his breath.

'And you let them think this?' I asked, incredulous that I was even involved in such a conversation.

298

'Christ, Joseph, who the hell d'you think I am? You think I have the slightest influence on what people think and do in their own time? No-one's breaking the law by having their own thoughts, and if they get talking over a few beers, if the women at these quilt-making circles start winding each other up, then what the hell am I supposed to do? You figure I should get myself invited to every social gathering in Augusta Falls just so I can overhear any slanderous words about Joseph Vaughan and give them a piece of my mind?'

I shook my head. I felt anxious and aggravated. I didn't know what to say.

'All I'm telling you is that you gotta take some slight degree of responsibility for how other people see you. You understand what I'm saying? You're not a child, Joseph. You ain't one of them Guardians any more. You're all grown up and people take you as they see you, nothing more or less than that.'

I looked directly at Dearing. I could feel how the color had drained from my face. I imagined I looked like a man haunted, maybe the ghost doing the haunting. 'You're saying that I have to fix myself so I look and behave like everyone else. Either that, or someone might come and torch my house while I'm sleeping. And while they're at it, hell, they might get the schoolteacher as well, and that don't matter a damn 'cause she's nothing more than the child-killer's punchboard anyway.'

299

Dearing frowned and shook his head. 'Shee-it, boy, you have a mouth full of piss and vinegar, don't you?'

I leaned forward. I was tired. Resolve was diminishing, like the pressure in a tire with a slow puncture. Heart like a fist that was clenched just for show. This fist wasn't planning on connecting with anything.

'What?' Dearing asked.

I frowned.

'Look like you're set to—'

'Kill someone?' I said, my tone sarcastic and bitter.

'You said it,' Dearing replied.

'But you put the idea in my head.'

'Devil puts ideas like that in folks' heads, Joseph.'

'Is that so?'

'Reckon it is.'

I nodded, looked toward the door. 'You have an inside line with him? He tell you to come talk to me?'

Dearing shook his head. Mouth turned down at the edges like he was going to fold it up and pack it away. 'Now you're talking plain crazy.'

'Well, if I killed some little girls and set fire to Gunther Kruger's house . . . oh hell, we can't forget leading the schoolteacher astray and—'

Dearing raised his hand. 'We're not having this conversation, Joseph Vaughan. I know you better than you think. I know you didn't kill no-one. I know you didn't burn the Kruger house, and I never said you did. I'm looking out for you, boy. I'm telling you that people get scared. These folks ain't the smartest, eh? That friend of yours, Reilly Hawkins. He sure as hell ain't the brightest light in the harbor, but he's pretty much the smartest one you know. All it takes is a word. You know the kind of thing I mean: Joseph Vaughan . . . hell, he don't look right . . . You hear about him and the schoolteacher? Sweet girl like that, looking after all them little kids. Heard he drove her out to Clinch County and done things to her in the back of a truck and Burnett Fermor had to come down and caution him . . . You get where I'm going with this, Joseph, or did you get out at the last crossroads?'

I nodded. I felt beaten down. I knew what was happening. I knew Dearing wasn't railroading me. I resented the fact that *who* I was had to be challenged, that I had to change my appearance, my manner . . . hell, I resented the fact that I couldn't just be whoever I wanted to be without people interfering.

'I understand,' I said quietly.

'Good,' Dearing replied. 'I'm sure glad you do.'

'I can go now?'

'You can. Trust we're still on speaking terms, Joseph?' Dearing rose from his long-suffering chair and extended his hand.

I took it and we shook. 'Sure we are, never been otherwise.'

'And you're gonna take a look at things and maybe—'

'Figure out how to convince people I ain't a child-killer?'

Dearing's eyes narrowed. He tilted his head sideways and looked at me askance. 'Not so much humor, Joseph . . . not the kind of humor folks around here can understand. You can't forget that you're a handful and a half smarter than most of them. They don't get sarcasm. You say things they can't figure out and they just get mean.'

'It's okay. I'm tired. I'm gonna go home.' I stood up and turned toward the door.

'You come see me if there's any difficulties, okay? Feel it's my duty to keep an eye on you considering what happened to your folks.'

'I appreciate that, Sheriff, but I don't think you need to worry.'

Dearing smiled. 'It's the worry that keeps me so young-looking.'

I shaved my beard. I hacked at it with scissors and then lathered my face with coal tar and razored it all away. The man that looked back at me had lost several years. I looked like the teenager I was.

For the week that Alex was away I pretty much stayed inside. I wrote a great deal. Sentences, paragraphs, random thoughts. I filled a notebook and then started writing on loose scraps of paper.

On January fourth I drove out to the bus station to collect her, and she double-took when she saw me standing there.

'Your beard,' she said.

I smiled. I felt awful young. She had on a silk dress – pale blue with ivory-colored trim on the hem and cuffs. She didn't look old, but older than when she'd left. The gap between us seemed to have widened.

We hugged in the cabin of the pickup. She felt warm and real and tangible. Loneliness did not suit me.

'I need you to cut my hair when we get home,' I said.

She frowned. 'Why?'

'Democracy.'

'Democracy?'

'A state of society characterized by tolerance toward minorities, freedom of expression, respect for the essential dignity and worth of the human individual with equal opportunity for each to develop freely to his fullest capacity—'

'Joseph!' she snapped. 'Enough . . . what is this? What's going on?'

'Democracy, what we're supposed to have in this country.' I told her about my meeting with Dearing the day she'd left. 'So you see,' I added. 'After the disappearance of Gunther Kruger I became Public Enemy Number One.'

She laughed. 'Drive home,' she said.

I shook my head. 'You don't understand.'

'I understand that you've been alone for a week. I understand that you have existed on root beer and hamburger, that you've more than likely stayed up all night scribbling furiously, that you need a hot bath, a damned good fucking, and then what comes out of your mouth will sound an awful lot less crazy and paranoid.'

'That's all you have to say?'

Alex turned and looked at me. She raised her eyebrows and tilted her head to one side. 'Drive,' she said matter-of-factly, shooing her hand toward the windshield. 'Shut your fool mouth and drive.'

The following day I went on an errand into town. I stopped at the public library, asked for newspapers dating back three years. I found those columns devoted to Rebecca Leonard and Sheralyn Williams. They told me nothing but the fact that they'd been found dead. I tore those pages out and stole them. Later, at home, I cut out the columns and put them in the box. Eight clippings. Eight dead girls. I imagined what Dearing would say if he searched my house and found them.

U.S. Forces arrested Ezra Pound in Italy and returned him to the States. He was declared insane and committed to St Elizabeth's Asylum in Washington, D.C. Rumor had it that fifty thousand English girls would be sailing into America, all of them 'war brides' of GIs posted overseas. There were riots in Paris over shortages of bread. The USSR reported the discovery of one hundred and ninety thousand dead bodies in Silesia. They were believed to be Russian, English, Polish and

French prisoners of war. Those Nazis who'd escaped trials at Nuremberg were seeking refuge in Argentina. I read the newspapers. I watched the world as it struggled away from the horrors of war. Such events were the mileposts of my life; the staccato punctuations that interrupted the rhythm of my existence.

I continued to work outside, mending fences, helping with seed-drilling and harvest. Alex and I spoke of moving away from Augusta Falls, but then she agreed to another two years continuance at the school. We did not argue about this decision, despite the fact that it seemed to contradict what we had envisioned. The truth was simple: though I had thought to move I had also realized that there was nowhere to go. Without a destination there had never really been a plan. Without a destination there was no disappointment.

When I wasn't working I stayed home and wrote. I wrote a short story about a man who missed death by inches, and forever after considered he had cheated Death of his due. He imagined he saw Death in the shadows, 'his eyes yellow, rich yellow like a sulfur flame, and about him the brackish snap and tang of hot metal, in His hands such offerings as pneumonic fever, pellagra, strangulation, gangrene, a suffocating fall from some interminable height', and when the story was done I posted it to the *New York Review*. They sent me forty-five dollars and published it in the third week of June. I received one reader's letter, forwarded from the office of the

Review, and the reader – 'Mr Repentant Lamb of God' – explained to me in no uncertain terms that I was advocating and furthering the work of Lucifer by supporting such a publication; and quoting from Ezekiel, 'Because you have made your guilt to be remembered, in that your transgressions are uncovered, so that in all your doings your sins appear . . . a sword is drawn for the slaughter, it is polished to glitter and to flash like lightning . . . you shall be fuel for the fire, you shall be no more remembered . . .' I thought to write back and ask how Mr Repentant Lamb of God had come by his copy of the *Review* but I did not. I kept his letter with the one from the Atlanta short story adjudication people. They were evidence that I had somehow reached the world, and the world had replied.

Toward winter I spent more time with Reilly Hawkins. He seemed to age two or three years for every one of mine. He had changed. His eyes were quiet and reflective as if long-exhausted from some unending burden, as if a daughter had vanished, or a wife departed in the company of some lesser man. Reilly possessed neither, but still his eyes spoke of some spiritual hunger never satiated.

'Had a sister too, you know?' he said one time. We were seated in his kitchen.

I frowned. 'A sister? I thought there was just you and Levin and Lucius.'

'Nope, we had a sister too. Just the one.' Reilly

smiled nostalgically. 'Real good-looking. Sandy-colored hair. Got hit by lightning when she was a kid.' Reilly looked up at me and smiled. 'After that she couldn't wear a watch . . . put a watch on her and the hands would just travel backwards. Hell of a thing. Strangest thing you ever did see.' Reilly shrugged. 'Hope . . . that was her name. Hope Hawkins.'

'And where is she?' I repeated.

'Hope? She's dead too.'

'How did she die?'

'Come off of a horse and busted her neck. Eleven years old.'

'Jesus, Reilly, why didn't you tell me about this before?'

Reilly lowered his head and exhaled slowly. When he looked up his eyes were glazed and rheumy. 'Seems to me there's some things you train your mind not to remember.'

I thought of how I had gradually erased my mother from my everyday thoughts. She would catch me unawares every once in a while. A smell, a sound, something at the back of a drawer, some small object of no consequence suddenly possessing sufficient power to return a memory in full color with all attendant emotions. Such things occurred, but as I'd grown older I believed I had made them occur with less and less regularity.

'I know how that is,' I ventured.

Reilly smiled. 'I know you do,' he whispered. 'I know you do.'

We didn't speak of Hope again, or of Levin. We drank some lemonade and then rigged a pulley in the barn to hoist the engine out of his tractor.

Later, Reilly said he'd read my story, that Alex had given him a copy of the *New York Review*.

'Should follow the light,' he said.

'The light? What light?'

'Some people got a light, Joseph . . . like a path, a reason for being. Something like that is rare, and when you got one you should follow it. Your story made a great deal o' sense to me. You can string all manner of words together in such a way as people can understand it. That's what you should be doing, not getting filth and grease under your fingernails fixing motors with me.'

'I like helping you,' I said. 'I like fixing motors.'

Reilly nodded. 'Suit yourself, Joseph Vaughan.'

He didn't say anything else, but later I spoke with Alex.

'So write the book,' she said.

'The book?' I replied, and thought of how I had started something so long before. I thought of Conrad Moody, of Providence and the Three Sisters.

'The one that's always inside people like you,' Alex said.

I laughed.

'I'm serious,' she said. She rose from her chair at the kitchen table. She came around and stood behind me. She massaged my shoulders and I felt the tension of the day drawn out like water.

'Everyone has a book inside them,' she said. 'Some people have two or three or twenty. Most people know it but they can't do a great deal about it. You can, and so you should. If you don't you'll be upset with yourself, kind of upset that comes back time and again to remind you that it isn't going away.'

The following morning I drove across the state line into Florida. Found a three-story bookstore in Jacksonville. Bought a copy of Hartrampf's *Vocabularies*, Polti's *The Thirty-Six Dramatic Situations*, a book called *Plotto: A New Method of Plot Suggestion for Writers of Creative Fiction* by William Wallace Cook. I sat in a soda shop on the corner of Cecil and Fernandina. I drank a 7-Up, read some paragraphs, tried to convince myself that this was what I would do; I would write a book: *The Great American Novel* by Joseph Calvin Vaughan. My confidence lasted a little more than twenty minutes. I bundled the books together and dropped them in a trash can on the facing sidewalk. I walked aimlessly for another hour, and then I drove back to Augusta Falls.

When I got back that late afternoon, in my hand a copy of *Mademoiselle* magazine for Alex, I learned that another girl had been murdered.

It was Thursday, October tenth, 1946, the day before my nineteenth birthday.

CHAPTER 16

The image of Virginia Grace Perlman invaded my dreams.

Sounds too . . . *like the sound of a heavy stick dragged along a picket fence, or down the stairs, but heavier than that, heavier like somebody whacking something . . .*

And feelings that were tight in my chest, tight like family; feelings I'd experienced when I saw her.

Lying down she was.

Lying down like she was taking a rest.

A long rest. Long rest of her life kind of rest.

Could see the soles of her shoes.

And no matter how hard I tried, no matter how many times I spoke to Alex, how many times I woke sweating in the cool half-light of nascent dawn, I could still feel those things, still see—

. . . fall leaves curling up on their branches like children's hands, infants' hands: some final, plaintive effort to capture the remnants of summer from the atmosphere itself, and hold it, hold it close as skin, for soon it would be hard to recall anything but the brooding, swollen humidity that seemed to forever surround us.

And thinking how she must have felt—
Stop it! Help me . . . oh Jesus, help me!

A girl like that, arms like twigs, legs like sapling branches, hair like flax, smell like peaches, eyes like washed-out sapphire stones.

And realizing that it had happened again.

And this time, just like the last time, there had been no-one to help her.

Her name was Mary. Same as my mother. Mary Tait. Hailed out of Surrency, Appling County, twenty miles northwest of Jesup, five miles beyond the Wayne County line. She was twelve years old, would never make thirteen. Four days after her body was discovered there was a picture in the *Appling County Gazette*. Mary Tait was a pretty girl, wide-eyed and expectant for what she believed the world would give her, what she believed she could give in return, and that expression would be all the world would ever know of her. I cut out the column, hid it in the same box with the others. Some of them were now fading, the print like something seen through a smoky haze.

The little that remained of Mary Tait's torso and head had been found in a shallow grave near Odum. Odum sat near the Little Satilla River, a tributary of its big brother that branched near Screven. Both her hands had been severed, as had her legs at the thighs. These were never found, and from what could be read in the earth

311

and rocks it seemed that the body parts had been hurled into the river and washed away. Odum was Wayne County, Mary Tait's hometown was Appling. Now there was a representative from each of the six sheriff's departments: Dearing from Charlton, Ford Ruby from Camden, Fermor from Clinch, Landis from Liberty, and the two new boys – John Radcliffe from Appling and George Burwell from Wayne.

Their first meeting took place in Jesup, a central point and closest to the location of Mary's body. It was Tuesday October fifteenth. Rain hammered the roads and fields, brutal and unrelenting, and the swollen breathlessness of the atmosphere lent itself to the dark melancholy of the gathering. They met in the mid-afternoon, but the overcast nature of the sky gave it the denser shadows of evening.

I thought of my mother; that she believed she knew the identity of the child-killer.

'I don't think so,' Alex said. 'She is . . . well, she is . . .'

'Crazy?' I ventured. We were seated in the kitchen of Alex's house. I knew of the Jesup meeting. There was little else I could think about. Six counties, six sheriffs, nine dead girls.

Alex smiled and looked away. 'There isn't an easy way to tell the truth, is there?'

'Why look for an easy way?' I asked. 'Truth is truth. Truth is whatever truth is. She's crazy. Don't know why, and now it doesn't really matter. Wherever the hell she went she isn't coming back.

That I know. She's crazy, Alex. Maybe the guilt made her mind head as far south as it could go.'

'Guilt?'

I laughed. The sound came out hollow, edged with bitterness, but I did not feel bitter – not now, not after all these years, all that had happened. 'The thing that happened with Gunther Kruger—'

Alex raised her hand. 'Yes,' she said emphatically. 'Yes, of course . . . sorry, I thought you were talking about something else.'

I didn't reply. I walked to the window. The rain, a dirty torrent, smacked vicious; a fluid raid. The sky was orange, graying at the edges like turned meat. Air was thick and tough to breathe. It seemed the sky had dropped a curtain between us and the rest of the world. Later, minutes perhaps – I didn't track with time – she asked, 'What're you thinking about?'

'Thinking about?' I turned. 'Thinking about the meeting in Jesup.'

'Is it because of the girl you found?'

I frowned. 'Is what because of the girl I found? What are you talking about?'

Alex looked at me unerringly. 'The fact that you can't let go of this. The fact that this thing seems to consume you.'

'It doesn't consume me,' I retorted. 'What gives you the impression it consumes me?'

She waved her hand nonchalantly. 'I don't know

where you've gone to . . . have a feeling you don't know either.'

I smiled. Alex had a way of gently reminding me when the edges between the inside and the outside had faded.

'What happened with your book? You were going to write a book.'

I opened my mouth to speak, closed it, shook my head. 'Don't feel like I have a lot to say right now.'

Alex was quiet for a time, and then she rose and walked toward me. Expression on her face was unreadable, skin pale yet luminous, an orchid's cantharus backlit by morning. Her eyes, well-deep, were narrowing as she approached me. I had seen such a thing before.

I opened my mouth to speak.

She reached me, raised her hand, pressed her index finger to my lips.

'Ghosts,' she whispered. She leaned forward and pressed her cheek to mine.

'Ghosts?' I asked.

'Everyone has ghosts, Joseph . . . ghosts of the past, ghosts of the present, ghosts for the future.'

'I don't under—'

'Ssshhh.' She leaned back a fraction and looked directly at me with her cornflower eyes that somehow still held a memory of the Syracuse sun. 'No-one knows what has happened. No-one knows except the killer himself. Your mother doesn't know, six sheriffs from six counties don't know. They will talk about it forever, but unless he does something to give them a name, a face, a clue to his identity, it will only ever be talking. Words are only so much use if they say something worth hearing.'

Alex paused; she gripped my right hand, raised her left and held it against my face. 'You have a great deal worth saying, Joseph Vaughan, always have done. Even as a child—'

'I don't want to be reminded of being a child—'

She laughed. 'Why not? Christ, Joseph, you're nineteen. You're a man now, not a little boy. There's a handful of years between us, and if you haven't come to terms with that now then you probably never will.'

She tried to pull away.

I reached out and grabbed her, held her firmly, pulled her toward me and kissed her forcibly.

Alex struggled against me, pulled away once more. 'Perhaps you should think about what you have, not what—'

I forced my mouth against hers again and silenced her. I sensed her eyes widen. I withdrew and looked at her.

'So?' she said.

'So what?'

'So, are you going to keep on being morose and tormented about something you can do nothing about, or are you going to be a writer?'

I smiled and shook my head.

'Is that recognition for your own stupidity, or is it uncertainty about your answer?'

'The former.'

'You admit your own stupidity?' she teased.

'I admit sufficient stupidity to make present company tolerable.'

'Is that so?'

'That *is* so.'

'And you think saying things like that is the kind of thing that charms a girl?'

'I don't have to charm you.'

'Oh, you don't, do you? And why not?'

I grinned. 'Because I own you, Alexandra Webber, because I own you.'

'Fuck you, Joseph Vaughan.'

'And fuck you too.'

'Not after the way you talk to me.'

'Is that so?'

She smiled wickedly. 'That *is* so.'

I grabbed her hands, held them close to her sides, and then turned her around to face the kitchen door. 'Upstairs,' I said, and leaned forward to bite her shoulder.

She yowled in pain and struggled to free herself. I held her even tighter, walked her to the bottom of the stairwell.

'You think you're gonna get me upstairs you have another thing coming,' she said.

'Oh, I have something that's going to come, sweetheart, believe me . . . I have something that's most definitely going to come.'

She laughed so much I nearly lost my grip.

★　★　★

That night, the night of the sheriffs' meeting in Jesup, we made love as if seeking revenge for an unknown crime.

Ten days later I returned from some work I had taken with Reilly. I walked from his house, back across the field and down the road toward my own place.

I saw Alex on the porch from fifty yards away. She stood motionless, and even though she did not move there was something about her, something I sensed . . .

I started to jog. I broke into a run. By the time I reached the end of the road and turned down the path I was breathing heavily.

She did not move. Even as I reached her, my hand outstretched, she did not move.

I opened my mouth to ask hcr what was wrong.

She started to smile. Within a moment she was laughing.

'No . . .' I said. 'For sure?'

She nodded, stepped back and sat down on the steps. 'For sure, Joseph . . . as sure as it gets.'

'Oh my God,' I whispered. I knelt down before her. I wrapped my arms around her waist, pulled her tight, and then – suddenly aware of the pressure – I released her. 'Sorry,' I said, suddenly conscious of how hard I had squeezed her.

'It's okay,' she said. 'It's okay.'

I felt overwhelmed with a breathless sense of elation; other things I couldn't even begin to describe. I felt – more than any other time in my life – as if I had *arrived*. 'Jesus, Alex . . . we're going to be parents.'

She ran her hand through my hair, she pulled me tight in return.

'I know,' she whispered. 'I know . . .'

Later that night, lying awake as Alex slept soundly, I thought of what had happened, and how it seemed to redress a balance. Like Alex had once said: a life created for a life lost. Another child had been murdered, and I was to be a father. At the time I was unsure which scared me the most.

At times I have believed that age is the enemy of truth.

As we grow older, with cynicism and bitterness heaped against us throughout the years, we lose our childlike innocence, and with it goes that element of perception that permits us to view the hearts of men. Look into their eyes, I would tell myself, and in looking you will see the truth of who they truly are. Eyes are the windows of the soul; look closely and you will see the darker aspects reflected.

Now I am old, and even though the truth is right in front of me, even though I am now closer to the truth of what happened than ever before, I find myself afraid to look. The thing I fear most is that I will see a reflection of myself.

I remember Alabama and Tennessee. I remember towns like Union Springs, Heflin and Pulaski. I remember the miles I travelled, the person I became, and to think of such things makes me feel that I have lived three or four lives simultaneously. I grew older with each journey, each mile, each step. I grew bitter and twisted, and saw things within myself that I hoped never to see. I saw the impulse to kill, but not just to kill . . . I saw the impulse to make this man feel such pain. An eye for an eye.

Now he faces me, and though he is dead I imagine he can hear my thoughts. I want him to understand what he has done, the lives he has ruined, the sadness he has brought to bear on innocent human beings. I need him to feel the terror that he inflicted, and though I know he feels none of these things, I can only hope.

I hope there is a better place for me.

A worse place for him.

CHAPTER 17

By the time Alex passed her first trimester we were struggling. Money came like drawing blood. She tired easily. Doctor Piper said there were indications of anemia and iron deficiency, recommended a high intake of green leaf vegetables and rare meat. Same as my mother. I wondered if Dr Piper possessed only sense enough for one prognosis, one diagnosis, one panacean remedy. We did not have the money for such things. Alex missed enough days at the school for the school board to call in a locum. The locum, a bitter-hearted spinster, seemingly more desperate than honest, wrote a lengthy report to the State Education Board detailing anomalies between the prescribed curriculum and Alex's term notes. An inspector came down at the end of January and interviewed some of the children. He found no cause for alarm, but Board policy dictated that any report had to be subjected to lengthy scrutiny before action could be taken or waived. Until such time Alex was on suspension. They maintained a salary, but it was one quarter of her official amount. The locum kept the job.

Alex sat around the house growing more despondent and pale. I worked as best I could, used the relationship I had with adjoining farmers and property owners to do some handiwork and chores. I thought to sell the house but could not. My mother, though committed to the care of the State, was alive and physically well. The law required an affidavit of intent, a sworn testimonial of proxy, before I could act on her behalf within the parameters of the law. In the spring of '47, as Alex entered the third trimester, we packed her things and moved them into my mother's house. We could not maintain the rent for Alex's house, and thus it was lost. Alex cried for two days straight, cried herself to sleep, and woke in tears. She barely ate. I called Dr Piper and he gave her iron injections. She suffered stomach cramps and there was blood in the toilet. She said nothing when I asked about it. She withdrew from me, from the people she knew, from the world. In May I drove her to Waycross Hospital, ostensibly to see my mother, and while we were there I stepped away for a brief moment and spoke to one of the orderlies. The orderly said he would have a doctor happen by us and comment on Alex's complexion, ask her how she was feeling, take her away for an examination. What I had arranged worked well, and in Alex's absence I sat and held my mother's hand while she watched me through eyes that seemed shrouded by smoke. I looked at her and knew she wasn't there. My mother had left some long time since, and to see her like that frightened me. I had driven out for Alex, not for my mother, and I did not believe I could see her again in such a state.

During the hour we spent alone she spoke of things that made no sense to me at all. She talked of people I did not know, names I'd never heard before, and when I tried to clarify something she merely looked at me with an expression that made me feel like a foolish and ignorant child. Only once did she say something that bore a connection to my thoughts, and the moment the words left her lips I felt myself grow cold inside.

She rambled and gabbled, her words falling over one another in their hurry to leave her mind, and in the midst of some awkward monologue about 'Edward John Tyrell, you know? Just like Edward John Tyrell he was, with his suit all pressed and his shoes shined bright as beacons, standing there looking like he'd done something wicked, you know?' And then she'd leaned forward, and the half smile folded into something altogether sinister, and she said, 'Like the children.'

In the moment her eyes were clear and blue and piercing.

'The children?' I asked.

'Ha! The children! You can't possibly know anything about the children! *I* was the only one who ever knew about the children . . . me, and him, of course. He knew all about the little girls because *he* knew who had done those terrible, terrible things—'

And then she stopped mid-flight and stared at me, literally pinned me to the chair. 'Who are you?' she snapped. 'What are you doing here? I'm not telling you anything until you tell me who you are!'

I frowned. 'I'm Jose—'

She raised her hand. 'Matter of fact, I don't want to know! I don't want to know who you are. I don't want to know anything about who you are or what you're doing. I want you to leave now . . . yes, I want you to leave now. I was doing just fine until you came and started pressing me for answers to questions, questions I don't even *want* to answer.' She paused to catch her breath. Her eyes seemed to cloud over once more and she turned her face away from me. 'They will not poison me, you know? They try to poison me with their lies and filth, the things they say . . . I hear them, you know? I hear them all, their whining voices, their crying, and they don't want to understand that there is nothing—' My mother turned to look at me. 'There is *nothing* I can do to help them. It's too late now, it's too, too late for anything to be done.'

She started to cry silently, her chest rising and falling as she suppressed her sobs. I rose from the chair, stood for a moment looking down at her, and believed that it would be better if she died. Such a thought did not seem a crime, but rather a moment of merciful compassion.

I left the room and went outside. I walked up and down the road for half an hour. When I returned I found Alex seated in the front reception area of the hospital. She looked as if she too had been crying.

She said little, but then Doctor Gabillard came through and took me aside. He spoke to me in hushed words. I had forgotten about him, had avoided looking for him each time I had visited.

'She will need to rest from now until the birth,' he said. His expression was grave and concerned. 'She needs to eat well and rest. She needs a good diet, a *very* good diet. She needs to eat for two, and until now she has barely eaten for one—'

'I understand—' I started, but the doctor interrupted me.

'She has explained to me the situation,' Gabillard went on. 'I didn't ask her, she just told me. I appreciate your predicament, what with your mother here and the fact that you have no legal foothold in this situation.' He shook his head slowly. 'The fact of the matter is that your mother is unwell. She does not respond to the treatment we have attempted, and the painful truth is that I don't believe she ever will. I cannot see that she will ever leave Waycross.'

Gabillard waited for me to speak, but there was nothing I could think to say.

'See an attorney,' he said quietly. 'Have an attorney draw up papers to transfer control of your mother's affairs to you, and I will do what I can to have her sign them.' He paused and took a deep breath. 'This is neither my jurisdiction nor my professional responsibility, but I cannot help the fact that I am human. Your mother . . . well, your mother is going to die before she leaves here, and I cannot stand by and let a pregnant woman suffer. Do this thing, Mr Vaughan, and whatever moral issues might be raised, whatever element of social obligation and expectancy may or may not apply, I also seriously – *very seriously* – recommend that you marry this girl before your child is born.'

I opened my mouth to speak.

'In fact, I am going to make that a condition of my help in this matter. Come back to me soon with a marriage license and your power of attorney and I will do what I can. That is all I can do.'

Gabillard, once again, waited for me to speak.

'I shall take your failure to respond as a sign of agreement,' he said, and then he reached out and gripped my shoulder. 'Marry her. Get the papers. We'll do what we can.'

He released me and turned to walk away.

'Doctor?'

He slowed up and turned.

'How long does she have? My mother. How long d'you think she has?'

Gabillard shook his head slowly. 'I think whatever time she had ran out a good while ago.' He held my gaze for a second longer, and then he turned once more and walked away.

I was motionless. I looked at Alex, seated there

326

on a chair, her head in her hands, her demeanor that of someone broken.

'Enough,' I said to myself, and started over toward her.

We drove back. I spoke of the future. I told her we would be married. I told her what Gabillard had said about the power of attorney and his wish to help us. Alex's manner changed utterly. She even laughed at one point. I did not speak of my mother, the things she'd said about the little girls. My mother's mind was a cat's cradle of lies, half-truths, imagination and paranoia. She could not know anything about the children. I had to believe that what she said was nothing more than the ramblings of someone without their mind.

I believed it so.

I *had* to believe it so.

I married Alexandra Madigan Webber on Wednesday, June eleventh, 1947, at Charlton County Courthouse before Judge Lester Froom. Witnesses were Reilly Hawkins, and Gene Fricker from the grain store. After the brief and perfunctory ceremony Reilly drove us to the offices of Littman, Hackley and Dohring, Attorneys-at-Law, and here, for three dollars, Leland Hackley drew up a letter of proxy. He worded it in such a fashion that all my mother would have to do was sign it, and the house would belong to me. Reilly drove us to Waycross, me in a suit, Alexandra in a pale cream skirt and blouse, her hair tied at one side and decorated with a flower, and there we met with Dr Gabillard.

'You don't wish to see her?' Gabillard asked as he took the paper from me.

I shook my head. 'No,' I replied. 'Not today.'

He nodded, smiled understandingly, congratulated us on our marriage and walked away.

'When shall I—'

Gabillard turned and shrugged his shoulders. 'I don't know,' he said. 'You'll have to leave it with me. I'll do what I can . . . no promises, okay?'

And then he turned once again and disappeared into the hospital.

The storm lasted for eight days straight. The ground swelled at first, and then it sank in defeat to reveal the clean roots of trees. Like gnarled and arthritic fingers they grasped with everything they possessed to hold the earth in check. The run-offs broke and swamped the crops. Reilly Hawkins made it across to see us a week after the wedding and did not dare to return for a further two days. He brought food and wine, what little provisions he could, and we talked endlessly of what we would do and where we would go. Had there been word from Gabillard it could not have reached us.

The storm abated on June twenty-first, a Saturday, and the sun broke high and clear from the bruised horizon. Nine people had drowned, seven of them Negroes in the fields, the other two a man and wife from Folkston who had attempted to reach Kingsland on the St Mary's River. Teams of volunteers came from the surrounding towns and surveyed the devastation. Many of them turned around and went home.

On Monday a letter came from Gabillard. Within it was the proxy document, signed and witnessed. Reilly drove me to see Leland Hackley and he notarized the paper and drew up a letter of authority for the bank. Within an hour a loan had been secured against the property, all of one thousand five hundred dollars. I took two hundred dollars in cash, stuffed them into my pockets, and Reilly and I went to the Falls Inn to spend some of it toasting our change of fortune.

'You'll have a new truck,' I told him. 'We can take your old one and drive it into the Okefenokee Swamp.'

We laughed about such an adventure on the way back to the house, and the way Alex would be unable to contain herself when she found out what had happened.

Reilly drew the truck to a halt at the end of the road.

'Come in,' I said.

'For God's sake, no,' he said, laughing. 'Go in there and share the good news with your wife, Joseph. You don't want me hangin' around half-drunk and stupid at a time like this.'

'No,' I said. 'You're as much a part of this as I am. I couldn't have kept any of this together without you, Reilly. Please come in, just for a little

329

while at least.' I turned and shouted toward the house. 'Alex! Alex! Reilly's out here and he doesn't want to come in and see you!'

'Hey!' Reilly said. 'That's just not true. You can't tell her that, for God's sake.'

I was laughing by then, had started walking away from the truck toward the gate. 'Alex! Come see what we've got! Come on out here and see what we've got.' I pulled handfuls of dollar bills from my pockets, held them like bunches of flowers for Alex.

Reilly was following me then, and when I turned to look back at him I noticed something. A flicker of something in his eyes. He shook his head, and then he looked up at the house and started shouting at the top of his voice. 'Alex! Alex! We're back!'

There was nothing.

My heart quickened. I looked at Reilly once more and he nodded his head. He started to jog toward the gate. I was there first, pushed through, almost broke the thing off of its hinges, and then I was charging up the path, Reilly right behind me, both of us shouting Alex's name.

I burst through the front door, stopped dead in my tracks, and then Reilly was right there behind me, collided with me like a freight train, but when he saw what was there I heard him inhale suddenly. I let go of the money in my hands. Dozens of dollar bills cascaded to the ground, floated out across the floor.

Had Alex gone with us things might have been different. She would have been present at the attorney's, then at the bank; she would perhaps have shared a drink with us at the Falls Inn. But she had not been well, had complained of nausea and dizziness. She had chosen to stay home, for we would not be long – an hour, perhaps two. Had we gone straight from the bank we might have been present when she fell, but we were not. She did fall, from the top of the stairwell straight down like a plumb-line, and when we arrived we found her unconscious in the lower hall, blood saturating her skirt, her breathing shallow and indecisive.

Later, I would remember the panic and confusion. Later, I would try to recall the exact thoughts that had filled my head, but try as I did they would not come. I remembered screaming her name at the top of my voice. I remembered the blood as I tried to lift her, the feeling of cool moisture on my hands, my arms, on my face as I pressed it to her chest to see if she was still breathing. I remembered carrying her to the truck, the way I held her head in my lap as Reilly bounced and jolted along rutted tracks to Dr Piper's house. I remembered blood-stained dollar bills adhered to her clothes, one in her hair, another stuck to her forearm. I remembered how Dr Piper, immediately overwhelmed by what he saw, urged us to drive directly to Waycross, and the way that journey seemed to swallow some interminable wealth of time. I remembered Gabillard coming as we carried Alex through the front doors, the cacophony of voices, the commotion that broke away from us like a wave. I remembered his face – grave and dark, the way he held his fingers to her wrist, her neck, the way he barked orders to nurses.

I recalled all these things vividly, and replayed them in my mind like some old bakelite record – over and over, until in time the grooves wore shallow, the sounds grew quiet, and nothing remained but the vast well of despair and grief into which I fell.

At six minutes past four, afternoon of Monday, June twenty-third, 1947, Alexandra Vaughan – mother-to-be, wife of twelve days – died. With her an unnamed child, a boy. My son.

It was Gabillard who told me, a man who had done all he could to rescue us from destitution and hopelessness; a man who had taken steps that would have guaranteed the survival and well-being of my family. He was my angel it seemed, at least on that day. He gave, and then he informed me that what had been given had now been taken away.

I was nineteen years old. Alex was twenty-seven.

I took to wondering what crime I'd committed that warranted such punishment.

Years later, as I looked back, the months following Alex's death seemed to blur at the edges and break up between my fingers. I buried Alexandra Vaughan, I buried my child, and with them I buried the first two decades of my life. People attempted to reach me – Haynes Dearing, Gene Fricker, Lowell Shaner, even Ronnie Duggan and Michael Wiltsey appeared at the end of the road near my house, paused, looked, shared a few words, and then turned to walk away. Their efforts went unrewarded. Reilly I saw frequently, but it was as if our lives merely intersected periodically, and for the duration of our time together those lives were put on hold until we separated once more. Our meetings became less frequent, and by the time the first anniversary of Alex's death arrived we were seeing one another no more than once a month. I did not visit my mother again. I could no longer face what she had become, and I didn't think I could face Dr Gabillard. It seemed that everything that could remind me of the past had to be cauterized or amputated cleanly. I had no shortage of money; when the first fifteen hundred dollars expired I merely extended my loan with the bank and signed over a greater percentage of the house. I waited for something to change. I waited patiently, trying my best to write, to keep mind and body together, but I felt the mooring rope wearing thin. Those things that had attached me to the world grew more insubstantial and transient: monthly visits to collect provisions, a visit to the Falls Inn once every five or six months, and beyond that I was insular and detached. Oftentimes I would feel the pull of company, but I would overcome it with the certain sense that whatever I might gain would soon be lost. Like Reilly Hawkins, never falling in love because he believed his heart could not stand to be broken twice, I gambled nothing in the belief that in such a way I could not lose. It was a pitiful existence, but the pity was not self-directed. I wore a veneer of resilience and fortitude sufficient to withstand the ravages of guilt and emotion.

Close to Christmas of 1948, Truman having retained his presidency against Thomas Dewey, I considered the possibility of leaving Augusta Falls. It was not the town or the county, or in fact Georgia itself, but myself I believed I could separate from if I travelled a sufficient distance.

'Where?' Reilly asked me when I mentioned it.

'New York.'

Reilly nearly choked on his beer. 'New York. New York? What in God's name would you want to go to New York for?'

'Because it is so completely different from here.'

'No other reason?'

'Seems as good a reason as any.'

Reilly shook his head and leaned toward me. We were in the Falls Inn, it was a Saturday evening. All around us the hubbub of voices, the clouds of cigarette smoke, the sound of someone playing the fiddle in the saloon. 'That's not a good enough reason to leave for New York,' he said.

'Maybe I don't need a reason. Maybe I could go on impulse.'

'You have to have a reason,' Reilly said.

'Have to?'

He nodded. 'Sure you have to. Has to be a reason for everything, otherwise there is no direction. Problem you've had is that there's been no direction for you. That's why your life is disappearing, Joseph—'

'My life is not disappearing.'

Reilly smiled, shook his head. 'You're right . . . of course . . . I'm sorry. There has to be something there in the first place if it's going to disappear.'

'You—'

Reilly raised his hand. 'Face facts, Joseph. Alex is gone. She's dead—'

'I don't want to talk about it, Reilly.'

'I don't care if you want to talk about it or not, it's the truth. Can't change the truth whatever happens. She's dead, Joseph. How long now? Eighteen months, right?'

'Eighteen months, yes.'

'And what's happened in that time? I'll tell you what's happened. Nothing. That's what's happened. Absolutely nothing. Saving grace is that you're not an alcoholic. Me? Hell, I would've drunk the county dry and then moved to Brantley. But that's the only thing I see, Joseph. You've got the house. You're alone apart from the odd time I see you. You spend that much time alone you lose your mind.'

'Which is why I'm thinking of moving, Reilly.'

'But to New York, of all places. What the hell is there in New York for you?'

'More to the point, what the hell have I got here?'

'Your mother?' he ventured.

I shook my head. 'She went, Reilly, she went a long time ago and you know it. My mother is not my mother anymore.'

Reilly was quiet for a time, and then he looked across the table at me, his expression compassionate, almost sympathetic. 'You're all grown now. I knew you when you were two, three years old. I've been there and seen it all as far as your family is concerned. I can't tell you what to do, and I sure as hell wouldn't presume to. You have some will, I'll give you that, and somehow you've managed to keep things together despite everything that's happened with your parents and now with Alex. I respect you for that, but part of the reason I respect you is that you think logical. There's sense and reason behind the things you do. This . . . hell, this New York thing seems to possess no logic at all . . .'

'Which is possibly the best reason for considering it.'

'You got a will, like I said. Doesn't seem to me that anything I could say is going to influence your decisions. You do what you feel you have to, Joseph Vaughan.'

'I haven't decided anything, Reilly . . . I've just been thinking about it.'

'Then think about it some more, and let me know what you decide.'

'Of course I will.'

'Hell, maybe if you go to New York you could find someone.'

I frowned. 'Someone?'

'Someone you could love.'

I shook my head, looked away for a while. 'Don't know that I could ever love someone like I loved Alex.'

'Sure you could. You're young. Your heart's strong enough to survive this.'

'Love like that,' I replied. 'You think something as good as that could happen twice in one lifetime?'

Reilly sighed, and it was then that I saw a weight bearing down on him, a weight broad enough to crush us both right where we sat.

'Twice?' he whispered. 'From what I've seen it most often doesn't happen at all.'

There was silence for a time, and then he looked up at me. 'Seems both of us have had a little too much unexpected and not enough predictable, wouldn't you say?'

'I would, Reilly, I would.'

We didn't speak of it again. I decided not to decide, that was all, and when it crossed my mind again it was February of '49 and they found another girl.

She was the tenth one, and she came from Shellman Bluff, McIntosh County. Her name was

Lucy Bradford. She was eight years old, had a brother of twelve called Stanley. I didn't know who she was, had never seen her before, but she – above and beyond all else – was the reason I finally left.

'You knew Alexandra, didn't you?' I ask the dead man before me. 'You knew her, but I can imagine that you never really understood her . . . never really understood anyone, right? Perhaps you thought you understood people . . . but you only imagined it. There could never have been anything compassionate or sympathetic about you . . . to have done the things you did for all these years.'

I want to stand and walk to the window, but I cannot. I feel myself growing tired. I wondered what would have happened had I not pulled the trigger, if I had somehow trapped him, tied him to a chair, made him explain who he was, what he had done . . . made him tell me what kind of person could have killed and killed and killed the way he did.

I want to reach out my hand and place it flat against the window. I want to look through the spaces between my fingers and see the city before me.

'She died, you know?' I say, my voice little more than a whisper. 'She was pregnant with my child and she died. For a long time I thought that it was my punishment for Elena. I promised I would protect her. I stood on a hill and looked down at Elena as she stood in the yard behind the house, and I swore I would protect her, that nothing would happen to her.' I pause, I look down and breathe deeply for a while. 'But it did . . . and it wasn't like the others.' I smile and shake my head. 'I can't believe that all these years have passed, and now, here I am, right here in the same room with you, and you don't even have a chance to explain yourself. How does that feel, eh? How does that feel? Isn't that what this has all been about? Hasn't this just been about you trying to say something to the world, trying to get everyone to understand whatever madness lies behind what you've done? And now you're here, now you have finally got an audience, and you cannot speak.' I laugh: a nervous, even frightened, sound. 'What irony, eh? What an irony this is.'

I lean down and retrieve my gun from the floor. I raise it slowly and press it against the dead man's forehead. I cock the hammer. The sound is loud, like a branch snapping, like a whiplash of lightning in some distant Georgia field.

'Speak,' I hiss. 'Speak now . . . or forever hold your peace.'

The silence roars at me, both within and without, and I wonder – just for a moment – if I haven't made another dreadful, dreadful mistake.

CHAPTER 18

Tears were not enough.
Little girl crying would've brought many a man to the brink of compassion, but not this one.

What a friend we have in Je-sus—

Praying in her mind perhaps.

On the vic-tory side, on the vic-tory side, no foe can daunt us, no fear can haunt us—

Words going round in her mind. Eyes tight closed like winter shutters.

Give me oil in my lamp, keep me burning, give me oil in my lamp I pray –

Smell of something like something dead. Smell of shoe leather, or something that smelled like leather, and after the sudden shock of being snatched, after the moment's expectation for laughter, that this was a game, just a game, just a fun game –

Yea, though I walk through the valley of the shadow of death I shall fear –

Like hide an' seek, catch-as-catch-can, ollie ollie oxen freeeeee—

But realization dawned *snap!* Sudden like a door

slam. *Bang!* One thing, now another, and then understanding that the pressure she felt around her neck, the fact that the other hand went beneath her skirt and touched her where she wouldn't have dared to touch herself, was never part of any game she remembered.

And then her breathing faltered.

Hitching, catching in her throat, and understanding that whatever was happening wasn't supposed to happen in any kind of world she'd imagined.

Feeling of hands – one around her throat, one beneath her skirt, and the smell of liquor, the smell of tobacco, the smell of leather or something like leather . . .

Struggling now. Muscles tensing. Nervous system charged with electricity, snapping inside her like a machine she once saw at the State Fair. Big silver globe, and sparks crackling away from it, and someone touching it and all their hair goes wild and haywire . . . and kids laughing, and the man standing there with his hair like cotton candy . . . and the smell, the brackish tang and hiss of energy releasing . . .

Give me oil in my lamp, keep me burning . . . keep me burning 'til the break of day –

And everything inside her screaming that she had to get away, run away, run like the wind, run like lightning across the field to home.

But the arms around her, holding tight, holding her ironbound and unrelenting, and the sensation of pressure increasing against her chest, her throat, and finding it harder and harder to breathe, and colors flashing behind her eyes, and wanting to scream, wanting to scream like she'd never screamed before, scream like a fire siren, like a great swooping bird of prey descending, like a wild horse, its mane flying behind like the colors of a hundred armies, unfurling and snapping in the wind . . . screaming like a little girl terrified for her life . . .

Eight years old. A quarter mile from home.

Opened her eyes a fraction. Could see the dip and sudden rise of the hill, the way the road wended east then northeast then east once again, and back of the rise to the right, back there where the tall tree stood with its shorter brother, was her house.

Had it not been for the dip and rise she could've seen the house, *her* house, from where she'd been walking when he came from out of nowhere.

Smelled like blackness, smelled like dark and deep. Smelled old; older than God and baseball.

Smelled like Jesus was nowhere to be seen.

A man behind her, arms like tree trunks, a man who *smelled* like he'd done this before.

And then she started crying, and that's when he hit her, hard, *smack!*, and the sound was like a whip, and the pain that lanced through the side of her head was like the time she fell from a tree and bloodied her nose and bruised her cheek, and felt the sound of the earth colliding with her head for three weeks in her right ear.

Started crying, and he smacked her, and she knew it was a *he* because no-one but a man could have held her so tight, and no-one but a man had such iron muscles and rough skin and callused hands.

Crying sound was swallowed by the darkness of evening, and every thought she had was more terrifying than the previous one, and when she realized what he was going to do it felt like her blood ran quiet and still in her veins.

Down on the ground now, hand across her throat, other hand tearing at her clothes, rending cotton and lace and a peach-colored satin trim, tugging the bowed pink ribbons from her hair . . . and she felt the press of cool air on her skin, and the ground beneath her head, the dampness of earth, breathed the smell of dead leaves and broken twigs, heard the labored breathing over her, her eyes screwed shut in the make-believe wish that if she didn't see it couldn't happen.

But it did.

Colors behind her eyelids like kaleidoscopic whirls, and the sound in her ears of blood rushing through her . . . frightened blood, blood trying to escape.

Hit her again. *Smack!* Stinging redness on her cheek, and opening her eyes, and through her tears seeing the light in his eyes – deadlight, redlight – and white teeth, and smelling his rancid, fetid breath, and feeling the roughness of stubble as he pressed his face against her stomach, as his hands buried themselves, as fingers pushed inside her and made her hurt like she'd never imagined anyone could be hurt, that someone *could* hurt that much. But they could.

And then deciding to lie still, barely breathing, barely thinking, barely hoping anything at all now, as he does *things*, bad things . . . things that men don't do to little girls . . .

Pain inside her. Lancing pain. Pain like her insides are being pushed up into her throat. Sensation of choking, and then the hand across her throat starts to increase its pressure, and feeling her eyes swelling inside their sockets, eyes fit to burst, and the sound of blood like a thunderstorm, like a black train, like those galloping horses across acres of night fields.

Struggling now, and as she struggles the weight and pain increase, and then she knows she's going, slipping away into somewhere cool and safe, where such things can't be felt any longer, and she welcomes the impending silence, the sense of motionlessness, the feeling of calm that invades every inch of her body.

Senses the man standing over her, a single pink ribbon in his hand. He pauses, and then he buries the ribbon in his pocket.

And then it all goes away.

All of it.

A feeling of nothing, of emptiness, a breeze like summer.

Figured she would have been a child a little longer.

That much at least.

McIntosh County Sheriff. Name was Darius Monroe. Father was a sheriff, his father before him, and before that their lineage went back to horse rustlers, thieves, drunkards and jackrollers. All of them on the muscle, tough men, men without conscience. Great-grandfather Monroe had sired the better part of twenty children out of four different women. Less a family, more a dynasty. Never married one of them. Earned a living playing cards on the steamers. Lothario glint in his gambler's eyes, waxed whiskers, hair slick with pomade, a life filled with shameful acts but never a shameful thought in his mind. Darius Monroe was fifty-three and tired. Never married, never would. Family line would stop with him, dead in its tracks, a deer with a head-shot. Face like a crumpled paper bag. Mouth tight like a widow's purse. Words out of it came in dimes and nickels, change from the last dollar and two weeks 'til pay day. Eyes like his gambler ances- tors, sharp and quick, never giving a thing away, saving everything until the moment came when he'd spread his hand and take the pot. Due to his station people had to trust him, but felt they shouldn't.

Darius Monroe's cousin on his mother's side, Jackson 'Jacko' Delancey, awkward-looking man, too tall by a head, all knees and elbows, and something in his color that spoke of a dalliance with Indians, something in the genes – plumbline-straight hair, black like a crow, nose almost Roman, features too proud for a man so humble. What Jacko found that Friday morning humbled him further. Spoke about it for months afterward – in bars, leaning on fences, walking horses to pasture, watering the herb beds his wife insisted on maintaining despite the taint in the earth that came from the swamp. What he found that Friday morning – February eleventh – made him turn cold and quiet, broke a sweat across his skin despite the unseasonably chill air, made him stand back and walk away, made him turn around and keep on going a good thirty or forty yards, and then return to make sure he wasn't hallucinating. He wasn't. Had known he wasn't. But the unreality of what was before him would've made any sane man think twice.

At one moment, kneeling there in the dirt, he even reached out and touched her fingers. Fingers attached to a hand. Hand attached to nothing much of anything at all. Body was in more pieces than he cared to count, and they were spread across the ground and took up as much room as the parlor of his house. But the blood that lay thick on the ground between them gave the appearance that they were all still connected. The little girl was all of twelve pieces they later confirmed, but looked like she was still one.

It was then that he vomited.

So Jacko Delancey, awkward man built from knees and elbows, ran like a hare from the scent of a dog. Ran the half mile to his house, where he untied a mare and rode straight as a rigging line to his cousin's house. Darius Monroe was home, had set his mind to showing for work after lunch. Jacko brought him to the front with a thunderous hammering on the door, and in staggered breaths and heaving whoops got the message delivered.

Sheriff Darius Monroe took the car, sent Jacko home with the horse, called on his radio and told Deputy Sheriff Lester Ellis to meet him out there.

Sheriff Monroe arrived a little before nine. Saw what he saw and was grateful he'd had the foresight to skip breakfast. Brought tapes and poles from the trunk and set a perimeter. Waited for Ellis to arrive. Smoked a cigarette and looked the other way the entire time. Perhaps nothing more than premonition, hearsay, something else, but he'd been there when the Leonard girl was found back in September of '43 and had wondered when his time would come again. It had. But forewarning, whatever it might have been named, had done nothing to prepare him for the dreadful grim reality of what Jacko Delancey had found.

Ellis appeared within twenty minutes, took one look, turned gray-green at the gills, heaved his breakfast and three-square from Thursday over the fence. Thought of his own girl, four years old two weeks before, and wondered if what they taught at Sunday School was true. God is merciful, God is just, God is all-seeing and protective of the innocent and the meek. God had sure been busy someplace else the night before, and he'd let another young soul pass into the hereafter. Ellis called the Sheriff's Office and had the desk call the Tri-County Coroner. Ten-thirty he came, rolling down the road in a beat-to-hell station wagon. Name was Robert Gorman. Gorman was responsible for McIntosh, Wayne and Pierce counties. Had been there for Rebecca Leonard in September of '43, Sheralyn Williams in February of '45; stood beside Sheriff George Burwell when Mary Tait's body was discovered in October of '46. Jurisdictions, both for police and coroner duties, were confused. Victims from one county had been found in another, and no-one knew exactly where to draw the lines.

By eleven the word was out. A meeting was arranged in Eulonia for three that same afternoon, and present were all concerned parties. Seven counties, seven sheriffs, their respective deputies and assistants, a gathering of seventeen men, all of them sober, all of them stunned.

Haynes Dearing from Charlton led the proceedings, asked questions, waited for answers. Few were forthcoming. None of those present had ever witnessed or been engaged in such a thing. What they had was a mass-murderer, because no-one thought there was more than one guilty man.

'It'll take a task force,' Burnett Fermor ventured.

'A task force can only be comprised of citizens from the different counties,' Ford Ruby said, 'but you get that kind of thing going and we're gonna have a witch hunt on our hands.'

'So what's your suggestion?' Fermor asked.

'Suggestion?' Ruby said, in his voice a tone of defiance. 'My suggestion is that we each take responsibility for our own counties and our own citizens. Break them all down into groups. Take the men aged between sixteen and sixty, exclude no-one, and go house to house asking questions.'

'Good enough,' Dearing said. 'Seems as good a start as any. And we have to establish a central location, somewhere where all files and records can be based so we all have access and can co-ordinate on this together.'

No-one had the gall to suggest that such a thing was long overdue.

Radcliffe from Appling suggested Jesup; previous meeting had been there in October of '46.

'Suits me,' Dearing said, and realized that this thing had been going on for ten years. First girl was Alice Ruth Van Horne in November of '39. A war had intervened. God knows how many millions of lives had been lost, hundreds of thousands of Americans amongst them on the other side of the world, and yet such an event seemed somehow insignificant in the face of this thing. This was at home, this was personal, this was an invasion of an entirely different land.

'So that's where everything goes,' Dearing continued. 'Every file, every coroner's report, every document, every interview, all of it goes to Wayne County Sheriff's Office by tomorrow morning.'

'You think Gus Young is gonna have an issue with that?' Radcliffe said, referring to Jesup's town councilman, a man renowned for his irascibility and short temper.

Dearing shook his head. 'Known Gus Young since I was a kid. Gus Young is gonna want to do everything within his power to help us.'

'Gus Young is Jesup's councilman,' George Burwell interjected. 'I'm Wayne County Sheriff. Gus Young is gonna do just exactly what I tell him.'

The meeting was closed. Each man returned to his car. Lester Ellis took a message on the radio. The girl had been identified.

'Oh, for the love of God,' Darius Monroe said quietly. 'Not the Bradford girl.'

'You know the family?' Ellis asked.

Monroe nodded his head. He looked more beaten and exhausted than ever. 'Oldest boy is my godson,' he said.

'You want me to go over there?' Ellis asked, hoping against hope that he wouldn't have to.

Monroe was silent for a moment, and then he turned to face his deputy. 'Now what kind of a man would I be to let someone else do this?'

Ellis didn't reply.

CHAPTER 19

The first I heard of the killing was late the following day. I heard it from Haynes Dearing's own lips, and it was then – in my house, right there in the kitchen – that he told me how he'd wanted to come and see me when he'd heard about Alex.

'It's not easy,' he said. 'Such things are never easy.'

I raised my hand and he stopped. 'It's over,' I said. 'She's gone. She died, and that's all there is to it. I've done enough thinking and talking for a lifetime, Sheriff. Seems to me I talk about it and it all comes back to haunt me. If you don't mind I'd really rather not go there today.'

'That's the way you want it?'

I nodded. 'That's the way I want it, Sheriff. Nothing personal.'

He conceded; sat there for a while, the sound of his thoughts almost audible, and then he told me about Lucy Bradford, the meeting that had taken place the previous day, the decision that had been made to give each sheriff responsibility for their respective counties.

'And I am on your list of suspects?' I asked.

Dearing smiled knowingly. 'Joseph, *everyone* is on my list of suspects.'

'But I am the first person you've come to, right?'

Dearing shook his head. 'As a matter of fact, no, you're not. Why, you think you should be?'

'I'm not playing any games with you, Sheriff, seriously.'

'This is not a game, Joseph, this is a serious business. Children have been murdered . . .'

'I'm well aware of that fact, Sheriff . . . and you want me to do what?'

Dearing leaned back in the chair. He had his hat in his lap and he nervously rotated it, fingering the brim. 'We had a discussion before—'

'We did?'

'No games, Joseph . . . set a rule then it applies to both of us.'

I fell silent.

'We had a discussion before, back at Christmas after the war ended, a few days after the Keppler girl was found.'

I remembered the day, the day I'd seen Alex off to visit with her parents.

'I asked you some questions. I told you some things. I asked you to keep your eyes and ears open as best as I can recall.'

'You did, yes, and you also suggested that I might be in amongst people's thoughts when they were thinking about who might have done these things . . .'

'I said what I said. What I said needed saying. I haven't spoken to anyone who's suggested such a thing.'

'So what're we talking about?'

'About the fact that another girl is dead. I don't even wanna give you an idea of how she was found, the state she was in . . . all I have is another dead girl and a county full of suspects. Three of them were from right here in Augusta Falls. Alice Van Home, Catherine McRae—'

'And Virginia Perlman,' I interjected.

Dearing nodded. 'And Ellen May Levine back in June of '41. Came from Fargo . . . found no more than a half mile from this house.'

'And what d'you want me to do, Sheriff?'

Dearing cleared his throat. 'I want your help.'

I leaned forward, raised my eyebrows. 'My help?'

Dearing nodded. 'Yes, Joseph . . . I want you to do something for me.'

I said nothing. I waited.

'I want you to go up to Jesup and visit with the Krugers.'

I didn't speak for quite a time.

Sunday I went to Alex's grave. I knelt on the ground, I read the words inscribed on her stone, and as I reached out to touch the smooth marble surface it started to rain. It came like a curtain across the world, and the force of it pounded on my head and my shoulders mercilessly. The flowers I had brought and set against the headstone were battered into handfuls of waterlogged petals. I held those petals in my open hands and watched as the rain washed them away once more. I stayed there until my clothes were almost too heavy for me to stand, and I thought about Alex, about the child we would have raised, and I shed no tears. I believed there were no tears left within, and thus the sky was crying for me.

The previous evening I had walked to Reilly's house and told him what had happened. I told him about the Bradford girl from Shellman Bluff, the visit from Dearing, the request he'd made.

'Ten girls?' he asked.

'Ten girls, yes.'

'And Dearing has his eye on Gunther Kruger for these things?'

'I think Haynes Dearing is a man adrift in an ocean of questions. He doesn't know anything, but he's the law, and now it's his job to do everything he can to end this.'

'And they had a meeting, all the sheriffs?'

'Yes. They've set up a co-ordination point in Jesup.'

'Why Jesup?'

'It's a central point, as close as it gets anyway. You've got seven counties involved, and that doesn't include the areas where bodies were found. Dearing explained it as best he could, said it was madness. There are case files coming from all over, more men involved than they can organize, and they need all the help they can get.'

'And you're gonna go up there . . . you're gonna go and speak with Gunther Kruger?'

I shook my head. 'I don't know, Reilly, I just don't know.'

'How can you not go, Joseph?'

I smiled. 'Easy. I just don't go.'

'But what if it is him? What if he killed all these girls?'

I sighed. I felt my mind and my emotions were stretched to their limit. 'Reilly, you know him as well as I. You were there when he used to come over and sit with us in the kitchen. His wife, his kids . . . Jesus, you really think he's the sort of man who could do something like that?'

Reilly Hawkins shook his head. His face was somber. 'I know one thing for sure . . . that you never really know anyone, Joseph.'

We didn't speak of it again, but the following day, as I knelt before the grave of my wife and child, a child I never saw, a child who was never named, I decided that I would do what Haynes Dearing had asked of me.

I would go to Jesup, Wayne County; I would speak to Gunther Kruger; I would see if his eyes reflected the faces of ten little girls as their lives had been extinguished.

Had I known at that point what would come, had I been aware how February of 1949 would in some way signpost the end of my time in Georgia, I perhaps would have made different decisions. That signpost was not visible to me, not there along the banks of the Crooked River, or on Jekyll Island or Gray's Reef; no indication amidst the flooded swell of islands, creeks, salt marshes or river inlets; nothing pinned to the trees, upon their coats of Spanish moss; no word in the grain of split-logs bound together to navigate the corduroy tracks across deeper swamps. Spanning sixty thousand square miles of history, a history I learned, a history I believed in, there was nothing that showed me the colors of what was to come.

Perhaps I longed to be a child once more, a child with a mother and father, a child possessing a quiet and unspoken love for Miss Alexandra Webber. Perhaps I was merely manufacturing enough compelling reasons for departure, for in leaving Georgia I could imagine that life would change sufficiently for memories of the past to be lost. They would not, and I knew it, but I believed that trying was better than nothing.

Morning of Tuesday the fifteenth I went to see Haynes Dearing. I told him I would go up to Jesup and see Gunther Kruger.

Dearing neither smiled nor thanked me. He sat behind his desk and looked at me for some seconds. 'You understand that I'm gonna need as much as you can get from him?'

'I understand what you want, Sheriff. I'm not sure you're going to get it.'

'I want you to do everything you can to determine his whereabouts, his movements. I want you to ask him about the girls that have been murdered. I want to know his reactions to questions, what he remembers of when they were found. I want to know what he heard and what he thought about it.'

'And you can't go because . . .'

'Because I'm the Sheriff. Because I am the law. Because any time I ask anyone a question they consider it's their duty to withhold everything from me.'

'And you think he'll let something slip?'

Dearing shook his head. 'I think nothing, Joseph . . . I just hope.'

'Scarecrow,' I said, and smiled as Mathilde Kruger hugged me.

'Sceercraw!' she echoed, and laughed exuberantly. She had changed a great deal. Only six and a half years had passed since the Krugers left Augusta Falls, and yet she seemed to have aged more than twenty. But their house, the one they now occupied in Jesup, Wayne County, was the same as the Kruger house in Augusta Falls. It smelled of sauerkraut and bratwurst and dark coffee, of generous hearts and the welfare of others. The Kruger house embodied the memory of my mother as she had been and the way these people had helped her. I could not imagine that Gunther Kruger knew anything of ten little dead girls and the terrible things that had been done.

I arrived in the late morning of Wednesday the

sixteenth. I had driven up from Charlton in Reilly's pickup.

'Should buy your own goddam truck,' he's said, and laughed, and there was something awkward in that sound that told me he understood how difficult the journey would be.

'Good luck,' he added as I leaned out of the window and raised my hand. 'Better you than me,' was what I think he said as I pulled away, but I was not sure.

'Gunther is out with the boys,' Mathilde explained. 'Aach, I say boys. They are not boys. They are men now. Both of them men, like you,' and once again she hugged me, took my hand and led me to the kitchen.

Mathilde Kruger busied herself with coffee and pastries.

'I'm not hungry,' I told her.

She laughed. 'Sceercraws is always hungry. You sit there. I make coffee, okay?'

I smiled, started to laugh. I pretended I wasn't nervous, pretended that my visit was nothing more than a social call.

'Your mother,' Mathilde said. 'I understand she is in this nervous hospital, yes? I am wrong, yes?'

I shook my head. Mathilde brought the coffee and set it before me. She sat down. 'You're not wrong,' I told her. 'She is in the nervous hospital. She's out in Waycross.'

'Such a woman,' Mathilde said, and there was something so compassionate and sympathetic in

359

her tone that a twinge of guilt invaded my senses; we were speaking of my own mother and for some considerable time I had thought little of her, felt even less.

'Such a woman, so many hard things in this life for her, eh?' Mathilde looked down, her complexion coloring as she fought back tears, and then she shook her head and smiled bravely. 'It will be hokay, all be ho-kay, yes?'

I nodded and smiled understandingly. 'Yes. I'm sure it will be okay.'

'So you are working in Augusta?'

I shook my head. 'Enough, yes. I'm surviving.'

Mathilde reached out and closed her hand over mine. 'Good. You are too thin, Yoseph, always too thin, but I can see that you are okay, yes?'

My attention wandered: I believed I could see through Mathilde Kruger, see right through her as if she were a window into the past. I looked at that past, the dark and awkward history we had survived together. I wondered if she knew about her husband and my mother. I wondered how much time she spent thinking of Elena, the way her body had been carried from the house the morning after the fire.

I remembered November of '45. I recalled speaking with Alex about the girls, the murders, about who might have done such things, and about the Krugers, the death of Elena, all that had transpired. I recalled how certain I was that Gunther Kruger was not involved. Back then there had been no question in my mind, but now . . . ? Now I was sitting in Mathilde Kruger's kitchen waiting for Gunther to come home. I was on an errand for Sheriff Haynes Dearing. An errand of investigation based on suspicion, backed by nothing more substantial than fear.

Perhaps I was wrong; perhaps my perspective, slanted and edged with mistrust, saw a reflection of something internal. Possibly my imagination wanted to create something in order to justify my visit.

Gunther Kruger arrived within the hour. He called to his wife from the front of the house and when he entered the kitchen I saw it.

I saw the guilt.

Later, hindsight my adviser, I told myself that it was the guilt he carried regarding his relationship with my mother.

That would have explained the element of surprise he manifested, and yet beneath that the evident shadow of unwilling recognition. His expression gave everything away: here I was, an image from the past – a face, a voice, nothing more than that, but sufficient to remind him of something long since buried beneath a shroud of justification. Joseph Vaughan stood before him, the son of a woman he had lain with while his own wife had stood no more than thirty yards away. Gunther the fornicator. Gunther the adulterer. Gunther the liar.

'Joseph!' He walked forward, his arms extended,

and with his hands he gripped my shoulders firmly. 'Ach! Nicht wahr? You are here! Joseph Vaughan. Ha!'

He pulled me close and hugged me, but there was something in the way his arms tightened around my back. He squeezed me, and at the point where he held me tight enough, he suddenly squeezed a little harder. I was caught off guard, surprised by the sudden pressure and I lost my breath. I am showing you how happy I am to see you for my wife's benefit, that gesture said. I am telling her that I have nothing to hide. But unbeknownst to her I want to hurt you for coming. For coming back into a life that is no longer anything to do with you or your people. I will pretend you are welcome, pretend only for appearance sake, and when you are gone you must not come back.

'Gunther,' I replied enthusiastically. 'It's great to see you! Lord almighty, it must be six years or so. Six years and you haven't changed a bit . . . neither of you.'

'Ach, so kind,' Mathilde crooned. 'I know you are being so kind. We are growing old . . . soon too old to keep the farm here.'

'Me?' Gunther interjected. 'I will never stop this. Me, I will pull a plow until I drop dead in the mud! Ha ha ha!'

We sat at the table and Mathilde brought coffee. Gunther stoked his pipe and proceeded to fill the room with bitter, acrid smoke.

'So you are living still in Augusta Falls?' he asked me.

'Same house, yes,' I replied. 'My mother—'

Gunther stopped me. 'I know, I know, Joseph . . . I understand that she was not well for some years, yes?'

'Seven years,' I said, and for some reason felt there was some significance in the fact that it had been February when Reilly and I took her to Waycross. February tenth, 1942. It was now February 1949. I'd been fourteen years old; now I was twenty-one. I'd lost a wife and a child. Seven more girls had been murdered.

'So things are well for you there, yes?'

I looked toward Mathilde, standing ahead of the sink. The woman never sat for more than a moment, she never ceased doing something; seemed she had managed to organize her mind in such a way as to exclude everything she did not wish to consider. Possibly she knew of her husband, his affair with my mother; possibly she thought of her daughter and how she'd been lost; perhaps she knew of the killings and said nothing.

'Things are fine,' I replied. 'Things are okay, Gunther . . . but there has been the same trouble . . .' My voice trailed away into silence. I felt awkward, as if here – premeditated and deceitful – I was attempting to trick Gunther Kruger into saying something that would somehow incriminate him.

'Trouble?' Gunther asked. 'What trouble?'

I shook my head. 'No,' I said. 'It's not something I wanted to talk about.' I looked up at Gunther, turned toward Mathilde as she stepped away from the sink. I smiled at her, but there was something in her expression – a shadow, a ghost – that defied description. 'I came here to visit with you,' I went on, at once unnerved by Mathilde Kruger's appearance. 'I came to let you know how things were doing, to find out about Hans and Walter . . .'

I turned back toward Gunther.

'Tell me what trouble,' he prompted.

I sighed and shook my head. I too was now a liar, and I really felt like one. 'These things . . . terrible things, you know?'

Gunther frowned and shook his head. He looked concerned, avuncular; he looked like the man who'd driven the length of the St Mary's River so we could spend the day at Fernandina Beach; the man who'd said that even I – Joseph Vaughan – should have some memories to cherish for when I grew older.

'These little girls, Gunther.' I looked up. Looked right at him. There was nothing but patience and curiosity in his expression. 'The little girls that have been killed.'

Mathilde stepped forward. She appeared behind Gunther and placed her hand on his shoulder.

'No,' she said. 'Still this is going on?'

I nodded. 'There have been ten now. Ten of them have died.' I looked at Gunther Kruger. If he knew anything – *anything* – then there was some clear division between his memory and his reaction, a division over which nothing crossed.

'Ten girls,' Gunther said, and once again his voice belied any knowledge he might have possessed. But then there was something. *Something?* Later, I couldn't even determine what I had seen. A shadow, a flicker of something in his eyes? I stared at him, so much so that I sensed him grow uncomfortable. 'I do not understand such a thing,' he said, and looked over his shoulder, up at his wife. It seemed then he did that simply to avert his gaze from me. Mathilde did not look back; she maintained her focus on me.

'And the police?' Gunther asked. 'They have nothing?'

I shook my head. 'There are rumors. People call them with all manner of reports about things they think they saw. I don't know how many false leads they've followed. I know that they've tried to get the Georgia Bureau of Investigation down here again but that never came to anything. Truth is, I don't think they are any the wiser as to who might have done these things than when they started.'

Gunther turned back to face me. For a moment he closed his eyes. When he opened them it seemed that he too was holding back tears. 'Such a world we live in,' he said, his voice cracking with emotion. 'Such a world where people can do such terrible, terrible things.'

'It is hard to comprehend,' I replied. 'But I didn't come to speak of these things. Where are Hans and Walter?'

Gunther smiled. 'They are out for much of the day. They are working over in Walthourville. I don't think they will be back before sunset.'

'A shame,' I said. 'I would so like to have seen them.'

'You must stay,' Mathilde said. 'They won't be happy if you come all this way and do not visit with them, no?'

'I can't stay long . . . I have work to get back to. I was driving over to Glenville and I thought I'd stop by.'

'So come,' Gunther said, starting to rise from the table. 'You must come and see our farm here.'

'Sure,' I replied, and stood also.

Gunther led the way to the back door. 'Make Joseph some food for him to take on his trip,' he told Mathilde. 'Some sausage and some rye bread, something to fatten him up!' Gunther laughed and I followed him out into the yard.

Ten yards from the house he slowed down. He took my arm and pulled me a little closer. 'I am sorry for your mother,' he said. 'You are a man now . . .' He looked at me for a second, and then he looked away as if embarrassed. 'There were things that happened many years ago—'

'Gunther—' I started, but he cut me short.

'Let me say what I need to say, Joseph. A lot of years have passed, and your mother has not been well. I have always tried my best to be an honest man, a God-fearing man, but there were things that happened when we were in Augusta Falls that would send even the best man to Hell, yes?'

'I think that's a little harsh, Gunther.'

'The Bible says what it says, Joseph. Lying with a woman other than your wife is a mortal sin. I have carried this sin in my heart for all these years. Mathilde' – he glanced back toward the house – 'Mathilde, she knows nothing of this thing, and she can *never* know, you understand?'

'You don't need to worry about me, Gunther . . . I would never tell a soul.'

'But you must understand that I have prayed for your mother's recovery. I have prayed night and day that the Lord would see to her recovery from this sickness she has.'

'I know, Gunther, and I appreciate your thoughts and prayers. Truth is that she will more than likely never recover, but they are doing what they can for her.'

'Ha! These people, these doctors, they know nothing. They can mend your leg if it is broken. They can stitch a wound and stop the blood. But the soul? They know nothing of sickness in the soul. It is only by the grace of God that such things can be remedied. Your mother was . . . your mother *is* a fine woman, a strong and fine woman. Such things are a crime against—'

'Gunther.'

He stopped mid-flight.

'Enough,' I said quietly. 'Enough now. It is too late for regrets. This is how the world is, and there is nothing we can do about it now. I came to see you, to let you know that I was okay. I came to see Hans and Walter—'

'And Elena,' Gunther interjected. 'You would have seen Elena too, if she was not snatched away from us as well.'

'I know, I know, and that's still so hard for me to think about. There are many things we can grieve over, but if we believe in God then we must also have faith in His decisions.'

'His retributions,' Gunther said.

I frowned. 'Retributions?'

Gunther looked down at the ground. 'The Bible tells us that all these things happen for a reason.'

'No,' I said. 'You can't start thinking like that, you can't punish yourself for Elena's death. How could you possibly consider that you had anything to do with what happened?'

Gunther was silent. He turned his back on me and looked toward the house. 'I did a terrible thing,' he said. His voice was almost a whisper.

'She was lonely. My father had died. I can understand human nature, Gunther, and you can too. If God made us in His own image, then He too must have made us feel what we feel. You are a good man, Gunther Kruger, and as far as I'm concerned you never did anything but help us, and I believe that punishing yourself for what happened with my mother is just as crazy as believing you

368

had some part to play in Elena's death. These things happen, and the real test of strength is to go on living despite them.' Even as I finished speaking I regretted having spoken at all. I wondered if the terrible thing he spoke of was his infidelity, or something else.

Gunther nodded. He looked up at me and there were tears in his eyes. 'Ach, you are right, Joseph. You have grown smart and clever in a few years, yes?'

I waved his comment aside. 'You have moved here and your family is well. Mathilde is happy, yes? The boys too, I should think.'

'Hans will be married in the summer,' he said. 'You must come to see him married. You *must* come to see him married, yes?'

I nodded and smiled. I reached out my hand and gripped Gunther's shoulder. 'I will come and see him married . . . I would be honored.'

'Good, then that is settled. Now you must go – or can you stay a little while?'

'I have to go,' I lied. I felt callous and hard-hearted.

'Very well,' Gunther said. 'Come say goodbye to Mathilde and get some sandwiches for your journey.'

Fifteen minutes north toward Glenville I turned the pickup around and headed home. By the time I arrived it was mid-afternoon. The sky was bleak and without feature.

I took Reilly's pickup to his house, parked it

outside, was grateful there was no sign of him. I walked home; it started raining, as if the God whose name I'd spoken in vain was attempting to wash away my guilt. Not a hope of such a thing. The guilt was within.

I had failed Sheriff Dearing. I had lost my nerve. I should have pressed Gunther Kruger, should have asked what he meant when he spoke of the terrible thing he had done. But in my mind I believe I knew, *must* have known. I remembered kneeling before my window that night so many years before. I remembered seeing Gunther standing out there in the darkness, his long coat like a shroud, and the way my breath had caught in my chest, the way a cool hand had gripped my heart and squeezed every last drop of blood from it. Could Gunther Kruger have done such things? Was such a man capable of such terrible crimes?

I wanted someone to be responsible. I wanted someone to pay for what had happened.

In that moment I tried to believe, tried to believe so hard that it hurt.

I stood at the kitchen window and looked out. I could see the old Kruger site, and with it came the image of Elena being carried beneath her shroud to the back of Frank Turow's waiting flatbed. Death had been there that night, neither walking nor floating, for He'd been in the shadows between the trees, the shadows of men that had walked with Elena, in the sound of heavy boots

370

as they'd crushed wet leaves and broken sticks, in the sound of gravel on the hot top, in the mist that had issued from their mouths as they'd cleared throats and whispered words, as they'd hoisted the body upwards and laid it on the truck. He had been there. I knew He'd seen me, and He knew I'd been watching Him.

I shuddered.

I asked myself if Death had come in the form of Gunther Kruger.

I knew I should walk over and see Haynes Dearing, but I could not face it. I decided I would visit with him the following day.

Had I gone he might have said something; might have done something that would have changed what happened. Later, hindsight casting a twisted reflection and showing me what might have been, I understood that I was viewing things just as I'd discussed with Gunther Kruger. I had told him how he was in no way responsible, that there was nothing he could have done. How quick we were to advise others, and then fail to apply the same advice to ourselves.

The truth *was* the truth, no matter how hard it was to face.

By the time I spoke with Haynes Dearing reality was irreversible. I told him what Gunther Kruger had said. I told him what I had thought, perhaps what I imagined. I see now that I told him what he wanted so much to believe. Reality, so much harder to face than imagination or conjecture, had driven home its point without mercy.

It was then that everything would change, and I – so accustomed to the worst that could be – found it hard to believe that my life would change for the better.

The wheels had turned. They ground between them the lives of people, and once their revolutions were complete there seemed to be nothing left at all.

It was a life, but so distant from what I'd wished.

Am I guilty for what I did?

Are we not all guilty in some way?

Did I say what I believed to be true, or what I wanted to believe? Did I say what I thought Sheriff Haynes Dearing wanted to hear, or did I say what I wanted him to hear?

Did I do this thing because I believed that everything would stop, that somehow the past would fade away quietly, never to haunt me again?

I cannot answer these questions. Even now, after all these years, I am still unable to answer these questions.

My sin. My crime. My torment.

I remember Dearing's face as I spoke to him, the way he raised his eyebrows but said nothing, the way his eyes widened, the glint of realization that I somehow lit inside of him. And I should have justified my words, I should have tempered them with doubt, with reservation, but I did not. I tempered them with fear and anger and grief; with the pain I felt for what had happened between Gunther Kruger and my mother, for the death of his daughter . . . for all the things I believed him guilty of.

I made him somehow responsible for the dissolution of my life. I made him carry the burden of my loss. I judged him for the death of my mother, the death of Elena, whom I had vowed to protect.

I was judge and jury and witness for the prosecution. I did not review the facts. I did not receive a plea for the defence. I determined guilt and considered no possibility of innocence.

I wanted someone to pay for what had been done. I just wanted someone to pay.

CHAPTER 20

It was still dark when I heard the engine at the front of the house. I rose. I stood naked at the edge of the window and peered down. The black and white vehicle was unmistakable. When I saw Haynes Dearing ease himself wearily from the driver's side, straighten his gunbelt, hitch his buckle; when I saw him reach in and retrieve his hat and set it atop his head like a punctuation mark; when I saw him take a moment, glance back toward the road, and then look up at the house like his own angel of death was planning to appear from within, I knew.

I *knew*.

I stepped back and reached for my pants and shirt. I dressed slowly, seemed that way at least; I figured Dearing would take his time making his way to the door despite the lack of distance. I sensed him pause several times, as if considering the reasons behind his action, and each time he thought to turn back there was something that spurred him on.

I was downstairs before he knocked.

I opened the door and said nothing. His

expression was blank. Beyond him the sky still slept; too early for weather.

'Figured you could take a ride with me,' Dearing said.

'Now?' I asked.

He nodded. 'Now,' he echoed, and turned to walk away.

'Where're we going?' I called after him. Dearing didn't slow or turn or respond. I went back into the house for my shoes and an overcoat.

On the way I spoke twice. Both times Dearing merely shook his head. I figured on a third attempt but gave up before I resolved what to say. He took a route through Hickox, Nahunta and Screven. I knew where we were going, and I guessed why. Watched Dearing's hands on the wheel, his skin like tanned hide, the scars and marks, the nicotine stains on his middle finger and the ball of his thumb. Once or twice looked sideways at his profile – much of it in shadow, little more than a silhouette, the way the muscles tensed and swelled along his jawline. Man was wound tight and tense. Wrong word, too sudden a motion, and he'd explode like a jack-in-the-box. I looked back at the road. Kept my thoughts to myself.

Roadside was littered with low-roofed shacks and weathervanes. Mailboxes every ten or fifteen yards, all of them hungry for something that would more than likely never come. Stack of tires like a wide black column, on it hung a sign – *FRESH EGGS* – and an arrow pointing down a meandering rutted path. A mile away from Jesup a burned-out tractor sat on the junction like a patient dog pining a fallen master. Windows without glass, colors long since eaten by rust and corrosion, grille at the front like an angry mouth chock-full of bitter words, unable to speak.

Seemed a sad and desolate country to me. Country of my childhood. Country of the past.

'They ain't here,' Dearing said as he pulled to a stop at the side of the road. We were fifty yards from the Kruger place. Already I had seen the lights, the flashing cherry-bars, sensed the hubbub and commotion that awaited us over the brow. I knew he was speaking of Mathilde and the boys.

Seven cars I counted. Faces I saw, recognized one or two. One of them was Burnett Fermor, remembered the little run-in we'd had Christmas of '45. Felt like a ghost, sitting in the front of Sheriff Dearing's car and watching the living through the windshield.

'They're all here,' Dearing said at one point. 'Ford Ruby, Landis, John Radcliffe, Monroe from McIntosh County . . . all of them. Seven counties.'

I said nothing.

Later, hours behind me, only then possessing some slim hope of understanding what had happened, I would think of him like a Jack O'Lantern. Head all swelled, eyes kind of lit up. Tongue turned blue and protruding from his mouth like a Hallowe'en party balloon. Trick or treat, I thought, and understood it was neither.

'Want to go down there,' I said to Dearing.

Dearing shook his head. 'No you don't.'

Considered insisting, but knew anything I said would fall on deaf ears.

'Hung himself,' Dearing said.

For a moment I tried to see nothing, but then I thought of him swinging by a rope, turning back and forth as the rafter that held him creaked and strained with the weight.

'Sometime this morning we think,' Dearing said. 'Walter . . . you remember Walter?'

I nodded.

'Walter found him.'

I didn't reply. I watched silently as the Tri-County Coroner left his car and started walking toward Gunther's barn.

'He had a pink ribbon in his hand,' Dearing said.

I closed my eyes, tried to breathe deeply. I felt emotion welling in my chest.

'There was other stuff we found . . . a shoe, a necklace that we think belonged to the Keppler girl . . .' His voice trailed away into silence.

After a while Dearing spoke again, something about guilt, about his concern that Gunther's suicide might upset folks all over again, stir everything up that they'd tried to forget. I heard nothing but the sound of my own frightened heart.

My mother, my sad and crazy mother, had lain up close and personal with a child-killer.

Ten little girls, all of them beaten and abused, many of them dismembered and scattered to the four winds . . .

Gunther Kruger – my friend, my neighbor, my mother's lover . . .

Gunther Kruger had walked out here to speak with Death and Death had hung him from the rafters.

I lost all strength at one point and started to cry.

'Enough,' Dearing said, and it was as if I heard his voice from some extraordinary distance.

'Finally it's over.' His voice like a whisper, and then he reached forward, started the car, and turned back the way we'd come.

Within a week Haynes Dearing told me to leave Augusta Falls.

'This is not a good time for any of us,' he said. He sat at the kitchen table his hat in his lap, his expression indecisive, almost nervous. 'This thing . . . this thing with Gunther Kruger has . . .' His awkward words fell away into silence and he looked away from me. 'There are some that think you might have had something to do with what happened out there.'

'You what?'

Dearing raised his hand. 'Don't get me wrong. This isn't coming from any official source, Joseph. We have a situation here, worst situation since I've been in Charlton County. Folks are scared. More from the shock than anything else. Gunther Kruger was a man well known, a respected member of the community. Thing like this people find hard to understand, and they get to believing that—'

'Believing what, Sheriff? What do people believe?'

'Hell, Joseph, this doesn't make any more sense to me than it does to you. I shouldn't have sent you over there. I shouldn't have asked you to go and see him. All well and good to look at what I might have done better. Fact of the matter is that I've placed you in a vulnerable situation. People would like to think this thing had more to do with your visit than any other reason.'

'You can't be serious. Christ, Sheriff, what the hell is this? They still think I had something to do with these murders?'

Dearing shook his head. 'Hell no, I don't think so.'

'Then what? What on earth do they think I might have done?'

'Maybe something to do with what happened to Kruger—'

'That I killed Gunther? Is that what you're saying?'

'I'm not saying anything directly, Joseph.' Dearing set his hat on the table and leaned forward, hands together, fingers interwoven. His expression was intense and serious. 'Maybe it's nothing more than the Kruger boys. Maybe it's nothing more than a rumor they've started. You imagine how they must feel? They don't want to think that their daddy's a child-killer for Christ's sake. They don't want to believe it—'

'So they're telling people it was me, that I killed those girls and made it look like their father did it.'

Dearing said nothing. His silence was all the confirmation I needed.

'You can't possibly think that there's any—'

'I don't,' Dearing stated emphatically. 'I know you didn't have anything to do with this. We found things in the house, things that were hidden beneath the floor in the barn. We found things that belonged to pretty much all of those girls.'

'So why don't you tell people . . . why don't you tell people the truth of what happened?'

'Because Kruger is dead and he can't refute any accusations.'

'You what?' I was incredulous. I could not believe what Dearing was saying.

'The law is the law, Joseph. We have a man hanged, committed suicide, no doubt about it. We find things that belonged to these girls in his house. There ain't gonna be any trial, no lawyers, no judges, no more police investigations. It is what it is. Whatever the hell nightmare this is, well, it's over. There ain't gonna be any more little dead girls in Georgia, at least not by the hand of Gunther Kruger. He's gonna go wherever the hell he goes and face his own justice. All I got is a lot of scared and upset people, and in a situation like that you do your best to remove any reminders of the terrible things that have happened.'

'And I'm one of those reminders, right?'

'People know you found the Perlman girl. They know you went out to see Kruger in Jesup. Twenty-four hours later he hangs himself. Whichever view you take of this thing you're part of it, Joseph. You're an unwitting player in this theater—'

'Don't get poetic, Sheriff. This is just so much bullshit.'

'I think it best you make a move, Joseph. There's nothing for you here in Augusta Falls. You're a young man. You've had your difficulties here. You ain't never fitted in with the slow country people that live in towns like this. Go somewhere you can make a fortune for yourself. Use the gift you've been given. Write some books, make yourself some money. Get yourself married and start over again. You could sell this place. I could have someone take care of that for you . . . sell up and take the money, make a new beginning. Leave all this bad stuff behind. I'll take care of what's here and you go get yourself the life you deserve.'

'And what life would that be, Sheriff?'

Dearing shook his head. 'Hell, Joseph, I don't know . . . seems it's about time you got yourself some happiness.'

Later, Sheriff Dearing long since gone, I sat on the edge of my mother's bed and cried.

I cried for her, for Gunther Kruger; I tried for

the ten little girls who perhaps deserved happiness more than any of us; I cried for Elena, for Alex, for the child I'd lost. I did not cry for myself. There was no point. Now I carried something inside of me, and it was not the ghosts of these children. I carried the truth of what had happened, and this was perhaps more terrifying than all.

I thought about leaving. I was not afraid of what people might say or do, not afraid of what they might think of me. I thought about leaving because it made sense to begin again. I thought of New York, of the book I had promised Alex I would write. I made believe I could survive such a change, and tried to convince myself that everything happened for a reason.

I wondered if the girls' parents had ever tried to believe the same thing.

'Go,' Reilly said.

It was the beginning of March. Reilly had come to eat with me, stayed for the night, much of the following day. We sat on the porch stoop, Reilly smoking, the late afternoon light reminiscent of every previous spring in Georgia. Winter did not leave indelible footprints on this land. There was an element of bleakness and solitude that was present regardless of season.

'Go . . . go to New York,' he repeated, and there was an insistence in his tone that reached me, even through my absent-minded wanderings.

'Like Dearing said, there ain't a whole handful of nothing for you here, Joseph. How old are you?'

'Twenty-one.'

He smiled awkwardly. 'That ain't even getting started.'

I turned and looked at Reilly Hawkins. 'You say there's nothing for me here. What makes you think there's anything more in a place like New York?'

Reilly smiled and looked down. 'Hell, I don't know. Place like this is nothing much of anything. Place like this you get born in and move away from, 'cept of course you got family or something.'

'You're here . . . you don't have family and you stayed here.'

Reilly laughed, something resigned and slightly sad in that sound. 'Me? I'm the best reason you got to get away from here. I'm you thirty years on if you don't do something, you know? Besides, you were the one who started this talk of New York.'

I looked toward the horizon. An ocean of low shrubs, chickweed, wintergreen, stunted cotton-wood and willow that had sucked too much water from the swampland and grown short and ugly; all of it punctuated by the low roofs of houses, houses that seemed to crouch across the earth, avoiding discovery, waiting to surprise whoever came visiting. I wondered if I was just afraid, afraid of the unknown, afraid of the future. I wondered what my life would come to mean if I stayed right where I was, and I could think of nothing. Up and marry some half-minded farm girl, rear some children, grow old resentfully and die from regrets and shortness of breath. Seemed there had never been anything but rough edges and sharp corners; seemed that whatever was gained ended up being taken away. New York beckoned like a loud and welcome noise at the end of a long, uncomfortable silence. I paid no mind to the Kruger boys, wasn't even certain there had been rumors, and figured Sheriff Dearing had his reasons for considering me better gone. I believed that he was the one who didn't wish to be reminded of Gunther Kruger. Nothing had been said – didn't see people often enough to know if they were looking at me strangely. I'd long since known that the only reason to stay was my mother, and even that I'd hidden from. Hadn't seen her since May of '47, the visit I'd made with Gabillard just before Alex and I were married. The better part of two years. I wondered how old she would look.

'Maybe I should go,' I said, and my voice carried out toward the trees and was lost amongst them.

'I think you should,' Reilly replied, and we didn't speak of it again.

In hindsight my life appeared as a sequence of connected incidents. Like a line of derailed boxcars, each one individual and yet coupled to the next. One car left the tracks – perhaps the death of my father – and everything from that point followed it swiftly, resolutely. I got to believing that

I was connected too, and if I failed to disengage myself I would hurtle over the edge of someplace into nowhere.

That, and the Poles, were the reasons I finally left.

His name was Kuharczyk, Wladyslaw Kuharczyk, and he came to the house in the first week of April 1949.

'Your sheriff,' he said, in remarkably good English.

'I come here because your sheriff says you are perhaps to sell this house and land and leave this town.'

Wladyslaw Kuharczyk was a good six and a half feet tall, but despite his size there was nothing intimidating about him. His features spoke of something gentle and sensitive.

'I have come with my wife,' he said. 'We have three children. My family . . .' He bowed his head and closed his eyes. 'Everybody is killed by the Nazis, everyone but us . . . I had seven children, now only three. I have parents, my wife too, and she has grandparents. All of them killed by the Nazis. We are just five people now and I come to America. We have money. My brother he is dead too, but he make much money in Poland before the war. I have money now to buy this house and this land . . . also this land where this other house was burned . . .' Kuharczyk glanced over his shoulder to the Kruger lot. 'So I come here with you and speak about this because your sheriff is telling us that you maybe go away from here and not come back. I come to see if this house is for sale.'

'Come inside,' I said. 'Come inside and sit down.'

'My wife . . . my children also . . . ?'

I frowned. 'They are here?'

Kuharczyk nodded. He grinned widely. 'Down there,' he said, and pointed to a knot of trees near the side of the road. He raised his hand and waved. A woman appeared, and within a moment a huddle of children were behind her, and for a moment I believed it was Mathilde Kruger, Hans, Walter and Elena. It was then, in that precise moment, that I knew I would leave, that Wladyslaw Kuharczyk and his family would take the position left vacant by the Krugers, that I would do what many had wished I would do for several years: Joseph Vaughan would vanish out of Georgia.

Kuharczyk and I agreed a price, a very good price, for the house and the land. I later learned that despite the document signed by my mother the proceeds of the sale would have to be held in trust until she died. I made an arrangement with the bank to issue further funds against the trust, and though it was not a great deal of money I believed it sufficient to get me to New York, to a place called Brooklyn. I had read of Brooklyn in magazines and books; I understood it was inhabited by authors, poets, artists, and others of a similar leaning and nature. Brooklyn was where

I would live and work, where I would write the novel that would encompass all that my life had been, and then herald all that it would become. Brooklyn was to be my spiritual home, perhaps the place Alex would have chosen for me.

I saw two people before I left: Haynes Dearing and Reilly Hawkins. Dearing was almost monosyllabic, shook my hand, gripped my shoulder so hard it hurt.

'You ain't gonna write no letter,' he said. 'You're gonna have better things to do than write letters, and I'm sure as hell gonna be too busy to read 'em. Get outta here. Place like this'll wind up pulling everything out of you.'

'Sheriff . . . I . . .'

Dearing shook his head. 'Hell, Joseph, I really don't have a mind to hear much of anything you gotta say. You an' me done all the talkin' we needed a long time ago, right?' He smiled, reached up and tipped the brim of his hat back on his head. 'I got word that someone tugged up thirty or forty yard of fence near Lowell Shaner's place . . . I gotta go tend to that now. You go wherever you're gonna go and make something of a life for yourself, okay?'

'Okay, Sheriff.'

Dearing nodded. 'Good enough, Joseph, good enough.' He smiled once more, reached out and shook my hand, and then turned and walked away.

'Sheriff?'

Dearing paused and turned back.

'You know I didn't have anything to do with Gunther Kruger's death, don't you?'

Dearing looked down. He raised his right foot slightly and started to dig a hole in the dirt with the toe of his boot. 'Seems to me we got a lot of dirty water gone beneath a few burned bridges. Seems to me it don't matter how such a thing might have happened, Joseph.' He stopped digging, looked up and smiled. 'You remember that ten-dollar word you used, the one about someone getting a kick out of someone else's misfortunes?'

'*Schadenfreude.*'

'That's the one. That's pretty much all I'm feeling regarding Mr Gunther Kruger right now . . . know what I mean?'

'I do, Sheriff,' I replied. 'Sure I do.'

'Well, okay then, Joseph . . . doesn't seem to me we got much else to say 'cept good luck and goodbye.'

I raised my hand.

'You take care, Joseph Calvin Vaughan, you take care.'

I stood silently as Sheriff Dearing turned and walked away. I waited for a little while, and then I made my way over to Reilly's house.

CHAPTER 21

Took a bus. Journey through five states ahead of me – both Carolinas, Virginia, Maryland and New Jersey. The Okefenokee Swamp, Altamaha River, Jekyll Island and Dover Bluff: these things behind me. Looking from the window as the wheels fought against rutted tracks and awkward angles, I passed out of Georgia like waking from a dream, watched as soft edges made way for intense light and harsh colors. Drove out of the past toward the future – the future that was waiting for me. I believed that; *had* to believe that.

Jostled against humanity in a cramped and airless vehicle, I met the sounds and smells of different people: a soldier behind me, tattered medal ribbons pinned around the brim of his hat, tunes from a cracked harmonica that he held in his hand, his mind lost somewhere in a dark memory of Europe that would forever haunt him. I believed I too heard their voices. An elderly woman, face like parchment washed clean of its message, eyes like holes punched through daylight to find the quiet darkness beyond. Wondered if she was leaving or returning. All of us – our lives

390

episodic, fractured by change – huddled together as night drew in, as we spilled from the bus into towns like Goose Creek and Roseboro, Scotland Neck and Tuckahoe and queued to register for austere rooms in cheap motels. Thin sheets and gray walls, blankets too scant to cover both face and feet, shivering awkwardly, challenging nature, resisting wakefulness. Hundreds of miles. Hours upon hours. Cramped in knee, elbow, shoulder and heart. Cramped for air, for space, for hope. Town limits and county lines, fields, forests, sunrise and sunset, angular windswept horizons that forever maintained their distance. A thousand miles, or two, or three or more. Changed buses, changed faces: a pretty girl with a tiny baby, a brash college jock with too many teeth, a middle-aged man who cried with his eyes closed and never said a word from Richmond to Arlington. Rite of passage. A travelog. A pilgrimage. This journey; *my* journey. Alex in my dreams, the child too, and waking with a bitter taste like copper filings in my mouth. Thinking of Georgia, of Reilly Hawkins, of Virginia Grace Perlman, of men walking side by side, an arm's length between them, beating a ragged path through undergrowth and swampland to find children lost and never to return. My mother: aged, infirm, crazy. A dead father, taken out along the High Road. Gunther Kruger swinging blue and swollen from a rafter. All these things; things of moment, of meaning, of dark and indefinable magic amidst the mundane and monotonous. My life. Nothing more nor less than that.

Road spooled out behind me. Took us days to reach New Jersey. Bus broke down outside of Perth Amboy. Stood at the side of the road, muscular twitch in my left leg.

'Smoke?' a man asked.

I turned, smiled, shook my head.

'Staten Island,' he said, and slanted his eyes northeast. ''S where I come from. 'S where I'm going. You?'

'Brooklyn,' I replied, and looked at the man's face suspended beneath a wide brim of a wider hat. Skin sallow and slick, waxy cheeks, pock-marked and ridged. Looked like a man who'd survived a terrible illness.

'Don't look like no trolley-dodger to me.'

'I'm from Georgia.'

'Georgia, is it? And what are you doing headed this way?'

'Going to be a writer,' I said. Heard the sound of distant bells, a church steeple over three hills and through a narrow valley. A ghost of a sound.

'A writer, is it? And what're you going to be writing about in Brooklyn?'

I shrugged and smiled. 'I don't know . . . I'll figure that out when I get there.'

'Gateway to the Hamptons,' the man said, and drew on his cigarette. 'Scott Fitzgerald, eh?'

'Something like that.'

'Well, something like that is gotta be something

good enough,' he said, and he drew on his cigarette once more.

We waited an hour for another bus. Came all the way from Linden to fetch us.

Through another night. Dark sky, heavy rain, sound of liquid thrumming against the roof of the vehicle, ceaseless and interminable. Slept with my knees against my chest, took ten or fifteen minutes to recover circulation when I woke. Williamsburg Bridge. Daylight weak and vacuous, feeling bewildered and empty. Pockets stuffed with dollars, didn't know east from west, ass from elbow. Figured I was old enough to work it out, find a place to stay, somewhere I could lie flat and straight like a board and not wake until I wanted.

And Brooklyn came at me like a wild thing. High-rise and hopeful; light smashing between buildings that reached further than the eye could see, the glass of a million Manhattan windows, and people, so many people, too many to see any of them as individuals. Broadway, Union Avenue, signs for schools and churches, medical centers, advertisements and hoardings resplendent in colors and messages; and more people, more along one sidewalk than passed through Augusta Falls in three seasons.

We alighted at the bus station on Lafayette Avenue. I carried my bag, must have weighed all of fifty pounds, and hauled it away into Brooklyn with no clear idea of where I was going. Three blocks and I could walk no further. I found a small hotel, it seemed clean and precise, and I took a room for the night. I unpacked some things. I washed my face and shaved. I dressed in a clean shirt, a creased jacket, and ventured out to a world that was both a stranger and my new home. I wandered for an hour, notebook in hand, felt sure I was lost, and then turned a corner to find myself facing the hotel. I felt foolish. I was a rube, a hick, a country-born farmhand. I was also desperately hungry, and in a narrow-fronted diner on Lewis Avenue I ordered enough food for two. Watched the new world through the window. Cars fender to fender, lights changing, drivers leaning on horns, traffic cop with a ruthless eye, stepping out into the rush of engines with no concern for his welfare. Passage of time, of people, of the past through the present into the ever-widening future. I smiled like the fool I was. Here was something worth traveling to; here was New York City, heart of North America, its streets like veins, boulevards like arteries, its avenues like snapping electric synapses, channeling, reaching; a million voices, a million more laid over them, everyone close up together like family but seeing nothing but themselves. Here was a place one could be somebody at the junction, and nobody by the time you crossed to the other side. New York pounded at me. Everything I saw was bright and bold and arrogant. The cut of suits, the scarlet lips of girls with faces from magazines and movies; the cars a mile of burnished chrome, wire wheels and snarling grilles, quarterlights like eyes and mirrors; children dressed in bows and brights as if for church. Majestic. Imposing. A clenched fist of a city. A thunderhouse of humanity.

New York took my breath away. I did not regain it for more than two days.

Monday, May second, 1949. Stood in the front hallway of the hotel where I was staying; newspaper on the porch caught my eye; a byline beneath the header, story about a man called Arthur Miller, a playwright, an icon it seemed; awarded a Pulitzer for *Death of a Salesman*. Concierge breezed past me, flung open the door, snatched the paper from the floor and headed back the way she'd come. I held her up momentarily, inquired after a boarding house, apartments or rooms to let. Middle-aged woman, squinted at me from beneath heavy-set brows that bunched in the middle.

'Throop and Quincy,' she snapped as if throwing small stones. 'Place on the corner of Throop and Quincy if more permanent is your requirement. My sister has a house down there. Name's Aggie Boyle, Miss Aggie Boyle . . . tell her I sent you down.'

I thanked the concierge warmly. Suspicious pebbles for eyes. Stepped back, looked me up and down for a heartbeat, and then she turned without another word and disappeared toward the back of the building.

After breakfast I ventured down to Throop and

395

Quincy. Streets were crammed with people. High-rise monoliths every which way I looked. Cars grille to fender at junctions, hunched like awkward beasts.

Found the house; sign in the window: Room To Let. Aggie Boyle was built with as much substance as her boarding house.

'Eight dollars a month, buy your own food, share the facilities, hot water between six a.m. and eight-thirty a.m.' Her tone was perfunctory and businesslike, her face like some old Tyrolean maid, childless, perhaps had never felt the hand of a man beyond simple courtesy as she climbed steps or alighted a train; very little resemblance between Aggie and her sister except in the eyes, squatting beneath verdant brows, darting this way and that as if expecting sudden motion. Beneath the acres of skirt were acres of flesh, and beneath that were sturdy bones, bones hewn from old trees, hammered together for permanence, sufficient perhaps to carry her into the afterlife. Aggie's hands were crudely fashioned, width of fingers preventing anything but a fan of digits, and when she turned her head it traveled in unison with her shoulders, as an elephant or a rhinoceros. But there was something about her that was likeable. Stationed on the earth to serve some purpose, to provide berthing and breakfast for the weary and restless. I imagined there was a past; imagined there were stories of Aggie and her sister, the years behind them, the things that carried them to Brooklyn.

'Four other tenants,' Aggie told me as we climbed the stairs to the attic room. 'Two gentlemen, two ladies. Mr Janacek. He's from Eastern Europe. Been here a good few months. Minds his own business, prefers it if we all mind ours too. Mr John Franklin. He reads copy for the *Brooklyn Courier*, makes sure they spell the words right and don't miss out the commas. Mrs Letitia Brock. She's been here for more than fifteen years. Elderly lady, helps out at the library Wednesdays and Fridays. Last, there's Miss Joyce Spragg. Assistant Registrar at St Joseph's College, over by De Kalb and Underwood Park, you know?'

I smiled, I nodded. I had no idea where St Joseph's College was.

'If you stay that's who you'll have for friends and neighbors, so it'd suit you to be polite and mind your manners 'til you know what they're about.'

The room was functional and clean, large enough for a bed, two chairs in the bay, a writing desk against the left-hand wall, a closet with a rail for hanging clothes.

I walked to the window and looked down into the street.

'I'll take it,' I said. I turned and looked at Aggie Boyle.

'You don't need to think about it?' she asked, in her voice an element of surprise.

'What's there to think about?'

She smiled, shook her head. 'Don't s'pose much of anything really.'

'Then we're done.' I reached into my pocket, took out a fist of dollars. 'How much do I pay you?'

'Two weeks' money now, and then I collect every Friday.'

I counted out sixteen dollars and gave them to her. The money disappeared into the pocket of her apron.

'I'm a writer,' I told Aggie. 'I'm going to be working here as well. You think the sound of a typewriter will bother anyone?'

Aggie smiled again, showed the kind of teeth that had been raised chewing sugar cane right from the ground. 'Don't think you'll find any complaints. Only one who concerns herself with noise is Mrs Brock and she's on the other side of the house.'

I nodded, smiled back.

'Bathroom's down to the right at the end of the hall. Faces Miss Spragg's room so don't be coming out of there as nature intended, okay?'

'Okay, Miss Boyle.'

'Aggie,' she replied. 'Everyone calls me Aggie.'

'Okay, Aggie.'

'Well, I'll let you settle in . . . you'll need to be collecting your things and bringing them back. When you're ready to leave come and fetch your key.'

'Thank you.'

Aggie Boyle stepped forward. She looked at me with her penetrating eyes and frowned. 'You carry a lot of weight for someone so young,' she said. 'That your writer's curse or you had a difficult time back wherever you came from?'

I laughed, taken aback. 'Writer's curse?'

'Hell, they all got a curse. I seen them come and go. Actors are the same. Carrying a hundred people around in their heads. Something to do with being creative and all that.'

'I don't know about any curse,' I said.

'Then you've had a difficult time of things.'

'Difficult enough.'

Aggie nodded. 'I could see that about you. Seems to me Brooklyn is the best place for you then.'

'How so?'

'Place is so busy you never have time to look anywhere but somewhere else, know what I mean?'

I thought of the people on the sidewalk, the smell of the place, the crowded diners, the thunder of humanity. 'I think so,' I said. 'I think I know what you mean.'

'Well, if you don't you'll soon find out,' Aggie replied, and with that she turned and disappeared into the hallway.

I stayed for a few minutes, my mind hollow, my thoughts contained. I breathed in the smell of new paint, of emptiness, of a room waiting to be filled by someone. I had arrived. Arrived somewhere from out of someplace else. A fresh start, a new beginning, a rebirth.

The ghosts were there, some of them – perhaps all – but for now they were quiet. I closed my eyes and tried to see my mother's face, but I could not. My father was an indistinct blur of monochrome, like the memory of a faded photograph. And the little girls – all of them, side by side somewhere, waiting for their wings perhaps: waiting to be angels.

It took everything I possessed to remember a little of Georgia, and in some way I felt that was good.

I was first seduced by Miss Joyce Spragg, Assistant Registrar of St Joseph's College, on the evening of Sunday, June twelfth.

Miss Spragg was forty-one, twenty years my senior.

'Come and share a bottle of burgundy with me, Joseph,' she said. I was seated at my desk, perhaps daydreaming, a half-hearted attempt to work, and I had left my door ajar.

I rose from my chair and crossed the room. As I reached the door she pushed it open with her foot. She stood there in a cotton-print dress, in one hand the bottle of wine, in the other two glasses. Her hair, dark and luxuriant, was swept back from her face. She was a fine-looking woman, her lips glossed in crimson, her eyes a haze of smoky blue.

'A drink,' she repeated. 'Unless, of course, I am interrupting your work.'

I shook my head and smiled. 'I'm not really working.'

'Then that's settled,' she said. 'We'll share this bottle of wine and talk of inconsequential things for the evening.'

I followed her across the hall to her room. Compared to my sparse habitat it was richly furnished with brocade throws and patterned silk cushions. Standing away from the wall was an ornate wooden screen, a gown draped over it, and to its right a deep high-backed leather armchair. Miss Spragg and I had spoken many times, a convivial greeting as we passed in the hallway or encountered one another in the downstairs kitchen, but it had never been more than that.

'You are a writer,' she stated. 'Aggie told me you've come to Brooklyn to write a book.'

I nodded and smiled. 'Yes,' I said.

'Please . . . sit down,' she said, pointing the bottle towards a chaise-longue at the foot of her unmade bed. She then uncorked the bottle with a degree of deftness that I could only assume came from familiarity, and filled both glasses.

'To a tremendous novel,' she said, 'and its great success,' she toasted.

I raised my glass and thanked her for the sentiment.

'So, you are Joseph Vaughan from Georgia,' she explained to me as she walked to the bed and sat down on the edge of the mattress. 'I understand that you have suffered some trials and tribulations?'

I shook my head. 'Trials and tribulations are a relative consideration,' I said. 'I am healthy enough—'

'But in the mind,' she said, 'and in the heart, that's where life invades with its shadows and edges, does it not?' She laughed. She seemed relaxed, self-assured, aware of her attractiveness and unafraid of what might be thought of her. I envied her her confidence.

'People are made of steel and whipcord,' I said. 'People survive far greater traumas and losses than those I've suffered.'

'So tell me,' she said. 'Tell me what happened in Georgia.'

'I thought we were going to talk about inconsequential things.'

She smiled. 'You are the one who's telling me you've suffered no great trauma or loss . . . so these are the inconsequential things we'll talk about.'

I talked for the better part of an hour. Once or twice she interrupted me, to clarify a point, to request a greater depth or detail, but for the entire time she seemed content to listen patiently as I spoke of my father, my mother, of Alex and the baby, of the child-killings, of Virginia Perlman, of the death of Gunther Kruger. I told her everything, even the letter from the Atlanta Short Story people, the collection of newspaper clippings I had carried with me, and when I was done she rose from the bed and refilled my glass.

She sat down again, her expression was distant and pensive.

'I have troubled you, Miss Spragg,' I said.

She smiled and shook her head. 'Not at all, Joseph, and stop calling me Miss Spragg for Christ's sake.' She laughed. 'You are how old?'

'Twenty-one, twenty-two in October.'

'And you have already lived the kind of life that could carry a book.'

I shrugged my shoulders.

'Have some more wine,' she said, and rose to fill my glass.

A quarter of an hour later she refilled my glass for a fourth time. Her dress rose over her knee as she crossed her legs. I glanced down, and when I looked up once more she smiled at me. She knew I had looked, and there was a moment of awkwardness.

'It is not a sin to look,' she said. 'Nor is it a sin to think thoughts, Joseph. And more often than not it's only someone else's conscience that tells you *doing* is a sin. If one lives life with an open heart and a sense of integrity . . . well, if one really lives life for the moment then there is never sufficient time to look over your shoulder and regret.' Miss Spragg leaned forward, and as she leaned she angled her chin toward me and closed her eyes for a moment too long.

'Are you ready to live for the moment, Joseph?'

I laughed, a little nervously perhaps. I could smell her perfume – flowery, sweetish, something beneath that, perhaps the musk of her body, and together they translated into promise, rendered into a language of seduction and sexuality.

I set my glass down and leaned forward also, our faces parallel. Our cheeks were merely inches apart.

'I am ready to live,' I whispered, and rose from the chaise-longue to embrace her. I remembered the sound of her glass hitting the floor on the other side of the mattress, considered it remarkable that it remained unbroken, and then she was over me, seeing to consume me like a wave.

Later, both dazed from the rush of passion, she lay across me, her head on my chest, and she told me that what had happened was of no great consequence or meaning.

She turned and looked up at me, and for a moment I saw through the veneer of her confidence. It was as if the real Joyce Spragg was visible through the outward appearance. The light of her eyes seemed dim, her skin tone fatigued as that of an aged courtesan. Each feature limned by small shadows, the narrow creases that spoke in epidernal tongues: here, a betrayal; there, a disillusionment; and finally, the outward sign of a broken heart. Her face told a story – or perhaps not so much a story as a saga of dreams drowned in alcohol before they'd earned strength enough to break free and walk unaided. Each aspiration had been anchored by her pessimism, her attempts to advantage opportunity maladroit and clumsy.

Here was a human being who believed the world would always owe her, and to her dying breath would stand testament to its failure to pay.

Or so I believed in that moment, believed and did not care. For Miss Joyce Spragg, Assistant Registrar of St Joseph's College on De Kalb, appeared to me as a small wish for perfection in a very imperfect world.

'Consequence and meaning are relative,' I whispered. 'Go to sleep.'

Each time I visited with Joyce, she would remind me that our union was of no consequence or deeper meaning. Each time I would smile. It was as if she viewed me through a telescope, my meaning infinitesimal, and yet when she wished to exhaust herself across my mattress I saw that I was all she really possessed. Joyce Spragg was a façade, her ambivalence a veil behind which she hid from the world. Perhaps she believed it necessary to be equivocal and ambiguous. Perhaps she considered such qualities attractive. I never loved her, never fooled myself that I loved her. Our relationship was a convenience, a means of company, and though we were friends we would never be anything beyond. However, for all her acquired manners and quirks, Joyce did introduce me to the narrow clique of literati who frequented the College Writers' Forum. Saturday evenings we would meet, my introduction in the first week of July 1949, and here I collided at last with the very people I had yearned to meet when I left Georgia for Brooklyn.

The College Writers' Forum was a haven for misfits and mavericks, those who could perhaps find company nowhere else; and though they proved to be some of the most intelligent and perceptive people I had ever met, they also proved to be the strangest. That first Saturday night I went with Joyce for the simple reason that she asked me.

'They will try to explain classic poetry that they don't understand,' she said, 'and then they'll drink copious amounts of cheap red wine and regale everyone with their own hideous attempts at iambic pentameter and free prose.'

The Forum was held in a meeting hall half a block from the college campus limits. Joyce, as Assistant Registrar, was permitted to bring as many guests as she wished as long as they were neither dullards, ignoramuses, or 'foreigners'.

'Foreigners?' I asked. 'You mean they consider only American literature of worth?'

She laughed. 'Foreigners are those who attend the rival colleges. Foreigners are not allowed in the Forum.'

Satisfied that I belonged to none of the excluded we went. We were met by Lance Forrester, second season chairman. The year was divided not into quarters, but 'seasons', and in turn they were 'winter's end', 'aurora', 'equinox' and 'solstice'.

'A literary license,' Joyce explained. 'Everything they do, and I mean *everything*, is granted a far greater profundity and significance than it deserves.'

Lance Forrester appeared, carrying a sheaf of dog-eared pages. Hair slicked back to the skull with apple pomade, center parting straight as a wheel spoke. Appeared to watch lips as we talked, hard of hearing perhaps, or maybe carrying shame enough to forgo eye contact in favor of mouths. Awkward manner, all angles and corners, a spilled jigsaw of body language packed tight inside the man. Seemed to me Lance Forrester needed a good woman to smooth down the edges, iron out emotional wrinkles, but such a woman would require three helpings of patience, perhaps ulterior motives. When he glanced at Joyce his eyes would spark like wood knots in a fire; lips would tremble as if fearing words would escape solely to humiliate him. His thoughts were his own. His alone. Would carry them home and look at them. The man seemed envious of beauty, of charm, of friends. Perhaps he'd think of girls and cry, or rub himself, or just hate them. The thoughts also, but mostly the girls. the absence they represented, the emptiness instilled.

'A rumor,' Lance told us, his tone hushed as if bearing news of suspicion or foul play. 'Just a rumor, but word was that Fulton Oursler could visit our little enclave.'

I frowned, looked at Joyce.

'Editor . . . was the editor of *Liberty* magazine—' she started.

'And *Metropolitan*. And a published author, you know?' Lance explained.

We smiled genially, Joyce Spragg and I, and we smoothed our way past Lance Forrester toward the makeshift bar against the furthest wall.

It was there, that same evening, that I met Paul Hennessy for the first time. A little taller than me, his hair dirty-blond, cut long on top, short in the back. He seemed to perpetually carry a wry smile, as if smirking at the utter ridiculousness of the world around him. He dressed exceptionally well, and later – having gotten to know him – I realized that his manner and appearance came not from money, but from the degree of care he applied to them. Hennessy had an infinite capacity to make the very best of everything, and with his rugged features, his strong jawline, his slightly brooding eyes, he could have gone to Hollywood. Had I known how significant a part he would play in my future, the future that was yet unknown, I would have left the Forum and returned to Georgia. Hennessy was an anachronism displaced both in time and location, and yet his charm was undeniable. That evening he was not alone. A woman stood beside him, seemed to hang breathlessly on every word he uttered. Her hair was fussed and lacquered into a brave and precarious crest, like a tree in full bloom suddenly petrified, and her eyes, low in her face, had a saddened and nostalgic weight to them. When she smiled it seemed she was expressing the deep and beautiful melancholy that could only be expressed in the company of living poets or dead opium addicts.

As the weeks followed one another, as I became as much a part of the Forum as any other guy, I grew to know Hennessy well. He addressed most men as 'Jackson' in some sort of hip, abbreviated jazz-speak; girls were 'twists' or 'squeezes', and he would refer to himself in the third person, a kind of grand *pronunciamento* – 'Hennessy wouldn't be seen dead in a place like that!' or 'Hennessy wouldn't take that sort of challenge lying down, you know?' He spoke of Nietzsche and Schopenhauer, of Gibran and Tolstoy as though each was a personal friend, and he quoted lines from *The Prophet* and *Thus Spake Zarathustra* as if they were the light-minded matters of common folk. When Hennessy entered a room, whether alone or accompanied, he acted as if Sam Falk himself might appear at any moment to take snapshots for the press.

'We were at the Top of the Mark, you know?' he would say. 'That little cocktail lounge on the penthouse floor of the Mark Hopkins Hotel in San Francisco,' and know full well that none of us had ever been to San Francisco, let alone the penthouse lounge. He would speak of drinking highballs and Tom Collins, and listening to a jazz ensemble: 'Extraordinary musicians, really extraordinary! Only problem was that each of them were playing different pieces of remarkable genius in eleven-four time, and me and Clara, you know she was my main squeeze at the time . . . well, I'll say me and Clara didn't know whether we were heading south from Carolina or north from Boston!'

Hennessy mixed his metaphors with greater aplomb than most Manhattan barkeeps mixed their cocktails, and when he was drunk he was merely louder, more insistent, aggressive like a Hearst newspaper-man. He would yawn constantly, giving all and sundry the impression of utter boredom.

'A medical condition,' he once confided in me. 'Low on vitamin E. My body fights for oxygen. Have to eat peanuts and shrimps all the time. If I don't I become lethargic . . . and *such* lethargy . . . and I'd be prone to terrible things like thrombophlebitis and diabetic gangrene.'

For a while I believed I sought out Hennessy for his humor, his incessant conversation. He seemed to be at least a panacea for my loneliness, the sense of hollowness I felt whenever I thought of Alex. After I got to know him I realized that there was something altogether magnetic about him, and through him I made acquaintances with people I would otherwise never have met. It was this whirlwind of activity that assisted me more than anything else. Hennessy was not the reason for any recovery I might have experienced, but he was certainly a signpost along the way.

For a while he made a habit of bringing another

older woman with him, a woman called Cecily Bryan. 'I have a catalog of ugly admirers,' she would slur at me, her breath rank with gin and cigarettes. 'But frankly my de-ah, I don't care how ugly they are as long as they continue to admire me.' And then she would laugh, and the sound she generated was not only harsh and styptic, it was sufficiently voluminous to fill the room and incite a need for escape.

In the fall of that year the parties started, parties that were instigated at the Forum and continued far beyond the walls of that building. People spilled out into New York, the city their playground as if class had ended. Paul Hennessy and Cecily Bryan would always arrive drunk, seemingly able to determine the existence of a gathering from any locale in the city. They gravitated toward alcohol as an apparently genetic necessity, and though they were rarely officially invited they always assumed that such an omission had been the fault of the Federal Mail, perhaps a messenger with the wrong address. So they came drunk, and they stayed drunk. After a while Hennessy would pretend he was sober, but despite neither moving nor speaking, his slackness of facial tone and laxity of mouth betrayed him. And Cecily: a lush of blowsy, swollen enthusiasm, everything swimming through her field of vision, her existence one of softened corners and indeterminate edges in which no word or action was ever too sharp to deflate the protective bubble of dipsomania. They would always argue, Cecily and Paul; argue about something meaningless and irrelevant, and then they would grow maudlin and sympathetic, and somehow find their way to the bathroom, and he would fuck her noisily as some sort of compensatory atonement for being such an asshole. And afterwards, perhaps in the kitchen or on the veranda, Cecily Bryan would drink gin and cry for the mothers of boys lost in the war. 'They could all have gone to Cornell,' she would say. 'They could have gone to Cornell and taken berthing in Ithaca . . . have you been to Ithaca? Do you know Ithaca at all? Perhaps . . . perhaps they could have gone to Notre Dame, I mean if they were Roman Catholics, you know? Roman Catholic football-playing dead boys, eh? Hundreds of them running through the streets looking for their mothers . . . mothers whose lives are now nothing more than unity in the American Gold Star or the Christian Temperance Union.' And then she would drink more gin, and she would cry some more, and much later Paul Hennessy would merely lift her from wherever she was seated and carry her to his car.

Others came along too – people who seemed 'literary' and 'cultured'. Later I learned that these were hangers-on, neither artists nor writers. Primarily they were ad agency people, working for such reputable establishments as Batten, Barton, Durstine and Osborn Inc., the company that held contracts for U.S. Navy Recruitment and Campbell's Soup. They quoted sections from the Starch Report, and they wore branded tweeds from Abercrombie & Fitch. They possessed the sort of rangy good looks and athletic frames that spoke of running for the high school track team, and when they could no longer hit a mile in five they'd run for the Senate. A blessed life awaited such people. Their downside was being blind to the magic.

There were three brothers who always came together and, though dissimilar in features, there was something quarrelsome and pugnacious about their manner that identified them as strains of the same gene pool. All three worked for E.I. de Pont Nemours & Company, and when they appeared Paul Hennessy would laugh and say 'Here come Beetle, Snorkle and Halftrack,' referring to the characters in the Mort Walker cartoon. 'Those boys know as much about literature as I know about French Impressionism,' he'd say, and then he would engage them in a conversation about Giovanni Boccaccio's *Decameron*, which resulted in nothing but embarrassment for everyone who had the misfortune to overhear. Our first party, at a tall house in Bedford-Stuyvesant, the address of which was as much a mystery to me then as it is now, Hennessy learned I was from the south.

'Not the Okefenokee Swamp!' he exclaimed, and when I allowed that the Okefenokee Swamp was no more than ten or fifteen minutes on horseback from where I lived, he goaded me by saying:

'Horseback? No more'n a quarter of an hour by horseback? Yo' sho' cannot be serious, massa! You musta hearda Pogo thay-un,' his voice slurring sideways in a vague approximation of accents south of the Mason-Dixon line. 'Pogo who lives in th' Okefenokee Swamp, Pogo the opossum?'

I smiled as sincerely as I could, thought the man was a complete ass, and turned to walk away, at which point he grabbed my sleeve and deigned to apologize.

Later I discovered that there was in fact a cartoon strip by a man called Kelly, and the character he drew was an opossum called Pogo, an inhabitant of the very same swamp. Then it seemed a matter of great hilarity to us, but I believe that our laughter was fuelled by liquor and not the humor inherent in an opossum.

The second party, he walked right over to me, thrust a glass of champagne in my hand, and said: 'You know the whole civil rights thing?'

I frowned at him. 'Civil rights?'

'Sure, civil rights . . . like this Martin something-or-other King fellow, young man, little more than twenty years old. Advocating passive resistance to segregation, you know? You must have heard something about this, surely?'

I allowed that I knew a little of it, insufficient to really hold an opinion of any worth.

'You know how all that stuff started?' Hennessy asked.

I shook my head.

'The Second World War.'

'What?'

'The Second World War.'

I frowned. 'I'm not quite sure I understand.'

'Negro soldiers were posted in England,' Hennessy said. 'They went over to England and the girls, white English girls, they treated them like human beings. Hear stories about dances, things like that, dances that were held every week, and white girls would ask Negro American soldiers to dance and the soldiers kept on refusing 'cause they figured if they danced with a white girl someone would come and lynch them.' Hennessy smiled, looked away for a moment. 'There was even a Negro soldier accused of raping a white girl someplace. Fella got court-martialed, found guilty, and the military were all set to hang him. Villagers knew he never did it, knew the girl that had accused him had fabricated the entire thing, and so they got together and signed a petition, sent it all the way to Eisenhower. Eisenhower quashed the court martial and reprieved the Negro fella three days before he was due to be executed.'

I shook my head. 'I still don't think I understand what this has to do with me.'

Hennessy smiled. 'Hang fire there, Vaughan, I'm not finished yet. Like I was saying, Eisenhower reprieved the fella, and the Negro soldiers, Negro American soldiers from the Southern states, they could not believe it, could not believe that a bunch

415

of dumb white folks would get something like that organized, and it was that, the way they were treated over in England, that made them realize that it wasn't right to be treated the way they were being treated at home. That's how this whole resistance to segregation thing got started up . . . that's exactly how it came about.'

Hennessy was like that: he held an opinion; he counseled no-one but himself, and when he felt you were ready to receive his opinion then he gave it you, both barrels loaded and a good spread of double-aught.

There was a time we went to see *White Heat*, ostensibly out of respect for James Cagney, in reality because Hennessy and I shared a mutual crush on Virginia Mayo. On another occasion I remember an impulsive and spontaneous trip to the beach at the far end of Staten Island near Perth Amboy, and there – sober as judges – we had frozen Florida juice popsicles, Eskimo Pie, and rock salt-encrusted hot dough pretzels. There was an ambience of convivial *bomhomie*, and at times like that Hennessy proved himself dry and sardonic, perhaps a little pessimistic, but always humorous without resorting to the coarse and boorish language that seemed the fad of the day.

'Hope,' he would say, 'is a tremendously over-rated commodity, Vaughan. You take the vast majority of those fellers back in Brooklyn. They *hope* for something better instead of recognizing that there is something right there in front of them that can be enjoyed for what it is.' He smiled and winked at me. 'Like now . . . right here and now. Here we are, two healthy young men packed to the brim with hormones, and what do we see? We see row after row of pretty young girls, any of them as cute as a George Petty pin-up . . . and we possess the nerve and charm to speak to them, to invite them to dinner, anything we like, do we not? Merely being here is pleasure enough . . . regardless of whether we actually do anything else. Those boys back there . . . well, I can tell you now, they would bemoan the sun, they would complain about insufficient funds to take a bus back to the city, they would needle one another about venturing an exchange with some young lady, and not one of them would have the gall to do it. And later they would wonder why the world was such a dark and disappointing place. Me? I don't give a red cent what people might think of me! I'm living life, living it every which way I can, and if I have nothing to show for it then who cares? Life isn't a dress rehearsal, Vaughan. It's the real thing, you know?'

Hennessy would laugh, and then he would search out Cecily Bryan and I would hear them laughing together. Their gauche irresponsibility was almost contagious, and I grew to love them for it.

When we were down on our dollars Hennessy and I would eat Cream of Wheat breakfast cereal, and then later – mid-afternoon, when the hunger gnawed like a mongrel at a bone – we would walk to a Horn & Hardarts Automat and share a bowl of soup and a sandwich. One time we both were stricken with influenza, and Hennessy – out of sheer desperation – stole boxes of Citroid and Superanapac from a Rexall Drugstore on the outskirts of Bedford-Stuyvesant. 'Trust me, Vaughan,' he would say, and his voice carried such momentous gravity it seemed he was preparing an auto-da-fe. 'No-one will see me, and even if they do what's gonna happen? They're gonna chase me for a dollar and a half's worth of cold remedies? Somehow I think not.' So Paul Hennessy stole them, and no-one saw him, or if they did they had neither the will nor the want to pursue him. We took the medication; we recovered.

When we were flush we would go up to Macy's Department Store, an eleven-storey monolith that consumed an entire block in midtown Manhattan, and there – amongst the basement bargains – we would find articles of clothing that we would wear no more than once. We bought flannel and seersucker suits at Hart, Schaffner and Marx, and then we would wander uptown to the Metropolitan Museum of Art and pretend we were Eastern European art students, barking at one another in clipped falsetto accents, pronouncing opinions as if we had something of worth to say, and then afterwards – Cecily, myself and Paul arm in arm – we would buy a bottle of Calvert whiskey and sit on a bench near Central Park. We sang 'Days of '49', and tunes by the Gershwins, watched as Buicks, Cadillacs and Lincoln Continentals made their way toward Broadway or across this better part of town – and never once did I think of my mother, of Gunther Kruger, of the past I had left behind. Alone, well, that was a different story. Alone I would think of Alex and the child that I lost. Sharing whiskey and laughter with Paul and Cecily acted as a panacea, seeming to blanch my mind of the past.

Later, much later, I heard that Cecily Bryan moved back to Missouri. Eleventh of September 1961, despite the successful evacuation of half a million people when Hurricane Carla brought floods and tornadoes to Missouri, Texas, Louisiana and Kansas, Cecily was one of the forty people killed. She didn't deserve to die. Despite her dipsomania, despite the fact that the Watch & Ward Society of Boston, Massachusetts, would have outlawed most of her language, Cecily Bryan was a swathe of blazing color in an otherwise predominantly monochrome world, and only in her absence did you realize what a fundamentally gentle, lost, bewildered soul she was. The last memory I had of her was of a trip we took to New Brunswick in New Jersey. Cecily wanted to see Camp Kilmer, the place where Hungarian refugees were temporarily housed. Thirty-seven thousand of them came to the United States, and Cecily figured there was something desperately romantic and terrifying about such people. She bundled armfuls of copies of the *Saturday Evening Post* and *American Weekly* into a battered suitcase and dragged it to the front porch. Paul tried to explain to her that the Hungarians more than likely spoke no English.

'But they speak American, surely?' she shrilled, and insisted that we take the magazines. 'They'll want to know something of their new homeland,' she went on, and Paul looked at me and shook his head resignedly. In Cecily Bryan's world non-English speaking refugees were tremendously interested in William Randolph Hearst's sensational reportage; perhaps they also took pleasure in the funny pages, the latest exploits of Homer Hoopee and Li'l Abner. I suggested we take a wireless. The Hungarians would more than likely enjoy *Dragnet* and *The Jack Benny Show*.

Paul laughed. 'All we want are the facts, ma'am,' he said, in a very passable Joe Friday accent.

'Ridiculous,' Cecily said. 'You boys are utterly ridiculous . . . that wireless has to weigh at least thirty pounds. You might wish to carry that on the train, but I certainly do not.'

Rumor had it that Cecily had come from a once very rich family, that they'd lost everything in the Wall Street crash of '29. Her father had put a flare pistol in his mouth and pulled the trigger. Had to have a closed coffin because his face looked like a handful of smouldering bakelite. Seemed to me, perhaps from personal experience, that death either consolidated or collapsed people. Some – challenged not only mentally, but emotionally and spiritually – found in the death of loved ones the will and resolution to reaffirm their presence and persuasion alongside everyone else. Others, their connections to the world already tenuous, simply fell away into a world of their own creation. So in some small way Cecily Bryan was a reflection of my mother, and perhaps this unspoken parallel gave me a sense of loss that was out of proportion to my emotional tie. Cecily Bryan was crazy, but beautifully, poetically, magnificently so, and for this I believed she may have become an angel.

Such were the weeks and months that closed 1949 and started 1950. A time of new faces and new experiences; different names and different places; a time of hope perhaps. It seemed I had passed through the walls of one world and entered another. It was a period of great change for me, coinciding with great changes for America, and from my room on the corner of Throop and Quincy, through my irregular and clandestine rendezvous with Joyce Spragg, and my friendship with Hennessy, I managed to establish some sense of who I was and why I had chosen to escape my past.

In July of 1950 I wrote to Reilly Hawkins. I spoke of New York: *A great swathe of noise, within which people rush and flood and overflow. It seems*

*there is insufficient room on the sidewalks or streets,
as though there could never be enough houses or apartments to cope with such a throng, but somehow they
press together in oblivious ignorance of each others'
feelings and fortunes. I find it hard to understand how
so many people can be so close, and yet remain so far
apart.*

And in writing I revealed my location, and in
revealing my location I created a window through
which Georgia could climb back into my life.

And that's what happened. October of 1950 a
letter arrived at Aggie Boyle's boarding house, and
Aggie herself carried it up and slipped it beneath
the door as I slept.

I remember the day precisely. I remember the
smell of fall in the air – the haunt of dying leaves,
the redolent funk of decay, the dissolution of a
season. Standing at the window, the letter in my
hand, the weight of it something far greater than
ounces or grams. The script I did not recognize,
save that it had not come from Reilly, and in
understanding this I understood also that this
dispatch would be an invasion. Before I even
opened it I knew that it would, in turn, open something within me. A wound. An aperture. A fissure
between the heart and the mind. Reason and deliverance had carried me away from my home. I had
sought remission from the weight and burden of
loss. Fooled myself into thinking that such a thing,
once achieved, could be maintained. As if I had
earned it.

I had not.

I had earned nothing.

I knew I would have to go back, all the way back to Georgia, to Augusta Falls; all the way back to where this thing had started.

And what scared me, scared me more than anything, was the belief that if I returned I would never escape again.

I opened the letter . . .

I believed myself a writer, a poet, a man of vision and foresight.

I believed myself strong, resolute, dispassionate and calm.

I believed I could go back home, and somehow remain distant. As if I would merely send my body, my mind. I would remain in New York and view everything from some thousands of miles away. My heart was strong. Hadn't Reilly Hawkins told me that? But strong enough to go back into the past? I was afraid – for myself, for my mother, for what might happen.

I was afraid that the memory of Gunther Kruger and ten little girls would haunt me forever.

I knew what had happened back then. I knew the weight of conscience that Dearing must have carried as he walked away from that barn, Kruger hanging from the rafters, his face swollen, his tongue blue, the thin pink ribbon woven between his fingers.

Perhaps I feared what might have been said, the rumors that would have wound their way through the people of that town. Seven counties, seven separate worlds, and to all of them I was as much a ghost as they were to me.

I forced myself to believe it was a test: my returning. Forced myself to believe that if I could survive this then I could finally lay the past to rest and continue with my life.

But I knew better. I knew all too well that they would always be there – the memories of girls, the sound of Alex's voice within the walls of my mother's house, the sound of my child crying in the darkness, how I would never understand nor believe that a life could have been so brief.

I faced a conflict and it challenged me. It threatened to break every bone in my body, every resolve in my mind. It assumed a nature and character all its own, and its nature was one of darkness, of loneliness, of some thin line drawn between who I believed I was, and who I feared I would become. I had tried to exorcise these things, believing that my escape to New York was a catharsis for the soul, but it was merely that and nothing more: an escape.

Had I traveled to some other distant corner of the earth it would have found me, for Georgia was not so much a thing of the external world, it was something within.

CHAPTER 22

'Going home is as natural as breathing,' Joyce Spragg told me, 'except if you happen to be drowning.'

I smiled. I reached out and held her hand.

'You'll come back . . . everything will be okay,' she whispered. She stepped closer to me. Right there in the lower hallway of Aggie Boyle's house. My suitcase at my feet, my coat buttoned against the cold, and she pressed herself against me, her lips to my ear. 'Everything I said before . . . I didn't mean it. It *was* something, you know? This thing we had . . . it *was* something.'

When she stepped away she was trying to hold back tears. I reached up my hand and held it against her cheek. 'I know,' I said. 'You are a terrible liar, Joyce Spragg.'

Our farewell was awkward. I believed that when I returned – if I returned – things would not be the same between us.

An hour later I stood in the bus station. I waited patiently. I shivered. I wished that the world I was returning to was a world I wanted. It was not.

The letter had been brief and succinct.

426

Dear Joseph,

I trust you are keeping well. Reilly Hawkins showed me your letter. I am glad he did, for otherwise I would not have known how to contact you. I write regarding your mother. She has not been well for a long time, as you know, and recently has slipped further away. I am afraid she will not make it through the year. I felt you should know this in the event that you wished to see her again. Sheriff Haynes Dearing visited a few times, but he has not been for a very long time. He spoke with her, but I do not think she realized who he was. I am asking if you would please come. She speaks of you often, though if she understands what she is saying I'm not sure.

My thoughts are with you, and I hope you will return. I write in anticipation.

Sincerely,

Lawrence Gabillard M.D.

In my mind I resented my mother – her illness, her madness, the way in which a simple note could carry me away from something for which I had so long yearned.

But I went; took the bus back toward my past, and my past waited there to meet me as if I had never left.

*   *   *

Georgia: darkest light of my heart.

The sun, once high and bold, now seemed stark and aggressive. Colors appeared insubstantial and vague, as if lacking assertion, as if the land itself had seen too many darkened days to possess the strength to continue.

I stood at the side of the road looking down at the house of my childhood. I did not see the family that now lived in it, but I sensed their presence, saw signs of their occupancy. It was dusk, early evening of October thirteenth, a Friday, and though I was never superstitious I did sense that here was both the end of one thing and the beginning of something else. Lights burned behind the windows. Smoke rose from the chimney like a specter. A dog barked.

I shuddered and turned away.

I took a room for the night at the Falls Inn. I had been away for eighteen months. I considered walking to Reilly Hawkins' place, but for some reason I could not. Frank Turow was dead, I learned; place was now owned by someone called McGonagle. A heavy-set man, wider than two regular men, but even with his size he seemed gentle, a gentle giant, with features soft and rounded, a thatch of gray-blonde hair, and pale eyes. There was something about him that was immediately likeable.

'Yes, Frank Turow went and died,' McGonagle said, his voice as gentle as his mannerisms, as I followed him upstairs to the narrow attic room. 'Stroke I think. You knew him?'

'A little.'

'I didn't know him at all . . . bought this place on a handshake back last winter and Frank Turow had been dead for a couple of months already.' I sensed a half smile in his voice. 'Odd . . . sometimes get the idea he's hanging around to make sure I take care of his place.' He laughed, almost nothing of a sound.

I did not ask further. Somehow I didn't want to know about Frank Turow or Lowell Shaner, Clement Yates and Leonard Stowell. The past was the past.

I did ask after Sheriff Dearing.

'Haynes Dearing,' McGonagle said, and he slowed and turned toward me. 'You didn't hear about that?'

I felt cool and loose inside. How had I known that my return would not be some joyous rush of nostalgia?

I shook my head.

'Tragic . . . really tragic.'

'What was?' I asked, in my voice an edge of anxiety.

'The thing that happened with his wife, you know?'

I shook my head.

'I don't know details,' McGonagle said. 'Let's see . . . I bought this place the winter before last. It must have been March . . . no, February of this year. Yes, February this year. Of course, details ain't my business, but from what I heard she . . . well, she took her own life.'

'She committed suicide?'

'Seems that way, yes . . . she committed suicide.'

'Why?' I was taken aback. I had never met Dearing's wife, but the idea that anyone would take their own life shocked and upset me.

McGonable shrugged. 'Like I said, mister, I don't know details. Why does anyone take their own life? Something they want they can't have. Something they got they don't want. Don't get an awful lot more complicated than that, eh?'

I couldn't speak, and for a few moments I couldn't move.

Why was Georgia so replete with the dead and dying? Or was it me? Was I some emissary of Death? Did I carry it with me like a scent, something imbued, a stain on the soul that permeated the air around me?

'And Sheriff Dearing?'

McGonagle shrugged. 'Left . . . outta here within a week or two. Resigned as sheriff and took off somewhere. That would have been in March. Understood he was a shell of a man . . . Drinking I think, though don't quote me on that . . . Don't know where he went. Haven't heard a word of him since.'

I stood there on the stairwell, my heart in my mouth, a cold sweat across my forehead, the backs of my hands, and made believe that I had never returned, that I could close my eyes and wish myself back in New York and everything would disappear.

'You okay there, mister?' McGonagle asked.

I nodded. 'Ye . . . yes, I'm all right.'

'Well, come on then. Let me show you the room.'

Later, an hour or more, I stood at the window and looked out toward the shadows of Augusta Falls. The world was silent but for the ghosts of the day, and they seemed afraid to come out.

Eighteen months, all but a fortnight. This place had swallowed some more of my past, and all of it beyond my awareness.

Tomorrow I would go to Waycross and see my mother.

Tomorrow I would face the darkness within.

The morning broke early. The sun angled high and full, white like snow, casting shadows crisp and definite. The night had cut cold, sleep came awkward, knees and elbows beyond the edge of the mattress, and when I rose my muscles ached with the dull thud of fatigue. This was no physical distress, but something else. Perhaps my bones, grown from this land, sensed their home, and in my sleep had tried to drag me down. They hankered for the earth, for the swollen damp and relentless humidity. I washed with cold water from the faucet in the bathroom, hoping that the snap and bite of ice would somehow refresh me. It did not. I clawed my way into consciousness, the world around me edged with the bars of memory.

'Sleep well?' McGonagle asked, as he set a plate before me in the kitchen.

I grunted some noncommittal slur, and faced as much of the meal as I could. My throat tightened with each mouthful.

I left quickly, didn't look back, and walked swiftly to Reilly Hawkins' place.

The house was unlocked but empty. His pickup stood in the yard, the keys in the ignition. In the kitchen I scrawled a note and then tore a hole through it. I hung it on the handle outside.

In Reilly's pickup I followed the meandering line of the Suwannee northeast toward Waycross, my heart like a clenched fist, my eyes seeing nothing but the thin strip of road ahead. I arrived at the town limits within an hour and pulled over. I tried to play the scene in my mind. A reunion with my mother. I thought of Alex and tears came. I rested my forehead against the steering wheel.

Fifteen minutes and I started the pickup once more. I made it to the hospital, a miracle in itself.

Gabillard was called. I waited for him with my head down, my hands in my pockets. When he came he seemed a much older man, his hair already white at the temples.

'Joseph,' he said, and in trying to smile he looked merely pained.

'Dr Gabillard.'

'You received my letter, then.'

I nodded.

'I am sorry—'

I raised my hand and he fell silent. 'Where is she?'

He tilted his head. 'Follow me,' he said, his voice a whisper, and then he turned and started walking.

I felt the hope of my future subsiding as I walked, sound of my shoes on the linoleum like the rhythm of a broken heart.

Her expression was lost. A vacancy of humanity. Her hair a white shock of fine wire, her skin folded tight around the eyes and the edges of her mouth, her pupils dilated with morphine. She was set up against the headboard with pillows, a blanket tucked beneath her chin like a shroud nearly arrived, and when she looked at me I felt more insubstantial than I believed it possible to feel.

'Mary?' Gabillard ventured. 'Mary . . . Joseph is here, your son, Joseph.'

I stepped forward, as if her field of vision could not extend to the foot of the bed.

My mother, all of forty-five years old, looked the better part of seventy.

'Joseph?' she croaked. 'Joseph who?'

'It's me, Mother,' I said, summoning everything within me to refrain from turning even then, turning and running away from that terrible death mask.

'Mother?' she said. 'Are you there, Mother?'

I took another step forward.

Gabillard was behind me with a chair, set it down so it touched the backs of my knees. I sat involuntarily. I reached out and placed my hand on hers.

'Joseph, you say?'

She turned her face toward me, and I saw that

my mother had long since left this shell to find some better, finer place.

'Yes, Mother, it's me . . . Joseph.'

I sensed Gabillard's retreat. I dared not look back over my shoulder.

'Joseph,' she said, and there was the ghost of a smile on her face. 'Joseph. Joseph. Joseph. I have waited a long time for you, dear.'

'I know, Mother, I know.'

'But I wanted you to come . . . wanted you to come so you could hear them.'

I leaned closer. 'Hear who, Mother? So I could hear who?'

She smiled again, and there was something in her eyes, something that made me think that we had connected, that she was aware – if only for a split second – of who she was and that her son now sat beside her.

'All of them, Joseph . . . I hear all of them now, you know?'

'Who? Who do you hear?' My heart thundered. My mind reeled. I believed that I knew what was coming, though how I could have known I could never comprehend.

'The girls,' she whispered, and the sound was like a breeze, a rush of wind, the snuffing of a candle, the movement of a cloud, the passage of someone through a field grown high with wheat.

My heart stopped. My eyes widened.

'Don't be afraid,' she said. 'They know you weren't to blame. You did nothing to hurt them.'

'Wh-who, Mother? Did nothing to hurt who?'

'All of them . . . all the little girls.'

She turned and looked toward the window. 'I knew it was him . . . knew it after the second or third one. Knew it was him out there in the darkness with his evil-minded thoughts. Knew he was killing those little girls with his dark thoughts and his dark hands, you know. I knew it right from Ellen May and Catherine—'

I shook my head. 'No,' I said, my voice weak and cracked with emotion.

My mother turned her hand and gripped mine, her fingers strong, grasping like claws. She seemed to pull me closer, for I felt drawn toward her, and within a moment my face was mere inches from hers.

'All along . . . all along I knew, and that's why it had to be done, Joseph, that's why it *had* to be done.'

'What?' I asked, and the terror flooded up inside me like a wave.

'Never meant to hurt her . . . only him. Couldn't tell anyone. No-one would have believed me. Had to exorcise the demon – exorcise the demon. Cleanse the ground. Cleanse the earth where he'd walked. Had to rout him out with the light of truth . . . had to bring light into the darkness and show people the color of his soul . . .'

Her voice trailed away. I tried to withdraw my hand but her grip was fierce.

'Had to rout him out with a cleansing fire, Joseph . . . had to . . . had to . . .'

And then I knew. Before she uttered another word, I knew.

Her eyes widened, and I saw then that she was crying. Swollen tears broke their surface tension and rolled down her cheeks.

'Had to burn him, Joseph . . . had to burn him out of that house.'

I closed my eyes. My breath came short and fast. I felt nausea rush through me like a wave.

'I had to, Joseph . . . I *had* to.'

I pulled my hand away from hers. I stood up, backed away.

'Joseph . . . no, Joseph, don't leave . . . you don't understand. You don't understand what happened. I had to do something . . . I had no choice . . . there was nothing I could do . . .'

'Enough!' I snapped. I backed away further, started to turn, and it was then that I saw Gabillard.

There was something in his eyes, something that told me he knew.

'She told you,' I said. My voice didn't sound like my own.

Gabillard did not respond, merely glanced away, and when he looked back at me his conscience was evident.

I began to shake my head. I pushed past him and through the door, almost at a run, and gathered speed in the corridor, thundering toward the exit as if everything I had ever wished to escape from was tearing at my heels.

I burst through the doors into the cold air. My breath rushed from my lungs, and before I had a chance to regain my balance I had fallen forward to my knees. I knelt there for a moment, trying to hold everything inside, but there was nothing I could do. I retched violently again, yet again, and felt as if my throat was being torn out through my mouth.

'No!' I heaved. 'No! No! No!'

But the truth was out. The Kruger fire. The death of Elena. My mother had murdered the child and paid the price with her sanity.

For a long time I did not move. No-one came out to help me. perhaps no-one saw.

When I moved, it was back to the pickup, and though I was in no condition to drive I somehow made it back to Reilly Hawkins' house.

I had learned a truth; a simple, painful truth.

My mother was as guilty as Gunther Kruger had ever been.

Twice I was sick in Reilly's house. He sat quietly, rubbed my back as I leaned over the sink and brought up nothing but further pain. He said nothing, not a word, until I gathered myself together and sat at the kitchen table.

When I looked at him he smiled. 'It was your birthday,' he said.

I frowned.

'Three days ago . . . your birthday, remember?'

I tried to smile. Shook my head. 'No,' I whispered, my voice hoarse, my throat like razors.

'Yes,' he said. 'And if I'd known you were coming I would have bought a gift.'

'If you'd known I was coming I trust you would have warned me to stay in Brooklyn.'

Reilly Hawkins smiled sympathetically. 'I could not have known, Joseph . . . how could I have known such a thing.'

'I was speaking hypothetically.'

'I don't know that we'll ever really know the truth—'

'I've had enough truth for a good while,' I said. 'I don't think I could deal with anymore truth.'

'You can't be sure that she did this thing. She's . . . well she's . . .'

'Crazy,' I said matter-of-factly. 'Yes, she's crazy. Crazy as they come. And I think this is why she's crazy.' I leaned forward and rested my forehead on the edge of the table. 'I don't know what happened that night . . . don't know that I'll ever understand what happened. Maybe she thought he was there alone . . . God knows, Reilly—'

'And God will judge her, Joseph, it's not our place to—'

I looked up and smiled. 'I can't deal with any religion, Reilly . . . not right now, okay?'

Reilly nodded. 'Okay, Joseph, okay.' He reached forward, closed his hand over mine. 'So tell me about Brooklyn.'

'Brooklyn?'

'Sure, Brooklyn. Is it everything that you imagined it would be?'

I thought of Aggie Boyle and Joyce Spragg. I thought of Paul Hennessy, Cecily Bryan, the St Joseph's Writers' Forum. I thought of the ragged handfuls of pages that were supposed to be the start of the Great American Novel. I thought of what Alex would think of the person I was trying to become.

'Brooklyn is a world all its own,' I said. 'Brooklyn and Augusta Falls don't even belong to the same world.'

'And you're working on something? You're writing?'

'Some,' I said. 'Nowhere near as much as I'd hoped, but yes, I'm working on something.'

'Called?'

'Just a working title,' I said. 'It's called "The Homecoming".'

'And there's some shred of autobiography in there, yes?'

'No, nothing autobiographical. Purely fiction.'

'So what are you gonna do?'

'Do?' I asked. 'How d'you mean?'

'About this thing . . . this thing with your mother.'

'I'm not going to do anything, Reilly. What would you have me do? Gunther Kruger is dead, Haynes Dearing has left . . . God only knows where he's gone . . .'

'Down the neck of a bottle someplace . . . at least that's what I heard.'

'Speaking of which, you have anything?'

'Bottle of mash,' he said, and rose from his chair. He fetched it down from the cupboard above the sink, brought a couple of shot glasses, and filled them.

He raised his glass once he was seated. 'To life. To the future of something other than this, eh?'

'Good enough,' I replied, and downed the whiskey in one. The raw heat filled my chest. It was a new sensation, something different from fear and nausea, and for this I was grateful. I reached for the bottle and refilled my glass.

'You're going to go back?'

'To Brooklyn? Sure I am. I have nothing to stay here for.'

'True,' Reilly said. 'And you're going to write this book . . . this homecoming thing?'

'I'm gonna try, Reilly, I really am gonna try.'

'So stay the night, okay? Stay just the one night and go back tomorrow.'

'That I can do,' I said. 'I can stay one night.'

'I have another bottle . . . we drink 'til we pass out.'

'There's a language I understand, Reilly Hawkins, there's a language I truly understand.'

CHAPTER 23

Over my head there are fall leaves. Leaves curled up on their branches like children's hands. Like infants' hands: some final, plaintive effort to capture the remnants of summer from the atmosphere itself. And hold it. Hold it close as skin. Soon it would be hard to recall anything but the brooding, swollen humidity that seemed to forever surround us. This winter was a thing all its own. A bold and arrogant enormity of a thing. Clenched fists and sourmash-breath.

The little girl.

She digs and scrabbles. Hands like tight little bunches of knives as she scratches at the ground.

Thinks that if she scratches at the ground some deep, almost subliminal message will be transmuted by osmosis, absorption, something, anything . . .

As if the earth will be able to see what is happening to her and relay the message through soil and roots and stems, through the eyes and ears of worms and bugs and things that go *scritch-scritch-scritch* in the night when no-one can see them, sort of things that cannot be seen with the human eye . . .

Something with a face like that . . .

Scratching, clawing, fighting, kicking, punching the ground . . .

That by doing those things someone might hear her . . . someone might hear her and come running and see the man.

Hunched over her. Bowed shoulder. Sweated brow. Rusty blade. Skin that stank of hole and outhouse and fetid swamp, of swollen river dirt, of raw fish, and raw chicken, chicken so raw and aged it's blue and withered and punky to the nostrils . . .

Someone would come and see.

Gunther Kruger hunched over. Working. Working hard. His job. A *real* job.

But no-one came.

No-one . . .

I collapsed into consciousness, a great thundering sound of nothing bursting inside me. Terrifying. Explosive silence. Like teetering on the edge of some dark abyss, and then falling upward, defying gravity, smashing against heat and darkness as I wrestled the sheets and blankets away from me.

A choking sound rushed out of me, and then I fell sideways and landed on the cold, hard floor. I lay there stunned and breathless for some time. I heard footsteps. For a heartbeat I believed that Death had come, walked down along the High Road to collect me. My dues paid. My debt for breathing in arrears. Carry me away on the black river, water like obsidian, water without reflections, shadowed faces looming up toward me, heart slowing, breathing staggered, falling silent now, closing my eyes . . .

'Jesus, what the hell happened?'

Reilly Hawkins standing over me, his hand outstretched, helping me up until I sat with my back against the bed.

I closed my eyes and looked down at my hands. They were shaking. 'A dream—'

'Nightmare more like,' he said, and then his hands were beneath my arms and he was lifting me until I sat on the edge of the mattress.

'You want a drink of water?'

I nodded.

Reilly hurried from the room and went downstairs. I held my hands out in front of me. It was impossible to keep them still.

I pressed them against my chest, felt like some great winged animal was fighting to break free of my ribcage. I closed my eyes and leaned back.

Saw my mother's face . . .

Had to rout him out with a cleansing fire, Joseph . . . had to . . . had to . . .

'No!' I shouted, an involuntary sound which frightened me. I was not in control of my thoughts, my muscular actions.

Reilly appeared in the doorway, a glass of water in one hand, the bottle of mash in the other.

He set them down on the floor and then helped me to my feet, steered me out of the room and down the corridor. He sat me on the edge of his bed, pulled a blanket up around my shoulders, and then returned for the glasses.

'Just the water,' I said, and took the glass from him.

He smiled awkwardly. 'Whiskey is for me,' he whispered. 'You scared the living Jesus outta me, Joseph Vaughan.'

He uncorked the bottle and took a swig.

'I'm s-s-sorry,' I stuttered.

'Don't be,' he replied. 'You have a right to be out at sea for a while.'

I nodded, tried to breathe deeply.

'Lay down,' Reilly said. 'Try to go back to sleep. I'll stay with you, okay?'

I said nothing. I handed him the glass and lay down slowly. I felt sleep tugging me back, and I was scared to go.

But I did go, eventually, and it seemed that whatever darkness was inside me had dissipated.

Homecoming, I thought, and drifted away silently.

Late the following morning, four days after my twenty-third birthday, my mother faded silently as well.

She was two months and four days shy of forty-six.

I was not present when she died, and felt somehow grateful, as if some small mercy had been bestowed on both of us. She had found her escape.

It was early evening before I learned of her death, seated there in Reilly Hawkins' kitchen, a meal before me untouched, my mind insufficiently strong to focus on anything, the day having stretched out behind me absent of all definition and clarity. Reilly had stayed with me but we had spoken little. He had not asked me about my departure, my intended return to Brooklyn, and had he asked I would not have been able to answer.

It was Dr Piper who came. Drove down to the Hawkins' place because he figured that's where I would be.

When he came I knew what he would say, but he told me well, and it seemed that such a thing was in the woof and warp of his being.

'Gone,' he said quietly. 'With peace, with a smile, Joseph, but she is gone.'

He did not know of her crime, and I would not be the one to tell him. I would tell no-one, and the secret she had shared with me would stay in my heart for as long as I could bear to hold it.

Perhaps there are scars – in the mind, the heart – that never heal. Perhaps there are words that can never be spoken or whispered, words to write on paper that fold into a boat that sails out on a stream to be swallowed by the tide. Perhaps there are shadows that forever haunt you, that close up against you in those moments of private darkness, and only you can recognize the faces they wear, for they are your shadows, the shadows of your sins, and no earthly exorcism can ever expel them.

Perhaps we are not so strong after all. Perhaps we lie for the world, and in lying for the world we lie for ourselves.

Later, Dr Piper's words nothing more than a memory, I cried for my mother.

Most of all I cried for Elena Kruger: the one I'd promised to protect.

Early morning. Sky like hammered copper. Heart like a blunted fist. Rain fine as dust.

Buried my mother. Same plain deal coffin as my father. This time there was no Southern wake. I did not tie her clothes to a branch of sassafras and burn them. Gunther Kruger did not carry her body down the country blacktop on a flatbed truck. Afterwards, there was no gathering in the kitchen of my childhood to tell tall tales and wider narratives regarding the life she had led.

This time there was nothing.

I did not cry for the woman who'd died; I cried for the woman I remembered. I stood over the grave and said some kind of prayer, a few words built on a thin hope for something better. Eyes closed tight, screwed up in wrinkles like twists of paper; mouth closed, a thin uneven line; fingers in my ears 'til it felt as if the tips would meet behind the bridge of my nose. The rest of the world was elsewhere, seven leagues before me and still ahead of the wind.

And then I walked away, Reilly Hawkins on one side, Dr Thomas Piper on the other.

It was Wednesday, October eighteenth, 1950.

'Maybe there's a better place,' Reilly said.

'Maybe there isn't,' I replied.

'Seems to me it'll be a good while before either of us finds out, eh?'

I nodded but did not speak.

Two days later, the afternoon of Friday, Reilly Hawkins drove me to the bus station in Augusta Falls.

I began the long journey back to Brooklyn.

I promised myself I would never return to Georgia.

CHAPTER 24

By the summer of 1951 I had returned to my writing. The money from the sale of the house had been released, and I had received more than three thousand dollars. I stayed on at Aggie Boyle's, but many things had changed. I had watched as my heart slowly healed, and of my mother's confession I said nothing. My relationship with Joyce Spragg, however meaningful – or not – it might have been, had died a slow but painless death. I still continued my allegiance to the Writers' Forum, and Paul Hennessy had become my closest friend. It was he who encouraged me to continue 'The Homecoming'.

'You just need a first line,' he said. 'Every great book begins with a great first line, you know?'

'Such as?'

He laughed. 'Hell, Joseph, you're the writer. I'm just a lowly reader. I know a great first line when I read one, but when it comes to writing I have a hard enough time filling out a job application.'

'I have a first line.'

'Which is?'

We were in my room. I was at my desk and Paul

was in an armchair in the bay. Against the mid-afternoon sunshine he appeared as little more than a silhouette.

I reached for the sheaf of papers upon which I had scrawled the beginnings of my novel so long before, and I thumbed through them.

'Here,' I said. 'You ready?'

'Hit me with it, Jackson.'

I smiled. 'There was never a time when I believed that life would be anything other than beautiful—'

He was shaking his head. 'No, no, no,' he said. 'It's clumsy. No poetry. It sounds trite as well.'

'Anything else wrong with it?'

Paul rose from his chair and walked to the book-case. 'Let's see what we have here,' he said. He reached for a volume. '*Cannery Row.* John Steinbeck.'

'That's not fair.'

'Shut up and listen.' Hennessy cleared his throat. 'Cannery Row in Monterey in California is a poem, a stink, a grating noise, a quality of light, a tone, a habit, a nostalgia, a dream.' He snapped the book shut and smiled. 'See? Poetry. A little magic. It conjures a whole atmosphere in one sentence.' He reached for another. 'William Faulkner. *The Wild Palms.*'

'Nobel Prize for Literature last year,' I said. 'You're setting me up against some stiff competition.'

'Which is probably exactly what you need. Here we go. 'The knocking sounded again, at once discreet and peremptory, while the doctor was descending the stairs, the flashlight's beam lancing on before him down the brown-stained stairwell and into the brown-stained tongue-and-groove box of the lower hall.' How's that for a little mystery, eh? Who's the doctor! Is he in his own house? What's the knocking sound? Someone at the door? Who would come knocking at his door at night? Is someone sick? Has someone died?'

'Enough already. I get your point.'

'So write me a great first line.'

'Now?'

'Sure now, why the hell not? What're you waiting for? You know what they say . . . ten percent inspiration—'

'Ninety percent perspiration, I know.'

'So I'll go sit over by the window and mind my own business until you're done.'

I leaned over the desk, pen in hand, and I closed my eyes. I thought of the opening scene. The arrival of friends at a house. Friends long since forgotten. Friends passing through a town who decide to call on the central character. He is surprised, taken aback, but their enthusiasm and charm seems to captivate him. He feels as though there is something here he has lost. He yearns for the past, a time when friends such as these were all that was important, and he decides that the life he has chosen has been a waste. He begins a journey, a journey back to his roots. He travels on foot, by train, on buses and wagons, and hitches rides. He crosses from the east to the west of America and lives life as it was meant to be lived.

He never does reach the town of his birth, but he does find his home. An allegory, a fable, a myth.

I put pen to paper.

'I hear no scratching of nib on parchment,' Hennessy said from his bay window seat.

'Ssshhh,' I hissed. 'Can't you see I'm working?'

A few minutes later I looked up, leaned back, turned in my chair with the paper in my hand and smiled. 'I have it,' I said proudly.

'Good. So let's hear it.'

'There was a time when it seemed each day could burst with passion; a time when life was swollen with magic and desire; a time when I believed the future could be nothing but perfect. There was such a time. And in my youth, my wide-eyed innocence and ardor, I felt that a path had been carved for me that could only lead higher—'

'Whoa, enough,' Hennessy interjected. 'That's more than one line.'

I looked up. 'I have more.'

'I didn't ask for more.'

'So what d'you think?'

'Better,' he said conservatively. 'Better than the other one. You get the idea there's some impending darkness. A disappointment. Something has happened to dampen this fellow's enthusiasm, right?'

'Yes, there is. Some friends of his—'

Hennessy raised his hand. 'Don't tell it, write it. Write it first, and then you can tell me.'

I smiled. 'You intend to be my muse,' I said.

'God no, Vaughan. A muse should be female, a woman of intellect and grace. Yes, we shall find you a muse, someone intelligent and elegant, but not so pretty that she's a constant distraction, eh?'

I had spoken of Alex with Paul so many times before. In that moment I could not bear to speak her name again, and so I said nothing.

'You are going to carry on writing?'

'Yes,' I replied. 'You have started me off now.'

'Then, Vaughan, my work is done . . . I shall leave you to the machinations and musings of your own mind. I am going to find a bar and drink until I can't see very well.'

'Enjoy,' I said.

'I shall, Vaughan, indeed I shall.'

I worked consistently. I found a groove, a rhythm, and somewhere between dawn and dusk I managed to discipline myself sufficiently to hammer out my words. I bought a new Underwood typewriter, set it atop a folded blanket on my desk to minimize the clatter it made, and shunted page after page between roller and platen. I took up smoking, a nauseating affectation which I promptly became addicted to, and oftentimes I would go out in the evening with Hennessy and we would try as many different drinks as we could manage until we were sick as dogs.

The past tried to leave me alone, but I would collide with it unexpectedly every once in a while.

I thought of the girls who'd been killed, and their names would come back to me: Alice Ruth Van Horne, Rebecca Leonard, Catherine McRae, Virginia Grace Perlman, others whose faces I had never known, would never know. I thought of the day I'd found Gunther Kruger in my mother's room, and then I would think of her creeping from the house that late August night to commit arson. I tried to convince myself that she could not have done such a thing, but I knew she had. She had tried to exorcise the demon from Augusta Falls, a demon she had permitted to enter her bed, her life, her heart perhaps. Guilt, anger, pain, her conscience, such things as these had finally over-whelmed her, and she had inflicted her own madness on the world. That madness had grown, had eaten her alive from within, and finally it had killed her. My thoughts of her were not heavy with grief, but a bitter sense of pity. I did think of my father. I often wondered what would have become of us had he lived. I took my emotions and I wrote them into 'The Homecoming', and somehow, some way, it seemed to make things better.

Early September of the same year, much of 'Homecoming's' first draft complete, I registered at the nearest library I could find. From here I borrowed *Worlds In Collision* by Immanuel Velikovsky, armfuls of the *Writer's Digest*, things by Ezra Pound, Machiavelli's *The Prince*, Fenimore Cooper's *Satanstoe*. And it was here that I saw her. Saw her for the first time, and though there was no discernible curve or line to her features, nothing particular that could be identified or highlighted; though her eyes were neither emerald green nor sapphire blue nor some depthless black, but warm, a color like mahogany, painstakingly sanded until the grain came proud, until the surface was as smooth as butter; though her face carried the familiarity of someone close but long lost, as if seeing her not only initiated a sense of affinity, but also the kindred ghost of nostalgia . . . Despite nothing to name or cite as *the one thing*, it seemed that everything about her carried with it an aura of magic. Later, looking back, perhaps it was the feeling that here was a woman who needed no-one, and this in itself was the quality that made her so unbearably attractive to me.

I saw her in the library, she too bearing up a handful of books, and I believed that some preter-natural selection had designated this time, this day, this moment, as one of great importance.

My words, ordinarily my strength, failed me with awkwardness. The first day I could say nothing of consequence or meaning. I merely smiled in the hope that she would smile back. She did not. I felt my heart snap like a greenstick twig.

I returned to the library each day for the better part of a week, and on a late Friday afternoon she appeared from behind a shelf with a copy of *Cannery Row* in her hand.

I remembered the line, the very first line, a line I had memorized following my conversation with Paul. I smiled; I cleared my throat; I spoke.

'Cannery Row in Monterey in California is a poem—'

The girl frowned, looked embarrassed.

'—a stink, a grating noise, a quality of light, a tone, a habit, a nostalgia, a dream.'

She shook her head. 'Excuse me?'

'The first line,' I said, somewhat proudly, though I felt like a fool. 'The first line of *Cannery Row* . . . the book you have there.'

The girl raised her eyebrows, peered down at the slim volume in her hand. 'Is that so?' she asked. 'I wouldn't know . . . I haven't read it.'

'I have.'

'So it would seem.' She lowered her hand to hide the thing, and then she moved as if to get past me.

'I'm sorry,' I said. I took a step back in an effort to be less intimidating, I tried to smile, a genuine smile, something heartfelt and warm, but my muscles tensed. I imagined she thought me quite crazy. 'I didn't mean to interrupt you,' I went on. 'It's just that when you see someone with a book you love you think there might be some—' My throat tightened. I didn't know what I'd planned to say.

'Some what?' she asked.

'I don't know,' I replied. My self-consciousness rapidly increased to near emotional distress. 'Really, I'm sorry . . . I wanted to speak to you last time you were here. I'll go now. I'm just making a fool of myself.'

The girl smiled. 'Okay,' she said gently. Once again she stepped to the left as if to pass by.

I knew that if I let her go then I would more than likely never see her again. Such were the Fates.

'I come here quite often,' I said. 'I've only just moved here . . . I don't really know anyone . . . I wondered . . .'

She looked at me askance. She seemed irritated.

I raised my hands and backed up. 'This is not going the way I wanted,' I said.

'And what did you want?' she asked.

'I don't know, miss . . . I just wanted to introduce myself. I wanted to say hello. I wanted to find a reason to speak to you, that was all.'

'And what did you want to speak to me about?'

I shrugged. 'Anything really. Books. Who you are. Where you come from. Whether or not we could . . . I don't know . . . whether or not we could get to know one another. I thought we might have something in common . . . literature, you know? We could discover that we have something in common, and then you could be the only person I know in Brooklyn.'

She smiled. 'What's your name?'

'Vaughan,' I said. 'Joseph Vaughan.'

'Well, Joseph Vaughan, it was very nice to meet you but I really am in a hurry. I have to get back home now, so if you don't mind?' Once again she took a step to the left to come by me.

'Could I see you again perhaps?' I asked. I had

reached a point of no return. I had nothing to lose. My dignity, my self-respect, everything had gone by the boards.

'You could,' she said. 'But then I could see you again. Wouldn't necessarily mean that I wanted to see you again. Like today . . . the fact that both of us happen to be in the same library at the same time means nothing more than we both come here to borrow books. Coincidence, yes?'

I did not mention that I had come every day in the hope that she would be there.

'I'm not a great believer in coincidence,' I said.

'Are you not,' she replied, a rhetorical question. 'Seems also that you are not a great believer in recognizing when someone doesn't have time to stand and talk to strangers.'

That was it. She had managed to crush me completely.

'I apologize,' I said sheepishly. 'I really am very sorry to have disturbed you. I didn't mean to come across as—'

'You came across just fine, Joseph Vaughan, and I'm sure it was very nice to meet you, but I really have to go now. I have things I need to do.'

This time she stepped toward me with greater determination, almost authority, and I stepped aside.

'See you again some time then,' I said.

'Perhaps,' she replied, and then she turned the corner at the end of the row and disappeared.

I stood there for a few moments, my heart

thudding, my nerves like taut whipcord, and I willed myself to do something. Anything.

I put the books I had selected on the edge of the nearest shelf and then hurried out of the library and down the steps to the street. A half block down I found a flower-seller, threw a dollar at him and grabbed the nearest bouquet. He hollered after me for change, but I was already at a run, back toward the library.

I was there as she came out of the door and started down the steps.

I stood my ground, breathless, red-faced, the bunch of flowers like a shield against her possible rejection.

She saw me, and for a moment she looked surprised, taken aback, and then she smiled, smiled wider, started laughing.

'You are a fool,' she said, echoing my own thoughts. 'What are you doing now?'

'I brought you some flowers,' I said, stating the idiotic obvious.

'What on earth for?'

'To apologize for upsetting you.'

'You didn't upset me.' She reached the bottom of the risers and stood on the sidewalk.

'Look,' I said, feeling something close to irritation overcoming my self-consciousness. 'I really don't know what it is about me that repels you. I'm sorry for looking the way I do. I'm sorry for stopping you when you obviously have better things to do, but my way of thinking tells me that if you don't talk to people, if you don't somehow start a conversation with someone, then you'll spend the rest of your life alone and regretful. I saw you once before. You looked like someone who would be good to speak to. I came here every day since then in the hope that I might see you again—'

'You did what?'

I realized I had taken my foot out of my mouth only to place it firmly back inside. 'I came here yesterday, the day before, the day before that . . . I came here until I saw you again and then I couldn't let myself not say something. The fact that I've said entirely the wrong thing is beside the point now. The truth is, that whatever might happen now, at least I won't kick myself for not saying something.'

'And what do you think should happen now?' Her expression was feisty and petulant.

'I . . . well, er . . . well, I figured we might go and have a soda or a cup of coffee or something. I figured you might tell me your name . . . that much at least.'

She smiled. She seemed to relax a little, let down her defences. 'My name? Sure I can tell you my name.'

I paused, waiting.

'Bridget,' she said. 'My name is Bridget McCormack.'

'Pleased to meet you, Bridget McCormack.'

She nodded. 'Reciprocated, Joseph Vaughan.'

'So would you like to go have a soda—'

'Or a cup of coffee?'

'Right, yes . . . a cup of coffee.'

'For annoying me, you got no points at all. For apologizing you get five out of ten. For the flowers?' She shook her head. 'The flowers weren't necessary.'

I put the flowers behind my back.

'But I'll take them anyway, just so you don't feel you've wasted your money.'

I withdrew the flowers and handed them to her.

'For persistence you get ten out of ten, and yes, I will go for a cup of coffee with you . . . but not today. Today I am actually on my way somewhere, and as a result of this little detour I am already considerably late, so if you don't mind?'

'So when?' I asked.

'When what?'

'When can I take you for a cup of coffee?'

'Monday,' Bridget McCormack said definitively. 'You can meet me here at noon on Monday and take me for a cup of coffee, okay?'

'Okay,' I said, and smiled wide.

'Though this does not necessarily mean that we'll have anything in common, or even like each other for that matter.'

I nodded. 'Understood, but at least we can give it a try.'

'That we can,' she said. 'That we can.'

'All right then, Monday it is . . . I'll see you then, Miss McCormack.'

She laughed and walked past me. 'You really are a foolish man, Joseph Vaughan.'

My heart soared. I said nothing. I stood there on the sidewalk and watched her walk down the street and disappear around the corner. She did not look back, and for this I was grateful; standing there with my hands in my pockets, a smile on my face as wide as the Mississippi was long.

Bridget McCormack was not Alexandra Webber. Bridget was similarly intelligent and well read, but there was something unique about her that made it easy not to be reminded. She did not look like Alex. Her voice was different, and when she laughed she seemed to possess such assurance and self-possession. No-one could ever have replaced Alex, no-one could ever take her place in my heart, but Bridget somehow managed to make me feel good about being alive. I experienced emotions that had been absent for years, and as I experienced them I realized how much they had been missed. Bridget was twenty-one years old, born of Irish-American parents, a lapsed Catholic, a student of the Humanities at Brooklyn University, and she intended to write poetry and essays, to write letters and articles for eclectic magazines, to study art, to live life, to be herself.

We met that following Monday. We walked three blocks and stopped at a deli. There we sat for the better part of two hours, and she let me speak of myself, of why I was in Brooklyn, of my work in progress.

'So tell me about this book,' she said, and I did, pouring out something of myself that would have seemed strange considering it was our first meeting.

'You are passionate about this, aren't you?' she said when I was finished.

'I'm sorry,' I replied. 'Once I get going it kind of takes me over.'

She reached out and touched my hand. 'Don't be sorry,' she said. 'Sorry is for the things you've done that you shouldn't have, not for the things you believe in. Next time, bring some of it would you? I'd like to read what you've written.'

I said I would. Anything to gain a second rendezvous. Thoughts of her pulled at me like gravity.

The subsequent months we met twice, three times a week. We went to the movie theater, we ate in a restaurant on the edge of Bedford-Stuyvesant, we walked in Tompkins Park until our hands froze, our noses were blue. We learned something new about one other each time, and she encouraged me to work at 'The Homecoming' the same way Alex would have done.

As Christmas approached we recognized that time together was so much better than time apart, and it was Christmas Eve of that year, a week or so after I had typed the last lines of my novel, that Bridget McCormack came to the boarding house on Throop and Quincy and consumed my heart.

Love, I would later conclude, was all things to all people. Love was the breaking and healing of hearts. Love was misunderstood, love was faith, love was the promise of now that became hope for the future. Love was a rhythm, a resonance, a reverberation. Love was awkward and foolish, it was aggressive and simple and possessed of so many indefinable qualities it could never be conveyed in language. Love was *being*. The same gravity that relentlessly pulled at me was defied as I rose into something that became everything.

I loved Bridget McCormack, and that night – Monday, December twenty-fourth, 1951 – she loved me in return.

For a while it seemed that the ghost of Alexandra Webber was there between us, and then I felt her leave. Her passing was quiet, almost intangible, and with her she took the memory of the child that never was. The past was like an eye, and sometimes I was ahead of it, sometimes behind, but it was always there . . . opening, closing, opening once more.

CHAPTER 25

Brooklyn was my new world. It was all here. Such things as I remembered from the moment I arrived: The high-rise and hopeful, the light smashing down, the multitude of people, the cars fender to fender, drivers leaning on horns, the passage of time, of people, of the past through the present into the ever-widening future. Here was *my* New York, heart of the Americas, its streets and boulevards like veins, its avenues like snapping electric synapses, chan- neling, reaching, a million voices, a million more laid over them, everyone close up together like family but seeing nothing but themselves. Here – as I'd imagined – was a place where I could be someone. New York pounded at me. My heart pounded back. In this clenched fist of a city I was a clenched fist too. Within this thunderhouse of humanity, I had finally, irrevocably, become the man I had longed to be.

And she was there. Bridget McCormack was there. She believed in me, and I believed back.

It was then that I believed I had finally buried the ghost of Georgia. Despite my memory and my conscience, despite the memory of my mother and all that had happened in Augusta Falls, I believed I had finally walked free. I felt it was not so much an escape as a pardon. My sentence had been served; justice had been seen to be done; I was reprieved.

It seemed fitting. It seemed right. It seemed just.

I met Bridget's parents. Her father a staunch Irish-Catholic, face liked a boiled egg dropped from a generous height, maintaining some semblance of shape despite the jigsaw of cracks and fissures. Nails bitten to the quick, fingers looking raw and sore and useless for gathering up anything smaller than shoes. Teeth angled and awkward, pier stanchions under salt corrosion. And when he spoke his thoughts came out as rough chunks of sound; had an ear for ten-dollar words: disposition, pivotal, exigent. Each phrase considered carefully, weighed and valued, like bluff or call for a thousand-dollar pot. Hair oiled and slick, could've rented it to kids; makeshift sleds from crown to brow, a straight run uninterrupted. Laughing as they went, scared but excited. Her mother slight and insubstantial, haunting the edges of the conversation, snippets of words as if cut from a magazine. We lied to them, told them I was as Catholic as they came. We laughed in private. We wore our faces for the world, and the world took to accepting us without condition or reserve.

For the first time since Alex I was truly happy.

Hennessy stood quietly on the sidelines, ever encouraging, ever patient. He neither questioned nor envied what I had. Showed his colors as a true and loyal friend.

Early in 1952, at the point where I believed things could get no better, Bridget came to see me at the boarding house.

'You will be sore at me,' she said as I opened the door and let her in.

'Sore at you? Why would I be sore at you?'

She stood in the hallway, her head down. 'I did something, Joseph . . . I did something without telling you . . . I did something and I think you might be mad at me, and I've been holding off coming over all day . . .'

'What?' I said. 'What's happened?'

She shook her head. Looked down again. Looked up. Eyes awkward in her face. Like a furtive thing. She shifted from one foot to the other, left to right, right to left.

'For God's sake, Bridget . . . what?'

'Promise first,' she said. A scolded child. Little girl lost.

'Promise what?'

'That you won't get mad.'

I huffed impatiently. I opened my arms, hands wide. *Look*, I said without words. *There's nothing here. Nothing at all.*

'I sent your book to someone,' she said, her voice reserved, little more than whispers.

466

I frowned. 'My book? What d'you mean, you sent my book to someone?'

'I sent it away to someone . . . someone at a company in Manhattan.'

'What company in Manhattan?'

'A publishing company, Joseph, what kind of company do you think?'

I lowered my arms, hands to my side.

Bridget put her hand in her coat pocket and took out a letter. 'They wrote to me,' she said. 'Here—' and she held out the letter.

I took it from her, withdrew a single sheet from the envelope.

Morrison, Brennan & Young, the heading read in cursive script.

Dear Miss McCormack,

Unaccustomed as we are to replying to a person other than the author of a submitted manuscript, we obviously have no means of contacting Mr Joseph Vaughan directly, hence we respond to your letter and enclosure with great interest.

After due consideration, we at Morrison, Brennan & Young would very much like to discuss the possibility of publishing 'The Homecoming', and would be most grateful if you could forward our details to the author and request that he attend these offices at his earliest convenience.

With gratitude for your forthright presentation of this manuscript, and in anticipation of meeting Mr Vaughan to discuss his work.
Yours sincerely,
Arthur J. Morrison,
Senior Editorial Director.

I read this letter twice. I started smiling. Couldn't keep my face on.

'You're not mad?' Bridget asked.

I started laughing. Seemed I laughed for a week. Laughed all the way to Manhattan on January twenty-fourth.

And Manhattan was there. Manhattan, there across the East River. Manhattan – a city that could have closed Brooklyn in its fist.

Corner of West Eleventh and Sixth – the Avenue of the Americas – there in the shadow of the Jefferson Market Library, myself and Bridget McCormack seated in high-backed leather chairs in the office of Arthur Morrison, Senior Editorial Director.

Hale and bluff, face round and generous; looked like the face of the wind, a cherubic, purse-lipped sketch that adorned archaic maps, sou'westerly gale through and around the Cape of Good Hope. Sailors beware. Rocks clawing up through foam and tide like Neptune's craggy grasp.

But his manner like a well-heeled uncle; charming tone through his words, generous with compliments of my prose and timbre.

'Artless,' he said. 'Simple, artless, unassuming, yet somehow complex, and such depth. A fine work, Mr Vaughan, a very fine work indeed.'

I thanked him.

'And so young,' Arthur Morrison said, and his face started laughing before the sound arrived. When it did it was like a train emerging from a tunnel, growing louder the nearer it came, and then he rose from behind his vast desk and walked to the mantel. He stood there for a moment, arm crooked and balanced on the ledge, and nodded his head back and forth like a wind-up thing. His movements were metronomic, hypnotic almost. Seemed he was elsewhere, lost for a little while, and then gently, effortlessly, he returned.

'It is hard to believe that someone so young could write something of such emotional depth.'

He talked a while longer, and then he said his piece regarding costs and competition, a few sentences that seemed rote and practised regarding the challenging nature of the publishing industry, and he arrived at his conclusion with deft aplomb.

I told him that yes, I would sign his contract, and yes, three hundred and fifty dollars would be an acceptable advance against the royalties to be earned from *The Homecoming*, and Arthur Morrison smiled like the stretched, pink cherub that he was, and we shook hands before the mantel and Bridget kissed me.

★   ★   ★

'I said it, I said it, I said it a hundred times, and I would have kept on saying it had you given me the slightest impression you were listening,' Hennessy announced.

The day after. Manhattan was a vague and pleasant memory. We sat in a bar on Van Buren Street – Hennessy, myself and Bridget – and we drank beer and talked a great deal of nothing important for a long, long while.

'And she believed in you too,' he added, and raised his glass toward Bridget, and Bridget beamed, and I beamed too, and it felt like the world had come to rights in Brooklyn.

The din of people, the faces on the street peering in toward us, envious, though not knowing why, and the smoke and chatter and rich rush of alcohol, and knowing that in something less than six months I would walk to the same library where I had met Bridget McCormack and be able to borrow a copy of *The Homecoming* by Joseph Vaughan. Paul and Bridget were the most important people in the world. A small world, but a world all the same, and for once it seemed to be a world of my own creating, something I had built with the sweat from my brow, with the strength of my own hands and heart.

This time it lasted. This time there were no white feathers around doorways, carried in narrow breezes from the sill to the floor. This time it seemed that all decisions had been made in earnest, and the world had responded with similar

470

resolution. I was to be published, and through editing, line-editing, proofreading, through one-sided discussions regarding covers and typeface, I maintained my sense of dignity and reserve. I made believe I was of significance, that beneath the exterior was a man of culture and balance, whereas – in truth – I felt like a seven-year-old child the night before Christmas.

The spring of '52 was a rush of color and inspiration. The Writer Forum became my second home, and some evenings there would be a small gathering of people who would follow Bridget and me back to Aggie Boyle's. Aggie seemed in her element, as did Joyce Spragg, for the house rumbled with the passage of young people, injecting life and love and levity into everything.

'You are the new Scott Fitzgerald!' Joyce called at me from the upper landing, and then she was grabbed from behind by some hormone-driven Lothario. There was laughter. There was drinking. There was magic.

It was in the latter part of May that I first met Ben Godfrey.

'North side of Jackson Heights,' he said. 'I'm a third generation Jew. Live out near Mount Zion and New Calvary Cemeteries.' Laughed, not just his face, his whole body. 'Literary-minded lot really, appreciate the sad nobility, the austere and grandiose performance of death. They all want to be Shelley and Byron, but they can't because they're Jews.' Laughed again, a rolling sound, kind of irritating like an empty bottle on the floor of the bus.

'But we do them all anyway. Rosh Hashanah. Yom Kippur. Succoth. Hanukkah. Purim. Pesach. Shavuot.' Laughed more, the sound rolling, rolling.

Hennessy was in the wings. Crossed his eyes, slack-jawed; made a face like a crazy man.

'You're a writer?' I asked Godfrey.

'I am, I am, I am,' he pronounced. 'Have a small thing gathering ink on the presses as we speak. A novella really, perhaps forty or fifty thousand words. Anything to drink around here, anything to eat except more goddamned matzoh?'

I handed Ben Godfrey a glass, a bottle of Calvert. He took them both in one hand and clapped me on the shoulder. I liked the man. He filled the room with something other than size and volume. He possessed a rough-edged charm, and by his dress it seemed he had no shortage of money.

'And you? I understand you are the head of this household?'

I shook my head. I reached out my hand for Bridget and she walked toward me.

Godfrey lit up like a jack o' lantern. 'Well, well, well,' he said. 'And who might you be, young lady?'

Bridget laughed at him. Godfrey perhaps believed she was laughing with him.

'Bridget,' she said.

'Well, hello there, Bridget,' he oozed. He ingratiated himself a little closer and peered down at her.

'Hello to you too,' she said, and slipped her hand beneath my arm. She pulled me tight. Her message was clear.

'So, what do we have here then? A gathering of like-minded literary drunkards, I think,' Godfrey said. 'Seems a perfect setting for people in our disreputable line of work, wouldn't you say?'

And Ben Godfrey became one of us that day. Me and Bridget, Paul Hennessy, and Benjamin Godfrey, third generation Jew from the north side of Jackson Heights. He was twenty-seven, three years my senior, and he flattered himself into the charms of Aggie Boyle and Joyce Spragg with ease. He even brought tea and baskets of fresh fruit for Letitia Brock, the elderly tenant at the end of the upper hall. Godfrey knew literature, and once you penetrated his blithe and convivial exterior, once you excavated the real man beneath, he proved himself to be good company, generous to a fault.

When his book was published we took the bus to Manhattan and bought two copies each. It was a slim piece entitled *Days of Winter*, and I enjoyed his language, the brevity and terseness of his style. I believed I had found a contemporary, and we talked of how we would become models of a new zeitgeist, the youngbloods, the bold talent of a new literary age.

My affair with Bridget grew in intensity. I loved her, was loved in return. Where once my nerves had tightened like turns of a ratchet, strung rigid until they hummed with the promise of breaking, and my heart was like a cold furnace – nothing but ash and embers, the scorched remnants of some earlier zealous warmth – where once I had believed myself hollow, incapable of passion, I now understood that I had truly healed, that Georgia was nothing but a sense of dark nostalgia, rarely considered, gratefully forgotten.

In Bridget lived the memory of Alexandra Webber, but that memory lived free of pain, without regret, without longing.

It was a high tide of euphoria, and when June arrived and we stood hand in hand between the narrow shelves of Langton Brothers bookstore on Monroe Street, when we carried a copy of *The Homecoming* to the register and paid our money, it seemed that my history had been some other existence entirely.

'The beginning of the rest of our lives,' Bridget said as we left the store, my arm around her shoulder, the sun warming our faces as we left the shadow of the awning.

Paul Hennessy and Ben Godfrey were at Aggie Boyle's when we returned. They had prepared a smorgasbord of cold cuts and cheeses, water biscuits and wine. We celebrated the day, the moment, the promise of the future.

That night Bridget and I made love, and I felt that then we each consumed some small part of one another. We became one – Bridget McCormack and Joseph Vaughan – and believed that it would be this way forever.

And it was that night that I saw the feather. Standing naked near the window, Bridget sleeping on the bed behind me, a cool breeze chilling my skin. I saw it then, watched as it graced the air with arabesques and curves, as it floated ever closer, as it settled upon the sill within reach of my hand.

I did not pick it up. I felt fear tighten my throat. I felt a shadow from the past inching through the open window and closing up against me.

I closed my eyes, my mind, my heart. I wished it to disappear. When I looked once again it was still there, but just for a fraction of a second, for I exhaled in anticipation and watched it vanish in the dark.

To walk backwards.

Given the chance to walk backwards I would, even now.

One by one, slowly, tentatively, I would retrace every single step, and my decisions would be different. I would forgive my mother her indiscretions, Gunther his infidelities; I would have kept Bridget close, as close as my shadow, and never let her from my sight; I would have been out there with the Guardians, and we would have seen the child-killer, and Sheriff Dearing would have run with us until he was ready to fall with exhaustion, and it would have ended, just as it has ended now, but different.

More than anything, I would make no promises that could not be kept.

Hindsight is perceptive, sometimes cruel, sometimes more honest than one can bear. Everything is easy in hindsight, and had I known, had I ever glimpsed a fraction of the ultimate truth of this thing, I would have fled New York . . . run like the wind away from it all, Bridget beside me, as close as my shadow, and I would never have looked back.

But I did not know, and would not know for many years to come.

Those years unfold behind me now. They stand as milestones and markers of the route I took, each step – whether brave or fearful, whether honest or deceptive – reflecting in all its facets the man I have become.

I am who I am. And who I am will never be as important as what I have now done.

Everything came full circle, turning about upon itself and taking me right back to the beginning.

The blood on my hands is dry now.

I have become what I feared the most, and it frightens me.

CHAPTER 26

Fall came swiftly. The months that preceded it seemed vague and tenuous. Later, much later, I would think of the weeks that separated June and November and they would possess a thin and insubstantial quality, as if they had never happened at all. Paul was amongst those memories, as was Ben Godfrey – forever laughing, teasing Bridget, making no mystery of the fact that he loved her too. Bridget dealt with him in a matter-of-fact and politic manner, always quick to point out that she was his friend, nothing more. For a while Ben brought a quiet girl along: Ruth Steinberg, a German Jewess whose parents had spirited her out of Munich as soon as National Socialism tightened its fervent grip on the nation. Her parents, her grandparents, her brother – they had not survived, and Ruth lived with a step-aunt on her mother's side, a resentful and bitter woman who bore the responsibility with something other than familial loyalty. I liked Ruth, but she did not suit Ben. They had parted company by the end of August, and once again Ben was the third wheel.

Mid-November came. We were planning a grand

478

Thanksgiving party at Aggie Boyle's, and on Thursday the twentieth I took a trip to Manhattan to see Arthur Morrison. *The Homecoming* had sold a modest eleven hundred copies in five months, but Morrison was not daunted. He wanted a second novel, something with 'spirit and passion'.

Bridget stayed behind, attending to some family matter. The first bus I missed, the second was delayed for some reason. I could have walked but chose not to. For a little while I looked in some bookstores, and then I sat in the station and read a discarded newspaper until we were asked to board. By the time I left I knew I'd be late by the better part of two hours.

Morrison waved aside my lack of punctuality. Was as generous and effusive as always. 'These things are built,' he kept telling me. 'We build these things slowly. We publish one book, and then we publish another. We make people take notice. We persist until we succeed.'

I returned in the early evening. The wind was sharp. I took a bus to the station near Throop and Quincy and stopped at a deli to warm myself before the walk home. I ordered a cup of coffee, struck up a brief conversation with the waitress, a middle-aged woman with a ready smile, and then walked the three or four blocks home. My meeting with Morrison had inspired me to write another book, to plow my heart and soul into it, and I was eager to speak with Bridget, to elicit her encouragement, her support, her bold ideas.

My thoughts spilled over. I found myself mumbling to myself as I walked, mumbling through my chattering teeth, and I smiled at my own foolishness. I was all rucked up inside, my thoughts twisted around and around like motel-room lovers' sheets. I walked faster. I knew Bridget would have arrived by now, would be waiting for me to tell her of Manhattan, of where our lives would now be headed.

I turned the corner at the top of the street. Within thirty yards I could see the house. The lights were on, all of them, and yet everything about the place – the eaves, the plank-board steps, the rough yard of hard earth between the sidewalk and the wall; everything gave off an atmosphere of being too late.

I stopped. Puzzled.

I heard a radio playing through an upper window behind me, the warmth of the crooner's voice:

. . . and for every broken heart there was a promise, and in every broken promise was a sigh, and with every sigh your face I did remember, and with every memory I bro-oke down and cried . . .

I started walking again, slower this time. Something was awry. Something challenged my sense of expectation.

It was than I saw the car. Black and white patrol car. Man inside. Policeman.

My heart quickened. Started running. Thought of Letitia Brock, her difficult hips, the way she swayed as she walked, the fierce grip that held her to the banister as she made her way down the narrow stairwell. My heart missed a beat. I went from the sidewalk at a sprint, hurtled across the road and through the gate. The policeman reacted faster than I could see, was out of the car, around the hood, and stood there in the doorway to bar my entry.

'Hold up there, goddammit!' he shouted. 'And where the hell d'you think you're going?'

'Inside!' I panted. My chest heaved. A film of sweat varnished my forehead.

'Not a hope, my friend,' he said. 'No-one goes inside . . . not without permission. Not without due reason.'

'I live here!' I said, and reached up to push past him.

His hand gripped my wrist as I extended my arm. The tension was vice-like, and held me steady.

'Name?' he asked.

'Vaughan,' I said. 'Joseph Vaughan.'

The policeman's eyes widened. His expression became stern. His grip on my wrist tightened, and he seemed to pull me closer. He leaned his head back and hollered at the top of his voice. 'Sergeant! Got him! Sergeant . . . I got him right here!'

Seemed to me in that moment that all things that took an age to build came apart in moments.

Two decades to build a cathedral. Half an hour

of dynamite and there was nothing more than a lungful of dust and a handful of memories.

Sergeant Frank Lansford. Face like a panel of raw steel, eyes like bullets, punched through, off kilter. Mouth a ragged-edge tear in the cloth of his features. Moved awkwardly in his clothes, hem too short, sleeves too long, as if some unique shape never witnessed by tailors. Nostrils uncommonly large, perhaps for the scent of blood, cordite, other indices of mayhem. Ears flat against his skull, glue applied and held until firm. Sat in Aggie Boyle's kitchen chair, a chair built for those of regular shape and girth. A man who sought comfort, found it rarely. No wedding band. Lonely manner that spoke of days filled with official and necessary acquaintance; no friends, no children, no lover, no humor. As if life was now viewed through the concave lense of a bottle bottom: a distended prism that slanted and skewed the world to rights. Believed such a man would have been wise to choose a profession that inspired respect, admiration, other such qualities. Someone, eventually, would have loved him for what he did, forgiven what he was. But no, he was a policeman. Bad choice. Lost before he had a chance to win.

'. . . and you came up here with no weight of family, or so your friend tells me.'

Voice-tone edged with suspicion. Everything suspicious. Everything accusatory, inflammatory.

I shook my head. 'I don't—'

I looked upward, up through the ceiling to the floor of my room. I wanted to go up there. I wanted to see her.

'Nothing to see,' Lansford had said. Said it earlier. When he'd come out to meet me on the porch steps. Came out there slow, like he was rolling himself out of the house, and he stood there for a while looking down at me.

'You're the girl's lover, right?' was his first question.

Eyes wide. Wondering what the hell had happened. 'Girl?' I'd said. 'What girl?'

Lansford smiled. 'Don't play dumb.'

'Bridget?' I asked. 'What's going on?'

'That's the one,' Lansford replied. 'Bridget McCormack . . . you're her lover, right?'

I nodded. Tightening in my chest. Sweating despite the cold. Heart thundering away, ready to burst. Grip on my wrist wouldn't loosen.

'And where the hell have you been all day?'

'Manhattan,' I said. 'I went to Manhattan to see someone.'

'Is that so?' Lansford withdrew a notepad from his pocket, a pen from inside his jacket. Wrote something brief.

'What the hell's going on?' I asked. 'Why can't I come inside?'

Lansford shook his head. 'No-one goes inside until I say so.' He wrote something else, something longer.

'Where's Bridget?'

Lansford stopped writing and looked down at me. 'You don't know?'

I shook my head. 'Don't know what? I don't understand what's happening. She's supposed to be here . . . supposed to be here by the time I got back.'

'And you can prove you've been in Manhattan, Mr Vaughan?'

'Prove? Why would I have to prove anything? Tell me what the goddamn hell's going on here.'

'Enough already,' the policeman said. 'This here is Sergeant Lansford. Brooklyn Police Department. A little respect from you, okay?'

I looked down at the ground. I couldn't breathe. 'Please,' I gasped. 'Please will one of you tell me what the hell is going on here? Where's Bridget? Has something happened to her? Please . . . for God's sake please tell me!'

'Something happened all right,' Lansford said matter-of-factly. 'Something sure as hell happened, Mr Vaughan . . . seems someone was upstairs in your room with her—'

'My room, yes. She would be in my room. That's where she was supposed to be.'

'And that's where she still is, Mr Vaughan.'

I exhaled. Relief flooded through me like a wave. I almost lost my balance. I started smiling, started to laugh. 'Thank God!' I said. 'Oh thank God . . . can I go and see her . . . please would you just let me inside my own house so I can go and talk to her?'

484

''S not gonna be possible, I'm afraid,' Lansford said.

'Not possible . . . why? Why would it not be possible?'

'Because she's dead. Mr Vaughan . . . your girl-friend is up in your room and she's dead. Seems someone did some things to her . . . what things the Lord only knows, but someone did some bad things to her and then they damn near cut her in half . . .'

It was then that everything fell apart.

I remembered nothing except the vice-like grip of the policeman as he tried to hold me up.

The kitchen.

Ahead of me a cup filled with strong tea, spoon-fuls of sugar stirred into it. Hands shaking too much to lift it, sickened by the sweet smell. Tried to light a cigarette, couldn't. Lansford lit it for me, handed it to me. Took a deep drag, inhaled, felt a rush of nausea fill my chest along with the smoke.

Eyes beaten red with crying. For a while unable to speak, to think, almost to breathe.

White feather. That's what I saw. Small white feathers. On the table, around my feet, there along the draining board, spilling out of the cupboards.

Everyone in the back parlor next to the kitchen. Aggie Boyle, Letitia Brock, Emil Janacek and John Franklin. Paul was there too, Ben Godfrey also. Could hear smatterings of words, small punctuations between the rasping breath coming from my own throat as I tried to gather myself together sufficiently to speak.

'So you left at what time?' Lansford asked, seemingly for the third or fourth time.

I heard footsteps upstairs, the boards creaking along the floors and hallways. People were up there. Other policemen. A coroner.

'Left here a little before eight,' I said.

'To get a bus at eight-fifteen, right?'

I nodded.

'Which you didn't board.'

'I missed it,' I said. 'I missed the bus and had to wait until just after ten.'

'Ten exactly?'

'Ten after . . . the second bus left at ten after ten.'

'And for the two hours between eight-fifteen and ten-ten . . . for those two hours where were you?'

'Around the bus station . . . read for a while, took a walk down the block, had a look in some bookstores.'

'You could have walked to your appointment. Or you could have come home to wait . . . why didn't you do that?'

I shrugged. Looked up towards the ceiling again. A dream. A nightmare. Nothing to place within any frame of reference. I would close my eyes later, open them, find it was all my imagination. I was still asleep on the bus from Manhattan. I hadn't even reached Brooklyn. I would shudder. Then I would smile. Then I would start laughing when I realized that my very worst fears were nothing more than some dark outgrowth of a tired and overstretched imagination.

'I didn't feel like walking anywhere. I didn't mind waiting and there didn't seem to be any point in coming home,' I said. 'Bridget would be out for the rest of the day . . .'

Lansford shook his head. 'Apparently not.'

'What d'you mean?'

'Apparently not is what I mean. According to Miss Spragg . . . you know Miss Spragg, right?'

I nodded.

'According to Miss Spragg, Bridget McCormack arrived here just before nine a.m. this morning.'

I shook my head. 'I don't understand . . . she said she had something to do with her family.'

'Which has also been confirmed by Miss Spragg.' Lansford reached into his pocket and took out his notepad. He leafed through a dozen or more pages. 'Here,' he said, consulting his own hieroglyphics. 'According to Miss Spragg she was leaving for work at St Joseph's at about ten minutes before nine. As she reached the hallway Bridget McCormack came in and spoke with her, said that she had been planning to do something with her family that day but it had been postponed so she figured she would come over and spend the day here. She said there were some things she wanted to read, that she would clean up the room a little. Miss Spragg believes that she

487

was referring to your room, Mr Vaughan. She said that yourself and Bridget McCormack spent most evenings here together, *living* together if you like?'

'Yes, you could say that. We spent more time together than we did apart.' I stopped. I looked at Lansford, at the policeman standing by the sink. 'This is crazy,' I said. 'What the hell is happening here?' I started to rise from the chair. The policeman stepped forward and held my shoulders.

'And where would you be going, Mr Vaughan?' Lansford asked, his voice stern.

'I need to see her,' I said. I felt the swell of emotion again, like a crowd of fists in my chest. Black things swam before my eyes. Feathers. More feathers. Now they were inside my head, right there behind my eyes.

I thought of angels.

I thought of my father. How Death had walked along the High Road and taken him. I thought of Gunther Kruger swinging from a barn rafter, a thin pink ribbon wound through the fingers of his right hand.

I thought of my mother, a child-killer herself, of how she had become exactly what she'd tried to prevent.

I started to sob, a great heaving retch through the middle of my body, and then I swung my arm wide, hit the teacup, sent it spinning across the room, its sweet tepid contents spattering on the linoleum.

'Get the doctor,' Lansford said. 'Get the doctor down here right now!'

The policeman jumped, released me, turned suddenly and went out of the room. I heard him running up the stairs. There were voices. I felt Lansford's hands on my shoulders, holding me right there in the chair. Right there in Aggie Boyle's kitchen.

I saw my mother's face. The mother I remembered, not the one I buried.

I saw the soles of Virginia Grace Perlman's shoes, saw them as they appeared over the brow of the hill.

Voices again. A sense of being manhandled awkwardly. And then there was a pin. Sharp pain like a needle in my arm. I fought against it, wrestled violently. But it came. Came like a cloud right through me and there was nothing I could do to assuage the feeling that it brought. A feeling like drowning in darkness, but buoyed up by feathers, a blanket of small white feathers that tried to hold me aloft but couldn't bear my weight.

I folded silently. Down I went into the darkness. It was a long time before I surfaced, and when I did I remembered that my world was gone.

I woke in a hospital, but no hospital I had ever seen. The walls were white, as was the ceiling, as were the sheets and bedframes. It was a dormitory of sorts, a single door at the far end with bars across the narrow window. When I moved I found that my hands were shackled to the frame, and it was then that reality came. Like a fist. Like a bullet. Like a thundering sound.

I closed my eyes. I could not bear to open them again. I believed I should die.

That – in hindsight – would perhaps have been the most merciful thing.

Hours later – I had no way of determining the time – Lansford came to see me.

'What's happening?' I asked him. 'Where am I? What the hell am I doing here?'

Lansford dragged a chair from the wall and sat down next to the bed. In his hand he carried a thin manila folder which he opened and balanced on his knees. 'Sedated . . . had to have you sedated,' he said matter-of-factly. His tone was dry and businesslike. I sensed the pressure of threat. 'You lost yourself somewhat,' he added. 'Back there in the house. Had to have the doctor come down and sedate you.'

'Where am I?'

'Hospital wing,' Lansford said. 'Brooklyn Prison.'

'Prison? What the hell am I doing in prison?' I tried to sit up but the shackles on my wrists held me down.

'Need to ask some questions. Need some answers. This is not a matter of negotiation. This isn't an issue for discussion. Time of death of the McCormack girl has demonstrated that you had more than ample opportunity to return to the house once you'd missed your bus, to have raped and killed her, and then to have made it back again in time to catch the second bus to Manhattan.'

'What? What the hell are you talking about? You don't seriously think—'

'I'm not done. Appreciated if you wouldn't interrupt me, Mr Vaughan. As I was saying, taking into consideration the time of death, you had more than enough chance to go back to the house and do this terrible thing, so opportunity is not in question. Method? Well, that seems simple enough. The girl was attacked, and there are indications that she was raped. Seems, at least from the coroner's initial report, that she was attacked with such violence that her neck was broken as she was pushed against the wall. Subsequently it appears that an attempt was made to actually sever the body in two. So that was method, Mr Vaughan—'

My mind was closing down. Images battered me. The sound of screaming, the vision of blood. The thought of Bridget . . . 'You're insane—'

'Mr Vaughan!' Lansford barked forcibly. 'I asked you once, politely I think, if you would not interrupt me. I'll ask you again now, and I will be most unhappy if you don't co-operate. Now, as I was going to say . . . if you understand anything of police investigative procedure, you'll know that the first facts that have to be established are threefold. Method, motive and opportunity. The first and the last are evident, but the middle one, the *motive* for this brutal attack, has yet to be determined, but we believe that we may have something substantial to consider.'

I said nothing. A thousand questions filled my mind. My entire body was wracked with anguish, a pain that was more than mental, a pain that drove right through me. I could barely breathe. I realized where this was going. I realized what this police sergeant thought.

Lansford seemed to be waiting for me to say something, but I was unable to speak.

'You understand, of course, Mr Vaughan, that in this democratic system of ours a man is innocent until proven guilty?'

He paused again. I still could not speak. Words were there, a multitude of words, but not one single sound came forth.

'So until we can demonstrate someone's guilt without doubt, we work on the basis that he has every right to defend himself, to seek legal counsel. In your case . . . well, in your case, Mr Vaughan, I suggest you attend to this right away. Secure yourself a lawyer, and be prepared for a lengthy interrogation regarding the death of this unfortunate girl. You are, shall we say, somewhat in the line of fire as far as this matter is concerned.'

Lansford said nothing for a moment, and then he rose from his chair, lifted it and returned it to its place against the wall.

'I . . . I don't understand what's happening,' I mumbled. My throat was tight. My head pounded mercilessly. 'I don't see what possible motive I could have had for doing this . . . this awful thing.'

Lansford smiled, it seemed at first a little sympathetically, and then his face hardened. 'The girl,' he said. 'This Bridget McCormack who was so brutally raped and killed . . . she was pregnant, Mr Vaughan . . . just a few weeks pregnant.'

I felt every ounce of life I possessed drain from within me.

'And in this day and age . . . well, it is a sorry state of affairs when an unwanted child provokes an act of murder, but the truth is what we see, is it not?'

Lansford backed up and turned toward the door. When he reached it he turned back to face me. 'I will send an orderly to make arrangements for you to call a lawyer. Like I said before, I would recommend that you do this immediately.'

I remembered hearing the door close with a metallic crash. Remembered the sound of the key grating in the lock, and then there was silence, silence but for the sound of my own labored breathing, and close behind it the wracking of grief in my chest as I felt my entire world come apart at the seams.

Perhaps I slept. Perhaps not. I think I dreamed. Bridget came to me. She stood over me where I lay and said nothing. I reached out my hand to touch her and she dissipated like a cloud. Every piece of her broke up and disappeared with the sound of a breeze.

The orderly came after a long time and told me it was Sunday. There was no-one I could call until the following day. He brought food which I did not eat. He asked if I wanted anything.

'My life back,' I said. 'I just want my life back.'

The orderly smiled. 'That, I'm afraid, is something I cannot do.'

I watched him disappear, and only then, as he closed the door with such finality, did I begin to face the truth of what had happened. I believed I understood what had taken place in the house on Throop and Quincy, but more importantly, I started to understand why.

CHAPTER 27

Monday evening a lawyer came. Thomas Billick, state-appointed Public Defender. My shackles had been released to permit me to sit up, and once Billick arrived I was allowed to use a chair.

Billick was a man out of place. Narrow eyes, wire-rimmed spectacles, face awkwardly adjusting to the discomfort of his surroundings. He carried a battered attaché case, clutched it fervently as if an object of defense, and when he spoke his words were faltering and hesitant.

'I . . . I am not at all too familiar with such things,' Billick explained. He shook his head, fiddled with the arm of his glasses. When he let go they were slightly lopsided. 'The charge has been made—'

'Charge?' I said. 'What charge?'

'Charge of murder, Mr Vaughan,' Billick said. 'You weren't aware that this charge had been made against you?'

'What are you talking about? You can't be serious—'

'Oh, it is most serious, Mr Vaughan, most serious

495

indeed. The charge was filed against you on Saturday—'

'Jesus, they've gotta be . . . no, this can't be happening. I wasn't even conscious on Saturday . . . you're telling me that they filed a charge against me while I was unconscious?'

Billick shrugged. 'I have nothing here that says you were unconscious, Mr Vaughan.' He awkwardly opened the attaché case. Papers spilled out across the floor which he spent a moment gathering together. 'Here,' he finally said. He held up a single sheet of paper. 'Says here that at ten minutes after one on the afternoon of Saturday twenty-second of November you were formally charged with the murder of Bridget McCormack, that your rights were read to you, and that you were advised to seek legal counsel immediately. Apparently you chose to do nothing until this morning.' Billick looked up from the page and frowned at me. 'Why was that, Mr Vaughan? Why did you choose to do nothing about seeking legal representation until this morning?'

'This is utterly insane!' I said. 'I can't believe this is happening. I wasn't even told that I should get a lawyer until yesterday, and as far as any charges being filed or rights being read . . . I can't believe they did that! They charged me and read me my rights while I was unconscious.'

Billick was shaking his head. 'Not according to this document.' He held the single page out toward me, and when I reached for it he swiftly returned it to his case. 'I need to keep that,' he said. 'That has to stay with the rest of your case file.'

'So what now? What the hell is supposed to happen now?' I asked.

'Tomorrow morning you will be arraigned, and once the arraignment is over you will be transferred to Auburn State Prison in upstate New York. There you will reside until a trial date has been set, and during your incarceration, which we hope won't be too long, the police will prepare their case for the District Attorney's Office, and I will be working on your defence.'

'Trial? I'm going to trial?'

'Yes, Mr Vaughan, most definitely. The trial date will be more than likely sometime in the next four to six months . . . meanwhile you should try to remember everything that happened that morning. My initial thoughts are that we should try for a plea of manslaughter, and if that does not hold water then we should attempt to plea bargain for a charge of second-degree murder.' He smiled sincerely. 'That way, as you know, we will avoid the death penalty.'

I couldn't speak. I looked at Billick as he closed up his case and rose from his chair.

'So until we speak again tomorrow, you take good care of yourself, Mr Vaughan.'

Billick smiled again, and then he walked across the room and knocked twice. The orderly beyond opened the door and let him out. He paused for a moment, looking through the bars that traversed the narrow window, and then he vanished.

A few minutes later the orderly came in and asked if I wanted to remain seated, or return to the bed.

I didn't move, didn't say a word, so he shackled me to the chair right where I sat.

Paul Hennessy was there, Ben Godfrey too, as was Joyce Spragg, Aggie Boyle and her sister, other people whose faces I vaguely recognized from the St Joseph's Writers' Forum. They were silent and expressionless, seated there in the gallery of the Brooklyn City Courthouse on Tuesday morning. The proceedings were perfunctory and brief. Thomas Billick said almost nothing in response to the representative from the District Attorney's Office, Albert Oswald. I was called before the judge, a man who looked no older than forty, a man who peered down at me with an air of condescending disdain. The D.A.'s representative, all three-piece suit and patent leather shoes, waved his hand in a dismissive fashion when Billick implied that the charge of first-degree murder was yet to be established.

'The charge has been raised and recorded,' Oswald said. 'While the defendant remains on remand in Auburn State there will be ample time for the Public Defender to present any information to the District Attorney, Your Honor.'

The judge nodded and indicated that the arraignment was at a close. 'I have heard everything I need to hear. Defendant is bound over to the custody of the Auburn State Correctional Facility until such time as a trial date is set.' He smiled nonchalantly. 'Mr Billick?'

Billick looked up nervously.

'If there are any questions regarding the veracity or validity of the charge as stated here then I suggest you present yourself for plea bargaining at the Office of the District Attorney with all due haste. The court will not be tardy in the execution of its duty. A great deal of time and money will be spent in the jury selection process and in preparation for trial. I will not take kindly to any unexpected surprises regarding charges or defense . . . you understand?'

Billick glanced at me and then nodded at the judge.

'Mr Billick?'

'Yes, Your Honor,' Billick said. 'Of course . . . everything will be arranged in a prompt and orderly fashion.'

'Well, I do hope so,' the judge replied. 'It is, after all, a man's life that's at stake, is it not?'

Two court officials stepped forward and hand-cuffed me. They turned to lead me away.

'Be strong!' a voice called from the gallery, and looking up I saw Paul Hennessy standing there, tears running down his face, his hands gripping the bar ahead of him.

I bowed my head. I was led away, Billick a few paces behind me.

I could not look back at my friends.

★ ★ ★

By Christmas Day of 1952 I had lost my name.

By the end of January I had forsaken my identity.

A month later I had ceased to be a human being.

From some vague recess of my mind I recalled words from de Tocqueville's *Democracy in America*: 'We felt as if we traversed catacombs; there were a thousand living beings, and yet it was desert solitude.'

He wrote these words about Auburn State Prison, Cayuga County, somewhere in a wilderness of humanity between Buffalo and Syracuse.

Upon arrival, that night at the latter end of November, my head had been shaved. My clothes were taken from me, and then we stood naked – myself and twelve others – as a doctor roughly and cursorily examined us. We were led through to an open courtyard circumvented by high walls, and in the bitter chill of dawn we were instructed to stand – legs apart, arms horizontal at shoulder height – and we were sprayed with a fine, acrid delousing powder. For a further thirty minutes we stood there, the acidic burning in nostrils and eyes, the urge to scream, to cry, to faint where we stood. One man did, a narrow-shouldered bald-headed man, and an orderly beat him with a stick until he stood once more.

From there we were walked down a long, stone-tiled corridor and into a shower-house. The water came like ice needles, stinging my skin until I felt blood was being drawn. Each of us was given a low-ceilinged white-painted room, colloquially known as 'the cubes', and on a thin horsehair mattress I lay shivering and stunned until sleep caught me unawares and made my nightmare vanish for the briefest of times.

My first day: a premonition of everything that was to come. We stayed within those narrow four walls, nothing to see but white paintwork and the weak shifts between daylight and darkness through a high porthole in the outer wall. Three weeks. No movement but for pacing the seven and half feet from one side to the next. Food came on a metal tray through a slot in the lower half of the door, and each time the narrow 'mailbox' grate was drawn, each time it was once again slammed shut, I felt that metallic clash reverberate through every bone, every nerve, every sinew of my body. Spiritually, mentally, emotionally I was elsewhere. I walked with Bridget, I sat at my desk and wrote a book for Arthur Morrison, something that possessed spirit and passion and human dynamics. I felt Joseph Calvin Vaughan slipping silently away. I watched him go. He did not turn back, for to turn back would have been to see me, to perhaps take pity on me enough to return. This he could never risk, and so he remained selectively blind.

After three weeks we were transferred to three-man cells. I was housed with a pair of brothers, Jack and William Randall, armed robbers from Odessa in Schuyler County. Eleven months apart in age, their resemblance to one another was

501

uncanny: blunt, porcine features, squint eyes, shoulders hunched forward as they walked, like gunfighters out of time and place.

I spoke to them of my innocence.

Jack Randall smiled, he placed his hand firmly on my shoulder. 'In here,' he said, 'there's only two types of people . . . the orderlies and the innocents.'

William laughed enthusiastically, and proceeded to punch me on the shoulder.

'We seen these places all too many times,' he said. 'You get used to it. It has its own ways and means of doing things, and as long as you sit tight and mind yourself you'll be fine.' He grinned heartily. 'Me an' Jack here, we'll keep an eye on you . . . make sure some brute from down the corridor doesn't make you his pony, eh?'

They laughed again, looking at one another, as if each was a reflection of his brother, and I closed down a little further, a little closer inside, and I pulled what little of myself remained tight to my chest.

Thomas Billick came in the third week of February. I was taken from my cell and shackled, both wrists and ankles. I walked a long way down featureless and identical corridors, shuffling awkwardly between two wordless orderlies. The chain between my ankles dragged heavily, and the metal bands cut into the skin of my heels. I was shown into a narrow poorly lit room, and there – seated quietly against the wall – was my defense lawyer. He looked as ill at ease and nervous as a man could be.

'You are well?' he asked unnecessarily.

I was pushed down in a chair facing Billick, and then the two orderlies stepped back and exited the room. The harsh grating of an external bar, the jangle of keys in the lock, the sense that everywhere I turned there was yet another means of preventing my free movement.

'So – we have good news,' Billick said. 'The District Attorney has heard our presentation of the case, and has agreed to accept a plea of guilty on the count of second-degree murder.' Billick opened his attaché case and removed a sheaf of papers. 'Second-degree murder is considered intentional but neither premeditated nor planned.' He looked up to see if I was paying attention. 'It says here that such a crime is not committed in the reasonable heat of passion, but is caused by the offender's obvious lack of concern for human life.' Billick smiled like he was giving a birthday gift to a small child. 'That means no death penalty, Joseph . . . isn't that good news?'

I lowered my head, looked down at the cuffs on my wrists.

'So all you need to do is plead guilty to second-degree murder, and not only will we remove any risk of a capital trial, we will also limit the length of the proceedings dramatically. A judge is always more favorable when such a case is presented. It is far less expensive to the state and the county when a straightforward plea of guilty is entered—'

I looked up at Billick. 'But I am not guilty, Mr Billick . . . I am not guilty of any kind of murder, and I will not plead guilty to something I have not done.'

Billick looked at first shocked, and then he became flustered and agitated. 'I don't think you fully comprehend the gravity of your situation, Mr Vaughan. There is a very strong case against you, and I would not be remiss in my trust of confidentiality if I told you that there are no other lines of investigation currently ongoing. The police have exhausted all their inquiries as to any other party that may or may not have been involved—'

'Meaning what?'

Billick cleared his throat. 'Meaning that your trial date has been set for March thirtieth, little more than a month from now . . . and you *will* stand trial for this murder, Mr Vaughan, let there be no mistake about it.'

I tried to raise my hands but the shackles prevented me. 'I don't understand what's happening here, Mr Billick . . . someone killed Bridget, someone came into the house where I was living and killed the woman I loved—'

Billick was shaking his head. 'To all intents and purposes, Mr Vaughan, that person was you.'

'No,' I said forcefully. I felt the swell of fear and anger in my chest. Once again I tried to move my arms, to somehow emphasize what I was saying. 'I didn't kill anyone, for God's sake!' I shouted. 'I didn't fucking kill anyone, Mr Billick . . . what the hell is it going to take to get someone to understand what's happening here. This is insane! This is a travesty of justice! I want to talk to someone . . . anyone. Go find Paul Hennessy. Ben Godfrey! Go talk to Ben Godfrey . . . he will tell you that I couldn't have done something like this. I have money, Mr Billick. I have three thousand dollars—'

Billick shook his head again. 'You *had* three thousand dollars, Mr Vaughan.'

I stopped suddenly. I frowned. 'What do you mean? What the hell are you talking about? I have three thousand dollars from the sale of my mother's house.'

'An account which has now been frozen by the state, Mr Vaughan. That money is no more at your disposal than it is at mine.'

'You can't do that! What the hell gives you the right to do that?'

'Me?' Billick asked. '*I* am not doing anything, Mr Vaughan. I am not the one who has charged you with a gravely serious crime . . . the crime of murder, and whether that murder was planned or not, whether it was first or second degree, it was still murder. The murder of a helpless and innocent young girl. A pregnant girl, Mr Vaughan.'

I felt the blood drain from my face. I saw their faces. All of them. Virginia Perlman, Laverna Stowell . . . all of them. I heard their voices somewhere. I glanced over my shoulder, half expecting to see one of them there, white and beatific, as innocent as Bridget, as Alexandra . . . and I believed that I might have been the envoy of Death.

My father, my mother, Alex . . . ten little girls . . . Elena, Gunther . . .

And now Bridget . . . consigned to the same fate, and that fate delivered by the very same hand.

I knew, I knew with everything I owned, that her death had been my doing. Indirectly yes, but I was nevertheless to blame. This was my punishment for what I had done in Augusta Falls. I knew that Haynes Dearing would be the only one to truly understand, but Haynes Dearing would be the very last person to come to my assistance.

I started to cry. I leaned forward and felt my chest heave. I was wracked with such pain I could barely breathe.

Billick rose from his chair and backed up toward the door. He knocked on it without turning, and within a moment I heard the grating of bars, the keys in the lock, and the orderlies released him. I looked up as the door closed once again, and Billick was there – his small white face peering in at me through the narrow porthole.

'Get me out of here!' I screamed at him. 'GET ME THE FUCK OUT OF HERE!'

Billick's face disappeared.

There was silence in the room but for my own labored breathing.

There was nothing I could do, no-one I could speak to.

I knew then – without doubt or hesitation – that the end was rapidly approaching.

My trial began on March thirtieth, 1953 at five minutes past nine in the morning. The charge was of murder in the first degree, for having refused to plead guilty to second degree I was at the mercy of the District Attorney's Office. It was a Monday, and the presiding judge was the same man who had overseen my arraignment. His name was Marvin Baxter. He seemed older than I recalled him, his hair cut scalp-close, his eyes set too far apart, his mouth a thin and bloodless line of determination and austerity. Prosecutor Oswald stood silent and determined, looking at me just once as I entered the court. Everything seemed ponderous and oppresive, and yet somehow insubstantial, as if with a wave of my hand I could have vanished it all away like a pall of mist. But I could not move my hands. They were cuffed to the arms of the chair.

Billick said little, raised few objections, even when the words spoken about me could only have been uttered about some other man entirely. The entirety of my past seemed to unfold from the lips of people I had never met, never spoken to. They talked about my mother, the death of my father; they spoke about how I had discovered the dead body of a little girl on a hilltop. They mentioned it in passing, as if it was nothing at all, but I watched the faces of the jury and they seemed intense and serious and very alert. They carried in boxes of papers, things I had written, and they read those things aloud as if they were references of my character. Questions were left hanging in the air like ghosts.

There was no word of Haynes Dearing, and he did not come to rescue me.

The days drew forward, one after the other, and at night I was remanded to a cell beneath the courthouse, lightless and dank, its very walls impregnated with despair and degradation.

Later, I could recall little of the proceedings: the back and forth of questions, the awkward cross-examinations, the appearance on the witness stand of Aggie Boyle, her sister, of Joyce Spragg and Letitia Brock. Bridget's parents came too. Her father spoke of his religious fervor, his commitment to the Lord, his vigilant adherence to the Ten Commandments, his hopes for his daughter, an only child, and behind me, three rows back and to the left, the hushed courtroom listened to the stifled sobbing of Bridget's mother.

The better part of six weeks dissolved without seam or juncture between one day and the next. During the weekend I was returned to Auburn and held alone in solitary confinement. A juror contracted influenza, and between April sixteenth and twenty-second, Judge Marvin Baxter initiated an adjournment. We returned on the twenty-third, and it was then that I began the first of four days of questioning at the stand.

I believed my soul had been wrenched away to some other place. I believed in nothing but a pure will to survive, beneath that the certainty of my own innocence. From the stand I could see Paul Hennessy and Ben Godfrey, other faces I knew from Brooklyn, and in the final week of the trial Reilly Hawkins appeared. It was then that I finally folded beneath the weight of what had happened. The past had come to find me in New York. A past I had lived to outlive, and yet now a past that would see me swallowed whole.

I cried on that stand. I held my heart in my hands and showed it to Judge Marvin Baxter, to Albert Oswald from the District Attorney's Office, but they did not believe me.

On Tuesday, May twelfth, 1953, a jury of my peers – eight men and four women who knew nothing of truth but my name – returned from their deliberations.

My heart, to that point nothing more than a small dark stone in my chest, was a red fireball of tension.

'The defendant will rise.'

I gathered what was left of me together as best I could, and with the help of the orderlies I somehow gained my feet.

'Has the jury reached a verdict?'

Blood thundered in the veins at my temples.

A cold sense of inner emptiness was suddenly replaced with abject and hopeless terror.

'Yes, Your Honor.' The foreman rose and stood silent.

There were words, so many words I wanted to say. Those words clawed up from the base of my throat, but as I swallowed I lost them all. My eyes wide, my face drawn and bloodless, my shackled hands grasped the rail ahead of me as if it was a life-raft.

'Very good. On the charge of murder in the first degree, that the defendant, Joseph Calvin Vaughan, did willfully murder the person of Bridget Sarah McCormack on Thursday the twentieth November, 1952, does the jury find the defendant guilty or not guilty?'

Heart like a hammer, crashing against an anvil.

The foreman, face like a Hallowe'en pumpkin, eyes incapable of looking at me even though he knew I was there, cleared his throat. The clerk of the court crossed the narrow walkway between the bench and the aisles, and took a folded slip of paper from the foreman.

He returned slowly, each step redolent of a funeral march.

He did not look at me either. None of them could. I thought to turn back, to look over my shoulder at Hennessy, at Ben Godfrey, at Reilly Hawkins. My mind screamed for release, for forgiveness for whatever I had done to deserve such a thing, but the only sound was the thin crackle as the judge unfolded the paper and looked down at the verdict.

'We, the jury, find the defendant, Joseph Calvin Vaughan . . . guilty.'

I stopped breathing.

I felt my knees collapse beneath me.

I started to scream, to cry, to sob, holding onto the railing as the orderlies tried to prise me away. I remember shouting at the top of my voice. 'It wasn't me . . . it wasn't me! It was him! The same one who killed the children . . . he killed Bridget! He killed Bridget!'

'Clerk!' Judge Marvin Baxter shouted above the tumult of noise. 'Clerk . . . clear the court at once!'

I heard those words. Beyond that there was little else to hear but a rushing sound in my ears, a rushing sound that filled my body, my mind, my soul.

And then there was a feather; a single white feather that drifted across my line of vision and disappered in a ray of light from the window.

I was going to die. That much I knew.

I prayed He would come quickly, quietly, work-manlike, methodical . . .

I prayed that Death would come soon, cold and unfeeling . . .

I saw myself as a child, standing there in the yard amidst the scrubbed earth and dry topsoil, amidst the carpetweed and chickweed phlox and wintergreen, but this time He would be visiting with me.

Soon now, soon enough, walking down . . . there He goes . . . no horse tracks, nor those of a bicycle . . .

Death would come to take me.

In my dreams I can walk all the way to Georgia.

In my dreams the walls hold me no better than mist or smoke, and I pass through them without effort or restraint, and the land rises, and the trees bank left and right away toward the horizon, and around my face is the orange haze of boxwood leaf miner-flies, and my spirit is adamantine and unyielding, and my thoughts – adagio and peaceful – belong to a time before my father, before the ten little girls, before Elena and Gunther Kruger, before Alex and Bridget and Auburn, Cayuga County.

In my dreams I am a free man.

The sky grows. The perspective of telegraph wires, birds like clusters of semibreves on staves, eyes winking, cawing their music, and bunches of withered grass and earth swollen with rain, and the sound of a dog in the distance pleading for home.

Wood cabins and ramshackle outhouses, and rusted signs reading *Mobil* and *Chevron* and *Red Parrot Diesel*; stooped men with heavy loads, yellow dirt, the smell of sowbelly pork, and clothes paraded along ropes to dry, snapping in the wind like the colors of some ghost legion, and the sound of horses, of feet pressing down on mud riges as

I walk, and flatbed tracks like the footprints of time, and the sweep of some lone silence that echoes the past, and the specter of fog, the haunt of fine rain against my face like varnish for skin, and I am nearly home . . . all the way home . . . all the way home . . .

And then I wake.

I remember Auburn.

A slow-motion descent into darkness, the sounds and smells of humanity divested of all value and identity. The stench of sweat and earth, the rolling interminable machine of men, the shackled lines of bowed shoulders and hunched backs, the changle of hoes and picks against unforgiving earth and stones and rocks; the sleepless nights, the hacking rasps of phlegmy, tuberculous chests, the swells and aches of dislocated joints and torn muscles; the creaks of cots and hammocks, the rush of rain against corrugated roof and thin wooden walls; the squeal of rats, the scritch of bugs, the hypnotic chant of cicadas. Trapped in the belly of the beast, and the beast was black and ravenous and never satiated.

I remember Auburn.

The whispers and moans of men admidst nightmares where guilt buried deep was never assuaged; the weals and welts of rawhide whips against exposed flesh, against sun-scorched skin, against broken spirits; the smash and rush of morning, the unforgiving thunder of summer, the waterlogged floors, the stench of rot, the fetid reek of undergrowth swollen with stagnant water; the filthy clothes, the absence of nourishment, the darkness, the pain, the longing, the despair.

I remember Auburn.

The box: standing out in the middle of the yard, too short for a man to sit straight, nor wide enough to lie on his side, knees against his chest. Twenty-four hours. Hunched down tight, forehead to kneecaps, the spine arched painfully, the roof against the back of the head. Louvers on the front, angled upward to let the sun beat through without mercy. No water. No words. No release.

Twenty-four hours and a man cried until salt lined his eyelids and stung like acid. Thirty-six hours and he heaved and retched and screamed through some awkward madness. Drag him out and he'd lie there for three or four hours before he could straighten his body. Escape attempts. Badmouthing. An orderly who took a dislike to someone, and he'd say 'In the box', and someone would disappear, return a different man.

I remember Auburn.

The Scales of Justice, they called it. Man had wooden slats bound to his legs so he could not bend. Burried to his thighs in the ground, earth packed hard, unforgiving, no hope of movement. Arms extended out from the shoulders, in each hand a billy can half-filled with a pint of water. Stayed like that, arms outstretched for two, three, four hours at a time. Spill the water and the time would start over.

'An hour on the Scales,' someone would say, and he'd be out there digging his own hole before the trustees bound his legs. Legend had it a man had stood for seven hours all-told. Slept forever after with his arms outstretched, didn't speak for nine weeks, and when he did he said, 'Billy-can, billy-can, billy-can' over and over until that became his name. Billy Can from Cayuga County. Billy Can from Hell.

Billick came one time. Looked pleased with himself. 'No death sentence,' he said. 'You're a very lucky man, Mr Vaughan. Your jury did not vote for the death sentence, but for life imprisonment. Count your blessings, eh?'

'Life means life,' they told me, over and over and over again.

'Life means life, boy,' they said, until it echoed in my ears, reverberated through my mind like the memory of the man I'd once been.

Images of Bridget, of Alexandra, of Elena, of my mother.

Images of some other pale existence that faded even as my thoughts touched them. Had to stop myself thinking. Think of them again and they would disappear forever.

I remember Auburn.

First month folded like a blanket around me, cocooned within. Second month like a straitjacket, tied tight, arms around my waist, buckled at the back. Third and fourth like a shroud so heavy I

516

could barely breathe. After that the months blended seamlessly one into another, claustrophobic, intense, unforgiving.

'Can't break a man's spirit,' Jack Randall told me. 'Something inside a man you can never snap. Break every single bone in his body and you'll still find something in there fighting back.'

Believed Jack Randall until he and his brother attempted to escape.

Late November 1959. Cloudless sky, the moon high. Gentle breeze from the south that crept between the cots and seemed somehow refreshing. Memory of a different time, a different place.

Sound of cicadas in the field beyond the wire. Jack and William Randall. Faces blacked with dirt, out through a hole in the floor and crawling along the earth. Made it fifteen yards along the edge of the compound and they were seen.

All hell broke loose. Dogs. Orderlies. Trustees. Searchlights. Mayhem and madness breaking forth like a thunderstorm.

Built another box they did. Built them side by side. A week inside for each man.

Whatever they might have possessed, whatever Jack Randall held inside of him, it was broken in half and stamped into nothing.

William slit his wrists in January of 1960.

Jack died of loneliness in the spring.

I remember Auburn . . . most of all the thought that followed me every moment of every day: that

I knew who killed Bridget, and that I knew why. I had no name, no face, no awareness of his identity, but he was there – in my dreams and when I woke, pressing his dark soul against me as a reminder of my betrayal.

CHAPTER 28

I am here for life. Until my body yields up its full and final breath.

Four walls, a stone floor, an iron bunk, a changeless day folding into yet another of the same color and rhythm.

Here for the rest of my natural life.

Joseph Calvin Vaughan, the murderer.

Through all those years I never heard from Thomas Billick again. I waited patiently through June, July, August, September. I followed the lines, the rules and regulations; I bided my time, but by Christmas I seemed to forget what I was waiting for.

In the New Year of 1954 I did hear word of the outside world, and it was Hennessy who came, Paul Hennessy, and he sat with his face in his hands in the narrow visitation room, and for a long while he could not look at me without choking back his tears.

Ironic, but I spent much of our time together consoling him. I asked him of Brooklyn, of where he lived, of the work he was doing, of his new friends, his plans.

'You must write,' he told me. 'You must write everything, Joseph . . . write down everything that happened and give it to me. I will make sure someone sees it. I will take it out there and make people understand the terrible thing that has happened to you. You must do this, Joseph . . . if not for yourself, then you must do it for me. I cannot go on knowing that nothing is being done to help you.'

'Nothing can be done,' I told him. 'What do you think will happen? According to everyone it was a fair and just trial. I could not defend myself. I could not prove where I was in those two hours that morning. They saw what they wanted to see, they believed what they were told to believe, and now I am here for the rest of my life.'

'No,' Hennessy insisted. 'I can't leave it this way. It's taken me six months to summon the courage to come and see you. I have spoken to the police. I wrote a letter to the governor of New York . . . I've done everything I can. No-one wants to listen. No-one cares what happens to you, Joseph . . . no-one but me. I *need* you to write it down. I need you to give me something I can use to help you.'

I told him once again that I could do nothing. I told him the same thing every month until the end of the year. Finally I gave in; I began to write. Late at night I scribbled words on the coarse paper that was used to wrap produce in the kitchens, and each month Hennessy would come, each month he would smuggle out a handful of folded sheets and would laboriously type them.

I began at the beginning. I started with the death of my father, and I detailed the events of my life.

One thing I chose not to write. One event, one memory. One thing that will stay with me until the moment of my death, and then when He comes perhaps I will tell Him, and He can exact His judgement.

Three or four pages a month, year after year, Hennessy pleading with me to write faster, to detail only those things that pertained to Bridget's death. But I could not. I had decided to tell the world who I was, and from this they could choose what they wished to believe.

I remember the words of my mother, a day in Augusta Falls a thousand years before.

'Don't stop,' she said. 'Don't ever stop writing. This is the way the world will find out who you are.'

Three days after the killing of John F. Kennedy, a cold November in 1963, I wrote my final words. The Randalls were dead. I believed I was also.

I was spent, empty, exhausted.

I believed my fate would pass into hands other than my own.

I had been in Auburn for ten and a half years. I was thirty-six years old, merely a year younger than my father when the rheumatic fever stopped his heart.

Perhaps I was nothing more than an echo of

him, and that echo would fade quietly into silence, and through the silence I would walk to meet the end of myself.

It would seem fitting; above and beyond all else it would seem fitting.

Encapsulated within those pages was a life.

Perhaps the worth of such a life was measured by the weight of paper, the quantity of ink, the depth of imprint on each individual page.

Perhaps it was represented by the significance of those words, the emotions they evoked and engendered.

Perhaps there was no worth at all save what I myself believed – and I believed there would have been no other way to convey the loss and despair that such events created.

My life began, it continued, and now it seemed resolved to closure.

If those words were all that remained, then so be it.

Perhaps some of us come back . . . perhaps some us will have learned enough to make a difference, to influence things for the better . . . to stand and watch . . . to wait until the moment is right, and then act . . .

And despite appearances, despite all indications to the contrary, despite reticence for fear of what others might think, I still felt we all possessed this quiet belief.

A quiet belief in angels.

★   ★   ★

Later, much later, Paul Hennessy told me of the events that followed.

He worked furiously, laboring often without rest for hours at a time. He filled page after page, neglecting his friends, watching his own life dissolve around him, and then in January of 1965 he travelled out to Manhattan to see Arthur Morrison.

Morrison, it seemed, received the book he had always asked of me, a book of spirit and passion.

Hennessy chose the title, and in June of the same year *A Quiet Belief In Angels* was published.

He came to see me in May of '66. The world beyond the walls of Auburn State was a different world. Men had touched the moon; a war raged in some South-East Asian jungle, a country called Vietnam, and America was sending tens of thousands of troops out there to lose their lives; civil rights marches led by a man called King, a man Hennessy himself had spoken of a thousand years before, resulted in that same man being jailed for speaking the truth; Kennedy was dead, a nation still mourned.

Hennessy sat facing me in the narrow confines of a visitation booth. Through the wire mesh he seemed distant, almost unreachable, but the words he spoke came through clear and succinct.

'An appeal has been lodged with the United States Supreme Court,' he said. As he spoke he suppressed his tears, but I did not know if they were tears of anticipated vindication, or tears for the seeming hopelessness of his task. 'Your book has sold and sold and sold,' he went on. His face was blurred. Everything was made from shadows and highlights, insubstantial, almost without definition. 'They can't print copies fast enough, Joseph. Morrison had to close his presses down and send the platens to a company in Rochester. People are up in arms. They are asking whether this book is fiction . . . they can't believe that such a travesty of justice could occur in America. Something will happen, Joseph, something will defintely happen.'

'I am disappearing,' I said. 'I don't know what day it is . . . I cannot remember how long I have been here.' I felt my face crease with an awkward smile; tension in the muscles that told me this was an unfamiliar expression.

'You can't give up hope,' Hennessy whispered. His voice was urgent, insistent, and as I watched his face I remembered Cecily Bryan, the nights we spent at the St Joseph's Writers' Forum, nights walking through Manhattan singing 'Days of '49' and drinking Calvert.

'I have done a terrible thing,' I said, and I closed my eyes weakly.

'You have done nothing,' he replied. 'That's the whole point, Joseph . . . that's the whole point . . . all the work we have done to get the truth out there, and we have succeeded against all odds. People know, Joseph, they know what happened. They can see how this thing was a terrible, terrible mistake—'

I rose slowly from my chair. I stood looking down at the only friend I had. 'I have nothing to say,' I told him. 'I am unable to feel hope, I am unable to see anything but what I have here . . .' My voice cracked, and I felt the weight of the past twelve years bear down upon me.

'You can't give up hope!' Hennessy insisted. 'You can't, Joseph, you can't . . .'

His voice faded as I walked away.

An orderly let me out of the door and into the corridor. I tried not to look at him. If I was seen to cry I would be sent to the box.

Hennessy came back the following day. They came to fetch me but I would not go. They told me later he had left a letter. I did not read it.

I lay on my cot and watched the shadow of bars on the ceiling.

Weeks unfolded into months. More letters came, more visits from Paul. I could not bear to see him. I lost track of time. I recognized the difference between night and day, but beyond that little else.

'Vaughan! Joseph Vaughan!'

My name was being called from somewhere out along the gantry. I turned onto my side and closed my eyes.

'Joseph Vaughan . . . out to see the Warden. Joseph Vaughan!'

I eased myself up and sat on the edge of my cot. My heart started beating more rapidly. I could not ask myself what was happening. I felt afraid, so horribly afraid.

An orderly stood before the gate. He nodded down the gantry. 'Number eight cell . . . open her up!'

The lock released, the gate was drawn back.

'On your feet, Vaughan. You're seeing the Warden.'

I hunted for my shoes. I worked my feet into them and stood cautiously. I felt sweat break out on my forehead.

'Move yourself, for Christ's sake!'

I started to walk; I stumbled and grabbed the bars for support. The orderly reached out his hand and took hold of my upper arm, pulled me out onto the gantry and shouted for the cell to close. It thundered behind me, and already I was being hurried along to the stairwell at the end.

Minutes later I stood for some interminable time in a windowless corridor. I stood silently, without moving. At the far end two trustees watched me through a grille in the door. Eventually the door behind me opened, and I was told to step through. I was faced with an outer room ahead of the Warden's office. My heart trip-hammered, missed beats, seemed too large for my chest. I closed my eyes and swallowed. I waited for something awful to occur.

A young woman came through. She smiled tentatively, but I could return nothing. 'This way, Vaughan,' she said, and her voice seemed strange.

I realized I had not heard a woman speak for more than a decade.

Warden Forrester. Imposing in size, in reputation. A brutal fist of a man. Eyes like headlights beneath thick brows, his nose askew to one side as if prizefighting was in his heritage. He rose from behind his desk and walked toward me.

'Joseph Vaughan,' he said, and the voice that emerged from his lips was altogether misleading. There was something almost compassionate in his tone.

'Yes, sir,' I replied.

'You have a guardian angel, it appears.' He smiled, turned to the woman and asked her to fetch me a chair.

'Sit down, Vaughan, sit down.'

Forrester returned to his desk. He perched on the edge of it.

I sat down also, looked up at him.

'I understand that you have been unwilling to receive any visitors or open any mail forwarded to you.'

I nodded. 'Yes, sir.'

'Perhaps you should have done, Vaughan.' Forrester turned and gathered a pile of envelopes from his desk.

'The majority of them come from a man called Hennessy, others from a certain Arthur Morrison. You know these people?'

'Yes, sir, I do.'

'And might I ask, Mr Vaughan, why you have

been so unwilling to receive any contact from the outside world?'

I cleared my throat. I blinked as if shedding sleep from my eyes. 'I don't know, sir. I . . . I felt it better to be unaware of what was happening outside.'

Forrester nodded. He started to leaf through the letters. 'This one here,' he said, 'would have told you than an appeal had been lodged with the United States Supreme Court in May of 1966.' Forrester put the letter at the back of the pile and selected another. 'This one from November of the same year would have told you that the Supreme Court had acknowledged receipt of the original transcripts of your case and were studying them. And from January of 1967 we have a letter, again from this Paul Hennessy, that the Supreme Court had agreed to a session and were ready to inter-view a certain Thomas Billick, a Judge Marvin Baxter, a number of key witnesses that were called for the prosecution.' Forrester looked up. I believed he expected a response from me. I had nothing to say.

'This one comes from the Georgia State District Attorney's Office. He has some very scathing things to say about the way in which your defence was handled . . . and here, from two weeks ago, we have another letter from Mr Hennessy to say that your appeal was being reviewed and they should have an answer within a week.'

Forrester dropped the stack of letters on the

table. He steepled his hands together in his lap and smiled. 'That answer arrived this morning, Mr Vaughan. Today, Monday, February twentieth, 1967, the United States Supreme Court has ruled that your conviction was based on nothing but circumstantial evidence. They have set a new trial date, Mr Vaughan.'

I stopped breathing. I felt the blood rush to my head, and it was all I could to remain seated.

'Do you understand what this means, Mr Vaughan?' Forrester asked.

I stared at him – speechless, without any real comprehension present in my mind.

'It means that your previous conviction has been overturned by the highest court in America, that there will be another trial.'

I started to cry.

Forrester nodded at the young woman and she came forth with a handkerchief. When I took it from her she seemed to touch my hand for a moment longer than was required. I looked up at her, and through my tears she seemed vague and indistinct. She smiled with such sympathy and feeling that it was impossible to respond.

Forrester leaned forward and placed his hand on my shoulder.

Thirteen years and nine months.

I was thirty-nine years old.

At ten minutes after four that same afternoon I was led out through corridors and offices that I had never seen before. I saw windows where there were no bars. I saw more sky than I could have ever remembered.

I was told to shower, to change into a clean shirt, denim pants, a cotton jacket. I was given shoes with laces. I was told to sign things, and those things were placed in folders that bore my name on the front.

I stood in a small room for a quarter of an hour. There were two doors, one to my left, the other ahead of me. Each was open, neither was locked. People walked through, some smiled, others merely nodded, and with each new face I imagined they would stop, look at me, frown awkwardly, and begin to explain that there had been a terrible mistake.

I believed I might wake, and understand that I had dreamed.

Eight minutes after five a man appeared through the door to my left.

'You're Vaughan, right?'

I nodded, tried to smile.

'We're here to transport you to temporary holding. You're up for a retrial, starts the day after tomorrow.'

I said nothing. No words remained. I followed directions as they were given. I answered questions when they were asked. I travelled silently in the back of a car, still handcuffed, still disbelieving, and was shown to another cell in another wing in another facility.

The edges blurred. I did not have to see them as there was always someone there to guide me. I saw Billick again, standing there in the dock answering questions about my original trial. Hennessy was there, Arthur Morrison, others I did not know. People from newspapers, people who wanted to take my photograph. Seemed every day I left the courthouse it was to face a barrage of flashbulbs.

Everything seemed to happen so fast, and then – before I knew it – I was once again being asked to stand, and someone was looking down at me, and someone was telling me that the past meant nothing, that what had happened had been in error, that there were miscarriages of justice, other such things as this. And then he smiled, and he nodded his head, and for a moment he seemed to close his eyes as if relishing what he was going to say, and what he said was 'Joseph Calvin Vaughan, you have been found not guilty of the murder of Bridget McCormack. You are free to go. Bailiff . . . see that the defendant is released.'

An hour later; standing in another office. A man faces me. 'This is your pay, Vaughan.' He hands me a brown envelope. 'Sign this docket here . . . and here . . .'

I sign the paper.

'Dollar-eighty a week,' he says. 'Ain't much, but it'll get you home, eh?'

He turns and disappears through the same door.

531

I open the envelope. Fifty-dollar bills, twenty-four of them, some fives, a couple of ones. Twelve hundred dollars or thereabouts.

'Don't want to make a display of that, Vaughan.'

I look up. Another man is in front of me. He smiles. 'Entirely the wrong place to make that kind of money obvious, wouldn't you say?' He starts laughing. 'Anyways, you're ready?'

'Ready?' I ask.

'To leave,' the man says, something of surprise in his voice. 'You got someone out here to collect you,' he says, and then indicates that I should follow him.

I fold the envelope with the money inside and stuff it into my jacket pocket.

I follow the man, and we walk through another office and down a long corridor. At the end he unlocks the door, steps aside, and before I walk through he extends his hand.

'Do some good out there,' he says, and shakes my hand. 'You understand me?'

I say nothing.

'So go,' he says, and looks to his left.

I follow his line of sight, and there – rising from a plain deal chair against the wall – is Hennessy.

CHAPTER 29

Manhattan was a vision from some other world. The cars, the people, the clothes; it seemed the universe had tilted on some unidentified axis and everything had changed.

I had changed too, perhaps irreversibly.

We drove that day, drove all the way from Auburn to Manhattan. Highway 20, Interstate 81 through Binghamton, southeast into Scranton, Pennsylvania; Interstate 380 to Stroudsburg, east through Morristown, Paterson, back across the New York county line and through the northern tip of New Jersey.

Sometimes we stopped merely because I had to. I stood at the side of the road and watched the horizon, and I could barely breathe. Hennessy stood beside me. He said nothing, merely holding my arm in case I fell. I was glad he didn't speak, for he seemed to understand that I could not have absorbed what I was seeing and also communicate. I felt lost, without anchor, and each time I closed my eyes and opened them once more I believed I would see dun-colored walls, the stain of damp; believed I would smell that stench of enclosed humanity – the sweat, the frustration, the madness. I came out of the catacombs into daylight, and the daylight burned impressions on my eyes that I knew I would recall for the rest of my life. Fields, ramshackle cabins, some clustered together, others further apart, as if randomly scattered by an unseen hand; cows and horses, grain elevators standing high and proud like temples to the land; acres of milo, maize and sorghums; railroad tracks that ran straight and true for hundreds of miles every which way I looked; all of it vast and awesome and breathtaking.

We drove on, stopped once at a roadside diner where I took a seat in the furthest corner from the door, my back to the wall. Each time someone crossed the room and entered the bathroom I watched them, and when they exited I watched them once more until they were safely ensconced at their chosen table.

'It's okay,' Hennessy kept assuring me, and I would nod, try to smile, and watch the people some more.

Hennessy ordered eggs, bacon, hash browns. I ate slowly, but I ate all of my plate and much of his. As we left I felt the rush of nausea, and I turned to retch and heave everything I had eaten in the car lot ahead of the diner. I was used to boiled potatoes, thin strips of boiled beef, oatmeal, sowbelly and collard greens. My body was not prepared for such a meal. Hennessy returned for a cup of black coffee, and I sat in the passenger seat, the door open, my feet on the tarmac. I watched the people come and go, watched them closely. Realized I was looking for someone I would never recognize.

It was late when we arrived in Stuyvesant, Brooklyn. The streets were as bright as day, sodium yellow lamps, neon signs, brightly illuminated shopfronts and store windows.

I followed Hennessy along unfamiliar sidewalks to a three-storey brownstone walk-up. Second floor, overlooking the new world, he had a comfortable apartment. He showed me his own room, a smaller room facing it where a bed had already been prepared. I stood for a moment, and then I turned toward him. I held out my arms, I hugged him, held him tight enough to stop him breathing, and then I walked into the room and lay down on the mattress. I slept with my clothes on, and when I woke it was the evening of the following day, and Hennessy had removed my shoes. Beside the mattress was a small cardboard box. I opened it cautiously, and what I saw inside stopped my breath in my throat. My newspaper clippings, dusty yellow in color, turned at the edges, and as I leafed through them I saw every face, read every word as if I was right back there. Beneath them was a photograph of Bridget, and as I lifted it from the box I believed the whole world would close up around me and I would suffocate inside. I did not cry to see her. I could not. I had exhausted myself of crying within my first month at Auburn. At the bottom was the letter from the Atlanta Young Story Writers' Adjudication Board. It was a box of dead dreams and distant hopes. And of nightmares. I put the things back inside, closed the box tight, and sat cross-legged on the floor with it in my lap.

'From the room,' Hennessy told me later. 'Aggie Boyle's place. I went there, later, you know? Afterwards—' He looked at me painfully. 'After everything was—'

I smiled at Paul Hennessy and he fell silent.

'It's okay,' I whispered. 'And thank you.'

I stayed inside for two weeks. I saw no-one but Hennessy. The little I said was meaningless and inconsequential. Hennessy tried to make me go out. He spoke of people I should see – Arthur Morrison, even Ben Godfrey. He said that newspapers had called, people from magazines and periodicals. They were asking for interviews. They wanted to speak with the man who had written *A Quiet Belief In Angels*.

I could not face them, and so I did not.

February became March. Leaves began to show on the trees in the street. Often Hennessy would be gone for hours at a time, and I would merely sit at the window and watch cars pass by, the people on the sidewalk. One day I saw a group of children, a young woman at the head of the line, and they held hands and made a crocodile to navigate the junction at the end. I cried when I saw them, and then I stepped away from the window and dared not look outside for another two days.

I felt I was being watched. I felt my every move was preordained and externally determined. Not an hour would pass without me thinking of Bridget, my unborn child, the man that had done this thing. I believed it was the same man, believed he had brought his madness all the way from Georgia, and with this madness he had destroyed everything I possessed. He had stripped away the innocence of my childhood, shown me a dark and depraved world where nightmares became reality, where children were taken from their families, were beaten and abused, raped and killed. This man had haunted Haynes Dearing, possessed his thoughts both waking and sleeping, and Dearing had been compelled to do something that he would otherwise never have considered. Dearing had seen to it that Gunther Kurger hanged. By his own hand, or by the hand of Dearing directly. I did not know what had happened that morning, and did not need to know. I knew that Gunther Kruger had not killed those children. I believed this in my heart and soul. My mother had been wrong. She had thought Gunther guilty, hence she had tried to rout him out by setting fire to the house. I considered that her guilt had been the predominant factor, that perhaps her mind had turned long before the fire, that she believed that ridding

Augusta Falls of Gunther Kruger was the only way to cease the daily reminders of her infidelity.

I believed that the child-killer was still out there, that he had followed me all the way to New York and killed Bridget. I also knew that whatever his motive might have been I would not understand it until I faced him. I asked myself why. Why me? Why had this life been chosen for me? But there was no answer, and I knew such a question would never be resolved until I found him. It was with this ghost that I existed, somewhere in a vague territory between living and dying, afraid to look at the world, afraid that the world would find me. I cared so much for Paul Hennessy; I understood that he had rescued me from Auburn, but I knew he would never comprehend what I had been through. When everything has been taken from you, then what fear is there in losing? There is none, and thus I resigned myself to leaving Brooklyn and returning to Georgia. I was adrift, without any real purpose or reason, and I knew I could not inflict such a thing on the person that cared for me the most.

Georgia stood at the center of my memories like some dark and poisoned tree – its branches wide, sufficient to enclose the sky; Georgia was my home, my nemesis, in some way my imagined salvation.

The third week of March 1967 I told Hennessy what I intended to do.

He shook his head slowly and looked away

toward the window. I followed his line of sight, and there through the glass were the myriad lights of a city I had forgotten the importance of. New York had beckoned me away from Georgia, and here I was wishing to return there. New York had represented the future, represented everything I had ever wished to become, yet here I was heading for the past. Fear sat inside me like a Gordian knot. Whichever way I turned, whichever way I tried to wrestle away from it, it grew tighter and more complex. They were all out there – the little girls, the memory of Elena, Alex, even Bridget – and sometimes, lying awake in the chill half-light of dawn, I would remember their faces, and then their voices would come, and I would understand that the fear would never pass until this thing was done.

'You can't go back, Joseph,' Hennessy told me. There was concern and pity in his voice. Perhaps he'd believed I would return all at once, that seeing New York would awaken me to who I'd once been. Perhaps he imagined I would walk back slowly, one tentative and cautious step after another, a man awkwardly balanced but nevertheless progressing. What he did not understand, perhaps would never understand, was that the Joseph Vaughan he remembered had long since vanished. I tried my best to remain implacable, but the past had a way of folding itself around me; Paul Hennessy was my anchor, and I was set to let go.

539

'I have to,' I said. 'I can't even begin to hope you'll understand—'

'I do understand,' he interjected.

We were seated at his narrow kitchen table. The window beside us was inched open and a breeze made its way through the gap. I shuddered.

'I don't profess to understand what you've been through, Joseph, but I know you as well as anyone. If you follow this thing it will wind up killing you. Let the past go—'

I shook my head, and already I saw in his expression the futility he felt. 'I can't let it go,' I said. I reached out and took his hand. 'I need some money.'

He nodded. 'You have endless amounts of money. The book—'

I interrupted. 'I just need a little money,' I said. 'I don't want a lot. The rest is for you.'

Hennessy laughed nervously. 'I can't possibly—'

'Yes, you can, Paul. The money is yours. Get me a thousand dollars, that's all I need. Get me a thousand dollars and the rest you can keep.'

'A thousand dollars?' he exclaimed. 'You have any idea how many thousands this book has made?'

I shrugged my shoulders. 'I don't want to know, Paul. I don't need to know. Get me a thousand dollars, that's all I ask, and the rest is yours to do with as you wish. This is what I want.'

'As your friend, Joseph . . . Christ, as your friend, I can't let you do this.'

I smiled. 'As my friend, Paul, the only real friend I've got, you *have* to let me do this. I can't stay here. I can't just sit in some apartment in New York while this thing haunts me. This is my life, you see? This is who I am.' I looked away toward the window and closed my eyes. 'Sometimes I think that this is the reason for my existence.'

'So where are you going to go?'

I opened my eyes and looked right back at Hennessy. 'Georgia,' I said. 'Back to Augusta Falls. I have to find Dearing . . . have to find him and make him do this thing with me.'

'And you think he'll be willing to help you?'

'I don't know. I don't even know that he's still alive. If he is I'll find him, and when I do I'll know whether he's willing to help me.'

'And if you get killed yourself? What then?'

'Don't you get the point?' I asked. 'If I die then a least I'll have died trying.'

Hennessy didn't reply for a while. He looked away into some indistinct space between the wall and the floor, and then he turned to me and nodded. 'I'll get the money,' he said.

'Good,' I replied. 'I knew I could count on you.'

Two days later, Friday the twenty-fourth, I stood in the hallway of Hennessy's apartment, at my feet a leather holdall packed with the few things I required. In my pocket was a thousand dollars, a collection of train tickets that would take me all the way back to Georgia, and the photograph of

Bridget McCormack. In an envelope in the bottom of my bag were the letter from Atlanta and the newspaper clippings, all of them in sequence from November of '39 to February a decade later. Lucy Bradford had died nearly twenty years before. Had she lived she would have been twenty-six years old, married perhaps, children of her own, remembering some distant nightmare from her childhood when little girls were taken from her hometown and brutally murdered.

I hugged Paul Hennessy, and I wondered if I would ever see him again.

'I feel I have to—' he started, but I released him and shook my head.

'Joseph—'

'I'm going now,' I said. 'I will call you if I can.'

'If you need money,' he said. 'I can wire more money to you if you need it.'

I smiled, leaned down and picked up my bag. 'Until next time,' I said, and then I turned and made my way quietly out of the apartment and down the stairs to the street.

As I reached the junction I turned and saw Hennessy's face there at the window. He raised his hand once, and then he was gone.

Pennsylvania into Maryland, through Virginia into the Carolinas. Wilmington, Baltimore, Richmond, Raleigh and Columbia. Faces changing as we made each stop. Through the window the expanse of the southeast. The sound of the train all around me, chuntering and thundering and crashing toward the horizon, through daylight into darkness, and out into daylight once more. Trying so hard to sleep, not to think, not to be afraid. Curled up in my sleeper car, each jolt waking me, each blast of the whistle tearing through my dreams and reminding me of where I was going, and why.

Thinking of Haynes Dearing, and what was done that awful day. Thinking of Reilly Hawkins and whether I would find him alive, or buried in a land that he'd never left. Hadn't seen him since the trial, all of fourteen years before. He'd be an old man, and the heart that had been broken by the pretty girl from Berrien County would not have healed. Time did not heal such wounds. Time did nothing but remind you that it was forever running out.

On Sunday the twenty-sixth we crossed the Georgia state line. I remember walking down the length of the train and standing at the window to watch the railtracks as they whipped out behind us like ribbons. I looked toward the horizon and felt the power of memory, and though there was something nostalgic about the images before me, there was also the tremendous sense of loss that Georgia represented. The land had changed, but never changed so much as to be anything other than what it was. This was my childhood, the death of my father, my mother; this was losing; this was the Krugers' kitchen, the smell of bratwurst and bundt cake; this was a Southern wake where my mother expressed her watchful silence, her kohl-rimmed eyes black like antimony. This was the Guardians and child-killer, the flyers posted on fences and gates, the curfews and warnings, the sight of Gunther standing in the darkness and scaring the hell out of me; this was Alex Webber, the schoolhouse, the tablet-arm desks, the soles of white shoes over the brow of a hill; this was ten little dead girls lined up and waiting for their wings. This was Augusta Falls, home of my heart, broken though it was.

I remember all these things in the third-floor hotel room. I ease sideways. My legs are almost without sensation. The blood is drying and clotting. I can smell it – thick and turgid, and I remember that smell from the day I found Virginia Grace Perlman, the day I went out to Fleming and found Esther Keppler. The present echoes the past, and in looking down at myself I wonder if I have not at last become the thing that has haunted me.

I close my eyes for a moment, and then I open them and look at the man facing me.

'I went back for you,' I whisper, and my voice sounds distant and faint.

I close my eyes again.

I want to sleep now, that's all.

I just want to sleep.

CHAPTER 30

Seventeen years I'd been away. Augusta Falls had not so much changed as attempted to become something else. The town was there – everything I remembered – but there were new things. A crescent-shaped motel out beyond the land that had once belonged to Frank Turow's brother; a small department store that already looked as if it had seen better days; Gene Fricker's grain store had vanished utterly, and in its place was a Mobil gas station, bright red pumps standing out in the forecourt like sentinels. Everywhere I looked I could see the ghosts of the past, the indelible footprints of buildings that had once stood. A visitor would never have seen such things, but I knew Augusta Falls, it was part of my being, an intrinsic element of who I was – so much so that new paint and different fencing and altered signs could not change what I recalled.

I stayed in the crescent-shaped motel. I paid in cash and took a key, and then I locked myself inside and slept for the better part of twenty-four hours. When I woke it was the morning of Tuesday, March twenty-eighth, and the motel

546

attendant looked at me with questions in his eyes that he would never have dared to ask. I wondered then if who I was, why I was there, my reason for returning, could be sensed or perceived. Did people look at me and see some personification of the rumors they'd heard about this killing town? Even now, the better part of twenty years later, did they watch their children with a weather eye, ever conscious of the fact that it had happened once, happened right here, and could so easily happen again?

I told the attendant I would be staying for at least one more night.

He looked at me askance. He couldn't have been more than twenty-five years old, and already there was something suspicious in his manner. 'Another night?' he asked.

'Maybe two,' I said. 'There's a couple of people I need to see.'

The attendant frowned. 'You're from round here then?'

'Used to be,' I replied. 'Many years ago.'

He nodded. 'I'm not from here,' he said. 'From out near Race Pond.'

I smiled, remembered the story Reilly Hawkins had told me of my father. He and Kempner Tzanck out beyond Race Pond to see a man in Brantley. How my father had leveled a brute of a man with a roundhouse and he'd bled to death.

'Anyone in particular you're after?' the attendant asked.

'Hawkins,' I said. 'A man called Reilly Hawkins?'

He shook his head. 'Don't know I've ever heard of him. Best thing you do is go over and see the sheriff. Name's Dennis Stroud. He's been here a good ten or fifteen years. He'll more than likely be able to help you.'

'Thank you,' I said. 'I'll be back later.'

I found the Sheriff's Office without difficulty. It was a new building, but from where I stood I could see the site of the schoolhouse. Perhaps its shell was still there, I couldn't tell, for the site had been extended with a low brick-built annexe with more windows than it seemed to need.

Stepped up toward the Sheriff's Office door, opened it and went inside.

Young woman looked up from a typewriter. Pretty girl, a head full of blond curls, smiled sweetly and asked if she could be of assistance.

'I'd like to see Sheriff Stroud,' I said.

'And may I tell him what it's about, sir?'

'Looking for some people . . . thought he might be able to help me.'

A handful of minutes later I sat in a chair facing Sheriff Dennis Stroud. His face was round like a child's, his eyes appearing too small, but there was a sincerity in his expression, a manner about him, that told me he was a decent man. After Brooklyn, after Auburn, after everything behind me, I believed I could tell such things.

'Vaughan?' he asked, and then he frowned and

scratched his head with the pencil he was holding. 'Vaughan, you say? Not *the* Joseph Vaughan?'

I smiled. 'Depends who *the* Joseph Vaughan would be.'

Stroud leaned forward and opened his desk drawer. From it he withdrew a copy of *A Quiet Belief In Angels*. He held it up. 'This is *the* Joseph Vaughan,' he said.

'Then *I* must be *the* Joseph Vaughan.'

He laughed heartily, and then he rose from his chair. He came around the side of the desk and extended his hand. I took it and he gripped my hand with both of his.

'Augusta Falls' famous son,' Sheriff Stroud said. 'Seems you're the only person who ever came out of this place and made something of himself.'

'I went to prison for murder, Sheriff Stroud,' I said. 'I spent nearly fourteen years in Auburn State—'

'For a murder you didn't commit, right?'

'Sure, for a murder I didn't commit, but—'

'Hell, Mr Vaughan, there's nothing that the American people like more than a man surviving against the odds. Round here you're something of a local hero.' He stood for a moment, and then he sort of tilted his head to one side, and said, 'For my wife . . .' He held out the book. 'Would you sign this for my wife? She's read it three times, I think, and it still makes her cry. She'd be so darn happy, Mr Vaughan, you have no idea.'

I took the book from him, and he handed me a pen. 'What's her name?' I asked.

'Name's Elizabeth, but I call her Betty. If you put it to Betty, then that'll make it all the more personal, right?'

To Betty, I wrote. *With my very best wishes to you and your family. Sincerely, Joseph Vaughan.*

I handed the book back. Stroud read it and smiled. 'That's mighty appreciated, Mr Vaughan, it really is. Now I s'pose you're not here just visiting . . . or are you?'

'In a manner of speaking,' I said. 'I came looking for some people.'

'What people?' Sheriff Stroud walked back to the other side of his desk and sat down.

'Reilly Hawkins—'

Stroud shook his head. 'He's gone, Mr Vaughan. Gone a few years ago. His heart, I believe.'

'He's dead?'

Stroud nodded. His expression was sympathetic. 'I'm sorry, Mr Vaughan.'

For a moment I could not think. I could not recall Reilly's face, and then it came to me, slowly but surely, and I closed my eyes. Just as Hennessy represented everything that was New York, so Reilly Hawkins had been representative of everything that was Georgia.

'Sheriff Dearing?' I said, anxious to change the subject. I would think of Reilly later, perhaps visit his grave, and only then would I let myself express what I felt.

'Haynes Dearing?' Stroud asked. 'And why would you be so interested in Haynes Dearing?'

'He was my conscience,' I said. 'He was the sheriff when I was a kid, for all the time before I left. I came back here in 1950 when my mother died and I heard that he'd left.'

'Hell, Mr Vaughan, that's a story all it's own. Yes, he left. That was many, many years ago. You heard about his wife, right?'

'She committed suicide, I believe.'

'She sure did. That would've been back around 1950 or thereabouts. When did you come back?'

'October of '50. I came back for my mother's funeral.'

'Right, right. So she would have committed suicide in maybe January or February, and Haynes, he upped and left in March right after. Transferred to Valdosta for a few years, maybe until 1954 or '55, and then he retired from the police department. Don't know where he went from there.' Stroud paused and looked at me. 'Out of school you know, but I heard word there was a drinking problem. That, and the fact that he seemed to be unable to work on anything else—' Stroud stopped mid-sentence. 'This is not something I should be discussing really, Mr Vaughan, you know. This is police business.'

I leaned back in the chair. I glanced away toward the window. 'I found one of those girls,' I said. 'Those murders. All those years ago. I found one of those girls, Sheriff.'

Stroud nodded. 'I read your book, Mr Vaughan.'

'And then I went to prison for thirteen years for a murder I didn't commit. I've lost most of my life, Sheriff . . . really, the very best part of my life has gone, and now I'm back trying to understand something of what happened, and why I had to be involved. You have any idea how that must feel?'

Stroud shook his head. 'No, Mr Vaughan, I don't.'

'I suppose I came back here looking for something . . . something that would help me make sense of all of this. Here is where I grew up, and I figure most of the people that grew up with me have left or died, or they've changed so much I'd never recognize them. Haynes Dearing was a part of that, a very important part. He knew my parents, and after my father died he was very good to us. He used to visit with my mother, even after the Kruger fire, even after the death of Elena, the Krugers' little girl . . .'

'What is it that you want from me, Mr Vaughan?'

I shook my head. 'I don't know, Sheriff . . . I suppose I hoped there'd be something . . . anything . . . that would help me understand what happened after I left. I went to New York. I met a girl there. She was murdered too, Sheriff, murdered just like the little girls in Augusta Falls, and—'

'And you think that it was the same man, right?'

I looked up at Stroud, surprised that he had stated the obvious so clearly.

'You figure that whoever did these killings in Augusta Falls also killed your girl in New York? I mean, that's certainly the impression you get from reading your book. That's what folks around here have got to believing as well, and I'd say that Haynes Dearing was perhaps the one who believed that the most.'

I frowned.

'You repeat any of this and I'll get my hide stripped and salted, Mr Vaughan, you get me?'

I nodded. 'Not a word, Sheriff, not a word.'

Stroud rose from his desk and walked to the back of the room. He opened a file drawer, reached into the back, and withdrew a slim manila folder. 'When Dearing retired, when he moved away from Valdosta to wherever he ended up, they sent me some files, paperwork that related to the Augusta Falls killings. This one here had some things in it that . . . Well, you take a look and see if it makes any sense to you.'

Stroud handed me the file. It weighed almost nothing, and when I opened it a collection of newspaper clippings spilled sideways to the floor. I gathered them up quickly, shifted my chair forward and laid them out on the edge of Stroud's desk. They were all there. It could have been the exact same collection of clippings that now sat in the bottom of my bag at the crescent-shaped motel. I leafed through them – read their names, looked at their faces: Alice Ruth Van Horne, Ellen May Levine, Rebecca Leonard,

Mary Tait . . . I turned them over one by one, and then my breath stopped in my chest. It was another clipping entirely, a clipping from a New York newspaper.

Girl, 20, brutally murdered in Brooklyn

I looked away. I could not read the article, could not bear to see Bridget's name in the same type-face as all the others.

I looked up at Stroud. He was peering over the desk at the sections of newspaper. 'There's more,' he said quietly.

I opened the file once again, and there were other clippings that had not fallen to the floor.

I took them out one by one.

Alabama, the Union Springs Courier, 11 October 1950: **Girl, 10, kidnapped, found dead.**

Once again in Alabama, a town called Heflin on 3 February 1951: **Child murder, police baffled.**

From Pulaski, Tennessee on 16 August 1952: **Local girl found dead.**

The last one was from Calhoun, right back here in Georgia, on January 10, 1954: **Missing girl discovered dead.**

'You see where he was going?' Stroud asked.

I looked up at Stroud.

'Shee-it, Mr Vaughan, you're damned near white as a bedsheet.'

'It carried on,' I said, barely able to find my words. Heart stopped in my chest, a feeling of claustrophobia, a tension that held me rigid in the chair.

'Certainly appears that Sheriff Dearing was of that opinion,' Stroud said.

'And he was still looking for him . . . after all these years Dearing knew he was still out there and he was trying to find him, wasn't he?'

Stroud said nothing for a while. The silence was tangible. Eventually: 'You were here when the Kruger guy hanged himself, right?'

I nodded. 'Back in February of '49. I left for Brooklyn a couple of months later.'

'You heard rumors?'

'About what? About Gunther Kruger?'

Stroud nodded. 'That he wasn't responsible for those murders . . .'

I shook my head. 'Gunther Kruger is dead, Sheriff, and there's nothing we can do to change that. I don't know whether Haynes Dearing had anything to do with Gunther Kruger's death, at least not directly—'

'But there were rumors, Mr Vaughan.'

'Rumors are rumors, Sheriff Stroud. I came down here looking for some kind of understanding that was reliable.'

Stroud shook his head. 'That I can't help you with. You're talking about things that happened the better part of twenty and thirty years ago. There aren't that many people left here that you'd remember. People moved on, went different places as they do. Other folks died, like Reilly Hawkins, Frank Turow. Even Gene Fricker . . . never met a man I considered healthier . . . he was hit by a car in Camden County. Killed him outright. His son's still here but he has a family all his own. Minds his business, you know? Don't know that I can necessarily speak for all of them, but its seems to be that they wouldn't want to go dredging up the past.'

'I'm not here to upset people, Sheriff.'

Stroud smiled, but there was a suspicious undercurrent in his tone when he asked, 'So why exactly *are* you here, Mr Vaughan?'

I thought for a moment of what to tell him. 'I don't know, Sheriff. I suppose I don't have a single understandable reason for being here.'

'These are simple people, Mr Vaughan. This town went through a terrible thing, but that was a lot of years ago. People have chosen to forget what took place, and though I can sympathize with your situation I cannot encourage you to go stirring things up that have no relevance to Augusta Falls as it is now. I can't stop you being here, and I have no wish to, but I can ask you to be discreet, to see whoever you came here to see, and then to move on.'

I gathered the newspaper clippings together and returned them to the file. I handed the file back to Stroud and rose to my feet. 'You have any idea where I'd start looking for Haynes Dearing?' I asked.

Stroud rose also, and I sensed in him a feeling of relief that I was leaving. 'Haynes Dearing? Christ, I wouldn't know where to start. Last place

I heard of him was Valdosta, like I said. You could go speak to the Sheriff's Department people out there and see if they know what happened to him. I wouldn't even know if he was still alive, Mr Vaughan.'

I extended my hand, thanked Sheriff Stroud for his help, and turned to leave. It was as I did so that I noticed a slip of paper beneath the chair where I'd sat. I leaned down to retrieve it, and turned it over. There, printed in Haynes Dearing's unmistakable script, was a single question: *Where did the boy go after Jesup?*

I held it out to Stroud. 'You know what this means?' I asked.

Stroud took the slip of paper, read the question, shook his head. 'Wouldn't have a clue, Mr Vaughan.' He put it in the file along with the newspaper clippings. 'Didn't the Kruger family end up in Jesup?'

I didn't reply. An image came to me. Gunther Kruger standing on the road that night, his long coat, the ominous sense of fear that had assaulted me when I saw him. And then he'd turned and hurried back to the house. Could I have been mistaken? Had it not been Gunther Kruger at all?

'I think so,' I said brusquely. 'I think they did, yes.' I wished Sheriff Stroud goodbye and left his office. I hurried back to the motel and into my room. I sat on the edge of the bed. I took a piece of paper and wrote down the names of the towns

557

from Stroud's file. Union Springs, Heflin, Pulaski and Calhoun. My mind was spinning. Everything I'd considered was suddenly upside down and back to front. Had it not been Gunther Kruger at all? Had it been someone else wearing Gunther's coat? And why had my mother been so convinced that the child-killer was in the house that night she set the fire?

I stayed motionless for some time. I could hardly breathe. I lay down and tried to close my eyes but image after image invaded my mind and made me feel nauseous. Eventually I crossed the narrow room and opened the door. I stood there taking deep breaths, trying to remain calm, trying my best to remain grounded. But the ground had changed and it was unstable, and I had to step back and sit down again. I held onto the edge of the bed and the walls buckled and swayed awkwardly.

An hour passed, perhaps more. I opened my eyes and realized that I'd lain back on the mattress and fallen asleep. The motel cabin door was still half open, and I stood up and closed it. I sluiced my face in the cupboard-sized bathroom, and dried my hands on a towel that was mottled gray and worn through in places.

I wanted to leave Augusta Falls. Everything that I'd imagined was here was now gone. It was not the buildings, it was not roads or landmarks, it was the spirit of the place. Perhaps because I was no longer a child, and thus I did not see these things the way I once did.

A little later I took the newspaper clippings from my bag and put them in my jacket pocket. I locked the motel cabin door and walked past the reception office toward the center of town. There was a launderette on the corner, and here I asked a woman if she knew the Fricker house.

'Maurice Fricker? Sure I know where he lives. Out of here, turn right, on past the Sheriff's Office to the end of the street. At the crossroads take a left, and down there about a quarter mile there's a house on your left. You can't miss it. It's got blue windowframes, and in the front yard there's a mailbox with a weather vane on top.'

I thanked the woman and left, followed her directions, and within a matter of minutes I stood before the Fricker house. There was a mailbox with a weathervane on top, and sitting on the porch steps was a girl, couldn't have been more than eight or nine years old, her hair tied back with barettes. She tilted her head, used her hand to shield her eyes from the sun.

'Your daddy home?' I called out.

The girl squinted at me, and then suddenly she turned, ran up the steps and banged her way through the screen door.

Moments later the inner door swung open, and through the mesh of the screen I could see someone standing there. 'You got business here?' he shouted, and immediately, without a doubt, I recognized Maurice Fricker's voice.

'Maurice?' I called back. 'Is that you, Maurice?'

The man hesitated, his hand reaching out to open the screen, and I started walking toward the house.

'Christ al-fucking-mighty,' he hissed through his teeth. 'Jesus Mary Mother of God. It's you, isn't it? Joseph Vaughan.'

Maurice Fricker swung the door wide and came down the steps. I came to a stop in the front yard. He'd always looked like his father, Gene, but now – at age forty – Maurice was a living, breathing image of the man.

Maurice hugged me until I was breathless, clapped my back enthusiastically. He stepped back, held my shoulders with his hands, and then he hugged me once more.

'My God, Joseph . . . I honestly believed I'd never see you again. Hell, come up onto the porch, we'll get some beers and have a drink. Goddarn lucky you caught me here. I'm on a day's layover before I go back to the job in White Oak.' He turned, started walking, and then he stopped and faced me once again. 'God, man, this is one helluva thing. I honestly believed I'd never see you again. Hell, I don't even know what to say to you.'

I followed him to the porch, and through and to the left was a veranda with some high-backed wooden chairs.

Maurice asked me to sit down, and then he backed up, opened the inner door, and called through to the darkness of the house. 'Ellie, be a sweetheart . . . go in the icebox and get daddy a couple of beers!'

The little girl with the barettes appeared within a few moments.

'Ellie . . . this here's Joseph,' Maurice said.

'Hey there, Ellie,' I said. I smiled.

Ellie looked uncomfortable, tried to smile back. She set the bottles of beer down on the porch, then turned suddenly and ran back into the house.

'She's the shy one,' Maurice said. 'Have another girl, Lacey her name is. She and her mom are over at the grandma's place in Homeland. You remember Bob Gorman, Tri-County Coroner?'

'Sure I do, yes.'

'Up and married his youngest daughter Annabel. You ever meet her?'

I shook my head. 'No, I don't think I did.'

'Helluva girl, Joseph, just one helluva girl.' He twisted the cap off a bottle of beer and handed it to me.

We sat in silence for a little while, and I could sense it around Maurice – the certainty of why I'd come, and beneath it the wish that I hadn't.

'So things went to shit, didn't they?' he said. 'Out in New York.'

I smiled, looked out over the veranda railing toward the fields in the distance. My childhood was out there, running through shoulder-high maize and wheat, carrying books from Miss Webber's class, listening to Reilly Hawkins tell tall tales in his kitchen. 'You could say that,' I replied.

'And that thing . . . the thing with the girl . . .'

'Bridget,' I said, and it felt so strange to be speaking with Maurice Fricker about something that he could never know anything about. 'You read my book?'

Maurice shrugged. 'Some,' he said. 'Never been much of a reader, you know?' He smiled, and he seemed tired, worn at the edges. 'My wife, she read it . . . but hell, she never knew you, so for her it was like reading a novel. Seems to me that those who weren't here could never understand what it was like.' He drank his beer. 'You heard about Reilly Hawkins?'

I nodded.

'My dad too . . . he was killed by some drunk-drive asshole out in Camden County. Have my wife, my two girls, you know?' He laughed. 'Keep me on my toes, twenty-four seven. Sometimes think there's so much of the present that I have no time to think of the past.'

'The others?' I asked. 'You ever see them?'

Maurice frowned. 'Others?'

'Daniel McRae. Ronnie Duggan. Michael Wiltsey . . . remember, the King of Fidget?'

'Hell yes, I remember him. He's still here, Joseph, but Daniel's long since gone. Joined the Army back in . . . hell, when was it? Must've been all of ten years ago. Wanted to see the world, figured it was best to do it on Uncle Sam's ticket.'

'The Guardians,' I said, and I felt the air suddenly chill and grow cold.

Maurice laughed, at least tried to laugh, but there was anxiety in that sound. 'That was . . . that was an eternity ago. We were kids, Joseph, nothing but scared little kids. We figured we could do something, but—'

Maurice Fricker turned to face me and there were tears in his eyes. 'There hasn't been a year gone by when I haven't thought of those little girls, Joseph. I got my own kids now. Annabel tells me I worry all the time, that I fuss around them too much. She tells me they have to learn their independence, have to make their own way in the world, but she wasn't there, right? She wasn't there when those girls were murdered. Her father was the coroner. Sometimes I wonder if she wasn't somehow hardened to it, but she's the kind of person who sees good in everything and everybody. I make her drive our girls to school, make her collect them when they're done. Other kids' folks don't do that. They let them walk half a mile there and back, even in the winter when it's dark in the afternoon. And sometimes I see things that remind me of how scared we all were. When they built all those extensions to the schoolhouse there was no-one who was happier than me. Before that the place used to remind me every time I went past it . . .' Maurice's voice trailed away into silence.

'I think it's still happening,' I said.

Maurice shook his head. 'No, it's not, Joseph. You're mistaken. They found out who it was and he hanged himself. The German. Gunther Kruger. He was the child-killer, right? Everyone knows that he killed those little girls and that's all there is to it. It's been and gone. It's over. That's all I've got to say about it, Joseph.'

I took another sip of my beer and set the bottle down on the ground. I rose slowly from the chair and looked down at Maurice Fricker. 'It's okay,' I said, knowing that any attempt I made to involve him in this thing would only serve to make him feel guilty for doing nothing. 'You're probably right, Maurice, you know? It's over. It ended all the way back there.' I smiled as best I could. 'Maybe it's all been a bit too much for me. I spent a great deal of years in prison. Maybe it made me a little crazy, eh?'

Maurice didn't get up. He looked at me as I made my way to the porch door.

'You have a beautiful daughter,' I said. 'You did the right thing, Maurice. Believe me, you did the right thing. You did what I should have done. Should have stayed here and gotten myself married, got some kids like you. Never should have gone to New York.'

Maurice shook his head slowly. 'You weren't the same as anyone else, Joseph Vaughan. You never were and you never will be. You got Miss Webber to fall in love with you, right?'

I nodded. 'Sure I did.'

'You were always the odd one out,' Maurice said. 'You were always asking questions about

564

things no-one else had a mind to find out about. Writing stories. Writing books that got published. Seems to me you're the one who's lived more life than all of us put together.'

'Don't have one helluva lot to show for it though, do I?' I said, and I reached out my hand and pushed the door open. 'I'm gonna go now,' I said. 'You take care of yourself, Maurice, and your wife and your daughters. And don't worry what she says . . . seems to me you can never take too much care of children, even these days.'

Maurice raised his hand. 'Maybe I'll see you again, Joseph. I'd ask you to stay for dinner, but—'

'Ghosts don't come to dinner, Maurice,' I said, and then I turned and walked away.

I glanced back when I reached end of the yard, and there – just behind the screen door – I could see Ellie watching me through the mesh. She could have been any of them – Laverna, Elena, Virginia Grace . . . My breath caught in my chest, and then she raised her hand and waved just once before disappearing into darkness.

I found Ronnie Duggan standing outside what was once the Falls Inn. It seemed his bangs had finally conceded defeat. His hair was thinning, swept back from a still youthful face, but there was a bitterness around his eyes that his smile could not disguise.

'Heard you were here,' was his greeting, and he sort of leaned back against the railing at the front of the building. 'Dennis Stroud gave me a call and said you'd come back.'

'Hello, Ronnie,' I said, and knew that my return was not welcomed.

'Hey there, Joseph,' he said. 'I called Michael, said he should come down and say hi, but he's got to drive his wife over to some bridge class or somesuch.'

'The Falls Inn,' I said, looking up at the building behind him.

'Not for many years. Frank Turow died, you know, and then there was a guy called McGonagle. Now it's owned by some company in Augusta and they serve warm beer and white wine spritzers. It ain't the place it was . . . hell, Augusta Falls isn't the place it was.'

'I gathered that.'

'It's good to see you,' he said. He tucked his thumbs in the belt of his jeans.

'I don't think it is, Ronnie.'

'Shee-it, no-one calls me Ronnie now, Joseph. That was my kid name. Everyone calls me Ron. Just Ron, nothing more than that.'

'I spoke to Maurice—'

'Maurice is a good man, Joseph. He has a wife and two daughters and a dog and a cat. He has a good job with the sanitation department out in White Oak. Man's made a place for himself here, gonna stay here until he dies. He'll see grand-kids, maybe even more, and I figure the last thing in the world he wants to see is you.'

I looked down at the ground. I remembered the Guardians. Seems I was the only one that did.

'I'll not be staying, Ron,' I said, 'but I wanted to ask you a couple of things before I left.' I looked up at him, looked closely, and despite the thinning hair, despite the wary expression, I could still see Ronnie, bangs in his eyes, always fussing with something – a stone, a marble, a piece of wood.

'What started here ended here, Joseph. That's the way I feel and I think that's the way most people around here want it to stay. I'm sorry for your troubles. I heard about Alex Webber losing the baby an' all, and then that trouble you had in Brooklyn . . . you know, the fact that you spent all them years in prison—'

'Do you think it was Gunther Kruger?' I interjected.

Ron Duggan snorted. 'Gunther Kruger hanged himself. Figure that's as good an admission of guilt as you're ever gonna get from anyone.'

'You think he did that, or you think he was hiding someone . . . you think maybe he knew who it was and he was covering for them?'

Duggan stepped forward. His thumbs came out from his belt and he stopped there, his fists clenching and unclenching. 'Seems it'd have to be a pretty tight arrangement for someone to kill themselves on behalf of someone else, Joseph.'

'Someone like family?'

'Family? What the hell're you talking about?'

'I'm saying that maybe it wasn't Gunther at all. Maybe—'

Ronnie Duggan raised his hand. 'Maybe nothing, Joseph. Maybe it ain't nothing at all. That's the thing I'm saying here. That's what I'm trying to tell you but it seems you're selectively deaf. That thing ended in 1949. That's the better part of thirty years ago.'

'I don't think it ended, Ronnie . . . and I think Sheriff Dearing felt the same way.'

'Enough now. This is a conversation I'm not having, not now, not ever. We aren't children anymore, Joseph. We have lives to get on with. There are people here who decided to leave the past behind, and I think it'd be real smart if you did the same thing. No-one wants this, no-one wants all these memories stirred up again. It's 1967. The world has changed. Augusta Falls isn't your hometown anymore. You should go back to New York . . . go back and sort out whatever you have to, but leave this thing alone, Joseph. For God's sake, let this thing lie.'

'We were the Guardians,' I said. 'We made an oath, a promise—'

'We were kids, for fuck's sake! That's all we were. We were never going to stop what happened, and we knew it. We were frightened and desperate, and we made believe that we could do something about it, but we couldn't – we couldn't then, and we can't now.'

'Now? What d'you mean, now! You know it never stopped, don't you?'

There was a flicker of anger in Ronnie's eyes. He took a step toward me and I could see the muscles twitching along his jawline.

'Look at me, Ronnie . . . look at me and tell me you *know* it was Gunther Kruger.'

Ronnie Duggan stared back at me with a fierce and unrelenting gaze. 'I *know* it was Gunther Kruger,' he said. 'You happy now? That's what you want me to say, then there you have it. I *know* it was Gunther Kruger, and the evil bastard hanged himself in his own barn, and they found a ribbon in his hand, all kinds of things that could only have come from those poor little girls. He killed them. He raped and abused them and killed them and cut them up. He threw bits of them around the fucking countryside, and then he died and went to Hell where he damn well belonged. That's what I'm saying because that's what I believe.'

'That's what you believe, or that's what you *want* to believe?'

He was silent for a moment, and then he looked away toward the horizon and smiled. 'I'm gonna go now, Joseph. Can't say that it's been a pleasure seeing you again, but for politeness sake I'm gonna say that it was a pleasure seeing you again. Appreciate it if you'd do whatever you have to do and move on out of here soon as is convenient. I'll pass on your best wishes to Michael, some of the other folks that you know, and I'll say goodbye.' He stepped forward and held out his hand. I took it, and he gripped my hand too firmly and looked me in the eye. 'So it's goodbye, Joseph, and I figure this is the last time we'll be speaking to one another.'

He released my hand, and then turned to walk away.

'What if it didn't stop, Ronnie? What then?'

Duggan turned back. 'Then it'll be someone else's kids, Joseph . . . not mine, not Michael's or Maurice's. Nightmare visited Augusta Falls, and then it moved on. I ain't calling up the ghosts just to see if it comes back.' He smiled once more. 'You take care now, Joseph Vaughan, okay?'

I nodded, watched silently as Ronnie Duggan walked away. The Guardians – whatever we might have believed ourselves to be – had died with the murder of Elena Kruger, the one I'd promised to protect, the one that had proved to the Guardians that whatever we did we could not make a difference.

I stayed there for some minutes, and then I turned back the way I'd come and returned to the motel.

Thinking back to that moment I cannot help but smile to myself. What had I expected? Who was I fooling?

We were the Guardians. Me and Michael Wiltsey, Ronnie Duggan, Daniel McRae and Maurice Fricker. The better part of thirty years on . . . what made me even think they would be pleased to see me?

We were frightened back then, each and every one of us, but time had passed and the kind of fear they'd felt had changed. Now they were afraid to be wrong. Afraid that the nightmare of the past hadn't ended. Afraid that if they stirred up the ghosts it would all come back to haunt them. Thirty years on and they hadn't forgotten. They would never forget. They knew that, and that – above all else – was perhaps the thing they feared the most.

I had assumed, and I assumed wrong. I walked away from the Falls Inn, and I knew who I was looking for. I thought of Gabillard, of Lowell Shaner, others that had been there, and I wondered whether they would want to know what had happened. I sat in that cheap motel cabin, the door ajar, a thin breeze making its way inside, and I realized that the end of this thing wasn't so far away. There would just be the two of us. Joseph Vaughan versus the child-killer. Like some old-time B-horror movie. And if I died . . . well, if I died there would be no-one behind me. There would be no-one holding ranks, marshaling forces, preparing themselves for a second strike. For some reason I felt an absence of fear. Of course, there was no doubt that I was afraid, but it appeared that the sense of closure I perceived was more powerful than the emotions it provoked. I would buy a gun, that much at least I had determined. I would find some backstreet army surplus store and buy a gun. There were always such places to be found – some uncaring, irresponsible citizen who would take fifty bucks and ask no questions.

I decided to head for Columbus, a big enough city to find such a place, and then I would cross the county line into Alabama. I would visit Union Springs, the first of those places about which Dearing had kept newspaper clippings. October of 1950 another little girl had died. Perhaps there would be people who remembered. Perhaps they would be able to tell me something to point me in the right direction.

I closed the cabin door. I lay down and slept in my clothes. I did not dream, and for this small mercy I was grateful.

The chill of early morning awoke me. I gathered my few belongings together and checked out.

I took the bus to Tifton, and there I waited at the

depot for a connection to Columbus. I passed out toward the Georgia state line like the ghost that I was. I believed that no-one would remember me, and if they did I trusted that they would forget.

CHAPTER 31

Reilly Hawkins filled my thoughts as we made our way to Columbus. I had thought to see his grave, perhaps to see the house where I'd lived, to find out if the Kuharczyks were still there, but I could not. I believed that seeing such reminders would provoke only anger, perhaps grief, almost certainly despair. Twice I had returned and twice I had lost someone I loved. I knew I could never go back.

And Michael? Ronnie, Maurice Fricker, Daniel McRae – who'd escaped just as I had, but had done it smart, had made his way half across the world – what of them? They belonged to a past that had stayed behind, and they had no wish to follow me. I was the fool, wasn't I? I was the one who had allowed it all to become a burden.

Columbus was a new city, a place I had never visited before. I appreciated the anonymity I felt, and when I checked into a hotel on the night of the twenty-ninth I stood at the window and looked out at the lights that burned in the darkness. The sky was clear, midnight blue, and the moon rose high and bright and full. I closed my eyes and thought of the house on Throop and Quincy, of Aggie Boyle, of Joyce Spragg and Ben Godfrey. I thought of Arthur Morrison and *The Homecoming* and recalled the day Bridget and I had walked into a bookstore and believed that the world and all it had to offer was right there ahead of us just waiting to be grasped. We missed the chance we were given. That was the simplicity of it: we were given one chance and we blew it.

I slept well. The sounds from the street below were unfamiliar, and that was comfort in itself. When I woke the day was clear, the street filled with traffic; reminded me of my first day in Brooklyn.

I walked until hunger assaulted me, and then I stopped in a diner and ate breakfast. I walked some more, down backstreets, alleyways, eyes open for a pawnshop. I found one on the corner of Young and Ninth Street, and there – behind a mesh counter – was exactly the kind of man I was looking for. Fifteen minutes and seventy-five dollars later I left the shop. I hurried back to the hotel, retrieved my bag, and walked downtown to the bus depot.

An hour and a half later I arrived in Alabama. It was raining lightly, and when I stepped down from the bus I knew instinctively that Union Springs had seen the same ghost that had walked through Augusta Falls. I sensed it. Something preternatural and intuitive. I believed it would be the same in Heflin, in Pulaski and Calhoun, and I knew then that visiting such towns would serve no purpose. The damage had been done. Whatever had walked these streets had long since left. But I knew there would be others. Recent towns, recent killings. I turned around and headed back to the depot. I took a bus to Montgomery, the nearest city where there would be a library of records. I was chasing a mirage, a phantom, a specter, and I was losing myself in the process. My mind was focused, single-tracked, unerring. I did not think to eat, to sleep. Necessity forced such things upon me, and without that necessity I would have walked until I dropped. It was after midnight when I arrived in Montgomery and hailed a cab. I asked the driver to take me to the nearest hotel and, seated in the back, I realized how bad I looked, how sour my odor. He set me down ahead of an imposing building with revolving glass doors. I waited for the cab to pull away and then hurried along the street until I found a decrepit-looking place with a broken neon sign. The first hotel would never have let me enter, but here they wouldn't care.

Once inside I stripped off my clothes and bathed. I washed my hair, shaved as carefully as I could, and then spent some time trying to gather my thoughts together.

Montgomery would have the information I needed; somewhere within its city library there would be newspapers from all over the state, and several states beyond, and there would be similarities. Always there were similarities.

I lay awake through the night, and when a thin, gray light seeped through the curtain I rose and dressed.

I was there when the doors of the library opened, and I asked for directions to the public records section. I started with Alabama; I found the Union Springs girl, an eight-year-old called Frances Resnick. Found murdered on Wednesday, October eleventh, 1950. Frances Resnick had been raped and decapitated. Her headless body had been thrown into a gully and covered with rocks and earth. Heflin, Saturday, February third, 1951, an eleven-year-old called Rita Yates was found dead after being missing for two days. Her arms had been severed from her torso, one of them was located, the other not. She too had been sexually assaulted. Pulaski, Tennessee; Saturday, August sixteenth, 1952, a local farm worker had found the scant remains of Lillian Harmond, the twelve-year-old daughter of the town's postmaster. Her body had been cut clean in two across the midriff, her upper half found in a shallow grave, her lower half left beneath a tree. The farm worker, a young man called Garth Trent, was quoted as saying, 'I couldn't believe what I was seeing . . . it was like she was sat there, just sat there, but there was just her legs . . . just her legs.' I thought of Virginia Perlman, and I understood – with far greater clarity than Garth Trent would ever know – exactly what he had felt. And then back to Georgia. The small town of Calhoun. Sunday, January tenth,

1954, the dismembered body of seven-year-old Hettie Webster was found by a group of children. First they found her left arm, then her right shoulder and most of her head. Then they ran away. Hettie had been walking back from Sunday school alone. It was late morning, a bright and clear day, and no-one had seen a thing. Police were baffled. The citizens of Calhoun felt much the same as those of Augusta Falls.

I found nothing for two hours. My eyes hurt. A headache raged between my temples, but I scoured the newspaper binders – page after page, volume after volume. I went through Alabama, Tennessee, Georgia and Mississippi looking for the child-killer. I found him in 1956 in a small town called Ridgeland, South Carolina. That town was a mere handful of miles from the Savannah River, no more than a hundred and twenty miles from Augusta Falls. The girl's name was Janice Waterson. She was nine years old; an only child. Her parents – Reanna and Milton – had told the world that she was 'a bright and inquisitive girl, always helpful, always polite, and not like we'd ever had to teach her to be polite . . . she just seemed to do it naturally.' Her feet had been cut from her ankles, as her hands from her wrists. She was buried without them, because they were never found. They had a closed coffin too, as much of her face had been taken away with a serrated blade.

It seemed then that I was tuned to his movements. I seemed to find them with greater ease, and I counted as I went, took note of names and dates and places; details of the manner of death, the way in which the girls had been found, who had found them and what they'd said. I felt like I was tracking him – Moncks Corner, Sparta, Enterprise, Alexander City, through '57, '58, '61, '63. I could see his face. I could see his pattern. Small towns, never far from the highway, girls no younger than seven, no older than twelve.

And I kept thinking of the scrawled note in Dearing's file: *Where did the boy go after Jesup?*

By the time I was done it was late afternoon. I had not eaten, or moved from the desk. The library attendant – a middle-aged woman, graying hair tied in tight bundles against the side of her head, aubergine lipstick, a loud flower-print skirt and a heavy woollen cardigan – had caught my eye a little after two o'clock.

'All right there?' she'd asked, and I'd smiled warmly and told her that everything was fine, that I was researching a book, that I tended to get a little obsessed with my work.

'You need anything there you don't hesitate to let me know,' she'd replied, and then she'd walked away.

I left Montgomery City Library with a list of nineteen names, the last one less than four months ago in a town called Stone Gap, no more than a handful of miles south of Macon. Twenty-nine killings in all, spanning the better part of thirty years. One a year it seemed, but I knew there were more. Those reported missing and never found. Even more tragically, those who disappeared and went unreported.

I made my way back to the broken-neon hotel. I knew I had to find Dearing. He was out there somewhere. He was out there looking for the next one. We were running the same track, parallel and connected.

The last killing had been in Georgia, on Tuesday, November twenty-ninth, 1966; a nine-year-old girl called Rachel Garrett. Memories would be fresh, people would perhaps remember a man like Dearing. No-one had witnessed the child's abduction, but a man coming after the fact, a stranger asking questions? Surely there would be someone who would recall such a thing . . .

Once in my hotel room I packed my things, then sat on the edge of the bed and let my mind run through everything that had happened. It was as if I was coming to the end of a chapter of my life, a chapter that had begun with the death of my father, my mother's alliance with Gunther Kruger, and the killing of Alice Ruth Van Home.

They were all out there, every single one of them, and I knew they were waiting.

Waiting for me to find their killer and release them.

In the night the Guardians came, and they came as children.

They came with hands held wide as if to welcome me, and as I reached them they turned their backs. There was the sound of laughter, and beneath that the sound of crying, and beneath that the sound of a serious man doing the Devil's work.

The sawing of bones, the letting of blood, the shame and guilt and fury and anguish.

And then there was a cool wind blowing, and inside of that wind I heard the sound of wings, and with it came a sense of calm.

I slept again. I did not dream.

In the morning it was raining.

CHAPTER 32

Saturday, April first. I sat at the back of the bus and rode away from Alabama. Once again I crossed the Georgia state line and headed for Stone Gap. I knew how the town would look before I arrived. I knew how people's voices would sound, the color of their eyes, the depth of their suspicion. Perhaps they would see me as I was; perhaps they would see me as something to fear. Now it did not matter. Nothing mattered but finding Haynes Dearing.

Stone Gap, as I knew all too well, was a small Southern town. The climate, the inconsistent humidity, the ordinariness of life. Nothing ever happened in places like Stone Gap; no-one famous hailed from its schools or small Methodist College. The roads were uneven, the cars ancient, the politics indefinite. It professed to be a religious-minded community, a community of tolerance and temperance, but the bars were crowded, and somewhere on the outskirts of town there would be a house owned by an unmarried woman, and living in that house would be two or three girls. Men would visit that house, as they had done for a hundred years or more, but there would be no metnion of this building in the town records. It was as if it did not exist, and never had, and such an omission would never raise questions in the land census. Beyond the immediate town limits the houses grew smaller and further apart, as if the people who lived there had been banished. The people of Stone Gap abhorred violence, but every man owned a gun and every woman had bloodied her hands around the throat of a slit pig. There was a way to do things, and it was an old way, but Stone Gap knew – would always know – that the old ways were the best ways. Cities like New York and Las Vegas, even such places as Montgomery, were representative of a different type of America, an America that had forgotten the land and its laws, the presence of nature, the inevitability of time.

Such a place would not wish to remember the murder of a child, but it would not be able to forget it. Such a thing would lie beneath the surface like an indelible bruise, mentioned only in looks and glances, each person knowing without words what the other was saying. And just like Augusta Falls, Stone Gap would know that such a thing could not have been perpetrated by one of their own. It would have been a foreigner, an outsider, and for years afterwards anyone arriving who was not a native of this place would find thin comfort and short shrift.

I stood outside the bus depot, nothing more than a plankboard lean-to with a corrugated roof, and

I knew Stone Gap as well as I knew my own home-town. This was the world I had sought to leave, but my leaving had merely tempted destiny to bring me back. Destiny had succeeded, more times than I cared to recall, and each time had been a reminder that that which I'd been given could so easily be taken away. Stone Gap had lost one of its own: I could feel it in the air, see it in the faces of people as they passed me by, and I tried my best to avoid eye contact, to be inconspicuous, to raise no questions.

The Sheriff's Office was a low brick-built affair at the end of the main drag. It stood alone, evident in its purpose and significance, and when I stepped up onto the porchway and opened the screen door I saw the sheriff himself through an open office door right ahead.

'My name is Joseph Vaughan,' I told him, 'and I'm a writer.'

Sheriff Norman Vallelly was somewhere in his sixties. His face was three-quarters wrinkled and the last quarter scattered with crow's feet, his eyes almost disappearing as he frowned. And those eyes were bright like pennies; eyes that had seen every-thing people could do, everything they thought. But there was something restful in his features, something that told me he would question a man, and that man would be unable to say anything but the truth.

'The murdered girl?' he asked me. 'And why the

hell would you be wanting to know about such a thing?'

I leaned back in the chair. I had not realized how exhausted I was. Had Sheriff Vallelly kept his silence for a moment I could have closed my eyes and slept.

'I'm working on a book,' I said. 'A book—'

'Like that Capote feller, right?' Vallelly nodded as if he now understood. 'That Capote feller with his *Cold Blood* thing . . . story about that family in Kansas. My wife has read that damed book three or four times.'

'Yes,' I said. 'Like Capote.'

'Well, hell, Mr Vaughan, I don't know that you're gonna get any kind of book out of this thing, but if you do then you must send me a copy for my wife.'

'Of course,' I said. 'Of course I will.'

'You know there was another feller came here asking about this murder.'

'An elderly man, about sixty-two or three?'

'Sure was,' Vallelly said. 'Retired sheriff, name of Geary or somesuch.'

'Dearing,' I said. 'Haynes Dearing.'

'That's the man! You know him?'

'Yes, I know him. He was the sheriff in Augusta Falls, my hometown.'

'He came here almost as soon as it happened. Couldn'ta been in the newspapers more than a day and he was at the door asking all sorts of questions.'

585

'Did he say that he was looking for someone?'

'Sure did.'

I raised my eyebrows inquisitively.

Vallelly shifted forward in his chair and rested his forearms on the desk. 'You want me to tell you who he was looking for?'

'Could you?'

'He didn't know, son. He didn't know who he was looking for, 'cept he said it might have been a German.'

'A German?'

Vallelly nodded. ''S what he said. Said he was looking for a German.'

'He mention a name?'

'No, he didn't give me any names. First I figured your Haynes Dearing might have been drafted in to help us with this thing, but he stayed no more than an hour or two and then he was gone.'

'He say where?'

'Didn't even say goodbye. In and out of here like rainfall.'

'And the investigation?' I asked.

Vallelly leaned back and frowned. 'I can't tell you where a current and ongoing investigation is headed, son. I just can't divulge that kind of information.'

'But no-one has been arrested, right?'

Vallelly paused for a moment, and then he smiled sardonically. 'Let's say that there haven't been any headlines about it in the *Stone Gap Herald* and leave it at that.'

'And you haven't heard from Sheriff Dearing since?' I asked.

Vallelly shook his head. 'No, not a word. He said he'd let me know if anything came of his investigation. You say you were from Augusta Falls?'

I nodded.

'And he was the sheriff there?'

'Yes he was, for quite a number of years.'

'And you had the same trouble there?'

'Ten of them,' I said. 'Between '39 and '49. Ten little girls were murdered.'

'All in the same town?'

I shook my head. 'No, some of them were from surrounding counties. By the end of it there were something like five different police departments involved.'

Vallelly whistled through his teeth. He reached for a pipe on the desk and started packing it with tobacco. 'And this is the same person?'

'We believe so.'

'We?'

'Me and Haynes Dearing.'

'Yes, of course. And you're trying to find this Dearing feller so you can investigate this thing together?'

'Yes.'

Vallelly squinted at me over the bowl of his pipe. 'And you're a writer, and he's a retired sheriff.'

'Yes.'

'And you have some kind of idea that you're

gonna do better than me and a whole bunch of other sheriffs through half a dozen counties?'

I smiled. 'No, of course not. This thing has been going on for thirty years. There's been killings in Mississippi, Tennessee, in Alabama and South Carolina. Far as I can gather there's been at least thirty in all, maybe more. Many of the original officers are no longer active. Can imagine some of them are retired, some have died. I don't think there's been any real understanding of the nature of this thing. It's spanned so many years and so many different places. Each town has had its own people and its own investigation, but they've never been co-ordinated.'

'And you're planning to write a book about it?'

'First thing is to find Haynes Dearing, see what he knows, then perhaps try and instigate some kind of task force operation that will pool all the information and see if there's a pattern, some kind of way to get everybody working on it in unison.'

Vallelly was silent for a while. He lit his pipe, and the crackle of fired tobacco was the only sound in the room. Arabesques of smoke curled toward the ceiling, and the light through the window turned them into ghosts.

'I don't know what to tell you,' he eventually said. 'I got a dead little girl. She was taken from right near her house in the middle of the day. No-one saw anything out of the ordinary, nothing that they remembered. She was found literally hours later—'

'How was she found, Sheriff?'

He frowned. '*How* was she found? You mean who found her?'

'No,' I said. 'I mean what had he done to her?'

Vallelly squinted at me again. 'I don't know that that's something I'd want to share with anyone.'

'I found one of them.'

Vallelly looked taken aback.

'When I was fourteen years old. I found one of them on the top of a hill near where I lived.' I felt the memory filling me, tightening my chest. 'When I say I found her, it's more precise to say I found most of her.'

'Jesus,' Vallelly said, and the word was sharp and sudden.

'I know what he does. I've seen it up close. I've read about it, talked about it, been carrying it for as long as I can recall . . .'

'He cut her through the middle, Mr Vaughan,' Vallelly said. 'He cut her right through the middle like she was a sack of nothing. Left her amongst some trees at the edge of the road where anybody could have found her, kids or anyone. Never seen anything like it in my life, and hope to God I never do again. That's what he did to her, Mr Vaughan, he cut a nine-year-old girl clean in half and left her at the side of the road.'

Neither of us spoke for some moments, and then Vallelly looked up and said, 'So what you gonna do now, son? You got any kind of a plan on how to find this friend of yours?'

589

'Nothing specific,' I said.

'Nothing specific ain't gonna do it, is it?'

'No, it's not.'

'You want I should put some kind of alert out for him for you?'

I was surprised, suddenly hopeful. 'You can do that?'

Vallelly smiled. 'I can do anything the hell I like. I'm the sheriff, ain't I?'

'What does that mean,' I asked. 'An alert?'

'I can send a teletype message to every sheriff's department in the state. I can give the man's name, his description. Can tell them he isn't wanted for any kind of investigatory purpose, but that he does need to be located. You want I should let them know to tell him you're looking for him?'

'Of course, yes,' I said. 'If someone sees him they can let him know I want to speak to him.'

'And they can give him your name?'

'Definitely, yes. That would be very, very much appreciated, Sheriff.'

'Consider it done, Mr Vaughan. I got one hell of a lot of people who want to find out what happened to Rachel Garrett, and if there's something that's gonna help make that happen then it's simply a matter of duty that I see to it, wouldn't you say?'

I thanked Sheriff Norman Vallelly profusely, so much so that I believed the man was embarrassed. I told him I would stay in Stone Gap for a day or so, that I may stay longer. He told me he would keep me informed of any information that came back, and that I should let him know my whereabouts if I chose to leave. He recommended the Excelsior Hotel on Fallow Road, three blocks down and to the right.

'Sounds like the Ritz or somesuch, but it sure as hell ain't anything like that. It's clean enough, a fair price for a room, and I'll know where to find you.'

I thanked Vallelly again, shook his hand, and left his office.

I walked three blocks down and found the Excelsior, a modest three-storey building painted an off-white color with cream-colored window frames. I felt as if something was happening. For the first time in as many years as I could recall, I really believed that there might be a chance. Thin and insubstantial, but a chance all the same. At that point I was grateful for anything, and chose not to question my hope.

By Wednesday the fifth I was climbing the walls of my small hotel room. Twice I had walked down to Sheriff Vallelly's office, the first occasion finding him absent, the outer door locked, the lights switched off; the second time, on Monday evening, he merely looked at me from behind his desk, those same squinting eyes, and shook his head. He said nothing, I was silent in response, and walked away.

From the window of my room I could see the

junction between Fallow Road and its neighboring street. To my right, slightly out of view, was the Stone Gap schoolhouse, a complex of small brick buildings with a field behind. At certain times I could hear the laughter and hubbub of children – first thing in the morning, around noon, and then in the middle of the afternoon when they were released for the day. A little after three on Tuesday I was lying on my bed, and the sound of girls laughing came drifting through the window. They were playing some skipping game, and as I moved closer I heard them. The sound of their voices chilled me suddenly, unexpectedly.

'Two-six-nine . . . the goose drank wine . . . the monkey chewed tobacco on the streetcar line . . . the line got broke . . . the mon-key choked . . . they all went to Heaven in a little rowboat . . .'

'Clap hands . . . clap hands . . . clap hands . . .'

I stayed there on my knees, my forearms on the sill, my chin resting on my hands, my eyes closed. Each time they sang through that chorus I felt the hairs rise on the nape of my neck. It was as if they knew I was there, and they were simply reminding me of my reason for being. Eventually, I could not have said when, I became aware of silence. I returned to the bed and lay down. My cheeks were wet with tears, but I could not remember having cried.

Wednesday at five I called again at Vallelly's office. I appeared at the screen and he called my name and waved me through.

'I don't have anything for you,' he said. 'I know this must be frustrating, but right now I don't know there's a hell of a lot else I can do. Your friend is out there somewhere, and unless he's already left the state someone's sure to see him.' He smiled sympathetically. 'Only thing we can't predict is when that will be.'

'I'm thinking of going back to New York,' I said, finding myself voicing something that I hadn't even seriously considered. It was a fleeting consideration, and even as it passed I wondered why I had chosen to say anything.

'Seems as good an idea as any,' Vallelly said. 'You can call me soon as you're there and let me know how to reach you. Maybe by the time you get back there'll be some word of him.'

I walked forward and sat down facing the Sheriff. 'I could be waiting forever,' I said resignedly. I realized that I'd spoken to no-one for more than three days. I wanted to speak, wanted to hear the sound of my own voice, to hear someone respond and converse in return. Loneliness had taken residence and I did not like it. 'It's vitally important that I meet with him, and yet I feel that staying here is accomplishing nothing—'

''Cept to remind me that I haven't got you what you wanted,' Vallelly said. He smiled, smiled like the Haynes Dearing I remembered from my childhood, and it hurt me to think of him, to think of all we went through, and here we both were – thirty years later – still chasing the same ghosts.

'Tell you something,' Vallelly said. Once more he reached for his pipe, went through the laborious ritual of stoking and tamping. 'You get to my age, all these years behind me in the sheriff's department, and you start to wonder if there isn't a percentage of the population that we'll never understand. Something like this, the murdering of children . . . and not just murdering, but the way they've been butchered and assaulted . . .' Vallelly closed his eyes for a moment and shook his head. 'You understand something like that, Mr Vaughan?'

'No,' I said. 'I don't understand it, and I don't know that I *want* to understand such a thing. Person like that—'

'Is the sickest kind of individual you're ever gonna come across,' Vallelly interjected. 'That's what I think.'

I smiled and looked at the floor. 'Seems to me it's been there all through my life. Started when I was a child, and . . . and hell, everything I've done since seems to have been tainted by it.'

'And that's the reason for the book?'

I frowned. 'The book?'

'Sure, the book you're writing. Seems to me writing everything down is gonna be like some kind of exorcism for you, right?'

I shrugged. 'Maybe,' I said. 'We'll see, won't we?'

'So tell me something,' Vallelly said. He leaned forward, squinted. 'What does that do to a child, seeing something like that?'

'Reminds you of the temporary nature of every-thing,' I replied. 'There were a group of us. We called ourselves the Guardians. Haynes Dearing posted these flyers around Augusta Falls. They were warnings to us, reminded us that we should stay alert all the time, look out for strangers. On the flyer they put this silhouette of a man. That's what it was all about. That was perhaps the most important thing I ever did. I got those boys together, and we made an oath. We even cut our hands and did the whole blood brother thing. We promised that we would keep the other children safe, that we would look out for them, make sure no harm came to them.'

'But it didn't stop, right?'

'No, it didn't stop. And I went back to Augusta Falls just a few days ago, and I looked up some of those boys—'

'And let me guess . . . they didn't have the time of day for you.'

'That's right.'

Vallelly smiled understandingly. 'Would figure as much. They're all grown up now, have kids of their own. Whatever happened back then isn't happening now so it doesn't have anything to do with them.'

I nodded.

'That's human nature, Mr Vaughan. Seems to me it never used to be that way, but it is now. World has changed. People have changed more. Don't necessarily know that I like the way it's

595

going, but I sure as hell ain't gonna stop it on my own.'

'So we do what we can do, and hope that it makes a bit of difference, right?'

'Right,' Vallelly said. 'Like you and your friend Haynes Dearing.'

I started to rise from the chair.

'Believe me, Mr Vaughan, I want you to find him,' Vallelly said. 'I want you to meet with him and see if there's something that can be done to stop this thing going any further. I'll do what I can. I'll send out another teletype message, and as soon as you get back to New York you give me a call and let me know where I can reach you, okay?'

'I will,' I said. I extended my hand, shook with Sheriff Norman Vallelly, and then I turned and left his office.

I walked back to the Excelsior and packed my things. At the reception desk I made enquiries about buses, was directed to take a connection to Atlanta, and there I would find a Greyhound that would return me to New York.

I did not wish to leave, and yet I felt I could not stay. Rock and a hard place. Leaving seemed easier, and so I did.

I left Atlanta for New York. Late afternoon, Thursday, April sixth, 1967. If I'd known then that everything would end within a few days, I wonder whether I would have delayed my journey. Strange to think now, but the question in my mind was what I would do when this thing was over. Whichever way it turned out, at some point it would be over, and then where would I go?

I took the Greyhound, slept as best I could. We drove for eight hours, and then we stopped for a little while. I stepped from the bus and stood at the side of the road. My body ached. My mind was buried inside some deep well of anguish. I looked at my fellow passengers: an overweight man in a pork-pie hat who smelled of dime-store aftershave and thirty-cent cigars; a pregnant girl, no more than nineteen or twenty, carrying everything she possessed in a worn-out Samsonite holdall; a shoe salesman, fifty-three and dog-tired, in his wallet a photo of the wife who'd left him, the son who hadn't called for eleven years; beside him a blond-haired, big-teethed college quarterback with a doubtful knee, finally resigned to life without cheerleaders and locker rooms and rubbing alcohol. These people were phantoms, images of those who populated some other world, a world I seemed to have stepped from, perhaps never to return. I tried to speak with them, but what could I say. 'I have come from prison for a murder I did not commit. I have lost more people than I will ever gain. I am crossing America to find a man who will help me identify a child-killer. Far as I can guess there are twenty-nine dead children. I can hear them all. Some of their faces are indelibly printed on the backs of my eyelids. When I close my eyes they are all I can see. Now what did you want to talk to me about?'

We came into New York on Sunday morning. New York had changed, but, just as with Augusta Falls, the New York I remembered was still there beneath the surface. I remembered the first time I had seen it back in April of 1949. How it had pounded at me. Everything bright and bold and arrogant. Majestic. Imposing. A thunderhouse of humanity.

I remembered how New York had taken my breath away, and had not returned it for two days.

Eighteen years had passed. I felt like an old man in comparison.

Brooklyn pulled me, magnetic and compelling, and I followed that pull.

I stood there on the corner of Throop and Quincy. Aggie Boyle's house had gone. It was no longer the same street, nor the same junction, but I felt Bridget's memory there. She too was a ghost that haunted me.

It seemed fitting to be here. To be right back where

my own personal nightmare started. For catharsis perhaps, or merely tempting fate, I took a hotel room no more than two hundreds yards from where I had turned the corner and started running that day of my return from Manhattan, running headlong into the worst day of my life. Or perhaps not – it seemed there had been so many. How had I deserved such a life? What crime had I committed that had given me such justice?

I did not know. I did not dare to ask. I let my mind fall silent, and sat at the window of my room and watched Brooklyn through different eyes.

In the morning I would call Sheriff Vallelly and tell him where I was.

CHAPTER 33

'We have word of him,' Vallelly said as soon as the line connected.

'Dearing?'

'The very same. One of the people in Baxley saw him.'

'Baxley?' I asked. Baxley was no more than an hour from Augusta Falls.

'Someone I know over there. We used to work together when I was in Macon.'

'Jesus,' I said through clenched teeth. I stood at the reception desk of the hotel. Behind me and through the front window I would have been able to see the Quincy junction. I turned my back to the receptionist in an effort to maintain some slight degree of privacy.

'Mr Vaughan? You there?'

'Yes . . . er, sorry . . . I'm here, yes. Okay, so he was in Baxley. How come they spoke to him?'

'He was pulled over with a flat. My friend . . . he's the deputy sheriff there, well, he stopped to give him a hand and they got to talking. Told him that he should contact me, that I had news of an old friend who wanted to look him up.'

'Did they give my name?'

'No, I didn't give your name out. I'm hoping that your man will call me, make some contact, and then I can give him your whereabouts.'

'He didn't say where he was going?'

'Said he was heading out of Georgia, going north I think he said. He didn't say much apparently, but he did say he would call me.'

I was silent for a while.

'This has come as somewhat of a surprise for you, Mr Vaughan.'

I took a deep breath, held it for a moment. 'Yes,' I said. 'It was a slim chance at best. Christ, I don't know what to say.'

'Well, there ain't a helluva lot to say until Dearing contacts me, and then we'll see where we go from there. Okay?'

'Yes. And thank you. I really appreciate everything you're doing to help.'

'Hell, Mr Vaughan, like I said before, if it brings this thing to an end any faster I'm more than happy to help. So you stay there, all right? And if Haynes Dearing calls me I'll make sure he gets in touch with you.'

'Thank you. Yes, as soon as you hear anything, call me here.'

'You take care now, Mr Vaughan, and hopefully I'll have some news for you soon.'

I thanked Sheriff Vallelly again and hung up. I told the receptionist to make sure that he fetched me down as soon as any calls came through.

The receptionist – a short, balding man called Leonard, awkward strands of hair jutting horizontally from above his ears, peered at me over half-moon glasses. 'Trouble?' he asked suspiciously.

I smiled, shook my head. 'A little excited,' I said. 'A very old friend. We haven't spoken for a lot of years and there's a chance I might find him.'

Leonard smiled, relaxed. 'Good luck,' he said. 'I'll make sure to get you if a call comes through.'

I returned to my room, sat on the edge of the bed. My head felt too heavy for my shoulders, and I lay down, tugged a pillow behind me and tried to think.

Augusta Falls. Sheriff Haynes Dearing. The Guardians versus the child-killer. I retraced my steps through everything that had happened, everything I could remember. I thought of Dearing's lecture in the schoolhouse, the way he looked at every one of us in turn, never mentioning our names but making it all too obvious who he was referring to. The violation of the curfew. The words of warning. My mother. The way she had slipped irreversibly into the depths of something terrifying. Elena Kruger. My failure to protect her. The oaths we had made as children, and how we had broken them.

And I thought of the killer, the little girls that had suffered at his hands. I tried to understand what would drive a man to such things. Anger. Hate. Jealousy. Some indescribable sense of madness that came from deep within the soul and could never be exorcised. A madness that Laurence Gabillard, irrespective of the number of letters after his name, could never hope to comprehend.

And then I thought of Georgia, of all that it had been, all that it represented. Of Reilly Hawkins, Frank Turow, one-eyed Lowell Shaner who walked with the seventy-man line and cried for a girl he'd never known. The smells and sounds of the Krugers' kitchen, of Mathilde and the children.

Of the question in Haynes Dearing's file: *Where did the boy go after Jesup?*

Where *did* the boy go?

The sudden hammering at the door startled me. I lost my balance on the edge of the bed. I stood suddenly, the blood rushing to my head and for a moment I was thoroughly disoriented. I walked to the door, snatched it open, and Leonard stood there – flustered, excited.

'Your call,' he said. 'Your call downstairs . . . your friend I think.'

I hurried past Leonard and bolted down the stairwell. I reached the desk and snatched the receiver from it.

'Joseph,' Haynes Dearing said.

'Sheriff Dearing?'

He laughed. 'Christ, no-one's called me that for as many years as I can remember. Hell, son, how are you?'

I started laughing. I felt emotion flood through

603

me. I felt dizzy, almost sick, and it was some time before I could find anything at all to say.

'I'm . . . I'm okay. Yes, okay. Sheriff. I've been looking for you.'

'So I hear,' Haynes Dearing said, and with the sound of his voice everything I remembered about him came back as if we'd spoken only the day before. I had everything to tell him, and yet I could barely string a sentence together.

'So where are you?' he asked.

'New York,' I replied. 'In Brooklyn.'

'Jesus, Brooklyn of all places. I'd have figured you'd have had enough of that place . . . you know, with everything that happened back then.'

'Everything in my life, Sheriff,' I said. 'I was hoping—'

'That we could meet up?'

'Yes, yes that we could meet up. Where are you?'

'Christ, all over the place. But I can come and see you,' Dearing said. 'I can come to New York and see you, Joseph . . . if that's what you want?'

'Yes,' I said, barely able to believe what was happening. 'Could you?'

'Sure I could. It would be good to see you again after all these years.' He paused for a moment. 'I heard about everything that happened. The girl in New York . . . the trial—'

'Enough,' I said. 'I don't want to talk about that. I want to talk about—'

'I know what you want to talk about, Joseph, and that's why I called you. I should come to New

604

York. I think that's the best thing under the circumstances. I could leave almost immediately. If I take a train I could be there tomorrow perhaps?'

'Yes,' I said. Every nerve in my body was jangling with anticipation. I felt fear, exhaustion, a sense of overwhelming anticipation. I would see Haynes Dearing. Between us we would make sense of this thing and bring it to closure. I knew it. I believed it. *Had* to believe it.

'Okay then, we're settled,' Haynes Dearing said. 'I'll come to New York. Tell me where you are.'

I gave him the address of the hotel. I told him I wouldn't go anywhere, that I'd stay right here and see him when he arrived. I thanked him for calling, for agreeing to come, for the possibility that we could at last speak and take some steps closer to the truth.

Haynes Dearing wished me well, and then he hung up.

I stood there with the receiver burring in my hand until Leonard took it from me and set it back in its cradle.

'Everything okay?' he asked.

I turned and looked at him. I smiled like a fool. 'Couldn't be better,' I said. 'Couldn't be better.'

A half hour later I went out and bought some provisions – some bread, cheese, some slices of ham, a couple of apples. I wanted no reason to leave the hotel. I carried them back to my room and set them on the table near the window. I closed the drapes and sat in one of the two chairs that were against the wall.

I could not sit still for long. I started to pace the room. I walked to the window and closed the drapes. I wanted it to be evening. I wanted to sleep, to think of nothing, to be already in tomorrow and seeing Haynes Dearing walking down the street toward the hotel.

I went back downstairs and called Sheriff Vallelly to tell him that Dearing had called, to thank him once again for his help. The phone rang out at the other end. No-one home.

Back in my room I paced between the window and the door to the small bathroom. I felt as if I was in Auburn again, counting steps to take my mind off everything. I believed I would explode, perhaps spontaneously combust right there in that room. The feelings that assaulted me were indefinable, but close, closer than anything. I tried to think of things I had read, movies I had seen. I tried to think of Alex, of Bridget, tried to see their faces to remind myself of why I was doing this. They did not come, almost as if they sensed my disturbance and wished to be no part of it.

Eventually I lay down on the mattress. I closed my eyes, and sleep pulled me down; I resisted, but it was strong; my body was tired, and my mind believed there would be nothing gained by fighting. And even as I lay there I imagined my reunion with Haynes Dearing, of the things we would speak about, of the years he had spent traveling this country looking for his redemption. He had killed Gunther Kruger, that much I knew to be true, and I wondered how much it had haunted him.

I am lost, he would say. I have been walking for thirty years and still I am lost. And I don't understand this thing now anymore than I did back then.

It's okay, I would tell him. It's okay, because between us we will make this thing end once and for all. You're here now, and that's all that matters, and I want you to tell me what you've seen and heard, what you believe, why you think these things never stopped. You can do that much, can't you? You can do that much for me?

And Dearing would sit in the chair by the window, and behind him the late afternoon sunlight would make a halo of his hair, and I would think of angels, and thoughts of angels would bring their faces back to me, and I would shudder in that moment of recognition, and realize for myself why I had let this thing consume me.

So speak, I would tell him. Tell me everything and I will listen.

And we would spread the newspaper clippings out across the coverlet of the bed, and we would look down at their faces together, and he would tell me why he believed they'd died, and why Bridget had been murdered no more than a hundred yards from where we now sat. And I would try to understand what he was saying, the conclusions he had drawn during all these years we'd been apart, and he would speak of how he too was haunted by the ghosts of the past, that he too could close his eyes, see their faces, hear their laughter and catcalls and childish games. And perhaps we would cry, and in crying together we would share some degree of fraternity, of camaraderie, and know that we had lived this thing together despite being apart. And then we would speak of what to do, of where we would go now, of how this thing would end.

We would speak of fear, of frustration; we would speak of anger, of hatred; we would speak of the nights we'd found ourselves facing this man, facing him in our dreams, and how we had killed him. Killed and killed and killed him a thousand times over. And how we had woken, and realized that the sense of justice we believed we'd earned was merely a phantom, a haunting, a ghost . . . just like the child-killer.

All these things, and beneath them would be the memory of those days in Augusta Falls, of the beginning of this nightmare, and how it really should have ended back there.

A circle, I would say.

And Haynes Dearing would look at me, and in his eyes I would see a younger man, a man who had in some small way cared for me, for my mother, who had visited her as many times as he could, who had spoken to her and given her a sense of resolve. When everyone else had disowned us, Sheriff Haynes Dearing had been there. He had never given up. A rock. A pillar of fortitude. A man of little compromise and reservation.

It has been hard, I would tell him. To suffer this much losing. My mother. Alex. Bridget. Elena and all the others. I don't know how someone could stand to lose so many people and still believe in the fundamental goodness of people.

That's because we have faith, he would say. That's because we believe in what we are doing, whichever way it comes down, we believe in what we are doing.

Leaning closer to me now, whispering perhaps, almost conspiratorial, as if only we two really understood the nature of what had happened.

And we have to do something to make it stop, I would say, and Haynes Dearing would nod and agree, and then he would tell me of the years he had walked through America looking for the next little girl, perhaps hoping against hope that there wouldn't be another, but knowing, *knowing*, that there would.

You remember the Guardians? I would say, and Dearing would laugh. That's what we called ourselves, the Guardians. Me and Hans Kruger and Maurice Fricker – you remember him? I saw him recently—

Recently?

Yes, just a few days ago. You know his dad is dead?

Gene is dead?

Yes, he's dead. Was killed in a hit and run some-where out of county. Maurice looks just like his dad. Always did, but even more so now he's older. And Michael Wiltsey? The King of Fidget we called him. Couldn't ever keep still. And there was Daniel McRae . . . and we always watched him closely, you know? Because his sister was one of the ones that died? We watched him like hawks, like any moment he would break down and we'd have a wreck on our hands. And Ronnie Duggan. You know Ronnie Duggan?

Yes, I remember him. Little shrimp of a kid, hair hanging in his eyes all the time.

That's the one. He was with us too. And you put those flyers up around the town, the ones with the silhouette?

I remember that . . . God, I haven't thought of that for so many years.

Yes . . . and it was the Guardians versus the child-killer, and though we knew we couldn't really do anything to stop him, we at least tried, right? We tried to do what we could to stop this terrible thing happening.

I know you did, Joseph, I know you did. And what did they say when you saw them?

They didn't want to know, Sheriff, they just didn't want to know. They tried to pretend that it was all in the past. That it stopped in Augusta Falls when Gunther died.

Yes . . . when Gunther died.

I know about that, Sheriff. I know what happened that day.

I know you do, Joseph. I know you figured out what happened.

And I understand why you did it.

You do?

Yes, I think so. Because you wanted everyone to go back to their lives. You wanted everything back the way it was before it started, and you thought that if they knew who was guilty they would stop worrying, they would stop being frightened, and Augusta Falls could be the town it was before Alice was murdered.

Dearing would be silent, and he would look at me with tears in his eyes and, just like my mother when she spoke of what had happened between her and Gunther Kruger, I would see that Haynes Dearing wanted me to forgive him.

I can try and understand . . . but I cannot forgive you, Sheriff. I can't absolve you of your sins. That's something you're gonna have to come to terms with when you seek your redemption.

I know, Joseph, I know. I wanted so much for it to end. I know you understand. I wanted everyone to go back to how they were before. I suppose I believed that if they had someone to blame it would be a sort of deliverance. I suppose I believed—

It's okay, Sheriff, it's okay. That's over now, and no matter how much we might talk about it, what happened will never change.

And now, Joseph? What now?

Now? Hell, I don't know. It all seems so long ago . . . so far back that I wonder sometimes if I haven't dreamed all of it up, dreamed it and then believed it so strong I really think it took place.

It did take place, Joseph, it did take place.

I know, Sheriff, I know.

So what are we going to do, Joseph?

I was hoping you'd have an answer.

Me? Why would you think I'd have any better answer about this than you?

Because you were there. All these past years . . . while I was here in Brooklyn, while I was in prison in Auburn, you were still out there looking.

Just because I was looking doesn't mean I have any better idea about what to do. I just saw more of it than you did, that's all. Nothing more nor less than that, Joseph . . . I just saw more of it.

And did seeing more if it make you better understand why it happened, Sheriff?

Silence for some eternity, and then through tear-filled eyes he would look at me and say, Because he killed the first child, and from then on he was ashamed. I think she talked to him, taunted him, followed him everywhere he went, and each little girl he saw reminded him of the first, and then the second, and then the third. And he had to stop their voices, Joseph. I think they talked to him and made him mad. They stopped him sleeping. They stopped him having any kind of life at all. He had to make them go away . . . and finally, at last, they all became the same, and they looked at him the same way, and their voices were like one voice, and the only way to make them silent was to kill them. Guilt, you see? The seed of guilt was planted, and from then on he could do nothing but try to make the guilt disappear.

You think that's what happened?

I don't know, Joseph. I don't know that anyone will ever really understand. I have tried, believe me I've tried . . . but the more I think about it the more I get confused.

Enough . . . enough now. We just have to decide what to do, that's all . . . we just have to decide what to do.

Morning of Tuesday the eleventh I woke suddenly. My clothes were drenched in sweat. Sunlight struggled to find its way into the room through the closed drapes, but the sound of the street told me that another day had arrived. I looked at my watch. It was gone eleven.

I rose and showered. I shaved, changed my clothes. I stood before the mirror and asked myself whether I was ready to meet with Haynes Dearing. If not now, then when? I asked myself, and tried to be strong, tried to retain some sense of certain resolve about what I was doing.

I tried to eat some bread and cheese but I had no appetite.

The room was nothing more than my new prison

cell, and though I could leave whenever I wished, though there was no lock on the door and no-one stood beyond to prevent my exit, I could leave no more easily than when I'd been in Auburn. Everything in the present seemed a mere echo of the past. Somewhere I had made a decision – perhaps something simple, even insignificant – and as a result of that decision everything from that point forward had slipped off kilter, some other axis. The real Joseph Vaughan existed within a parallel world, a world without dead children, a world where he had grown old with Alex Webber, where his mother had lived to some ancient age, where she was ever present, ever beautiful, ever pleased for the life she had created for herself and her son. Or perhaps even earlier. Some other life where Earl Vaughan's heart had been sound and strong, the heart of a giant, and nothing so inconsequential as the rheum had afflicted him. He was somewhere even now with his wife, and though they'd never had more than one child, that child, their son, was an inspiration for them. He was a writer, and people knew his name. He was the son of Augusta Falls, and Augusta Falls would be remembered for that son.

Some other world. Some other life.

Not this one.

By two I had opened the window, sat there on a chair with my forearms on the sill. Watching and waiting, praying that Dearing had not been overcome with second thoughts. He was coming. I had to believe that. I willed him to come. I placed everything within a single thought and sent it out there. I wanted to see him turn the corner at the junction. I wanted to see him make his way down the sidewalk with that unforgettable gait. I wanted him to look up at the window and see me, to raise his hand, to smile, and start speaking to me even before I could hear him.

I watched cars and cabs crawl down the street, wishing any one of them would draw to a stop against the curb, that the rear door would open, and after a moment's hesitation Haynes Dearing would appear, and I would see nothing but the top of his hat as he emerged, but I would *know* it was him. No doubt. No uncertainty. Haynes Dearing in Brooklyn and at my hotel.

By the time the sun began to set I was beside myself with agitation. I could not speak. I tried to look at myself in the mirror, pretend I was someone else, start a conversation just so I could hear a voice. *Any* voice. Nothing but a strangled sound emerged from my lips, and I closed my eyes and breathed deeply.

I am an exile, I thought, and wondered if here I would stay. Forever trapped within a prison of my own making, caught in some hiatus of time and place, waiting for someone who would never arrive.

I am an exile, and no-one knows I'm here except

the man I'm waiting for. And he will never come. Never intended to come. Made a promise and then broke it. Just like the promise I made to Elena. Broken words. Broken oaths. Worthless vows. This is who I have become, and I have created this for myself. No-one else has done this but me. No-one else but me.

CHAPTER 34

It was dark. Through a thin gap in the drapes I could see the moon, high and full. Shone like a single eye into my room and found me there sitting on the floor, back to the wall beside the bed.

I heard the car pull up. I heard an exchange of muffled words. I heard the door slam, the engine start, the car pull away.

My body fought against me, but I dragged myself up from the floor and made it to the window.

I pulled back the drapes, tugged up the window, and I looked down. I looked down and it could have been the same day.

Thursday, February seventeenth, 1949.

He looked the same as he had then. When he came to drive me to Jesup.

When I saw him take a moment, glance back toward the road, and then look up at the house like his own angel of death was planning to appear from within, I knew.

I *knew*.

He raised his hand.

I extended my hand through the open window.

'Joseph,' he said, and his voice was almost a whisper.

'Third floor,' I said. 'The room at the end of the hall.'

He nodded, took a moment to set his hat on his head like a punctuation mark, and then he walked slowly, funeral-slow, toward the front door.

I rummaged through my bag. I gathered the newspaper clippings and put them out on the bed. My heart was thundering in my chest, my hands were sweating. I could feel my pulse in my temples and my head was ready to burst. I took the chairs from near the window and set them facing one another in the middle of the room.

I stepped toward the door.

I could hear his footfalls on the stairwell. I stood for a moment. I tried to breathe deeply. Tried to gather myself together. I stepped back, sat down in the chair, and closed my eyes.

The door ahead of me started to open. I could see the handle turning. I almost passed out, believing for a moment that I would lose myself completely. I watched the door open inch by inch, and then Haynes Dearing was standing there in front of me, and he was smiling, smiling high, wide and handsome, and though he had aged, though the better part of thirty years had passed since I had seen him, I did see him. I *saw* him perhaps for the very first time.

'Joseph,' he said, and he stepped into the room and closed the door behind him.

'Sheriff Dearing,' I said.

'It's good to see you.'

'Is it?'

He glanced at the bed as he turned, saw the newspaper clippings spread across it. He smiled understandingly, even compassionately. 'These are our ghosts, are they not?'

'I believe so, Sheriff,' I said, and somewhere within me I found some deep well of resolve and inner strength. 'Come and sit down,' I said. 'Come sit down and tell me how you've been.'

Dearing did not carry a bag. He wore a long coat, and he took a moment to remove it. He folded it neatly and placed it on the small table beside the bed.

'You been here long, Joseph?' he asked as he walked forward and sat down.

'A couple of days.'

He smiled, started to laugh. 'Smells like someone died in here, Joseph, it really does.'

'Perhaps someone did.'

There was nothing between us for a moment, and then Dearing reached into his jacket pocket and withdrew his gun. He pointed it unerringly at my chest.

'How long?' he asked, and his voice sounded caring and sympathetic.

'How long?' I said. 'I don't know, Sheriff. Everything's blurred together and there are no seams. I look back and see everything as if it happened yesterday.'

'You understand anything of what has happened?' he asked.

'I understand that you turned my mother against the Krugers, that you made her believe that Gunther Kruger, perhaps even Walter, was responsible for the children that died. I think you were the one that shot a bullet through Kruger's window, and you killed his dog as well. I think you fired the Kruger house, and then you visited my mother all those times at Waycross and made her believe that she had done it.'

Dearing stared back at me implacably. There was a twitch along the line of his mouth, and this was all that told me he was alive. His eyes were dark, lightless and deep. I could see my own reflection there, and what I saw frightened me.

'And you went out there and hanged Gunther Kruger. You used me, didn't you? Used me as your scapegoat. You went there and killed him, and you put that ribbon in his hand, and you put those things beneath the floorboards . . . your evidence that Gunther was the child-killer.'

Dearing's eyes closed for a moment, and when he opened them he possessed a vague and distant smile on his face.

'I think you put that note in the file you left in Valdosta. You wanted to find the Kruger boys, perhaps were afraid that they would realize you murdered their father. People saw that note and believed you suspected one of them. Walter? Was he the one you were afraid of?'

620

Dearing didn't respond. I felt my heart hammering relentlessly in my chest.

'You feared him, and you wanted to find him too, didn't you? And you feared me as well . . . what I knew, what I might say. I think that you came to kill both me and Bridget that day, and as I wasn't there you just killed her. I believe you spoke to the police, that perhaps you made them think I was not only responsible for Bridget's death, but that the Augusta Falls killings had never been solved, that they had continued and therefore Gunther Kruger could not have been the one. I think you put doubt in their minds and made them hate me enough to do anything. You convinced them to look no further, and they didn't, and because of that I lost nearly fourteen years of my life . . . a life you had already as good as destroyed.'

Dearing raised the gun and pointed it at my face. 'Enough,' he said. 'I don't want to listen to you anymore—'

'And the little girls,' I said, my voice faltering as I stared at the barrel of Dearing's gun. 'So many of them. And you took them all in broad daylight. You kept your uniform, didn't you? Put your uniform on and drove from town to town, and people saw you and paid no mind because you were a police officer. Even the little girls, even they never suspected who you were. I'm right, aren't I, Sheriff Dearing? That's what happened, didn't it?'

I sensed his hand tighten on his gun, and I raised my own gun from down beside the chair and pulled the trigger.

The shots were almost simultaneous. Even as I saw the impact of the bullet in Haynes Dearing's chest I felt the sudden and intense pain of that same impact across my shoulder, my chest, my heart.

I dropped my gun, as did Dearing, and for a moment we sat there staring at one another.

Dearing opened his mouth to speak, but already his eyes were closing. He mumbled something unintelligible, and then his head lolled forward.

The room was silent but for my own labored breathing, and that breathing was weak, faltering, and I felt myself slipping toward something from which I believed I would never return.

The darkness came then – grey waves of pain, scarlet flashes within, and beneath that some well of blackness that seemed to swallow me. I slipped back and forth, in and out of consciousness, and I heard the sound of my own heart, and beneath that the sound of breath shuddering through punctured lungs, and I knew that I wouldn't be there for long.

I forced myself to stay awake, to concentrate, and I looked at Haynes Dearing and started to talk to him.

'I am an exile,' I said, and my voice was frail, little more than a whisper.

'I take a moment . . . to look back . . . across the

span of my life . . . and . . . and I try to see it for what it was . . .'

I spoke to him for a long time, and then I could not speak anymore.

At one point there was a cooling breeze that came through the window and seemed to fill the room, and then I closed my eyes and felt nothing at all.

My mother was there, my father too; Elena and Alex and Bridget. They were all there, and they watched for me to take the first step toward them.

And then there was light, and there were voices, and people were shouting, and for a moment I believed I opened my eyes and saw Rcilly Hawkins standing over me laughing about the fool that I was. And when he opened his mouth he started screaming at the top of his voice, and what he said made no sense at all . . .

'For fuck's sake . . . someone get a fucking medic! This one has a pulse for Christ's sake! Get a fucking medic!'

For the life of me I did not know who they were talking about, and for some reason it did not matter.

EPILOGUE

New York Times Literary Supplement
Monday, August 15th 2005

Reclusive author enchants New York

Yesterday evening, before a packed Brooklyn Academy, Joseph Vaughan (77) – reclusive author and literary enigma – gave a reading from his latest publication, a companion work to his controversial 1965 novel *A Quiet Belief In Angels*. Entitled *The Guardians*, the book tells of Vaughan's life subsequent to his release from Auburn State Prison in February 1967. His first work, a novella entitled *The Homecoming* was published in June 1952, and then nothing further was heard of Vaughan until his wrongful arrest for murder in November of the same year. Vaughan was tried, convicted, and subsequently sentenced to life imprisonment. With the aid of a friend, Paul Hennessy, Vaughan's autobiographical work *A Quiet Belief In Angels* was handwritten in prison, smuggled out and typed for publication. Its release sparked an outcry which resulted in Vaughan's case being heard before the United States Supreme Court. His conviction was overturned and he was released after having served more than thirteen years.

Upon his release Vaughan committed himself to identifying the perpetrator of more than thirty-two known child murders spanning five states and more than three decades. Vaughan's investigation resulted in his eventual discovery and shooting of a retired Georgia sheriff, Haynes Dearing, an action taken in self-defence as Vaughan himself was shot. Vaughan then disappeared once more, and did not surface until last fall when rumor had it that another book had been written. The capacity Brooklyn Academy audience were present for the first reading from this work. Before speaking, Vaughan dedicated the book 'to Elena, to Alex and to Bridget . . . also to my mother who would have told me that I'd waited too long to write this.'

The Guardians is due for release next Monday, and is already tipped to be the number one best-seller of the year.